MONSOON IN THE MAKING

CLIVE RADFORD

MONSOON IN THE MAKING
Copyright © 2021 by Clive Radford

ISBN: 978-1-953735-52-2

Melange Books, LLC
White Bear Lake, MN 55110
www.melange-books.com

Published in the United States of America.

Cover Design by Caroline Andrus

CONTENTS

1. Surf's Up — 1
2. Unexpected Encounter — 5
3. Realisation — 26
4. The Die is Cast — 46
5. A Martyr in the Making — 59
6. Ship's Company — 71
7. Embarkation — 102
8. Sages and Seers — 112
9. Preparing to execute Allah's will — 153
10. Searching for Passage — 169
11. Escapism and Beyond — 182
12. Spying on Poseidon — 205
13. Into the Tunis Night — 212
14. Colonel Nassar — 238
15. Majid's Cruiser — 257
16. Back on Poseidon — 280
17. Clear Blue Water and Clear Minds — 289
18. Final brush with Neptune — 308

Appendix A: New World Order — 315
Key — 316
Thank You For Reading — 319
About the Author — 321

1

SURF'S UP

Tunis, Spring 2009

Glyn Sumner flinched at the funsters and hustlers parading by. Far from what he knew back in Blighty, they challenged his perceptions, cast doubt on certainties and opened his psychic valve, paving the way to paradise. An explorer by nature, and in more recent times a borderline anarchist, savagely decrying the acerbic effects of twenty-first century modernity, he had embraced the trials afforded by a Mediterranean venture, hoping they'd neutralise the sterility of his home life.

Absorbing more of the carousel, he watched evening's jubilant emissaries race down Avenue Mohammed V, their incessant noise drowning out calls to prayer at the minarets, leaving Glyn torn between the need for modern innovations and a desire to stay planted in the cultural past.

Overhead, cobalt turned to Prussian then graphite-steel blue, the city retaining a soft, balmy feel from the day's luxuriant heat. Neon signs flashed honeyed words, their carousing messages lost on souls more abstracted by the city's drones and murmurs. Hosing down the last remnants of discarded food packaging, street cleaners swapped gossip, their sights fixed on the night ahead. Glad to have finished their daily toil, shop workers hurried home to families and a nourishing meal. Reminding Glyn that a change of location did not necessarily bring a change in required daily actions, he conceded every city must host a common conformity adhered to by its residents. Tunis was no different from London in that respect. It ignited the question, had the venture he embarked on really provided any differences from what he knew in England, apart from sampling local traditions and habits?

As commerce subsided, Tunisian nightlife rose up, inviting reckless abandonment and nocturnal curiosity, its biting beguilement flushed with swollen distraction, Glyn tramping in limbo regarding whether to become a practitioner or stay as an impartial observer.

Buzzing and bubbly, the Tunis rich parked their Mercedes' then leapt into the night stalking excitement. Wanting temporary release from sombre or taxing lives, they hoped to elude colossal fate and sticky betrayals, at least under the cover of darkness, their searing self-confidence boundless and on high alert. Wives and girlfriends giggled, preened coiffed hair and licked glossed lips, their smiles encouraging tactile and furtive contact. A throng of pleasure seekers in fleeting escape, the dynamic though short-lived, still treasured, always sought, never neglected, no matter what the cost.

Drifting on the wavering breeze, traces of freshly smoked kif found its way into receptive nostrils familiar with the candied scent. A forbidden indulgence, its liberating affect overcame visions of confinement, the transgression worth the risk.

As nightclub doors opened, the sounds of chanteuses and raconteurs modulated the background melee noise, their calls freeze-dried from another epoch, dipped in mellow blarney and sent through the ether like a travelogue fishing for green custom. Beckoning the crowd, Glyn witnessed them plying their trade, selling silver coke spoons, unconditional love and offering an Arabian Disney.

Further down the track, gimlet-eyed nighthawks gathered for clandestine liaisons, their ravenous wantonness brimming over with anticipation. Amazed by street conjurers' tricks tourists caught their breath, the easy deception having them spellbound while street urchins picked their pockets. Mosquitoes and moths vied for air space; the party goers oblivious to their feeding frenzy. Dogs howled at the weeping moon. The screech of tyres announced someone narrowly avoided death. Others, less fortunate, were already Hades bound, an unforgiving hiatus with an infected needle ensuring fulfilment of his daily quota.

Blistering colours and shades beyond garish imagination, Tunis, everyone's delight, brought up to order by room service, sassy and sumptuous, always available, but sometimes, as Glyn found, unpredictably surprising.

～

Away from the street life confabs and powwows, after reviewing recent enigmatic and unsettling chronicles, Poseidon crew member Glyn Sumner and his fellow argonauts cogitated on the next stage of their voyage.

Relaxing in the Hotel du Lac's terrace garden with libations working their magic, they floated away, immune to distraction and insulated from the passage of time. Despite reverberations made by the backdrop hubbub, both swept by with enormous regularity, but neither impinged on their idyllic state. Gazing at the cloudless night sky, their sense of satisfaction and achievement became heightened, North African charm enhancing the cosmic lift, impressions of Arabic mystique proven. Hovering further away into the warm glow of the nonaligned zone, they caressed fulfilment in the knowledge the Med had been tested, and they'd found tenacity and won through, conquering their demons, and discovering veritas, its elixir virtuous and soul cleansing.

As had become the custom during the evening of shore visits, they happily discussed the next stage of the voyage, howbeit their volition still partially entranced by the peerless heavens above. In preparation for sailing to Marsala, Sicily, Jeff and Ed, the senior crew members and boat owners, assigned tasks to the crew for execution the next morning. Known as newcomers, Glyn, Steve, Tom, Bill, David and Colin accepted the duties with relish, their enthusiasm still sharp after six weeks sailing.

During their conversation, the ship's company became peripherally aware a figure stared at them from the hotel balcony steps, leading down to the terrace garden.

"Beware, chaps," Glyn advised, shifting his gaze to swiftly assess the gate crasher. "Its sales time again."

With the rhapsodic spell broken, his comrades avalanched out of equanimity and into consummate actuality. Taking Glyn's lead, they eagle-eyed the interloper.

2

UNEXPECTED ENCOUNTER

Poseidon's crew had grown used to the often-unwanted advances of Arab peddlers in ports from Tangiers to Port de Bejaia, Glyn naturally assuming here was yet another dealer attempting to dispense his vocation.

People in Tunis dressed European, Arab-Tunisian, or a combination of the two styles, the stranger falling into the last category. He made his approach.

"You are English, yes?"

Unwilling to engage in what usually turned out to be a sales pitch, none of the crew answered. Finally, Glyn's close friend Steve Fleming broke the silence.

"Yes, we're English," he confirmed glimpsing around his comrades. "Is there something we can do for you?"

"My name is Saleh bin Tariq bin Khalid Al-Asfour," informed the oddball. "That's my full family name. Allah has blessed me. I am a disciple, a devout Muslim. I pray many times each day. My prayers have brought me to you."

Quite an opening speech, it drew the crew's attention. Their inspection revealed Saleh appeared to be in his early twenties, just short of six feet in height, jet black, imbued with large brown merging into russet eyes set in an impish face, and in all probability, he was versed in the art of concealment. Contrastingly, his slim frame, narrow shoulders and grave expression made him come across as vulnerable. Unkempt, his dark hair had been allowed to grow into a thick morass touching his collar, and his hands were indented with many scratches and scars, the stamps of fatalism and finality upon him. Every inch the archetypal Sub-Saharan, the Englishmen judged him to be a transient, a wanderer attracted to the city in the hope of finding easy pickings. However, the combination of a European jacket worn over traditional Arab garb did not suit him, the former seeming out of place like an inappropriate postscript, a garment hurriedly put on without redress to balance. Therein lay the dichotomy, the glitch betraying the devotion claim, the ship's company alerted to possible trickery.

Unsure of his next sentence, Saleh gawped at them, testing receptiveness.

"Go on," said Jeff.

"I have come from Nazret in Ethiopia." Halting, still trawling for reassurances in their features and body language, he became shaky, his status disarranged, his mouth left open.

"*Yes*," Jeff prompted.

"I," he began, before again losing his train of thought, his physiognomy a peck of conflicting facets.

Becoming fidgety, Glynn noticed Poseidon's crew exchanged glances.

North African experience to date had taught the newcomers to be wary of unwelcome accosts, apparent conviviality invariably concealing hidden agendas. Through their long and eventful tenure in the Med, it was a given for the seniors. They always reminded the newcomers to be watchful when leaving the schooner for any shore activities.

Continuing to ogle blankly as they gauged him, Glyn assessed Saleh realised their demeanour neither promoted nor indicated they wanted to undertake a protracted discussion. He had to take the initiative with conviction or be dismissed by them.

"I can both read and write English," he blurted. "I was taught by a Western aid agency in Dire Dawa. I have been in Tunis for over three weeks."

Like many Arab and Sub-Saharan English speakers, his

clipped dialect made each syllable clear and discernible, further fostering Poseidon's crew to appraise him. Clearly, he banked on a favourable response, but having applied prudence in similar situations until suspicious chancers got to the point, their vigilance persisted. 'In North Africa's backyard, it's always best to play the human chess game with subtlety, until clarity distils true intention', Jeff had briefed earlier in the voyage, his edict now resonating in the newcomers' minds.

"I heard your voices," Saleh spilt, yearning to keep them engrossed. "I knew you must be English. I want to ask you if…"

Trailing away to nothing, the idiom made the Englishmen feel more uncomfortable.

Shifting in their seats, they gaped around the terrace garden, twisting their heads to see into semi-concealed nooks and crannies, wondering if the stranger was truly alone, or whether other cohorts were about to reveal themselves, and descend upon them with menace. Often creatures of the night hunted in pairs or packs, a successful sortie more easily accomplished through numbers, rather than a single player. Unlike the Avenue Moncef Bey café waiters the crew had met earlier in the day, plainly he did not intend to make small talk, nor did he possess merchant characteristics or credentials.

What does he want, Glyn postulated?

"You were saying," Jeff pushed, his granite-like chin thrust forward, a defence the newcomers had seen on previous occasions when danger lurked, and their safety became compromised.

Wringing his hands, Saleh developed a sheepish manner. Espying back at the terrace steps then out onto Avenue Mohammed V, the ship's company followed his eyes, their concern for self-preservation amplified, accomplice-abetted robbery still a possibility. Licking his lips for moisture, Saleh watched them full-on, his gaze blooming with trepidation. Jittery in the exposed surroundings, his hands fell to his sides. Shaking involuntary, his temperament segued into unsteadiness, perspiration building over his forehead.

"He's a singleton," Jeff whispered to Ed. "But is he being pursued?"

"Well," Ed barked, a glint of steel in his tone.

Belligerent as ever to suspicious persons, Ed had already made his mind up about the intruder. He and Jeff had seen identical drifters emerge out of the shadows in other North African ports, their schemes habitually fraudulent. The outcome never pleasant or agreeable, the trick was to get them to move on quickly, without knives being drawn or the authorities summoned, the latter always a tenuous affair resulting in drawn-out interrogation for the plaintiffs.

Surprised by Ed's precipitous burst of assertion, Saleh refocused on his mission.

"I have money," he bellowed, showing them a thick roll of Tunisian dinar. "You have a boat, yes?" he posed, optimism beating in his intonation.

"Huh, so much for devoutness," Ed underwrote, turning to Jeff.

Perceiving a definite miscreant, Poseidon's owners returned perturbed sulks. They had dealt with many testing affairs in North Africa, but given the choice remained risk averse, a cavalier *modus operandi* to the unknown invariably resulting in trouble.

Leaning frontwards Jeff narrowed his eyes. "We're not interested in human cargo," he icily counselled. Flicking his head, he betokened the Ethiopian to quit bartering and move on.

Formally presuming Poseidon's owners were open for business, the bolt dispelled Saleh's short-lived elation, his jaw dropping, disappointment covering his face. Sighing as Jeff's non-negotiable kickback hit home, his head hung heavy to one side, his peepers widening in reaction to grating cognizance.

Advancing from the balcony unnoticed by the crew, a hotel waiter blazed at Saleh, ready to act if requested. "Sir," he said to Jeff, "is this man bothering you?"

Usually reserved, reflecting carefully before taking part in a potentially dicey debate, Bill tapped Jeff on the arm. "Allow me," he requested. "A round of drinks, please." Dwelling, he scrutinised the stranger. "Saleh, you've made me curious. Have a drink with us, and let's see what transpires."

"Yes, have a drink," the equally inquisitive David urged. "I'd like to hear more."

With an eye on broad-mindedness, the unknown a factor to be confronted, Bill and David had begun to pity the Ethiopian, their intrinsic neutrality and a Christian upbringing making allowance for conspicuous insincerity, particularly when the incomer radiated duress.

Back in Blighty, overcoming obstacles had its own rewards, but here in the radically divergent regime of North Africa, the same rules did not necessarily apply, as the seniors had repeatedly channelled to the newcomers on previous occasions. Everyday European directness did not always result in plain speaking from local counterparts. Often sidestepped to disguise ulterior purpose, many the crew spoke to from Tangiers to Tunis became hesitant regarding a definitive comeback, fearing discovery of whatever caper they played.

"Just some orange juice," Saleh spluttered, his vocal cords taut with apprehension. "Thank you."

Before scurrying off, the waiter's blaze at Saleh became a sneer, the outlander reacting by turning away.

Exhaling noisily, catching Bill's and David's attention, Jeff lowered his eyes, the action designed to convey dismay. Sensing a can of worms had been unlocked, they blushed with regret, their inexperience breaching a tried and trusted convention, obdurate consequence rapidly arriving on the back of curiosity.

Rising, Jeff cast an indifferent look at the uninvited guest. Stepping onward, his gaze became probing. "Okay, Saleh, *what* exactly do you want from us?"

Sitting on a low garden wall opposite the crew's semicircle, the outsider detailed his history. Deserted by his parents at age three, he told his listeners he had been taken to Dire Dawa on the leeward side of the Ahmar Mountains by Western missionaries. As well as Arabic, he spoke Amharic and considered himself to be a member of the Amhara ethnic group, a once nomadic, Semitic-speaking people, inhabiting the central highlands of Ethiopia for thousands of years. Predominantly Christian, in more recent times, the Amhara embodied tight-knit family and community values. Saleh had attended Ethiopian Orthodox Tewahedo Church services, but when he moved to Nazret hunting for work, he converted to Islam under the tutelage of a local mullah.

Going on to brief them he had joined a Muslim fundamentalist faction, rebelling against the secular doctrine of the Ethiopian military junta, he confessed to being a wanted man, with ambitions of claiming political asylum. He had appealed for shelter to the Tunisian Department of Immigration and Border Protection, without success. Like the Ethiopian establishment, the Tunisian Government resisted Muslim fundamentalism, instituting laws to forbid its teachings, and enacting campaigns to purge Tunisia of its pernicious mavens. Saleh admitted most Ethiopians were likewise disposed, often turning in atrocity-committing fundamentalists to the authorities. Concluding his address, he insinuated the Tunisians were intent on sending him back to Ethiopia, but he'd managed to evade their weak security, and had sought refuge with a band of Muslim fundamentalists in Tunis. Now he wanted to get to Europe, preferably England.

Returning to the terrace with the drinks, the waiter scowled at Saleh. Dipping his head slightly in a gesture of courtesy to the Englishmen, he then receded back into the Hotel du Lac, grouching under his breath about gullible Europeans stupidly pitying fake exiles.

"Why don't you stay with the Muslim fundamentalists in Tunis?" Glyn asked.

On the face of it baffled, he lowered his head. "It's difficult to say."

"You mean, they don't want you?" Jeff proposed.

"No…no, it's not that. No, it's…"

Dissolving into Arabic mutterings, the sentence left the ship's company doubting Saleh's authenticity. Though novices when it came to North African proceedings, even the newcomers surmised their undesirable guest played his cards without honest certitude, his inability to come clean neutralising any built-up sentiment harvested from his doleful review. Enduring his story unconvinced, they uttered a few notions of suspicion and disbelief to each other, Saleh left agog, still unable to summon up cogent truth.

Since the Ethiopian arrived in their midst, Steve had listened to the dialogue without comment, Glyn knowing he'd been evaluating the stranger during his early interchanges with other crew members. After some bitter personal affairs, Steve had cultivated a careful tack before connecting.

Waiting until he felt sure of his interpretation of the quandary, and thereby able to rate truth, he gave Saleh a perceptive gander, then posed, "Is there really any legitimacy in your story whatsoever?"

"What do you mean?" Saleh retorted, put on the defensive by the softness of the inquiry.

"I mean, are you being truthful?"

"Yes," Tom supported, "I'm wondering about that, as well."

"Me too," Colin declared seconds later.

An imposing soul should circumstance demand, Tom had begun to see the contrariness in Saleh's story, and thereby its flaws. Evolving exceptional personality evaluation skills over decades of man-watching, to his mind, the Ethiopian's account did not ring true. Conversely, Colin was a methodologist, versed in the law and the applied sciences. Using the litmus test to find fact and certainty, few grey regions existed within his determination palette. Both shot glares at Saleh, their accusing mugs further increasing his fragility.

"You appear to be extremely nervous," Steve ascribed. "That's usually associated with those having something to be afraid about, or alternatively—" He bore deep into Saleh's phizog. "Those pulling the wool."

Confident his crew had begun to doubt their dubious guest, Jeff sat down, still annoyed in spite of his protestations some of them still strayed into rickety waters, allowing the unqualified unknown to impact their security.

Indicating his own approval, Ed growled, "Thank Christ for that." Directing an apprehensive grimace at Jeff, his carriage suggested the happenstance be brought to a swift conclusion, and Saleh sent packing.

Clocking signs of alarm beyond the obvious, Glyn guessed the encounter had brought recalls to the forefront of the senior's minds. Perhaps, he calculated, comparable occurrences had indented their good natures, the upshot closing off any further approaches without exception. Though outwardly fully open on all matters, nonetheless, Jeff and Ed had sufficient gravitas to cloak barbed issues without being pretentious. Soon after the voyage began, Glyn divined they dodged burdening the crew with legacy baggage for yet to be outlined reasons.

Dogging for a hook to restart their kindness, the Ethiopian searched the Englishmen's faces for renewed consideration.

"You *have* to believe me," he implored. "*Please*, I cannot begin to tell you how important it is you take pity on me and help me." As if Charon the ferryman stood at his shoulder, his mien became bleached of autonomy, Poseidon's crew arrested between patronage and dismissal.

Earlier, balance had made Glyn empathetic to Saleh. Now he recognised something very doubtful about the interrupter, his story just too pristine to be totally true. He'd been musing about his ex-wife Suzy, and a time when like Saleh, they should have made the grand move. With his ruminations wayfaring into the past, he'd failed to see the warning signs. Free from ambiguity, he counted they reeked of capricious fiction, and ominously, Saleh's agitated condition flagged probity and the Ethiopian rarely collided. Assaying the gate-crasher with a dispassionate appraisal, his sensitive nose told him Saleh held back from a full explanation.

"Saleh," he began in a measured note.

Snapping his head around to look at Glyn, his gills became charged with escalating hope, the aspiration for understanding clear to see.

"Trying for emotional blackmail won't work, especially when you leave the imprint that you and the truth do not coexist."

Startled by the accusation, Saleh's lips parted slightly, his gaze traversing about his inquisitors sending out spikes of fretfulness, classic signs of hidden confessions yet to be disclosed.

"What haven't you told us?" Glyn probed. "What is really driving this quest to flee from Tunis?"

Anguish crossed the Ethiopian's face. Briskly ascending to his full height, he peeked about the terrace garden in a jerking motion, his mettle blunted but escape still an option. Steadying himself and ignoring Glyn's query he pleaded, "Aahh, I'm…I am really desperate. If the Tunisian police don't get me, the Muslim fundamentalists will. You must believe me. If I don't get out of Tunis…I will be *killed*!"

Normally a statement of such dire punch attracted anxiety, even abhorrence. However, the path Saleh trod in terms of fractured accuracy apropos his plight progressively made Poseidon's crew distrust him, his latest incendiary revelation reinforcing the impression.

"What is it you want from us?" Glyn persisted.

"I want you to…" Quivering, unable to complete the request, he rested.

"*Answer the question*," Jeff reiterated in a stern overtone. "What do you want?"

"I want you to take me to Sicily with you," Saleh blurted out regaining confidence. "I have money. I can pay. They're after me. They will kill me. You *must* take me." Hopping from foot-to-foot with nervous tension, he showed them his thick wad of readies again.

"Hah, just as I suspected," Jeff scoffed.

"Who is after you, and why do they want to kill you?" Glyn prodded, sweeping his gaze around at his comrades for advocacy. Reengaging Saleh, he duplicated, "*Why?*"

Terminating the hopping, Saleh froze, holding his breath, his eyes lodged on stalks. Wringing his hands again, he began to perspire.

"You stole the money from the fundamentalists, didn't you?" Ed grilled.

Hesitating, he responded, "Yes."

"And the jacket?" Ed appended inspecting his attire.

"That as well," the Ethiopian conceded.

Shrinking into lost sullenness, the scraps of initial confidence and composure he had displayed oozed away. He had confided his pickle, cocksure it'd be received with compassion, but a touch of solemnity would not have gone amiss far earlier in the conversation.

"Why do you want to go to Sicily?" Colin quizzed. "Why not go back to Ethiopia?"

By then, the Englishmen inwardly anticipated the phoney justification. Saleh's end objective seeped out like an advanced forecast. Wanting them to see it and make it easy for him, he wished them to discharge the invitation, bequeath the gold-plated parachute, and let him float gently onto cloud nine. Whispering their misgivings to each other about his true intent, it led to the balance of the encounter being an affirmation of the all too explicit suspicion.

On the edge of self-discipline, Saleh scrunched up his kisser, his bartered proposal lingering indeterminately. Simulating the swinging pendulum of a topsy-turvy grandfather clock, his panicky hopping started again. Petrified, he meticulously scoped the hotel grounds left and right, then peered out onto Avenue Mohammed V, horn squawks from irate motorists involved in ill-judged overtaking manoeuvres dragging his circumspection further down the road. Every odd commotion accentuated his immersion, as if he expected an imminent disagreeable clique to fall upon him.

"You have to help me," he beseeched. "I haven't got much time. I have to get out of here." Overwhelmingly anxious for his wellbeing, he looked about once more, then thrusting the dinar forward again, tendered, "You can have all this money."

"Why Sicily?" Bill needled. "What's so special about Sicily?"

"As well as officialdom, I'm being pursued by the fundamentalists," he claimed while the hopping mushroomed. "If I'm caught, they will torture me, then kill me. I have to get…"

Again the sentence faded away into Arabic mutterings. Vacant and panting, uneasy about his fate, and desperately seeking to conjure up his next play, Saleh's spirit went further down the well, close to spent.

Gathering together, Poseidon's crew broke into a hushed

parley to decide what to do, their tenor not hopeful as far as the stranger was concerned. Regarding him equitably, Glyn ascertained no mark of the manacles were on the Ethiopian, or any portent of persecution, yet he desired their sanctuary. Originally unreadable, his true nature had started to emerge.

As he reflected further, Glyn surveyed Saleh again, determining he possessed the elegant, wasted comportment associated with lovelorn poets, combined with feint grace and mystery. But something else became transparent, bipolar in its clout. Brittleness was patent, but could it be a front hiding a very dissimilar beast? Perhaps his outer layer contained the softer incumbency. Further back in his lair, there might be another side, capable of the atrocities he alluded to earlier. Given the opportunity and the motivation, could he be a future bomber with appetites turned testy in pursuit of carnage? Just the tonic needed to mask off morality in favour of terrorism, his wide-eyed glare hinted he condemned Anglo-American interventionism in the Middle East as indefensible, while concurrently seeing no backpedalling of the ethics code, when it came to applauding Muslims executing kidnapped Westerners live on the internet. Befitting a phlegmatic resolution, Glyn figured hypocrisy inhabited his realm of filmy contradictions.

Sensing the crew's reticence, Saleh agonisingly bleated, "Okay, okay," curtailing their deliberation.

Ogling him from their senate-like semi-circle, the ship's company awaited his rejoinder. Taking a large gulp of orange juice, he then wiped his mouth and breathed out making a hissing noise. Balancing himself, he stopped panting as if preparing another monologue of woe but let fly with unforeseen aggression.

"You owe black people," he spat out, timidity of alleged pursuers temporarily stowed away. "I am a devout Black Muslim. Your crusaders did immense wrongs to us. We want revenge on the infidel. It's my time to get justice from you. I want to live in England. You used to be great, but now we know your politically correct politicians have made you weak and feeble, ripe for exploitation. It's the duty of all true neophytes to inflict havoc on the West, abuse your pathetic human rights laws, destroy your civilisation, and make you our slaves."

Aghast at Saleh's rapacious outpouring, the crew sat back, stunned by the suddenness of his diatribe. Proud of his inflammatory outburst, he stood tall, hands on hips and head impelled forward, his aggressive body language challenging them to respond.

Preliminary dialogue with Saleh had revealed his devotion to Islam. Evidently an unshakeable proselyte, he adhered to the Koran's teachings and practiced its canon verbatim. Now it became clear the fundamentalist's acerbic creed had been superimposed on the baseline belief, making Saleh a potentially dangerous and deranged being, if not a ticking time bomb, ready to explode on command. If faith was his master as he professed, he had a propensity to meander in and out, using it to maximise effect when the occasion necessitated, his reference to crusaders shining a thousand grudges and complaints.

"*So*," Colin proclaimed, "everything you said earlier really was a lie."

Sustaining his impudent look, Saleh stared to infinity, his lips sealed.

"Why are you referring to crusaders?" Glyn cross-examined. "Do you mean, the Crusades?"

Grabbing Glyn's attention, the stranger vehemently said, "*Yes.*"

"Are you saying, all the Muslim atrocities we have seen in recent years, like nine-eleven and seven-seven, are founded on what happened nearly a thousand years ago?"

"Yes. We must take our revenge on and defeat the descendants of the crusaders. We have to—"

Before he could go any further, Ed stood up, almost knocking over his chair, blood rushing to his face, anger consuming his calm. Curtly interrupting Saleh, he grouched, "You mean to tell us Muslims still harbour a grudge for something that happened hundreds of years ago?"

Remaining silent, Saleh's arrogant body language showed his

nerve. Sitting down, he curled his upper lip at Poseidon's crew, emanating a disgust for non-Muslims.

"*Good god*, man," Ed boomed, "the English have suffered multiple defeats over more than 2,000 years. Worse still, we have lost tens of millions in two world wars. In cosmic terms, that happened just yesterday." Ceasing his rebuke, he waited for a retort, but none came from the Ethiopian. "Muslims were the aggressors when they invaded the Holy Land. Just because they got a massive spanking from the crusaders, you think it gives present-day Muslims the right to wage jihad against the West in the twenty-first century." Not far from losing restraint and applying his huge hands to Saleh's scrawny neck, he gulped in air to keep himself calm. "Using your rationale, the English should be waging war on the Pope, for what the Romans did to our ancestors, but that's ridiculous...*isn't it?*"

Saleh's indifference remained, his stare directed toward infinity again.

Taking a few short steps towards the malcontent, Ed leaned over him fuming, Saleh aflutter under his presence. Cowering in abject guilt, he raised an arm over his phiz, assuming a beating to be coming his way.

Desisting, Ed calmed himself but still smoldered. "There comes a time," he powerfully promoted, "when all reasonable people put wars behind them and try to repair the damage done. Following your rules, we English should be killing Germans and Japs for the atrocities they inflicted on our people during World War II, and as I say, that was just yesterday." Resuming the vertical, Ed tried to preserve his stiff composure before advancing the argument. "But we don't. We try to forgive and forget. But maybe that's the difference between Western Christianity and Islam. Because we can forgive, we presume other people wanting to enter our realm, will behave the same way, but you Muslims are beyond that...*aren't you?*"

Hunching himself up in an act of self-loathing, Saleh lifted his knees into his midriff, burying his head in them, shutting out the senior's image. Ending his attack, Ed returned to his seat, breathing heavily and beside himself because anger had got the better of him.

Though eminently intelligent, Glyn knew Ed's hackles could speedily rise in response to wrong doers. Free-loading transgressors, something-for-nothing dogma, and mendacity coupled with hypocrisy, all appalled him. Back in Cadiz at the start of the voyage, Jeff had told the newcomers about Ed's short temper, and how he'd pledged to try and turn the other cheek when accosted by rapacious ingratitude or downright deception. Saleh had driven him through the sanguine barrier, Ed annoyed with himself for falling into the trap.

The more the Englishmen gave Saleh the third degree, the more he began to fit the fictitious asylum seeker profile. Finally, he confessed he was not an orphan, and his parents and many brothers and sisters were back in Ethiopia. Acting as an advanced guard, his sole purpose was to accomplish asylum in England. Once established, he planned to tell the authorities, his family were being persecuted by the Ethiopian Government and must be allowed to join him.

Doubtless real, the familiar hallmarks of something the crew could read in the *Daily Mail* about duplicitous bogus asylum seekers were prevalent. Also intent upon wholesale deception, Saleh told them, there were hundreds of thousands just like him, massing on the North African coastline, waiting to cross the Med. Further, a passing fancy plotted to solicit sympathy, engender Western guilt and play the mythical tribulation card, Saleh conceded he was not a member of a Muslim fundamentalist cabal, and the Ethiopian administration were not after him. Bolstering their rebuttal, the crew maintained it was unlikely his family were being persecuted, Saleh acquiescing on the false story as well. Notwithstanding, the more they dissected his claim, the more Glyn and his friends reckoned the Tunis Muslim fundamentalists wanted Saleh for theft, and being an illegal, doubtless the Tunisian administration had him on their radar.

Contesting why he and his fellow countrymen did not try to make a better life for themselves in Ethiopia, instead of freeloading off other people, the Englishmen's rebuke only served to reignite Saleh's intolerant bearing and desire for vengeance. Returning to the thought that the world at large owed black people, and the Muslim revenge for defeat by the crusaders was legitimate, he gave stock vindications to their counter viewpoints. Plainly someone else's words, he echoed them verbatim.

"I can see your dilemma," Glyn underlined, "even empathise with your situation, but in place of fleecing England, why don't you work to improve the economics of your own country?" Lowering his voice, he continued. "Contrary to what you believe, the world does not owe black Africa a living. You already get huge amounts of taxpayer funded relief from the West, England in particular, but I'm sorry to say, we distinguish it mostly ends up in the pockets of corrupt officials or funding executive jets for tin-pot dictators." With the crew making affirming nods in agreement, Glyn produced his final prescriptive remark. "You should toil for self-sufficiency, economic independence, and originate an honest statute we can respect. Surely you can see the entire world could be bankrupted bailing out blacks, and nothing will change in Ethiopia, or any other black African country, would it?"

With his head tilted down as if gazing at his navel, Saleh acknowledged what Glyn said to be unarguable.

Reaffirming their beliefs, Tom notified him it had only been since the end of WWII that relative prosperity had been consummated by ordinary English people through hard work, dedication to task and self-reliance. "Wind back the clock to the nineteen-thirties and you'll find the English people, like most Western Europeans and Americans, were out of work, homeless, and starving in the Great Depression. They could not, or did not, avouch phony economic asylum rank with more prosperous countries. They had to work their way out of it, fight the Nazis', win the war, and then start a programme of social and economic prosperity, resulting in the baby-boomer generation becoming better off than their forefathers."

"Those sacrifices made by our parents and grandparents were not done so fraudulent asylum seekers and carpetbagger economic migrants can milk the welfare system they tirelessly strived to create," Colin reinforced. "Neither was it done to transform the ethnic makeup of England, so her indigenous people feel under great threat." Distressed by the implications of his words, he defended, "I'm sorry to be so frank, but go back to the nineteenth century, and even further back in our history, and life expectancy for most English people was very short, with life extremely tough and harsh."

Taking up the theme, Bill stipulated, "Yet the Third World assumes England has streets paved with gold, and every Englishman has lived in the lap of luxury since time immemorial. Right now, England like much of Western Europe and North America, is heading for severe economic recession." Eyeing the Ethiopian critically, he took a long pull on his drink, then finished saying, "England is already the most densely packed country in the developed World. For social and economic pretexts, we simply can't take any more economic migrants or asylum seekers. The populace won't stand for it. If not impeded and reversed, the country could be goaded into Bosnia-style civil war through the sheer desperation of its indigenous people."

Appeasement written into his complexion, Saleh became shamefaced, aware the valuation to be undeniable. What his contenders had said was not new to him. He'd been well educated and had access to the internet back in Nazret and Dire Dawa. He knew the score. He knew if his own country had wealth resultant from diligent work, and European economic migrants flooded Ethiopia, his outraged people would throw the intruders out by force, just like Idi Amin did to Asian migrants in mid-nineteen-seventies Uganda.

His guilt laying ploy had failed to gain acceptance from Poseidon's crew, let alone transit to Sicily. With his ulterior motive uncovered, Saleh became downhearted, contrition replacing dogged defiance. Taking a seat between Steve and Glyn, he began to talk about his life, the audience softening to his predicament, even stern-faced, implacable Ed became kindly.

Telling them about his family, his delinquent father, more about Nazret and Dire Dawa, he then admitted taxpayer-funded Western aid agencies had provided for his welfare and education.

Working for a Western independent charity as a translator, life was good for Saleh compared to most Ethiopians, and clearly, the Ethiopian authorities did not want him for being a Muslim terrorist. In truth, Poseidon's crew were right. He had portrayed himself to be a cheap asylum seeker, currying favour with Tunisian Muslim fundamentalists, and gaining their patronage before stealing money to fund his intended getaway to England along with the jacket and other items.

"How did you get from Ethiopia to Tunis?" Glyn asked, furrowing his brow. "It must have been a torturous journey travelling across Sudan, Egypt and Libya."

At once, Saleh's confidence reignited. Almost nonchalantly he replied, "Oh, I actually came by plane from Addis Ababa."

"*What*!" the Englishmen exclaimed in unison.

Saleh's subterfuge foundered again. His caution had slipped, lies accidentally traded-in for truth. Realising he had made a titanic *faux pas*, he became stage-struck sensing a further bout of rebuke.

United stringency resurfaced amongst the crew. Jeff stood up, followed by Ed, Tom and David, all towering over the Ethiopian, Saleh staying silent, head bowed in regret as if stupefied by a cobra.

"You mean to tell us," Jeff began, "you had enough money to go by plane, yet you pretend you are a persecuted asylum seeker?"

Fuming, David blasted, "And you have the gaul to sit there, trying to lay a guilt trip on us, when you're not destitute?"

Consternation overcame Saleh. On the verge of fleeing, he rapidly verified his breakout path, but his nerve held. Attack becoming his best defence, he challenged their moral right to judge him. It got predatory, dirty, his vicious tongue once more delivering a scathing assault.

Thundering up defiantly, he berated, "You criticise me when your country backs the Israeli fascist regime murdering my Palestinian brothers, and the world's biggest anti-Muslim aggressor, the United States, bombing Muslim cities." Regaining his mercenary instincts, the boldness returned. "The urge to rip off the English welfare scheme and exploit your civil rights laws, is part of my revenge for all Muslims." Fixing the ship's company with unmitigated disdain, he shrieked, "I *hate* the West, I want it destroyed. I want the uncut world to be ruled by Muslim fundamentalists, and everybody subjected to Sharia Law. I want to see England, America and all the other anti-Muslim states wiped off the face of the Earth. The Holocaust is a lie, put about by Zionists to promote sympathy for the Jews..."

For sure, he wasn't going anywhere. If being tracked, his pursuers had decamped from his mind. He wanted to fight, more so than just blowing off steam. Intoxicated for the physical, he clenched his fists. If he'd had a sword, he'd have used it, glorious martyrdom within touching distance. Certainly, Ed would have obliged him.

As his anti-Semitic bombast boiled over, Poseidon's crew expressed their distaste of his two-faced tirade, and disgust of his self-righteous indignation and hypocrisy. Saturated in vitriol, Saleh remained inattentive to their reprimand.

Walking up and down in front of the Ethiopian, holding his chin with his left hand, the Holocaust remark brought Steve to the plate for batting action, Saleh remaining in full-rant mode, transparent to his movement. Halting, Steve pointed at him, the Muslim zealot quitting his gushing anger.

"You know—" Steve sniggered. "You're absolutely right about the Holocaust."

Astonished, the crew gasped at the inconsiderate remark, but Glyn knew his long-time friend merely fished, tempting Saleh to rise.

Glowering at the kibitzer in their midst with a piercing intensity, Steve pronounced, "It's just like slavery was a myth in the Americas, brought about by failed black asylum seekers and economic migrants, sent back from the plantations to Africa for being jumped-up, untrustworthy troublemakers." Stepping forward, he pressured, "Don't you agree?"

Enraged by the deliberately rendered mockery, Saleh's inflexible standpoints made him blind to its satire. "No, no...it's *not* true," he stubbornly rebuked. "Black slavery did happen. It *did* happen."

"How do you know?" Steve questioned.

"Because…because everybody knows. I've read about it. It's fact."

"Could just be lies propagated by black political opportunists to hold the West to guilt ransom?"

Coasting into silence, Saleh's lower lip quivered. Had Steve hit a sore spot?

Grimacing at the moonstruck Ethiopian, he continued, "Anyway, as Ed said earlier, our people were enslaved by the Romans, but you don't see us banging on the Pope's front door and bleating, 'hey buddy, you owe us for what your Roman ancestors did to my people'…unlike the way you blacks constantly do. We have more pride, whereas the only weapon in your arsenal, is to try and lay guilt." Turning serious, Steve shot a dagger-look at Saleh. "Won't work. It is blacks who owe us. If Hitler had prevailed, we wouldn't be having this conversation." Moving further onward, he finished only inches away from Saleh's dampened puss. "The Nazis' would've wiped you lot out, and you know it. So, it is *you*, Saleh, who should get down on your knees, and be thanking us for holding out against Hitler, and conclusively defeating him."

Recoiling, totally dejected, Saleh sat back down, open-mouthed, and perspiring profusely. He knew what Steve singled out to be totally true. Time to grasp at straws.

"Black slavery did happen…it did happen," he whimpered in a near-to manic intonation, the words formed full by a mouth misshapen with blazing fury, his outright being looming into rage. With delirium welling up inside of him, the ignite flame flowered again. "*It did happen, it did happen*," he shouted.

"Yes, you are quite right," Steve consented, releasing the tension. "It did happen. Just like the Holocaust happened. The evidence is incontrovertible. Only you are highly selective in your truth. You dismiss the Holocaust, but you buy into black slavery in the Americas, because it suits your political agenda." Turning away from Saleh, he rejoined his comrades. "Scarcely an objective position, is it?" Steve posed. "Oh, and by the way, if you want to milk somebody, go to Kuwait where the streets are paved with petrodollars, and everyone gets an annual income from the government equivalent to thirty-thousand pounds, regardless of if they work, or not."

Still incensed by the Ethiopian's easy duplicity, Ed pressed home the assertion. "Yes," he endorsed, "why don't you go to Kuwait, Saleh? Or do you admit, they won't want you there either? Damned right! Get real, the Kuwaitis despise artificial asylum seekers as much as any other country."

Rubbernecking back, a blank condition written into his visage, his eyes transfixed by bitter truth, and his forehead dripping beads of perspiration, Saleh knew he had flunked achieving his primary goal, embarkation to Europe. Awkwardly shifting about in his seat and twisting his body in an angular frenzy as if constrained by a straitjacket, his demeanour became volcanic. He stormed to his feet again.

"You are all devils. You are all white, Christian bastards," he bawled in a cold inflection. "When we rise, you will all pay for your crimes against black Muslims." Hoisting a wavering arm at Poseidon's crew, as if it held a sword, he wailed, "I will personally kill every one of you, gouge out your blue eyes, and hack you to pieces when we…"

As the haranguing babble went on, his targets sat cross-armed exchanging glances, not quite conscious of what to do next but tuning out his condemnation of anything not Muslim, his grandstanding just too verbose to warrant serious assessment. His eruption intensified, smoking out the real Saleh bin Tariq bin Khalid Al-Asfour, the boosted performance jagged and flailing.

Jeff turned to Ed. "I just can't hear this guy anymore."

"Can I shoot him?"

Sticking his tongue almost through his cheek, Jeff said, "Best not to, it will only upset the locals."

Catching on to the humour, Colin played an imaginary violin, as Tom hummed Chopin's *Piano Sonata No 2 in B-flat minor*.

Oblivious to the Englishmen no longer taking him seriously, Saleh continued decimating all things Western and Christian. They could have evaporated away into nothingness, but he'd have tarried blind to their departure, his craze on automatic, but unpersuasive.

Turning his head slowly from side-to-side, Steve quipped, "He couldn't sell food to the starving Biafrans, could he?"

"Never seen anyone less convincing," Bill commented. "He couldn't sell himself out of a wet paper bag."

Joining in, David gibed, "His ability to be compelling is about as likely as a certain Wigan Athletic striker scoring a goal for England."

"Yes," Glyn agreed. "He couldn't hit water if he fell out of a boat."

Staggered by the onslaught, Ed started laughing. Soon they were all lost in hysterics, the spectacle of Saleh in full broadside fashion, arms thrashing about to emphasise his stream of hate, but without any sense he had lost them, comic. In the short time they had known the Ethiopian, he had become a parody of himself. Attempting to inform Saleh they were no longer receiving, Colin waved his hands in front of his chest, but the demagogue saw nothing. He had gone, lost in the *de facto* standard clichés of enmity learnt from radical mullahs.

As his voice reached a high-pitched crescendo, in the background Poseidon's crew heard their drinks waiter chime out, "There he is. That's the man."

Expeditiously terminating his bluster, Saleh gawked at the balcony. Frozen to the spot, his jaw dropped. Turning about, the Englishmen's laughter died away as they saw Tunisian police officers stood next to the waiter. One of them gestured and issued an order, but before his colleagues could start down the balcony steps to apprehend the illegal, Saleh fled, the police following in hot pursuit.

Agape, the ship's company awaited the next incendiary act.

3

REALISATION

While the police bustled around the balcony summoning witnesses for statements, and Hotel du Lac staff righted chairs pushed over during Saleh's escape, Poseidon's crew debated the unexpected encounter.

"Wow, I'm all for excitement and the shock of the new," Glyn attested, "but I didn't foresee coming across anything like that."

"Well, I suppose if you put yourself into the outer limits, you're more likely to find the unanticipated," Steve chided. Ogling the seniors, he petitioned. "That's right, isn't it, Jeff?"

"No two ways about it. Ed and I have had more bombshell moments in the Med than either back home or in the Caribbean. It's an area constantly throwing up surprises. But I must say—" He turned to address Ed. "We've never met an ingrate quite like Saleh before, have we?"

Shaking his head, Ed affirmed, "No. To say it topped our list of formidable verbal flukes, is an understatement."

"What will happen next?" Bill asked, studying the police reconstructing what had occurred by talking to the waiter and other hotel staff.

"Difficult to say," Jeff submitted. "The one thing consistent with North African brass, is inconsistency itself. Procedures for dealing with crime vary widely. The police could just send us on our way, or—" Glancing at the officers going about their duty, he made an ambivalent pout.

"Or," Bill repeated.

"Or, they could hold us for questioning."

"It depends on how much of Saleh's tale was real," Ed contended. "But judging by the way the police charged off after him, I can only surmise the latter half of his story held water, and he is wanted by the authorities."

In their minds, the newcomers were still circling overhead, yet to drop down to *terra firma*, the sudden arrival of the police making hearts pump faster and the jitters produce an adrenaline rush. They had got sucked into Saleh's theatre, drawn in headlong fuelled by revulsion of his sickly doctrine and future blueprints. Depleted by the intensity of the event, from the wanderer's mellow entrance, through his momentous central period, and his volatile exit, they were captured in the web of incredulity he had generated. Emphatically the antithesis of nearly everything else they had experienced prior to Tunis, taking Saleh's wrath head-on and fighting fire with fire had brought out some hidden demons and prejudices *vis-à-vis* his antagonistic say-so. Unquestionably, there had been some hairy moments, particularly at sea, but all paled in significance compared to the latest incident.

Beyond the odd hirsute flash, the focus of their flutter primarily centred on sailing Poseidon, light-hearted fun, inner space communion, and cultural appreciation. Fleetingly discussing thorny or contentious wrangles when occasion demanded, but invariably in an academic vogue, their indignation had never risen above mild stimulation. A floating rock and roll circus for maverick adventurers prowling for life fulfilment, in the main, Poseidon offered a platform for them to act out their fantasies. None of the newcomers had signed up for the trip with finding controversy in mind. Collectively, they sought quiescent pastures, empowering them to saunter through landscapes and seascapes in the knowledge dissension and disharmony had been left far behind in England.

"It's definitely not over yet," Glyn advised signalling to the police. "Studying the body language of those officers, they're not going to just dust us down, and wave us on our way."

"Yes, I dare say you're right, Glyn," Colin backed. "I've got a feeling there's much more to come."

"*Oh*," David exclaimed. "What makes you say that?"

"There's more to Saleh than he showed us, something fitting into a bigger picture, we're yet to understand."

Combing for solace in pro tem alcoholic retreat, Tom announced, "I need another drink, chaps. Anyone else want a snorter?"

Drawing the waiter's attention, Jeff requisitioned spirits all round. Casually resettling on the terrace, the ship's company circumvented suspicious police glances by sustaining their cool, giving the appearance they were in no way part of Saleh's masquerade.

"The more I think about it, the more Saleh reminds me of Charles," Jeff stated, gaping at Ed.

Earlier in the voyage, Jeff had told the newcomers about Charles Seagrove, a family friend going back more than three decades who had converted to Scientology. A contemporary of Jeff's at Cambridge, Charles had majored in theology, becoming a Church of England parish vicar. After initially finding strong vocation, he began to lose his conviction when his young wife perished in a road accident. Though retaining some Christian beliefs, eventually he left the priesthood to lead a secular life in commerce. His outlook became frail, his life meaning severely retarded, Jeff losing contact with him for many years. Then out of the blue, he resurfaced, joining the seniors and their families in Montserrat for a Caribbean summer voyage on Poseidon 2.

Quite by chance, Charles had met a scientologist, became inquisitive about the lore, and began attending the East Grinstead Church of Scientology. Traversing a fine line between Christianity and Scientology, never positive on which side of the demarcation zone he might fall, Charles hovered, impounded between two stools. Definitively, the latter prevailed, his Christian ethos deconstructed and reformed in the ideology of L. Ron Hubbard.

Jeff became aware of the divinity conversion before Montserrat, paying little attention to his friend's Saint Paul on the road to Damascus moment. However, during the voyage, if an occasion arose to his advantage, Charles constantly plagued other crew members about Scientology, speaking of his admiration for Hubbard, and how he had studied the scientology exposition at length.

Jeff knew Hubbard had a tainted past. Despite being jailed for fraud in France and becoming the subject of intense press speculation stoking his lack of credibility, he launched the Scientology creed in 1952 based on his own dubious Dianetics religious philosophy. To many onlookers, Hubbard was a monumental conman, gaining a multi-millionaire standing by coaxing large monetary contributions from his followers in return for Scientology's secret gospels and practices. When Jeff enumerated the shortcomings, Charles had none of it, freely yielding, without reservation he'd brought out the cheque book on many occasions.

Relentless in his drive, there was no absconding for the Poseidon 2 crew from his badgering campaign to convert them to Scientology. Ultimately requested to leave the boat at Barbados, Jeff had not heard from him since.

"Yes, I see what you mean," Ed confirmed. "Now you mention it, I recognise the parallels with Charles, and thereby the problems. Saleh is a matching creature apropos blinkered patronage, though I could never accuse Charles of having the easy duplicity the Ethiopian exhibited."

"Religion is fine, if gauged in context, and used to add richness to life without diminishing everything adjacent it," Jeff argued. "But like Scientology, Islamic fundamentalism crosses over the boundaries of reason, and the shared space for coexistence with other religions and the secular world. It makes it very troublesome for non-confrontational people to tolerate, notably when in recent times, unreciprocated broad-mindedness ends up with Muslim terrorist atrocities becoming the vehicle to try and make the world submit to the will of despot, self-appointed, Islamic evangelists."

Scanning the crew, he noted their agreeing body language acknowledgement, their own analysis of the Muslim problem in sync with his.

"What you say is true, Jeff," Glyn concurred, heavy-hearted with misgiving. "These tenets are not passive, like say Buddhism. They are hostile and corrosive, unfluctuating on eradicating all competition by domination and violence." Still unsure of what he had witnessed, he peeped back, distrustful of the vacant space where Saleh had embarked on his rant. "Indeed, they are both examples of neo-fascism. I hear a lot of zealous pundits bandying the word tolerance about back home, but they never ever apply it to Muslim terrorists. Somehow, they always excuse their dreadful deeds with some fashionable politically correct excuse to legitimise atrocities."

"Yes, I got the distinct hint, like Charles, Saleh could never be rational, let alone objective," Jeff replied. "The outright, unconditional codex given to him by Islamic extremists would repulse alternative explanation and unorthodox sentiment, including no place for tenderness, generosity or equity afforded to non-believers."

"But at first sight," Tom advocated, "he hardly looked like a terrorist, did he?"

"What should terrorists look like?" Bill queried. "Most of history's villains looked very normal. It's not how they look, its' what's in their mind. That can be hidden and disguised, kept at bay until they've wormed their way, or been allowed to worm their way into a society, before committing terrorist crimes."

"Where's the salvation in it?" Steve contested. "To kill civilians *en masse* and abducted soldiers in cold blood without just cause, is as heinous as the barbaric acts committed by Hitler, Stalin and Pol Pot. And for liberal, do-gooder elitists to pretend these crimes are justified, puts them in the same category. They might not have pulled the trigger or wielded the sword, but they sure as hell inaugurated the social and political frameworks, making Muslim terrorism a near-to everyday occurrence in Europe."

Employing a clinical perspective, Poseidon's resident historian

Colin proposed a motive. "Gentlemen, you must appreciate to Muslim jihadists, we are the blue-eyed, fair-haired devils, the progeny of the crusaders who rid the Holy Land of Saladin and the Muslims. There's been resentment ever since."

While Colin extended his commentary, the ship's company noticed the police searching the terrace garden grounds for evidence of Saleh's presence, and taking official testimonies from hotel staff. Returning from unsuccessfully apprehending the fugitive, the officers involved explained to their colleagues how he evaded their grasp. Summoned by the officer at the helm, the hotel manager arrived on the balcony steps. Interrogating him about the Englishmen, the officer took his formal admission. Weighing up his defensive flags and surprised facial expression, Poseidon's crew guessed the hotel manager evinced he had never seen them before. Gawking in their direction during the process, the officer exhibited doubt about the declaration. As more accounts were taken from hotel staff, police suspicions relating to the crew's involvement sharpened. Soon they'd be coming for them.

"The concept of holy war or jihad to expand oppression aims was embraced by the followers of Islam, when the Muslims seized Jerusalem in 638 AD," Colin particularised. "Later, the Church of the Holy Sepulcher on the site of Christ's crucifixion, burial and resurrection was destroyed in 1009 by Hakim, the Fatimid Caliph of Egypt. Then a new wave of Muslim aggression by the Seljuk Turks led to Christian persecution in the Holy Land, and the invasion of the Byzantine Empire."

"I didn't realise it was as deep as that," David remarked, smiling facetiously at the explanation. "I should have listened to my school history lessons more intensely."

"Quite," Colin returned, impervious to the slight mockery. "Their scorched earth offensive massacred millions without mercy or regret. Constantinople became vulnerable, and pilgrimages to the Holy Land ended abruptly. Byzantine Emperor Alexius Comnenus appealed to Pope Urban II for help. In turn, the call went out from Rome to Christendom, leading to five crusades, finalising with the Holy Land reclaimed by the crusaders and the Muslims defeated."

"Are you saying, Muslim fundamentalism was born out of this defeat and humiliation?" Glyn enquired.

"Yes. That's a judicious interpretation."

"And, it's been in play down the succeeding centuries?"

"It has, and therefore?" Colin unfolded his eyes wide at Glyn, signifying he desired the corollary.

"So, in the struggle for worldwide Muslim domination," Glyn avouched, gathering his valuations, "the latest generation of Muslim jihadists are using it as a means to fire up the young and the susceptible, to make the ultimate sacrifice."

"Precisely, hence Saleh's references to the crusades. He must have become easy meat for the mullahs. They've indoctrinated him into the brotherhood's unethical credo, with ends to use him for their own itinerary."

Conspicuously, Colin's factual narration made for an uncomfortable zero hour regarding Saleh and his caustic principles. But in a parallel province, though his methods were deplorable, Glyn could see why the Ethiopian wanted to re-launch his life in England. As the discussion ensued, he mentally recalled people he had met, telling him about life-changing decisions, turning out to exceed their wildest fictions. Those moving to Australia and New Zealand to continue their careers, or retiring in the Dordogne and Tuscany, and even more buying second homes in faraway places, had found a new way in life. Such daredevils had disclosed their natural itch to want to switch surroundings, take a calculated risk, and achieve a higher level of familiarity with wisdom.

Since the late nineteen-sixties, low cost air travel had made the wanderlust craving a reality for a generation of young Westerners, whose parents had seldom strayed far from their place of birth. Approaching the millennium, the I.T and communications industries had brought the opportunity to explore the possibilities in depth via internet services, enabling argonauts to trek around the globe, only armed with a credit card and an email address. Conversely, global news broadcasts picked up in the Third World on television receivers and personal computers, had acted to energise and further increase Third World bulk migrations. From the information received, they perceived the grass to be greener in the Western democracies, the temptation to pretend persecution in their countries of origin, just too juicy to resist.

In Saleh's case, the freeloading, easy-life choice became his main incentive, the prospect of living in a hotel under the guise of an asylum seeker, his subsistence covered by taxpayers, the supreme wasters' dream.

As the rest of the crew reviewed the Ethiopian affair in more detail, Glyn drifted off again figuratively replete with financial and universal communication credentials, revisiting his contrivances about the divine move he conjured up earlier, when Saleh made his intent clear.

During a visit to Key West in 1990, Glyn and Suzy met a family originating from New York, residing in Hemingway's backyard for over twenty-five years. Back in the mid-sixties, George and Beth were married with a young family. He spent his days as an equities trader at Morgan Stanley, whilst she brought up their two infants. They had never set foot out of New England, so decided to vacation in the Keys. Proving to be a massive eye opener, the trip brought to light profound lifestyle differences. Whereas New York was exemplified by breakneck speed living, they found Florida to be laid back, all the family enjoying the novel backdrop. On return to the Big Apple, it became arduous to get back into their daily routines. George found himself preoccupied with lazy afternoons spent in Fort Zachary Taylor State Park, gazing out over the Caribbean while sipping Bahaman rum under a parasol, or messing about in a dinghy off South Beach.

Early in the fall, George broached a move to Key West to Beth. She had been waiting for the overture since the day they arrived back in New York. Six months later, George quit Morgan Stanley, and the family pulled up roots and bought a small guest house in Duval Street, Key West. By 1990, they owned two hotels and a water sports and boat hire business. When Glyn and

Suzy met them, George and Beth were both age forty-seven, but appearance wise resembled thirty, irrefutable evidence the seed change had paid dividends by way of enhancing health. Anticipating tiring of the Keys or wanting to go back to New England, once their children reached adulthood, all had remained, the ex-New Yorkers found they wanted to be part of the family enterprises.

Visiting New York in the mid-nineteen-eighties, they found many of George's ex-colleagues on Wall Street had either suffered strokes or fatal illnesses. Many of their friends had divorced, and they couldn't find anyone they knew truly happy. George told Glyn, forsaking New York for a new life in Key West was the smartest determination he had ever made. No equal of the New York Met existed in Key West, and Miami housed the nearest AFC club, but local compensations were plentiful and rewarding. Setting Key West apart, lifestyle made for athletic, happy people, content in their work, and dazzled by a lot of social activities, the ideal place to fulfil hungers and raise a family.

It made Glyn think. Symbolically speaking, his and Suzy's compass was hinged more on New York than Key West. Though they basked in the whole Keys ambience, at that juncture they had ambitions elsewhere and in a different world, London their main habitat, social orbit, and channel for calling fulfilment, thereby their prime haunt.

Concluding his inner musings, on reflection, Glyn deduced taking a big leap of faith is what they should have done.

Settling into his shipmate's conversation again, momentarily he revisited the caprice, pondering if England was Saleh's Key West, and thereby his great move.

"I'm not persuaded Saleh is really a devout Muslim," Bill slammed. "My inkling is, his so-called divinity dedication was an act of convenience, something to browbeat us with. Devotees do not steal from their own kind. In reality, he's a user."

"I see what you are driving at," Steve responded. "He had the seal of someone selling their granny down the Swanee River, if it meant furthering his own cause."

"Well, we could hypothesize forever," Ed added. "One thing

is certain, he is an illegal."

Participating in the forum, Glyn enquired, "What's the protocol in relation to illegals in Tunisia, Jeff?"

Musing for a moment, he replied, "Its complex. Illegal immigrants and economic migrants from the Sub-Saharan provinces have been entering North Africa's major cities for the past twenty years, either intent on going on to Europe, or stopping in Algeria, Tunisia, Libya and Egypt. Scaling up every year, it's a major headache for both Europe and North Africa. Like her neighbours, the Tunisian Government is under severe pressure to halt the flood by both its own people, and the European Union. Tunisia has become reliant upon the EU for trade but dealing with the pickle is not simple."

"You mentioned the EU," Steve reiterated. "How does Brussels see it? I mean, we get such conflicting reports in Blighty. It's tricky to judge if the EU has a solid counter to the swarm migration threat. I'm convinced the impact of the issue is being kept from us."

"Ahh, that's even more knotty," Jeff stressed. "Flushed with visions of claiming asylum under the EU's ultra-weak, open to unchecked abuse Human Rights Laws, there's been a huge rise in economic migrants and asylum seekers crossing the Med. I've heard tell, North African administrations complain the EU is making it easy for Sub-Saharan asylum seekers, and thereby exacerbating the pain for countries like Tunisia." He shrugged his shoulders. "As I say, it's not simple."

"You mean," Glyn began, "the EU castigates the North African nations for allowing bogus asylum seekers to set sail from their shores, but at the same time, weak EU Human Rights Laws encourage the deluge?"

"Precisely. That's politics for you," Jeff vilified. "No other philosophy can hold two contradictory views simultaneously, and sanction both have unexpurgated coherence with truth and credibility."

"But *why*?" Tom disputed. "Serves no practical end, and in due course, it will lead to widespread social unrest throughout Europe."

"To keep the deceitful politicians in charge," Ed ruefully retorted. "If immigrants see one camp of lawmakers make it easy for them to become citizens, they will vote for them. It's a vicious circle, the more immigrants settling, the larger their voting sway. Someday, they'll become the majority, leaving the Western European indigenous peoples as outcasts in their own lands."

"But surely the political classes can see the trend," Glyn argued. "Conceivably, they'll lose dominion to the snowballing throng of immigrants filling grand posts and taking over the principal institutions. Europeans will be marginalised, just like native North American Indian clusters have been virtually wiped out by mass inward immigration into the United States."

"They don't plan that far ahead," Jeff countered. "Modern day politicos only consider the near-future and feathering their own nests. The consequences of their short-sighted doings are conveniently ignored in the name of political correctness."

As per most English people, the newcomers were not specifically *au fait* with the illegal immigrant conundrum in the Med. Such weighty, far-off hassles never touched their radar, their lives dominated by domestic, career and social relationships. Saleh had brought the self-evidence and thereby the jam to the forefront of their minds, though they were yet to altogether comprehend its intercontinental implications.

Taking up the subject, Ed built on Jeff's perception. "If asylum is granted and most are, the asylum seeker can live on state handouts for the rest of their lives, much to the fuming annoyance of those having to pay taxes to cornerstone their freeloader lifestyle. Once the beachhead is installed, the asylum seeker engages a human rights lawyer, also paid for by taxpayers, to plead the case for getting the rest of his family over to the receiving country, to also milk the benefits system." Grinding his teeth at the notion, he then plugged, "it must be the basis of Saleh's plan."

Making disparaging comments in accord, the newcomers foreshadowed their joint disapproval of the obvious abuse.

Strange how if not directly involved, Glyn conjectured, *current affairs often wash over the sensory system virtually undetected, little registering, let alone sticking. But when confronted by those same chilling contentions head-on, the shock hones the mind to train on the far-reaching sequels.*

Ill-thought-out policies and half-baked tilts at magnanimity had become oversimplified, their doyens and perpetrators either conveniently ignoring the outgrowths of their actions or sweeping them under the carpet for future generations to inherit and deal with. Those promoting such naive one-world rules, either motivated by their desire to implement PC politics for pluralist longings, or to traitorously clinch the decline and fall of Western civilisation, knew such statutes could definitively cap in tragedy for all concerned. Philosophers had tendered, enforcing unpopular and undemocratic edicts on any people without consultation or consent, and treacherously denying them the opportunity to vote on such life-changing elements for their children's, children's children, inevitably results in *ad initio* unrest, then conflict, and irrevocably, bloody civil war.

"Am I right," David posed, "that any objection to this malpractice by the indigenous population is met with howls of racism by the PC industry?"

"Yes, quite right," Jeff verified. "Such crucial and climatic data is fed back into the Third World. So-called asylum seekers then find it extremely easy to make the case to stay in the receiving country. The 'Promised Land' for most is England, because the good nature, tolerance and fair shake of her people is easily defrauded by both asylum seekers, and the PC vote-catching, political classes."

"But more importantly," Ed attached, "the English welfare and blessings cadre is the major attraction, the uppermost target they're desiring to milk and feed on, *ad infinitum.*"

Digesting the bitter dialogue David advanced, "The international rule for asylum seekers is, the first country entered and deemed to be passably democratic, with a UN approved human rights record, must cosset the asylum seeker. That's right, isn't it?"

"At least as an interim measure, it is," Ed authenticated, "until his home country can be sorted out by the UN. However, it infrequently works out in usage. Somehow these apparent destitute and persecuted people, not only manage to get to North African ports, but also to mainland Europe, then on to England with Sangat used as a staging post for the final illegal trip across the English Channel."

"We've all seen those histrionics," Colin clarified. "Remarkably, the television pictures from Sangat reveal virtually all the asylum seekers are young single men from the Sub-Saharan region, other parts of Africa and the Middle East." Purposely hesitating he quizzed, "Why is that?"

"Yes, it does seem juxtaposed to newsreel films of WWII," Glyn suggested, "showing undivided families of refugees fleeing the Nazi war machine, doesn't it?"

"Precisely," Colin propped. "The puzzle is, where are their families? They can't all be orphans."

~

Beyond the consensus of democracy, Glyn knew New Labour and the EU had levied strict and severe laws designed to limit or terminate free speech, and thereby objections being tabled to the horde influx of economic migrants and asylum seekers into Blighty.

For him and Steve, England had not felt like England for over a decade, its demography inexorably altered in favour of rising immigrant numbers, its institutions corrupted by foreign dockets, and its media, prominently the BBC and Channel 4, acting as a clarion call to fuel the indiscriminate invasion by egregious interlopers, out to socially reengineer the country in their image.

"Everyone knows it," Glyn put forward to Steve over a lunchtime get-together in Kensington's swish Launceston Place restaurant, "but most tow the party-line, afraid of being tarnished with the racist brush, if protests are disseminated."

"You don't pull your punches," he responded. "That said, manifestly, all the Western European indigenous populations are paying the social and economic price for multinational inward migration. They don't like it. They feel threatened without recourse; the predatory aliens are not wanted."

The state of play continued, then all at once, an augury of national preservation overtook fear. Glyn noticed a substantial 'we're not going to take it anymore' movement sprung up, people no longer terrified to candidly discuss the nettlesome aftermaths. Pressure on the EU to end mountainous immigration into Western Europe intensified, subsequently going on to be the number one vexation for English voters. No matter what the politicians and media bosses said to justify immigration, the voters were not buying it.

Reviewing the polarity, Glyn said to Steve, "Publicly admitting it had got the open doors immigration policy wrong, New Labour had presumed a few tens of thousands, whereas they got millions, the trend irreversible and preserved in concrete by the very laws they instituted and legitimised by EU membership."

Distressed by the goings-on, Steve bemoaned, "Gone are the unequivocally great people, Churchill's immense legacy watered down and bastardised by political opportunism, greed, and the lust for supremacy. Now in discernible decline through their own stupidity, humans wallow in a quagmire of false ethics and 'one world', phoney beyond belief prophecy."

"Yes, when the Western commonwealths should have rebelled against the new totalitarians in our midst, as instincts told Westerners we must," Glyn replied, "instead, the lamentable majority became collective sheep, capitulating through fear, lethargy and naivety. Sheep get slaughtered, go to idiots' heaven."

"Undoubtedly," Steve supported. "What makes the world's various race and culture makeups unique is meticulously being coalesced and forced together to produce a muddy mix of human specimens, in the compulsion to make them perfectly socialised into the one-world of PC internationalism, containing no nations, no races, and certainly, no individuals."

The friends knew only one immutable stereotype existed in this social laboratory created realm, going about its daily life as a pre-programmed android, easily governed and dominated, in short, human robots. Engineered by the PC brigade, and probably funded behind the scenes by universal commerce, the phantasm of every totalitarian dictator became a reachable reality. But *why*, Glyn postulated?

Undeniably, the objective of international mercantile is to make the unabridged world's population customers and consumers. Because his software sales management role fortified the intention, Glyn knew this to be true, his job requiring him to execute corporate globalisation strategies throughout Europe and beyond. Diverse political and devotional dynasties limited the proficiency to carry out the directive. Countering the bottleneck, the UN, the World Bank and the EU had their own one-world index for harmonising and standardising mankind.

Glyn speculated, "By default, its unifying progression provides the platform for transnational enterprises to meet their own corporate wish list, in a win-win bonanza for both international politicians and corporations alike."

"Absolutely," Steve agreed, "and rumour has it, the latter feed vast amounts of capital into the former, so a single entity planetary autocracy can be created."

Contributing to the hubbub, Glyn and Steve worked out expansive immigration from the Third World and the ex-Soviet Union Bloc into the West suited the lineup. Weakening and marginalising indigenous peoples' resolve to uphold sovereignty, it provided the final nail in the coffin of Western European invention and advancement in the arts and sciences, building the world ensemble over the past 3,000 years. They noted objecting voices were drowned out by the sheer, overwhelming numbers of immigrants, and most essentially, those same intruders swelled the purchaser catchment area courtesy of state handouts, providing a huge windfall for big business. Nonetheless, they knew it neglected the possibility of social strife peaking in comprehensive societal breakdown, and as a result, the demise of widespread consumerism, and in the end, the abyss and mortal pandemonium.

If they could see it, as could millions of others, evidently the informed collection must include the politicians and ministry mandarins responsible for the impending mayhem. But the gravy train beckoned the policymakers, integrity and veracity conveniently slipped into back pockets. If the flier succeeded, nationhood, individuality, and pivotal human attributes such as dauntless character and tenacity, might never see the clear light of day again, return to the dark ages a racing certainty, resultant from a combination of contrived overpopulation Armageddon and consequent social bedlam. Howbeit, Glyn and Steve marked that renegade economists predicted the step input of enlarged buyer spending for multilateral trade would be transitory, enterprise-scale companies crashing down as societal and economic systems collapsed, taking medium to small combines with them.

"One such manifestation of combined political and commercial globalisation," Glyn proposed to Steve, "is the burgeoning rise of cash-rich, Third World multinationals acquiring Western European blue-chip companies, and re-branding them under their own banner."

"Eminently true of India and China," Steve tabled, "both nuclear powers and still recipients of vast sums of international aid paid for by English taxpayers, it begs the question, who is exploiting who? Further, who allowed and authorised the blatant counterpoint, and who gained from it? How have these new boys on the block got so big so quickly, and why are they on a vast shopping safari in downtown Europe?"

"Most old-moneyed companies with late nineteenth century origins do not want the wholesale internationalist panacea," Glyn testified. "Satisfying customer demand through traditional pipelines, sound transactional precepts, and above all, honesty, their motivations are firmly national. They have no aspiration for world domination, whereas the new-moneyed brigade, notably those from the I.T, telco and communication industries, have always been keen on the one-world concept, their M.O invariably associated with a liberal, do-gooder public facade hiding an exorbitant profit-driven prospectus. It's helped them conquer global markets quickly and efficiently, en route eradicating selling price differentials between sovereign states."

A vital endeavour to maximise profit, the pinnacle twin goals of a single ecumenical price expressed in a universal currency, and the elimination of salary differentials country-to-country, the latter, factored down to the lowest common denominator, were achievable. Often spurred on by self-possessed guilt conceptions of benevolence and philanthropy, some observers theorised it likely the new-money players sponsored the rise of Third World companies to procure old-money detractors, thus eliminating any opposition to political and commercial internationalism.

Glyn had read and heard from the media many times, that proponents of the EU often cited a close and fulsomely integrated association, embodying a common currency negated the possibility of another European war. Though many had their hearts in the right place, they failed to envision the upshot as sovereign power became devolved to the EU mega-state and overarching taxpayer-funded organisations, embracing the UN. Politically incited to achieve a worldwide totalitarian PC federation, or to front for multinational consortia wanting to run the world through the vehicle of these world dominion oligarchies, inevitably, political opportunists found their way into such dominating organisations, soaring to the top then dictating policy and compendium.

Either way, Glyn and Steve figured it spelt the end of national sovereignty and democracy on a global basis, the horrors of and sacrifices made in WWI and WWII by English people, laboured for in vain. Prevailing through the side and back doors, the totalitarians took ascendancy at the expense of true democracy, the nations' unwittingly bedding them via the ballot box, their totemic bill of fare instituted with complete detachment of all upright judgment by the self-interested, its everlasting negative end product seismic and terminal, nothing spared in the pursuit of absolute power. Primary advocates of the cunning and perverse deception, Blair and Brown, brazenly outlined their autocratic conspectus, their forged legitimacy upheld by PC stormtroopers, principally the UAF with links to al-Qaeda, and described by some journalists as a Muslim-supremacist group, charged with exterminating dissidents and loyalists by any means, just like Hitler's Brownshirts in the nineteen-thirties.

"All sociology students know Marx maintained economic power always leads to political power," Glyn reviewed during a visit to Whitstable Sailing Club with Steve. "In this context, national regimes backed by international organisations are teaming with intercontinental businesses to produce a macro-establishment surpassing Marx's wildest dreams, or could they be nightmares?"

"True," Steve concurred. "Internationalism bombed when branded as communism, its acerbic cargo too ghastly and grievous to be universally accepted. Whereas, political correctness, with its self-righteous, one-world agenda and social piety as major weapons, coupled with corporate bedfellows with a discordant schedule of ends is accomplishing the same gory end."

A gold-plated money spinner, Glyn and Steve perceived it strange Hollywood had never made a movie about the possibility. But behind the glitter and gloss, the PC-led movie moguls were part of the oppressive conspiracy. Because it would cut their own throats, and in the process incur the wrath of the one-world republic, they never produced a single film exposing the probable truth.

Hitting Glyn and Steve like a thunderbolt, the blended national and international conspiracy realisation had them reeling. Clearly, it had been in play since at least 1997 when New Labour came into office, but they only became aware of its greater ramifications within the year preceding their Mediterranean sojourn, after Lehman Brothers bellied up leading to the cosmopolitan financial meltdown.

"Conspiracy theorists are convinced a global, power elite cabal of mega-rich fraternities, freemasons and other secret societies exists, and is known as the Illuminati," Glyn advanced post Lehmans, after Gordon Brown actually used the term, 'New World Order', in his advocacy for a comprehensive reform of the global financial network. "They control national governments and international organisations incorporating the UN, the World Bank, the IMF, the WTO, and thereby the world."

"Yes, after Brown let his totalitarian ideal out of the bag, I investigated the Illuminati," Steve shared. "They're emulating the power of the Knights Templar, a Catholic military order founded in 1119, to fight in the crusades and manage vast financial frameworks throughout Christendom. In that respect, the Illuminati or New World Order, is a fast-emerging, clandestine domineering world government, with a globalist itinerary intent on replacing sovereign states with an all-encompassing propaganda, whose ideology hails the construct of the NWO as the culmination of history's progress. In actuality, the EU is a microcosm model of the despotic creed, presumably with links into the Illuminati."

"For sure, and operating through frontline structures, and activists with both left and right-wing objectives, the NWO has clearly orchestrated significant political and financial events, ranging from causing systemic crises, typically the pandemic effect of the Euro on southern Europe's economies, to pushing through controversial policies like overseas aid at both national and international level, as steps in an ongoing plot to achieve world domination. It's a kind of *Brotherhood of the Bell* dogma, if you're familiar with that Glenn Ford film."

"I am, and yes, the film does portray an example of the crowning totalitarian nightmare, but it seems tame compared to the unambiguous power of the Illuminati. And…" Waggling a finger, his timbre dropped into a scornful vein. "The spillover from that clique are felt by all, but paradoxically, they remain invisible, cloaked behind a robust grid of elected or power-usurped, national officialdom."

Backstage, the rise of the Illuminati was far more momentous than Glyn and Steve had been able to determine. Adopting the principles of eighteenth century Bavarian Illuminati founder, Adam Weishaupt, the latest incarnation had been advantageously launched post WWII on the back of international organisations, in particular, the UN, WHO, NATO, and later, the EU, various regional alliances including the African Union, plus bi-lateral trading agreements like GATT. Above those pan-worldwide instruments, national governments and global blue-chip conglomerates lay the Illuminati matrix, a coterie of narcissistic, mega-rich individuals, families and cartels, owning the lion's share of world wealth, and correspondingly, the principal investors in the financial services sector. As Glyn had speculated, in reality, liberal internationalism began to take a dominant role in the Illuminati with the rise of high-tech industries in the nineteen-fifties, finally spawning a raft of multi-billionaire philanthropists from the I.T industry in the nineteen-nineties, with a platform of conspicuous altruism but at their price, meaning ruling nations and creating a one world/NWO economic and political supremacy.

Devolving into unreserved rottenness before the imbalance could be corrected, ultimately, outright revolution might be necessary to wrestle economic and political power away from the Illuminati and their lower echelon structures, like the EU, back to the national level.

Consequently, when pressed, even the free-thinking Poseidon crew knew they were being conned by the immigrant-loving PC brigade and the counterfeit political and media classes. Appalled and dismayed, they became very fearful for the long-term future of their country, as did most ordinary Western Europeans.

~

"*Hey*, you Englishmen," the lead policemen called, waving for Poseidon's crew to join him on the balcony steps.

Though disinclined, they duly obliged, reluctance and foreboding making for slow steps. When accosted in that part of the world by authority, there were no choices for Europeans, no opportunity to request legal representation, let alone make a telephone call to the British Embassy. Jeff and Ed had seen it before, and back home the newcomers had read about it daily, or seen it flashed across their TV screens. Now they were bagged in its tentacles.

His verbalisation ablaze with cynicism, he told them, "The hotel manager says he is not acquainted with any of you. We're taking you to central headquarters for questioning. You're going to meet our chief of police, Colonel Nassar."

4

THE DIE IS CAST

Somewhere to the east of Dire Dawa, Saleh's Christian mother Gabra had given birth to him during a drought crisis, its derivatives relentlessly driving millions of rural Ethiopians to the country's major cities, scouring for food and safeguard. Following the track of most Sub-Saharan men, his Muslim father Jasim participated in multiple affairs and concurrent sham common-law marriages to many women, the feckless lifestyle producing twenty-eight children over a ten-year period, most dying in infancy through disease and malnutrition.

Jasim's latest offspring had arrived in the world at a time when he indulged in the pleasures of the flesh elsewhere. While Gabra fended for herself and her five surviving children during the last few months of pregnancy, Jasim had gone off to Dessie, north of Addis Ababa, to be with another of his women for a few months. Making her pregnant as well, he repeated the same shiftless and irresponsible practice moving further north to Mek'ele.

Undiminished by Western civilised liability teachings, the depraved and reckless impregnation ritual and the gross sexual abuse of women had been a feature of Sub-Saharan societies for thousands of years. Though the mullahs insisted on undisputed obedience to the Koran, a convenient blind eye allowed Muslim men to do as they pleased with the female gender. Those women objecting to the inequitable treatment were beaten, and if they continued to protest, often killed. In defiance of alarming high infant mortality rates, the men pretended prodigious procreation was necessary to sustain the Sub-Saharan races. In truth a convenience, it allowed them to flit from fatherless-family to fatherless-family, multiplying their number, while failing to fulfil both husbandly and fatherly responsibilities.

When the European Christian missionaries arrived in the nineteenth century with medicines, and morality as their byword, infant mortality reduced, but rampant procreation subsisted unabated. A hundred years later, Western aid agencies had taken on the thankless task, their efforts making little impression on the overpopulation cephalalgia, or reducing starvation in the wake of famine.

Making contraception freely available to both men and women, the agencies tried in vain to alter convention and instil a virtuous maxim, Western taxpayers funding the programme along with the endless black hole of food and shelter provision to little avail. In the calculation of reducing, let alone reversing the boundless poverty and unwanted offspring trend, it dramatically flopped. Though hundreds of billions of pounds, dollars and euros poured into the Sub-Sahara, in the main, the production of needless babies and parentless children accelerated. Aware Western politically, self-imposed pressures pivotable upon ancient history, could always be relied upon to featherbed the lives of their offspring, the men saw the opportunity to be even more negligent and flighty about fathering children.

Despite being the recipients of free education from relief agencies, those males making it into adulthood merely carried on the business as usual culture, unconditionally neglecting what they had been taught, whilst preserving their iron-fist will over women, and propagating the never-ending procreation cataclysm.

Though many women saw contraception as a way to get away from more or less a life of perpetual pregnancy until they died, most men abhorred the provision. If caught taking the pill by husbands or live-in boyfriends, women were beaten, even murdered.

No matter what charity workers did *ad modum* sex education and basic family economics, it resulted in little modification to entrenched behaviour. Widely disseminating absentee father status to their multiple children, the men carried on with their recalcitrant conduct regardless, the women perennially too scared to refuse sex, or take the pill.

Jasim formed part of a huge aggregation of brash, egocentric and negligent men, responsible for disorderly Third World overpopulation, and the knock-on irritations it brought to the world at large *in toto*. A selfish vagabond, capable of feigning hardship and conning the gullible into bank rolling his excesses, additional to his begetting agency, his life C.V comprised of a series of scams and dodgy deals, most illegal, and a propensity to evade honest work at all costs.

~

Charged up by the society-changing effects of mass immigration into England, Glyn had researched the causes behind the phenomena. Raiding multiple information sources he established by Christmas 1945 the newly created United Nations and every Western government had gone on record corroborating the biggest hazard to the Earth centred on mushrooming overpopulation, especially in Africa and Asia.

"If allowed to go on unbridled," he informed Steve, "statisticians predicted within the next hundred years, the entire Earth's natural resources would be exhausted, and farming craft swamped by incalculable demand."

"Doesn't surprise me."

"Further, they forecast African and Asian famine instigated by extremist political and religious factions constantly occupied in war would culminate in super-mass migrations into an already bursting at the seams with its own social problems Europe. Cautioning widespread indigenous population resentment and ubiquitous hue and cry could result in race wars, the learned prognosticated the total inescapable and irretrievable breakdown of all the Western societies."

"So that's the diagnosis. What did they prescribe as the antidote?"

"That's just it. There is nothing on the public record summarising their recommendations."

"Too hot to handle, hey?"

"Probably. Though political correctness was decades away from invention, I doubt those in power at the time took any notice of possible advice from those conducting the case study."

"But surely it leaked out into the public domain somewhere?"

"Maybe. By way of illustration, Aldous Huxley produced dissertations in the early nineteen-fifties warning of Third World overpopulation chaotic impact on the world's assets in general and Western societies in particular. Later, the theme became used for disaster novels predicting the draconian aftereffects of Third World overspill, Christopher Priest's *Fugue for a Darkening Island* foretelling of a time when black Africans invaded Europe, before driving on and colonising England. Like locusts in search of rich pickings to feed on, raiding the economy and the State of all its assets, never to be replenished, it spelt out in no uncertain terms, the everlasting fallout of the black invasion; the global economy collapsing, the unabridged world falling into a bedlam-like plight where no food or material goods were produced, and public services plunged into non-existence."

"So just as everlastingly stringent in its protracted backlashes as a nuclear holocaust," Steve put forward. "Presumably, the tragedy would climax in the Earth regressing back into pre-historic times, those left over from the race wars, scavenging for sustenance and refuge like Neanderthal Man."

"Seems likely."

Right about their prognostication, few in the Western democracies had paid any attention to either the statistical projections or writers' forecasts, preferring to ignore the ordained in the lame and wild hope it went away. As the economic boom of the late nineteen-fifties gave way to nineteen-sixties liberalism, the empirical evidence pertaining to immigration became hard to ignore, the ethnic composition of the European confederations and the United States beginning to radically change, its negative affects plain to see. By the time Poseidon's crew were on Med sabbatical in 2009, the migration had reached epidemic proportions, but still the politicians' heads remained firmly planted in the sand.

Sometime after his first excursion into the thorny subject, Glyn unearthed more data, sharing his findings with Steve.

"Not new or even remotely surprising to successive generations of historians, the 1945 revelation paralleled what they'd been documenting along the lines of world demographics and their wakes on corporeal wherewithal and social structures, since the time of the famous renaissance."

"I remember from my geography lessons," Steve recalled, "as far back as the early nineteenth century, Western economists had ascertained the world's natural resources were finite. Though farming food stocks could be replenished, if overpopulation outstripped manufacturing capacity, it spelt the beginning of the end of civilisation." Pausing, his review became prescriptive. "You see, like for any enterprise built on supply and demand, the historical message is crystal clear. The planet's ability to linchpin life has its' limits. Beyond the maximum point, any increase in population numbers are unsustainable."

"Yes, just like in Priest's farsighted dystopia, if not restrained, and the trend reversed, a runaway disaster inextricably follows, its spread reducing the modern world to a permanent combat zone. Those outlasting armed conflict scrounging for the basic necessities to preserve life and fighting to the death for jurisdiction not over land, but essential resources."

With London straining at the seams and south-east England's transportation systems reduced to a daily log jam, well before joining Poseidon Steve took a turn at researching the overpopulation enigma.

"I've discovered," he shared with Glyn, "no one versed in logical rumination, ranging from social anthropologists to philosophers dispute the 1945 prediction, but it was not always the case. Back in the nineteenth and early twentieth centuries, Western politicians were more agitated about European wars and empire building, and intellectuals about the meaning of life to treat the subject with the seriousness it justly demanded. Precariously, though well-equipped as a human science discipline to analyse, predict and warn the powers that be about the impending repercussions of world overpopulation, sociology swiftly became corrupted by a left-wing synopsis, purity of fact conveniently shelved, or critically, rashly ignored."

Glyn and Steve learned the collectivism germ plus the obsession to install an all-powerful, holistic and progressive republic, with the covet of exhaustive mastery over all human cogitation and activities, roosted as a central plank to its purveyors in the twenty-first century.

"No national government organisation or world authority embracing the UN," Steve later recounted after more digging, "ever use the word, overpopulation, let alone discuss it. Instead, as the world population climbed from one-billion in 1800, to three-billion in 1960, and over-doubled forty-eight years later to six-point-seven-three billion in 2008, such august bodies made sanctimonious noises about the need for wealth redistribution from the developed West to the Third World, a politically impelled ploy to conveniently sidestep and ignore the central crux of dangerously out-of-control Third World overpopulation."

"Very enlightening," Glyn praised, "however, and this really is a showstopper, I found out from the *National Geographic* archive, arising from its own bulging and untenable population growth, nineteen-sixties Red China invoked a one-child-per-family policy, the instrument having an all-inclusive, positive corollary over the next forty years, culminating in China becoming a top-three world economic superpower." Resting, he furrowed his brow. "If the Chinese prudent approach had been adopted by Third World countries, explicitly those in the Sub-Saharan region, then the famine impediments of the late twentieth century might never have happened, not that famines are a modern phenomenon. Scandalously, egomaniacal Western politicos make the world believe famines in Ethiopia and Eritrea are somehow a consequence of modern worldwide economics, but in reality, famines have been sweeping across the Sahara, as they had been in some of parts of Asia, the Americas, and even Europe, for thousands of years."

Turning on the aid tap actualised little, apart from quelling Western liberal elitist sensibilities and consciences. As had been classified to Saleh by the crew of the Poseidon, the World could be bankrupted pouring money into famine torn Ethiopia, and nothing altered. The preeminent and superior force of nature was at work. Mankind could never hope to equal, let alone bewitch and exceed its mightiness. A self-regulating miracle, Steve had pinpointed as part of his survey, nature monitors the Earth's healthiness in connection with Homo sapiens gross overuse of its riches.

"When nature uncovers the Earth is in peril," he told Glyn, "it generates extreme weather conditions, aimed at culling the infestation gnawing at its well-being. Hence Tsunamis, hurricanes, flood, and intense hot and cold temperatures, resulting in the destruction of basic food stuffs, thereby producing famine and reducing overpopulation."

Supposedly, the only two things capable of defeating nature were a nuclear holocaust and, overpopulation exceeding critical mass and enveloping the Earth from A to Z. Though the cause and effect criteria were very well known at the UN, generation after generation of reality-avoiding politicians ignored or side-stepped the overpopulation dilemma, jumpy any debate led to the familiar but crass taunts of racism. Glyn and Steve concluded, they were willing to preside over the slow strangulation of the planet, but indisputably did nothing about addressing its central cause; overpopulation.

~

Gabra understood her fate from an early age. Born into an extended family and brought up on the Christian teachings of the Ethiopian Orthodox Tewahedo Church, she knew the never-ending motherhood cycle awaited her. Unable to counter Ethiopian male dominance in the domestic sphere, chiefly procreation, she feared severe maltreatment by reason of any noncompliance with the age-old code. Though also a Christian, her father's infernal heritage of child-bearing aspirations saw to it many of Gabra's sisters and brothers died at birth or in early infancy, the family's meagre income not capable of underpinning his offspring, her mother constantly acquiescing to her father's sexual urges.

Made of sterner stuff, Gabra managed to survive early childhood without attack from life-threatening diseases or malnutrition. For a short period in her nascent years, she found life to be tolerable. Then the suitors came-calling, much older men taking their brides or common-law wives before they had barely gained puberty, and crushing them into a life of servitude, bordering on bondage. In Gabra's unfortunate case, Jasim, a so-called family friend, over twenty years older than her, became her ruination. Comprehending she had no choice but to tolerate her fate, as did millions of Ethiopian girls of her age, she complied with her father's wishes. Just about into her teens, her inaugural child had been born in the wastelands to the north-west of Dire Dawa, while Jasim allegedly worked on a farm near Jijiga, but in fact cavorted with one of his other concubines at Asaita in the Mile Serdo Wildlife Reserve. Since, Gabra had been pregnant every year for the past twenty-two years, many of her new-born dead soon after birth, or within a few years.

For countless women, the extreme burden of too many children coupled with husband abandonment became too much to bear. When the missionaries started arriving, followed by multi-national aid organisations, they too abandoned their offspring, to be doted on by Westerners. Going against her Christian teachings, Gabra could not do that. She loved her children and cared for them to the best of her abilities. She was a good mother.

Never expecting to make it to forty years old, Gabra's only yearning became endurance from one day to the next. Her surviving children, Makeda, Girma, Ayana, Dawit and Iskinder were all malnourished. She knew at least two more of them could die before attaining adulthood. Twelve-years old Makeda, the eldest daughter, had already become the patsy of suitors at least twice her age. Not wanting Makeda to go down the same conception path from a tender age, her mother encouraged her to take birth control precautions, albeit conscious as soon as marriage, or worse a common-law alliance happened, and Makeda did not get pregnant, the man in her life would beat her and cut off any contraception method. At least for a while Gabra prayed, her eldest daughter could escape childbirth and enjoy her youthhood. All the same, Makeda and her sisters were doomed to follow in the same sex-slave-like footsteps, as that of their mother, and her ancestors.

Professedly, Jasim had some distant Arab blood flowing through his veins, often using the distinction to differentiate himself from other Ethiopian men, on the basis Arabs were superior to pure-bred blacks. He pictured cultivating the Arab breeding in his bloodline might benefit his standing, making his requests for inclusion in Arab society more likely. During Gabra's latest pregnancy, he had nurtured loose relationships of convenience with Arabs, self-confident he'd capitalise on his part-Arab genealogy to gain auspices from them. Yet another ruse to con upwardly mobile Arabs into funding his shameful slacker's lifestyle, he took the step seriously. During the final months of pregnancy, Gabra normally named the children in his habitual absence, but her husband had left instructions to name his latest offspring, Saleh, an Arab name.

Like for many Sub-Saharan children, Saleh survived early life by the skin of his teeth. Close to death on numerous occasions, principally through disease rather than malnutrition, careful nursing by his mother nailed down his recovery and future wellbeing.

Returning to Gabra twice over the next two years, each time Jasim made her pregnant, raising the child count to eight with the births of Yenee and Kassa, a number well beyond his wife's competence to care for in his continued absence.

Then luckily, by being in the right place at the right time, Gabra and her children were taken into an evacuee camp run by a Western famine relief agency on the outskirts of Dire Dawa. Thankfully, for a few years Jasim was unable to find them. Not being constantly pregnant allowed Gabra's health to improve, and the relative security of the camp guaranteed her children were fed and clothed, even educated.

Things started to perk up for the fatherless family. No more of Gabra's children died. Becoming fit and healthy, they also received fundamental schooling and social grounding. Then Jasim found them again. Realising the family's placement and security could be jeopardised, Gabra renounced having any more children with him. Receiving a brutal beating from her vicious husband, for what he considered to be refusal of conjugal rights, he left her severely bruised and broken.

When Makeda alerted Western charity workers, they called in the Ethiopian police, Jasim arrested and jailed for his heinous act, though subsequently released within a year, on the promise he left Gabra alone. Though bed-ridden for eight weeks and having to be cared for by the charity's medical team, eventually, she recovered.

Saleh grew up within the confines of the Dire Dawa camp, but notwithstanding his good fortune, he was always a difficult child. His mother and elder brothers and sisters often chastised him for ingratitude, bad manners, and a poor attitude to both his family and their guardians. Even from an early age, for some obscure and unfathomable justification, he favoured his delinquent father, ignoring the obvious maltreatment of his family and leading a thoroughly negligent life. Falsely, Saleh clung to the idea Arab blood raced through his veins, setting him apart from other Ethiopians, and making him a superior being. It became the foundation of his mentality, his personal belief system, and in the end, his nemesis and downfall.

In an attempt to identify the source of his contempt, Gabra and Makeda recurrently spent hours talking to Saleh, but no plausible explanation came back. Grudgingly, he offered up excuses for his stroppy ways, laziness, general dismissiveness of his easy life at the Dire Dawa camp and the denunciation of Tewahedo Church Christian credos. Prevailing in being belligerent and contrary about all things, from his place in the family pecking hierarchy to playing tricks on aid-workers, because they refused to give him the special treatment he craved, he progressively became more and more the outsider.

Saleh had few friends, and those young Ethiopians gravitating towards him rapidly found his estimation of friendship meant exploiting them. Assessing him to be dishonest and unnecessarily quarrelsome, when his peers cross-examined his moral ordinance, or criticised his objectionable behaviour, he got into fights with them. Though his assailants were often bigger, Saleh never shied away, his compunction spurring on a physical response well beyond his slender physique. In itself, that impressed those supposing they had a similar kinship brand with him. But when befriending Saleh, they found he maliciously abused the pact for his own selfish ends, capping in more strife. Remarkably, his unpopularity never bothered him. In fact, he revelled in the maelstrom of enmity and rancour thrown at him. Putting aside his malevolence, Gabra hoped her son's abject behaviour was temporary, and as he matured, his white angels might shine through.

At the camp school, the charity workers adjudged him to be very bright, even clever, but unreliable, crafty, and incessantly in hot water for minor misdemeanours and stealing. Disruptive in class, tetchy and crabby with other schoolchildren, and always on the verge of squabbling with his teachers for no valid vindication, Saleh received numerous d-minus fitness reports. Warned unless his bad behaviour ceased, Gabra grasped Saleh would not only be expelled from school, but also from the camp, the charity management team confirming there were plenty of other children to take his place, who were not an invariable torment to them.

Taking a tongue-lashing from his mother, she instructed Saleh to make profound apologies to the aid workers and promise to improve his decorum. Possessing a heightened natural sense of survival, he complied, but the repentance became short-lived. Returning to his anti-social ways, he caused trouble and interminably peeved others. Complaining about his arrogance, derision of virtually everything they beheld to be good and true, and exhibiting an extremely manipulative and conniving behaviour with little or no humility, his teachers washed their hands of him. Once more given an ultimatum by those in charge of the camp, this time he appreciated they had reached their tolerance limit. Something inside Saleh told him to quit, then he coldly deliberated other opportunities to execute the rogue persona could unfold downline.

Much to Gabra's relief, Saleh knuckled down to school. His natural cleverness divided him from most young Ethiopians, his flair to learn reading, writing and arithmetic fundamentals elevating him to the top of the class, most of his contemporaries trailing in his academic wake. His aptitude to understand basic science, delight in world geography and history, coupled with an ever-evolving logical mindset to solve mathematical brainteasers, were way beyond his years. Presuming he had passed through his early scallywag period, his teachers had high hopes for his future. Even his classmates and his family saw a huge transformation in his temperament, Saleh apparently relinquishing his innate inclination to play the rascal.

Already fluent in English and Arabic, as well as the Amharic language, by his mid-teens, he had appended computer skills to his canon. It led to the Western charity giving him a job as a translator and performing office duties. Easy meat for Saleh, well within his academic capabilities, he finalised all his delegated undertakings with commensurate ease. So as to act as a role model and even a mentor for younger Ethiopians, aid-workers talked about promoting him to a more responsible position.

Then his old habits returned. Unruly in his dealings and disorderly in his conduct, he generally disrupted the execution of everyday necessities required for the camp administration to function properly. Worse, he became short with people, upsetting the fine symmetry between the relief staff and the evacuees the camp needed to flourish and retain stability. Finally, he was caught with his hand in the till, and given his marching orders. As far as the camp administrators were concerned, this time, there was no way back for him. Shocked and disappointed with her son's appalling failings, Gabra administered a stout, uncompromising dressing down. He had brought the family name into disrepute, further shame piled on when Saleh repulsed acknowledgement of his misdeeds. In comparative Ethiopian terms, he had been given an extraordinary start in life, and had bitten the hand feeding him. Telling him to make his own way in the world, his mother said not to come back until he had learnt the value of his good fortune.

Collecting his belongings, Saleh stuffed them into an old, battered suitcase, then stormed out of Dire Dawa, shouting abuse back at his family and camp officialdom.

5

A MARTYR IN THE MAKING

Indignantly sloping off, devoured by enmity and impulses of retribution, Saleh headed for Nazret, vowing vengeance on the Dire Dawa camp aid workers. In his eyes, they'd brought him down and ridiculed him. He even contemplated some form of hurt for his family. Scorching with bitterness at what he calculated to be unjustified treatment, he cursed aloud as he walked along the dusty roads, making other travellers turn in his direction and chastise him for his blasphemy.

At Karamile, he managed to thumb a lift from a passing truck and proceeded to gripe about his 'woe is I life' to its driver. Fed up with Saleh's moaning and bitching, the driver halted the truck, kicking him back onto the road outside the Aledeghi Wildlife Reserve, leaving the Ethiopian stranded. Saleh's animosity intensified. Hoisting a clenched fist, he shouted insults and obscenities at the driver as he drove away. Still having over a hundred miles to go before he landed in Nazret, Saleh started walking.

Dusk arrived. Exhausted, he faltered before falling to his knees. Not far from the road, he saw an outhouse on the wildlife reserve. Unsteadily making for the relief, he settled down for the night in its sparse interior. Going over the day's events in his mind made his anger well-up again. Weakened by his self-imposed ordeal, he slumped in a corner before falling into a restless sleep. With the rising sun stimulating his eyes to open, early the next morning he awoke disorientated, before remembering the turn of events bringing him to the sorry pickle he now found himself in. Eaten up by the gravity of his predicament, his fury rose again. Stomping around the outhouse, he roared with unabated rage before collapsing down, his meagre energy spent. Hearing the occasional vehicle pass by on the road dissipated his hostility and stiffened his grit to make it to Nazret. Learning from the previous day's mistake, he decided if he could thumb another lift, to remain calm and not be confrontational. After walking a few miles, a truck picked him up. Two hours later, he alighted in Nazret, a town also traditionally titled, Adama.

Though bringing money with him from the Dire Dawa exile, something inside told him to exploit others to boost his stash. Abusing peoples' good intentions to accomplish his singular designs had become ingrained in his nature. Far better than the grind ethic, as far as Saleh was concerned, somehow in his unbalanced mind, he perceived it to be more satisfying, like money won by chance is deemed by some to be more rewarding than money earned through honourable sweat and toil.

Looking churlish and bedraggled, he walked about the Adama Health Centre area, occasionally obstructing passers-by to solicit money from them. He had little success, most he harangued instantly disgusted by his slovenly shot at feigning poverty. After producing disapproving faces, they reprimanded him for his impertinence, Saleh acknowledging he needed to improve his down-and-out act to succeed in hoodwinking his victims. Annexing an unconvincing alms-for-the-poor mantle, with a pained expression he crouched on his knees, sobbing and crying to attract attention. Few were persuaded of his claimed lowly origination, or his sincerity, many spitting on him or throwing stones at him.

As a last resort, he resolved to try for casual work in the market, only to be repulsed by stall owners, suspicious of his integrity and true purpose. Shocked they had easily seen through his masquerade, he apprehensively pondered what to do next.

Then hunger overtook him, his stomach churning and wheezing. While ruminating on his future, he spent a few birrs on a sparse meal in a nearby café. Running out of tangible alternates, and very unsure of his next move, he fretted about how he'd fair in Nazret.

Disembarking at the bus station, a bunch of students came into his line of sight through the café window. Reckoning they must be going to Adama University, he followed them at a discrete distance, envisaging the university and its campus consigned easier pickings from susceptible students, rather than trying to overcome the wise realism of the town's people.

Recognising the need to come across as inconspicuous, he strolled all over the university attempting to blend in with the students. Though receiving some curious ogles, mainly from those he assumed to be academic staff, no one stopped him to test his endeavour. Circumstantially, he found a hideaway in an unsecured structure used for waste disposal and rested up. Opening his battered suitcase, he poured over his belongings, amounting to very little, and even less in terms of tradable value. Rolling his eyes upwards in a gesture of admission, he mulled over ways to improve his life stock, without harnessing himself to the conformity of regular Ethiopian life. Coming up short of any key-opening solutions, he parked the conundrum.

During the succeeding days, he passed himself off as a student, attending lectures and frequenting the refectories begging for money, again with skimpy success. Soon, the university authorities became aware of his presence. Warning him off, they said if they found him on university premises again, he'd be reported to the police. Reluctantly Saleh left, swearing at and cursing the officials as they chased him away.

Finding refuge in an Ethiopian Orthodox Tewahedo Church, he told its priest, he was an outcast from Dire Dawa needing stopgap sanctuary from those pursuing him. Fortunately, the imaginary tale worked, the priest allowing him to stay in a refuge behind the main church. However, the empathy crashed when church cleaners nabbed Saleh raiding the parishioners' collection box. Banished by the priest for theft, again he left issuing a hail of profanities and threatening revenge on those reporting his foul deed.

Spending a few nights under the stars, the outcast perused what had happened to him during his maiden few days in Nazret. Failing to derive a plan to make his life easier, his plight took on insoluble dimensions. As a makeshift rouse, he decided to try the market area again, preying on easy pickings with his begging routine. Found wanting in his trickster deception, he got a sound thrashing from a man witnessing him conning an old woman into giving him money.

Beaten and blooded, he neared desperation, theft a last resort. Licking his wounds, he judged when the market reached the height of its business activity at noon, with stall owners engrossed in serving throngs of customers, it offered the opportunity to purloin goods and either pawn them for currency or go to an unfamiliar part of the town and bid to sell them.

Edging around the periphery of the market, he assessed his best options, inexorably setting his sights on an antiques stall containing a plethora of mid to high-priced items.

About to pilfer a silver-plated goblet, he heard someone say, "There is no need to steal, my brother. Allah tends to the poor and the oppressed."

Swinging around, breathless and alarmed, Saleh fancied he'd see a uniformed market inspector. Instead, a gaunt man, with dark brooding eyes, deep-set cheeks, and a greying moustache and beard confronted him. He wore white robes with a silk belt, leather sandals and a traditional Arab keffiyeh headdress. Though not an official, he possessed the zest of someone with gravitas and authority, capable of persuasion and making a cogent argument. So startled by his abrupt appearance, Saleh's mouth flopped open, but he could not speak, his countenance a cluster of uncertainty.

"Do you have somewhere to stay?"

Saleh shook his head nervously.

"Are you hungry?"

Nodding, he uttered, "Yes."

Taking Saleh in like a dairy farmer assessing a cow at a cattle auction, the bearded man asked, "Are you itching for work?"

Nodding more vigorously, Saleh indicated his appetite for employment. "Yes," he upheld. "I am."

Taking a few steps frontwards, the man enquired in a friendly but firm tempo, "Are you a believer?"

"A believer?" Saleh repeated, perplexed by the term. "I was brought up on the teachings of the Ethiopian Orthodox Tewahedo Church."

"What is your name?" the man pressed.

"My full name is Saleh bin Tariq bin Khalid Al-Asfour."

"That is an Arab name."

"Yes, my father is part Arab and a Muslim."

"Where is your father?"

Reluctant to reply, Saleh bowed his head.

"Where is your father?" the man pushed.

Summoning up courage, he riposted in a frail modulation, "He's in prison."

By then, Jasim had long been released from penile servitude, but sensing imprisonment might impress the stranger, Saleh felt the need to lie.

"For what crime?"

Hesitancy overcame him. "He, he beat my mother."

Smiling, as if condoning Jasim's act, the man coaxed, "Come, we will take care of you."

Walking out of the market, he gently put his left hand on Saleh's shoulder, and whispered more soft reassurances to him.

For some reason he could not explain to himself, Saleh designated a courteous manner with the stranger. "Excuse me asking, but may I know the name of my benefactor?"

Turning to face Saleh with a riveting air, the man stopped them from walking. Gazing into his eyes like an adroit magician about to perform a wondrous trick, he advised, "My name is Mayhar bin Ishak bin Massood."

"Then you are also an Arab?"

"Yes." Pausing for a moment, he added, "I am also a Muslim mullah."

"Where are we going?"

"You need to be among your own people," Massood wrote back. "We are going to the mosque."

~

Massood went to the market most days searching for outcasts and strays he could groom into Muslim devotees and followers of Allah. A Syrian by birth, he had been brought up a strict and staunch Muslim, rejecting the material world of secular societies, and devoting his life to serving the faith and obeying the Koran. Though at one time tolerant of other religions, and by no means a Saddam Hussein supporter, he had been heavily influenced by the radical Muslim Brotherhood and al-Qaeda, particularly after the first Gulf War. On joining the Muslim Brotherhood his charitable tendencies evaporated, and he became intolerant of all non-Muslims. Directed to go to Ethiopia, his mission became radicalising young, persuadable men, and making them into instruments of death, pointed at the West. Never killing anyone himself, his charges had massacred many hundreds at his behest, Massood coldly having no qualms about slaughtering Western Christians in the name of Islam.

Forthwith, Saleh came under the mullah's spell. Ditching his Ethiopian Orthodox Tewahedo Church ethos, he became a practising Muslim. Instructing him in the ways of Islam, Massood brought restraint and rule to his staccato mind, instilling him with deep application.

"Mostly," he stipulated. "Without strict dictum and dedication to a just and righteous cause, nothing of any significance can be affected, apart from making facile protests and demonstrating discontent." Ridiculing such passive approaches, Massood insisted they achieved nothing in relation to status quo revision, and only affirmative practices resulted in change.

Every day, Saleh and other young, disenfranchised Ethiopians prayed at the mosque, read texts from the Koran, and listened to the mullah telling his stories of Islamic tradition, history, and their grievances against Western Christian and secular societies. Accrediting their collective efforts were focused on the universal advancement of Muslim certitudes, and the creation of a transcontinental Islamic state republic, he rammed home the ruthless, ethnocentric aphorism without forethought of consequence. In this heaven on Earth, all peoples and nations were to be constrained by the will of the mullahs, imams and other Muslim clerics, acting on behalf of Allah.

To bring about the intent, they'd mercilessly persecute Christians to the brink of extinction, notably in traditional Muslim autonomies such as Pakistan, eradicate secular societies by mass genocide subjugation, and implement Sharia Law on all the world's citizens. Insisting the weak, liberal sovereignties of the West were to be systematically victimised by playing the race card, raiding their welfare and health schemes, and infiltrating their political frameworks to the fulcrum whereby immigrant Muslims formed a dominant majority, enabling them to dismantle democracy, he forecast with pride the enforcement of an unyielding, pan-worldwide Islamic dictatorship.

In truth, Massood fed his young brethren a bumper book of gibberish Islamic bunk, wittingly misinterpreting and spinning the holy text to act as the springboard for dissatisfied and gullible men in their nascent years to enact the Islamic leadership's mandate. Seizing transnational supremacy through a combination of terrorism and fifth columnist infiltration, they'd end consensus government and institute an overarching cruel and callous autocracy.

Muslim leaders had been expounding their evil orthodoxy for over 1400 years. Nothing altered in the baseline objective, apart from the method of execution. They had waged holy war across the Middle East, India, North Africa and Southern Europe for centuries, only to be repulsed and forced back by national armies. After the success of three Christian crusades to the Holy Land, in the main, Muslim aggression lay dormant until the rise of the Ottoman Empire resulting in Greece, the Balkans and the lands foremost around the Black Sea being conquered, then colonised by Muslim invaders. Therewith, millions of Christians were uniformly persecuted, tortured, enslaved, and murdered for rebelling against the intruders. Its savage legacy on the indigenous peoples of the Balkans was never forgotten, revenge for centuries of Muslim tyranny the prime catalyst behind the former Yugoslavian and Balkan wars of the nineteen-nineties. Progressively multiplying in leaps and bounds since the mid-nineteen-eighties, the same Muslim colonisation of Western Europe, expressly in Holland, France and England, premeditated the same endgame. Though ostensibly passive in nature, nonetheless, the implications for those realms subordinated to Muslim wants, brought about by an overdeveloped discernment for entitlement, were crippling. Abetted by the weak, liberal elitist political and media classes, it resulted in indigenous populations feeling like strangers in their own countries, and if not curbed and inverted, signalled an inevitable Balkans-style war.

~

For month after month, Saleh followed Mullah Massood's strict instructions, observing stringent prayer time diktats, reading Koran scriptures out aloud to his fellow novices, and in general, leading the life of a good Muslim. Then the day came when Massood's daily sermons mutated into how his disciples of Allah could destroy Western Christian and secular societies and help establish worldwide Muslim ruling governance. Charging up the devotees, he told his captive audience about the concept of jihad, and to enter paradise, a devout Muslim must make the ultimate sacrifice in the offensive to see Islamic regimes installed by brutality and coercion in all domains.

Whether the young followers became convinced through faithfulness to the cause, or through recognition of the sequels to disobedience, made no difference to Massood. So long as they did the Muslim Brotherhood and al-Qaeda summons channelled through him, the effect was the same.

If things were taxing for Saleh back in Dire Dawa, they were about to get ratcheted up with respect to life fluctuating sways in Nazret. Naive and wide-eyed, he lapped up the Islamic radical syllabus with a fork and spoon, repeating back phrases and slogans parrot fashion, and accepting the global view without contradiction. In his mind, he still weighed he had been unfairly mistreated for a minor transgression by the Dire Dawa Western aid workers and by his mother for refusing to give him any further chances. Telling this to the mullah and attaching his father had also been given short shrift by the camp management, unfairly ending up in jail for beating his wife, he hoped to further ingratiate himself. Just the kind of revenge motivator Massood sought to turn Saleh into a disciple of hate, he piled fuel on an already blazing fire.

Capitalising on Saleh's disenfranchisement, the mullah's indoctrination intensified. He told him Western crimes against Muslims were not to be tolerated, and they had no right to make judgments on Islamic traditions, especially the way men treated women. Saleh incorrectly deduced his grievances against the charity, and maybe even his family were warranted, and thereby vengeance was justified.

Inevitably, Massood commanded Saleh to become a Muslim fundamentalist, make his way into the West, and take revenge on Christians by carrying out the orders of the Muslim Brotherhood and al-Qaeda.

Obsessed with anti-Western rhetoric, Saleh fully embraced the trenchant doctrine at the onset, equating glorious martyrdom with the highest salvation. Then his natural portent for self-preservation kicked in. Without doubt, Saleh was a me-person from birth, the cooperative only a vehicle to further his own needs and hankerings. He did not really want to permanently affix his colours to any flagpole or die for any cause. On the contrary, he wanted to live and enjoy the good life. Like many so-called, virtuous and devout Muslims, he craved the scope Western freedoms could deliver, licensing him to indulge in his own chosen abridgment of fleshpots and desires. To Saleh, life was exclusively for enjoyment. Albeit he didn't grasp it, his natural constituency fell into the Dionysian strain. Exemplifying its ecstatic, orgiastic, and irrational nature, he easily became frenetic and delirious.

In the cold light of day, Saleh discerned in his spur to find shelter and the wherewithal to wreak revenge on those offending him, he had slid unerringly into the fiery turbulence of jihadism, resignation from the guild, not an option. He knew too much about their plans and their members to be set adrift in contemporary Ethiopian society, any attempt to leave, checkmating in his death at the hands of those befriending him. His natural ability to play the hungered part without any real authenticity came to his rescue. Appearing to uphold Massood's decrees, when the opportunity arose, he intended to flee, bailing out into calmer waters to reengage his desire to find the easy life at the expense of others.

Foxing the Nazret mullah and his fellowship of followers into deeming he was one of them, he went through the initiation processes, outwardly projecting the symbol of a staunch and dedicated Muslim. Still to be defined by way of a terrorist act, they prepared him both physically and mentally for the labour ahead. Nevertheless, until he was in the required place to execute their commandment, nothing specific about the target was disclosed to him. Taught how to use weapons, make explosives, handle communications, adhere to the required security protocol, and how to take his own life should he be captured and interrogated, he became empowered to perform the sortie. Like most things he had been shown in his schooling, he caught on right away, acquiring the skillsets crucial for him to discharge his duty. Though appearing impelled and enthused, privately Saleh went through the course in a perfunctory mode, his natural fraudulence persuading his instructors of his impulse to succeed with his assignment.

Riddled with misgivings and emotionally pulled in many directions, Saleh began to have guilt pangs about his family left in Dire Dawa. Telling Massood he wanted to see his family again before exiting Ethiopia to begin his undertaking, the mullah agreed to his request. Ordering him to say nothing about his jihadist involvement to anyone he met, Massood allocated one of his trusted lieutenants to drive Saleh to Dire Dawa, on the face of it to ensure his security, but in reality, to guarantee he did not get cold feet about pursuing his commitment to the cause.

While his minder retired to a discreet distance at the camp, Saleh found Gabra, informing her he had the facility to get to Europe, and when he succeeded in gaining political asylum, he'd send for his family. Shaking her head dismissively, she told her son, he had learnt nothing from either his education, or from Ethiopian Orthodox Tewahedo Church philosophies. Appalled by his deceitful plan, she lectured good Christians did not swindle others, and she was ashamed about his premeditated trickery. Knowing his mother would see it as yet another observance of the something-for-nothing trickery he had adopted from an early age, Saleh refrained from telling her he had converted to Islam.

Captivating his siblings, some of his brothers and sisters were quite enthusiastic about the prospect of going to Europe, but Makeda, and Girma his elder brother, were highly censorious, castigating the delinquent Saleh, and saying with his intelligence, he should be putting his efforts into making Ethiopia a better and more prosperous place. Criticising his draft reeked of sneaky and devious inclinations, Makeda had no hesitation in condemning such scheming as unworthy of his Christian upbringing.

Reacting very badly, Saleh sparked into volatility, screaming at his family he elected to do what was best for him, and he could not care less about Ethiopia.

Much to the disapproval of the rest of the family, though some of his younger kin said to send for them when he got settled in Europe, he returned to Nazret under a cloud. When his minder grilled him about the meeting with his family, Saleh gave the impression, they had wished him well.

Secretly, Saleh did not fathom why the easy life way he proposed had been met with such hostility by his mother and elder brother and sister. Having no societal morality or affinity for others, essentially, he was a loner, cheating anyone to implement his ends. Whether Western aid workers or Muslim fundamentalists, to him, they were all pawns to be played and immolated in a greater cause; his ambitions, his thirsts.

Continuing to play the devout Muslim, Massood and his followers were convinced of Saleh's devotion to act out their edict to the letter. Finalising preparation for the task ahead, in parallel, he concocted stratagems to extricate himself from the monolithic fix he had gotten into once out of Nazret.

The time came to begin his quest, Massood giving him money and forged travel documentation, and sending him on his way to Addis Ababa for onward embarkation to Tunis by air. Instructed to contact a band of local Muslim fundamentalists, and await further instructions from them, Saleh launched his trek north-west to the Mediterranean coastline. Maintaining his pious and devout worshiper charade to impress upon them his readiness to make the hindmost forfeit, he rehearsed the glib angle in advance to gain the Tunis Muslim fundamentalists advocacy.

On reaching Europe, he planned to melt away from their grasp, claim asylum seeker capacity, then send for those members of his family wanting to join him. Knowing calling for asylum seeker classification in Blighty was very easy, and the welfare and health systems were ripe for defrauding, his craving became to live in England. In Saleh's mind, easy street beckoned for the rest of his life, courtesy of the English taxpayer.

6

SHIP'S COMPANY

Buoyed up by the proposition of a Mediterranean voyage well in advance of the event, the newcomers' perceptions of sailing the mighty Poseidon and exploring North African ports made for colourful deliberation about shipboard life and delving into an exotic part of the world. Arrangements had been made for limited detachment from their civilian lives, affording the life-long lodestar to be fulfilled.

Back in January, Steve had seen an advertisement in a boating magazine outlining a Mediterranean voyage on the schooner Poseidon beginning Easter Day. Bringing it to Glyn's notice, they discussed the opportunity at length. Meeting the schooner owners in London, after going through the interview convention, they wanted the gig more than ever. A few days later, the pair got the green light.

"Do you think those guys are strictly chicken soup?" Glyn probed.

"*Huh!*" Steve spluttered, unsure of the phrase meaning.

"Kosher."

"Oh yeah, I've already audited them."

"What?"

"The day after we met them, I did a company's search in *Dunn & Bradstreet*. They are, who they say they are, and yes, they're loaded."

"What about the schooner?"

"Did that too," he validated, showing disbelief his friend imagined his hunt imperfect. "Lloyds of London confirm Poseidon is registered with them. In fact—" He sniggered. "Those boys have two schooners. The other one is in the Caribbean."

"So they're the real deal then?"

"Seems so."

"Time to start withdrawal doings and begin packing."

"Oh," Steve chimed, grinning mischievously, "I began on that before the research."

"*What!*"

Bashfully, he admitted, "I decided to go, even if they weren't—" Dawdling, he playfully tapped Glyn on the shoulder. "Kosher? The risk is worth it, just to get away from Führer Brown for a while." Scowling, his rhetoric turned into a complaint. "With every passing day, that charmless Celtic bastard does more harm to England then the Luftwaffe ever did, and we are helpless to halt him. I need a holiday to get away from his regulated, thought police impelled state apparatus."

Surprised by the preciseness of his friend's forthright grievance, Glyn retorted, "I didn't conceive you felt so strongly about it." Absorbing Steve's words, he then said, "I loathe him, his predecessor, Blair, and their PC sycophants as well, but I've resigned myself to not being able to get rid of Brown until the next general election."

"Geez!" Disgust spread across Steve's face. "I'd like to get rid of him sooner, and permanently."

Needing to shelve the contentious issues for re-examination on their return, coupled with desperately yearning to de-clutter their minds and revive vitality; the primary goal of the voyage, they agreed to make the Blair-Brown destruction of Blighty a strictly verboten topic during the voyage.

Changing jobs in the software industry, Glyn made a special agreement to delay starting his new post until the following July. Taking an extended sabbatical, Steve left his brother to run their partnership. Both felt release sprint through their bodies at the very notion of severing from levied conformity, and hopefully finding an egalitarian Eden in the Med.

~

The same reflex to the sensation Glyn foremost experienced relinquishing home for university enlivened his final preparations and centralised his zip. He was soon to discover his crewmates were comparably disposed. Galvanised with resolve, they to contrived to feed on the grail elixir and the ambrosia of the gods, then segue into unbeatable warriors, discharged from regularity to enlist in physically and spiritually exhilarating pursuits. Their intent a pilgrimage, not a sightseeing tour, whatever the Med threw at them, they planned to take it without vacillation. Explicitly, the threshold had to be crossed. Wanting to see what lay on the other side, they hoped for blessed escapism.

Steve and Glyn journeyed from Heathrow to Madrid, then on to Cadiz. Last to arrive portside, just as the sun set over the western horizon, Jeff and Ed met them and introduced the rest of the new crew in Poseidon's saloon.

Glyn had known Steve for over twenty years. After working in a civil engineering job with Ove Arup & Partners, he ran his own construction firm with his elder brother. Fed up with the tortures of daily commuting and largely being office based, Steve decided to join the family business as assistant managing director.

Well-built with Nordic gracility and a deep resonating voice, for a sturdy man he moved like a gazelle, quick off the mark and with the necessary stamina to carry out any imposed function. Philosophically open to counsel, he never erred to pre-judgment, always dissecting data before making any conclusions. Like Glyn, he also had a sensitive nose, able to detect potential skunk and take countermeasures accordingly. Rarely giving up on any trial, his solid and reliable mentality made a matchless attribute for crewing a schooner and surviving an extensive jaunt in the Med.

"I used to race motorbikes in the 250 and 500cc classes at Brands Hatch amateur events in my late teens," Steve told his new companions during initial introductions. "Won a few trophies, but during one race, I could have been killed when I came off, narrowly missing advertising boarding."

"You're a bit of a dare devil then?" David remarked.

"I'd not go as far as that, but I do like to test myself to find my limits."

"You'll get plenty of testing on the voyage," Ed specified.

"What happened next, Steve?" Tom pumped.

"I was university bound, so a combination of disquieted parents and a very frightened girlfriend persuaded me to quit the bike game. After graduation, I resumed risky pursuits. Not on the racetrack, but with hang-gliding and bungee jumping." Marking the crew's approving smirks at his exploits, he grinned back. "I still ride road bikes for fun. Currently I get my kicks on a Yamaha YZF-R1. Glyn's been on the back of it, and it scared the living daylights out of him."

"Yep, perfectly true," he confessed. "Next to sex, the thrill of being on the Yammy comes a close second."

Tempering his natural bent for hazardous pursuits when he married, he astonished Glyn by telling their new-found friends about his wife's infidelity.

"Judy had an impromptu affair with an old flame, reported to me by a nosey neighbour," he informed with candour, not wishing to shock, but more to illustrate for him, frankness and truth were programmed to be his watch words during the voyage. "Although she regretted the deception, I felt betrayed. The marriage had been sullied and broken. I couldn't go on, so I filed for divorce."

Not foreseeing such a high scale of intimate disclosure, the crew shrank away, the encumbrance of shared distress a jarring touchstone, but cryptically, they admired Steve's courage to be transparent.

"You see," he expressed, "loyalty is a mainstay for me. It can't be watered down in any kind of pact. Without sincerity, there is no foundation, just shifting quicksand. I'm a civil engineer by trade. You can't build on shaky *terra firma*. One fine day, the edifice will come crashing down. It's the same with human relationships. If we can't trust our partners, friends and professional colleagues, or in the national sphere our government, then there's no aggregate values and communal sentiments to bind us together."

At the time of the parting, his action came as no surprise to Glyn. His job, to favour Steve, but being genial, he also liked Judy. He knew malice did not exist in Judy's indiscretion, just lack of prudence, probably fostered by boredom born out of cosiness. Steve worked augmented hours and had an active sports life outside of marriage. A manuscript reviewer, working from home after her publishing office moved from Maidstone to Reading, Judy felt alone and neglected, hence the possibility for temptation. Howbeit Glyn's calls for clemency, Steve remained adamant, repair impossible. Glyn's longer loyalty to him meant he shied away from further contact with Judy. She soon found a new mate. Though Steve had many girlfriends prior to Judy, after the failed marriage, he became very cautious with the ladies.

"I take your point *vis-à-vis* loyalty," Jeff comforted. "You engage a creed we should all adhere to. Yet most people gloss over such a deep-seated virtue, at least in today's flaky world." Raising his eyebrows, he appended, "And occasionally, it includes me."

"Something has definitely been lost in recent times," Ed insisted. "That precious something axiomatic to our parents and grandparents binding and well-being at the family, community and national level, has somehow seeped away. Whether it reflects modern society, or is resultant from the liberalisation of the nineteen-sixties, I can't say, but standards have markedly declined, and like Jeff—" Tarrying, he earnestly eyed his sailing partner. "I also have not been immune from self-indulgence at times."

"You mean, you've had affairs?" Bill asked.

"No, nothing like that," he affixed, cracking into a broad smile. "As you get to know us better, you'll find Jeff and I are in no way unblemished. I don't mind telling you, we've both forsaken conventional domesticity to indulge our sailing passions."

"Your wives are sailing widows then?" Tom asked.

"Something like you infer."

"Sorry, Steve," Jeff apologised. "We seem to have deviated from what you were telling us."

"Quite alright. When I decided to open-up, I knew it might draw comparable stories."

Hand gesturing, Jeff prompted, "Please, go on."

Advancing his account, Steve brought in more C.V minutiae, incorporating how his life had panned out since Judy, and why he had seized the Med opportunity with both hands, anticipating Poseidon dispensing another vehicle to test his mettle, thereby satisfying his lust for excitement. During the junket, Steve was to climb the mainsail mast more than any of the newcomers and became comfortable with sail-rigging duties in the bows, even in perilous weather. Glyn knew his friend had to find his limits, a trait in the blood inherited from his late father, also a risk taker.

In the course of the premier evening aboard Poseidon, Glyn and Steve got familiar with the other crew members in no time. For some peculiar inkling, after Steve laid the trend with his marriage failure concession, everyone became predisposed to reveal their sins and motives for joining the select group, any holding back somehow inappropriate. Amongst strangers, like being under the spell of a psychoanalyst, they confessed their shortcomings and tragedies, warts and all, the cupboard left bare of skeletons. They had no clue if previous crews had the same need to come clean upon arrival, but the all-out honesty and thereby inferred safekeeping with new companions made for instant comradeship, adding to the comradery.

Twice married, with a third scheduled for later in the year, professedly, Colin Napier epitomised the archetypal serial husband, the ladies going for his studious air of sophistication, rather than his medium build, square-jawed, angular face, and a handshake gripping like a python. For all that, the ship's company soon found it had not all been the stuff of male folklore.

Though scholarly in outlook, Colin had boxed for his school and could still handle himself behind his professor-like facade. A lawyer by trade, the universally unpopular profession drew good natured boos from his crewmates. Duplicated throughout the voyage, in contempt of the superficial ribbing, Colin abounded jovial fellow credentials, his ready smile dissipating any circumspection of deep insult.

"A lawyer with a personality," Glyn earmarked. "Borders on the atypical."

"It's why he passed muster back in London," Jeff certified.

"After law school, I acted at the Lord Chancellor's Office," Colin relived. "But I was a fish out of water, my frame of mind simply not in-line with operational parameters."

Whereas Colin's colleagues struggled to get to grips with concurrent toils, his superior productivity set him apart. They were unalloyed civil servants, their careers predetermined to traverse upwardly. Destined for the private sector, Colin found his lively posture alien to public-sector dictums. Qualities making him a noteworthy company law professional, also cast him as a poor civil servant.

"They considered me to be a free thinker, a *very* dangerous trait in the Civil Service," he sheepishly confided. "They wanted clones, but I didn't fit the bill. I left Whitehall for a senior legal post with Arthur Anderson, specialising in company law, then I joined Ernst & Young. Those moves made me a significant amount of money. By my late thirties, I'd fired up my own law firm."

Soon, the crew accredited Colin was also a walking, talking encyclopaedia, knowledgeable on a wide variety of academic schools encompassing history, a subject proving invaluable during their trek. They also discovered a capable sage, able to interpret data and make plausible deductions. Some of the crew had come across people adept at regurgitating stored information, but paradoxically, incapable of understanding, let alone deciphering intelligent conclusions from it. They were sheep, easily manipulated, easily moderated, ideal for Brown's auto-compliance dominion. An unruly maverick like the rest of the crew, and certainly not of the brainwashed breed, Colin's exceptional dynamism put him on the outside, a thorn in the doctrinaire PC cosmos, never submitting to thought control.

His wealth of assets combined with a breezy persona made

him first-rate crewing material, his onboard forte, recounting quick fire jokes, mainly about lawyers.

"I'm also serious about cooking," he told them. "The kitchen has become my centre of excellence for invention."

"So, your future wife will never be allowed into the kitchen then?" Glyn proposed, the rest of the crew grinning at the light gibe.

"Hah, it's why she finds me so attractive," Colin boasted tongue-in-cheek.

When on galley detail, his new friends were to find the corporate lawyer's piquant starters, delicious meat and fish entrees and lavish desserts were a sheer delight.

Shifting further down culinary avenues, the cheerful conversation prospected cookhouse capabilities, everyone forwarding some speciality bringing taste bud pleasure.

Then to their complete surprise, Colin altered tack, saying in a restrained modulation, "I have two children from my second marriage, Melinda and Adrian." His head fell. "But I seldom see them."

Facial features avalanched from toothy laughter into solemnity, the sudden testimony dispelling the bouncy mood.

"When we divorced, my ex got child custody, and moved to Carlisle from Horsham, where I still live. In terms of character, she transformed so strikingly after they were born, it broke the *affaire de coeur*. We ceased communicating. There was no way back after that. She wanted to be by herself with the children. It left no room for me. I'm sure you can work out the rest."

The bombshell left the ship's company gaping. Colin's effervescent attributes and ebullient charm hid his agony so effectively, that if he had not told them about the break-up, they could not have guessed what hurt lay beneath. Going on to unveil his first marriage was not a bed of roses either, it dispelled their initial Don Juan picture of him. The second marriage dark episode had happened five years before Cadiz, Colin indefatigable about one final adventure to cleanse its' stinging aftermath from memory, before settling into his third, and hopefully everlasting marriage.

Comprehending his tale demonstrated supposed playboy fortune reposing on stereotypes often fell dramatically short in reality, Glyn concluded not all serial husbands were the stuff of barroom banter imaginings.

Unmindful of being in his late-fifties, Bill Cressey, or Bill the brain, as the crew grew to call him, passed for forty with ease. A human dynamo, blessed with boundless energy, it imbued him with eternal youth. Sporadically supplemented by extravagant meals and a penchant for quality French wine, his wiry frame honed on long-distance running, mainly lived on nervous energy and adrenalin generating a weight to power ratio enabling him to accomplish physical deeds the casual onlooker assumed beyond him. When the on-watch flagged under challenging sea conditions, the ship's company were to find Bill still had the reserves to keep going. Quickest up the mainmast by a country mile, he gave the vastly proficient seniors a run for their money.

"My background is in software," Bill told his shipmates. "I've been in the business for over thirty-five years, and currently I'm an independent consultant. I left school with meagre qualifications before joining ICL as a trainee. It's where I found order and life aspirations. Without that, I wouldn't be here today. I floated my own software consultancy over two decades ago, but I'm virtually retired now. I leave the running of the firm to a dependable team of professionals, only getting involved with special clients or challenging problems, just to keep my hand in."

While the others discussed their I.T skills, or lack of them, Glyn had a 1-0-1 with Bill.

Their brief interlude finished with Bill saying, "By the time you're my age, you should have left the software industry and be probing other schemes. Keep yourself busy by doing business consultancy, but don't let the bits and bytes consume you."

A well-balanced recommendation Glyn had heard on many occasions, but from the eminent Bill, it had the full ring of credence.

Ostensibly an ideas man, Poseidon's crew were to bring to light when soliciting Bill's opinion, he came out with a stream of consciousness containing no commas or full stops, just a string of characters fused into coherent meditations, like Dylan reciting *Subterranean Homesick Blues*. Hence, Bill the brain.

"This might seem strange to you word processor advocates," Bill implied, "but I've been a Dictaphone user throughout my career. I'd rather speak into these devices, then have a secretary convert to the written word."

To preserve the sanctity of the odyssey without any back-home distractions, the seniors had advised the newcomers, mobiles and other communication devices were banned from Poseidon. Consequently, Bill had not packed his portable Dictaphone, the ideas he gushed on the voyage flying into the ether, lost forever.

Furthering his exposition, Bill amused them with anecdotes about his career. Then focusing on his home life, as if the earlier report had been a gentle trailer graduating to the main film event, his affectation became faithful, his facial expression wounded.

Taking a deep breath, he testified, "I lost my wife to a severe illness fourteen years ago," his voice breaking at the declaration.

Still jammed in laughter by Bill's witty stories, the unpredictable articulation had miens frozen by the severity of the remark.

"At the time, it just about destroyed me. Unable to serve her in any way, I had to watch her slowly dissolve into nothingness." Careening his head, the recollection hit him harder than he desired. "Afterwards, I funneled my energies into mechanising work initiatives and preferred pastimes. If it hadn't been for those distractions, I couldn't have gone on."

Hauling himself out of foggy despair, his recital took a positive surge. "I have three children," he brightly recounted. "My son Kyle moved to Australia a few years ago, but my two daughters Bridget and Christina, still live close by. They're all married." Pausing, he elatedly chimed, "Christina made me a grandfather last year," the announcement making his eyes light up with pride. "I just wish her mother had been around to see her grandchild."

His loss still too arduous to bear without sadness, the short-lived sparkle faded from Bill's face. Nevertheless, with a forced effort he regained his spirit, telling the ship's company more about his family, and his orienteering and hiking exploits. He also liked jazz and blues, something else he had in common with Glyn. Talking enthusiastically about the depth of pleasure he found listening to Miles Davis, Dave Brubeck, and a host of other modal-period jazz luminaries, his normal bubbly aura shone through, Glyn speculating he might have seen him at Ronnie Scotts.

"It's possible," Bill replied. "I've been known to frequent Scott's, especially when dining semaphore is on offer."

"Dining semaphore," Glyn repeated. "Defined as?"

"Oh, that's my software developer speak for *haute* cuisine, meaning, tasty jazz."

Bill scarcely spoke first in debates, but the crew readily appreciated his often-flamboyant rejoinders marked him as a person with wit and charm.

Swarthy, with a very smart hairstyle, and often mistaken for an Italian, Tom Parker never looked out of place in the Med. Annihilating sustenance like a hungry wolverine, remarkably, it did not burden his athletic build, his high metabolism naturally burning off calories. A babe magnet when Poseidon's crew were ashore, Tom was never short of female admirers. Possessing a wonderful matter of fact, free-will, nothing seemed to upset him, or be beyond his ken. Professionally, a rock-solid entrepreneur, aboard Poseidon he preferred to show his easy going and gregarious side.

"I've taken to fiction writing in recent times," he told the crew. "But I also own an electronics design and development firm, serving the motor vehicle and other industries. It's what pays the bills and covers my fleshpot itches."

His early calling had been with Aston Martin, where he worked as an electronics systems designer. Sustaining the association, as well as owning a vintage 1954 Jaguar D Type, he currently drove a DB9, much to the envy of the sea-sailing newcomers.

"Regarding your writing," Glyn prompted. "Have you had anything published?"

"After several years of rejections from agents and publishers, I've had two short works published by a boutique press." Hesitating for a moment, he continued, "I hope you don't mind Jeff and Ed, but I want this sea caper to provide the raw input for a full-length novel."

"Not in the least," Jeff responded. "Just promise you'll send copies to Ed and me."

"Will be a pleasure."

Throughout the voyage, Tom subsequently harvested substance by documenting events and talking to the crew about their estimations and observations. Proving to be a kind of diary mirroring goings-on, deals and dangers, he'd come up to his shipmates at the most irregular or inopportune moments enquiring, 'How did you feel about climbing to the top of the main sail mast?' or, 'What was going through your mind when that wave nearly pushed you off the bows?' Like Alan Whicker interviewing the lost tribes of Papua New Guinea, Tom's riveting manner ensured everyone cooperated.

Also a serial husband, currently separated from wife number three back in Wiltshire, unlike Colin's matrimonial tragedies, his attachments bounced along with both parties out for a good time, and neither surprised when the boom came down on the affiliation. Tom told his conquests up-front what he was like, so they were under no illusions pertaining to his wandering eye.

"I usually trade them in every two to three years," he jested with a wicked grin in their introductory session.

Doubtless just alpha-male bluster, notwithstanding, his marital yarns made for hilarious discourse. Wife number-three, Trudie, had chased him out of the house when she caught him philandering. The DB9 got him out of the way of a vicious tongue and a thrashing from a country walking stick. Not the first time he'd been on the receiving end of a ferocious rebuff, he decided to beat a hasty retreat for a while, gravitating in the direction of Poseidon.

There had been no unusual misfortunes or catastrophes in Tom's inside life. Unfailingly symbolising the utopian vision of charmed, carefree living, his dalliances with the opposite sex produced satirical farce to challenge anything Henry Fielding and a string of comedy writers could conjure up, his partners giving as good as they got with only egos bent temporarily out of shape. Though Tom had no children, for Glyn it became easy to see other compensations filled his days, making him philosophical and gratified with his lot.

"If children do come, they come," he conceded. "Under the covers, I've already reserved an unmatched side of me to manage child rearing. Gone will be the life I lead now, but until that day, I'll continue to bask in the fleshpots."

His artless self-appraisal drew agreement from the ship's company. Covertly, they fancied, what man given the right physical attributes and opportunity, did not indulge in Tom's flamboyant lifestyle?

Everyone exhibits dual or even multiple personalities. Some make their owners proud. Others remain perplexing, human frailty confounding and challenging even the most erudite of minds. Though flaky in his romantic life, the other side of Tom's coin revealed him to be a skilled strategist, making professional judgments in a flash contingent on facts, an attribute periodically producing benefits in his private life.

"On many occasions, I've seen people reluctant to make rulings for fear of repercussions," he said. "Making no decision in the engineering world leads to events overtaking those owning the bane. Invariably, it has knock-on fallout. What I call, house of cards syndrome."

"You're right on that score," Jeff proclaimed. "At sea, often there's no time to postpone determinations. Procrastination is the enemy of endurance."

"Oh, I can see the comparison. It's half the reason why I presumed I could ascribe some value to this voyage."

"It's not quite act, don't think," Ed cleared up. "But making the quick and right choices is often the difference between survival at sea and sinking."

"Quite," Tom approved. "For me, it's qualifying the information, then deciding. It has become my guiding light. Too much time to cogitate and worry, might produce incorrect conclusions, post-graduating in a poor, if not fatal outcome. But at sea, wow." Grinning broadly he rubbed his chin. "I can see the modus has to be speeded up even more."

Resolutely, the principle drew flawless agreement from the crew, chiefly the seniors. Indecisiveness often produced ruination at sea, whereas swift and steadfast cerebration usually eschewed disaster. Glyn chanced if Tom had introduced the quick decision code during his interview, the champion sailing facet must have made the seniors beam with delight. Plausibly, he was immediately given the consent signal to join Poseidon.

Flourishing events promoter David Reader managed a services firm, specialising in large outdoor music and cultural spectaculars across the UK. If a man's success can be measured by the size of his girth, then David's mushrooming waistline illustrated he had been extremely successful. Poseidon's crew grew to treasure his warm decorum, his never say die attitude, and his endless optimism, the glass always half-full, never half-empty. In his world, there were no quandaries, only solutions needing to be found to address unforeseen issues. Never short of a generous simper, and a pleasant word, David's onboard 'good mornings' emanated a cheeriness and relish for the day's call ahead. By nature, a bodacious explorer, he'd become a detective tracking for unturned stones. Never satisfied with convention, he found interests beyond conformist pursuits, sincerely inclining towards the obscure, and always posing w-questions.

On that initial evening, he told the crew stories about his dubious dealings with other promoters. Often, they were perverse, poignant, and exceedingly funny. Always ending the lurid tale with, "they're all cunning bastards you know," a rakish sneer glinted across his playful face.

"Before my promoter vocation, at the tender age of sixteen I joined the British Army as an officer candidate. Then—" David patted his stomach. "I was extremely fit with my girth restrained by exercise."

Representing the Army in a tri-service outward bound competition at RAF Cosford, David put his fitness to the test. Comparatively, at age fifteen, Glyn was one of four ATC cadet

NCOs sponsored to attend a Cosford five-day outward-bound course with RAF entrants. Embarking on a dedicated fitness drill, he prepared for the test ahead, but on a far higher physical plane than anything previously undergone, the Cosford event damn near wasted him. Returning home a week later, he was fit but near-to skeletal in semblance, when they met him at Lancaster rail station his mother and girlfriend in tears calculating he had been starved. In contrast, David breezed the Cosford tri-service competition, won it, and went on to reach the rank of captain before decamping from the army after a five-year commission.

Becoming serious, he divulged, "I saw action in the Falklands, the thorny bailiwick toughening my bottle to make the rest of my life successful. You see—" His aspect swallowed up in sadness, he wobbled his head. "Many of my comrades didn't make it back to Blighty."

"It must have been a gruelling ordeal," Glyn jabbered.

"Yes, but interestingly enough, its significance has hit me more in recent years than at the time. Back in 1982, you just had to get on with it, and hope you survived, but when we returned to England, few soldiers discussed the war. Subconsciously, we wanted to bury the bloody episode in the figure of what we saw, and what we were part of. It's the same for any soldiers, in any war."

None of the ship's company could table a parallel circumstance equalling David's war zone bulletin. Rendering most of them incapable of truly rating his baptism of fire, they cast confounded looks, unsure how to give a leisurely response. Seeing their discomfiture, Jeff took the lead.

"We can only surmise what went on at Goose Green and in those other battles," he assigned, his resonance deliberate and respectful. "My father fought in the Second World War, but he seldom talked about his wartime escapades. When he did, it always erred on the upbeat side, something about camaraderie, or the surprising good times he had, never about the fighting. That's the part he wanted to forget."

"Soldiers have been doing that since Julius Caesar embarked on his conquest of Europe," David submitted in accord. "I've never met anyone glorifying battle and speaking of it in glowing terms. It's much more that obligation spurs on the soldier, killing the enemy a consequence of the belief, and acquiring the dedication needed to protect the homeland and her territories from aggressors. But after the heat of battle, I didn't see many victorious British soldiers celebrating. Many were physically sick." Resting, he then clarified, "Oh, we did the PR bit for the cameras, but it was laboured, an expectation drawn out by the politicians."

"It was finalised in a few months, but washed over as incredibly intense," Bill remembered. "That is true, isn't it, David?"

"Absolutely, extremely intense. But if we didn't treat it as a full-blown, must win the war mentality, the Falklands conflict could have gone on for a very long time." Breaking off to summon up the strength to go on he asserted, "You see, wars are only won by decisive and concentrated exertion. Containment strategies do not defeat the aggressor, and result in the conflict going on, sometimes for decades without a resolution and agreed terms of surrender."

"No doubt, we can all see what you're driving at," Steve specified. "The policy of containment in Afghanistan was always doomed to failure, and the conflict has been in play for longer than the Second World War. I could never see why Blair combatted in Afghanistan anyway. There have been so many justifications tabled by his legislature over the past eight years, none believed by a clear majority of English people."

"Quite right," Tom supported. "Being led to swallow the invasion was justified to curtail huge Taliban created supplies of heroin finding its way into England, simply didn't square. It could have been fulfilled by denying access to the perpetrators. Beefing up homeland security by bringing down the boom on trafficking and defending our shores properly might have prevented the Taliban using legal and illegal immigrants as pack mules to bring the stuff in." Clearly miffed, he chuckled cynically. "Blair and Brown would rather see British military personnel killed in an unwinnable war, than be accused of racism by denying admission to the Muslim carriers."

"And, if you're going to go to war," Bill backed, "do it properly. Don't try to appease the do-gooder brigade. If the allies had done that on D-day, the Second World War might still be going on! As David says, to conclusively win a war and safeguard there is no aftermath of revenge attacks, it has to be done mercilessly." Self-assured of the valuation, he sat back. "Surely both world wars showed that. After Germany surrendered in 1918 and 1945, the fatherland laid down its arms. There were no afters, no renegade army units still fighting. Peace reigned."

"Correct," Colin concurred. "The value of history is what can be learnt from the past. Our own history is littered with many abortive containment misadventures resulting in elongated conflict, those in charge at the time prognosticating it'd be over very quickly. But often, containment strategies have gone on for decades, with more people killed, and at a higher economic cost, than if a search and destroy operation had been instigated to eradicate the enemy in its entirety."

"*Sweet Jesus*," Ed piped up, scrutinising the crew. "In all our lifetimes, we've been impacted by the pernicious offshoots of IRA terrorism and then Muslim terrorism. It just seems to go on *ad infinitum*, with more and more civilian atrocities. Terrorists see negotiation as a weakness to be exploited, while they prolong their bombing campaigns, and execute kidnapped civilians without regret."

"Beyond question," Bill okayed. "Back in the nineteen-seventies and eighties when the IRA bombed English cities, many people said the British Government shouldn't equivocate with the terrorists, or fudge and evade the closed book with dodgy rhetoric. Security services knew their identity, and where they were located. The SAS should have been sent in to wipe them out."

"Well, that's modern politics for you," Glyn jeered. "Somehow, the top brass deems a regular stream of coffins arriving at Brize Norton from Afghanistan will be more acceptable to the public, than doing the job properly and blanket bombing the out-and-out region where the Taliban are based. I mean hell—" He fabricated assurance in his lineaments. "The military have the sensor technology and the weapon delivery platforms to pinpoint precisely where the Taliban hierarchy are holed up, yet the British Government handicap our armed forces by instructing them to adopt the same tactics to hunt down enemies used a hundred years ago. What's the use in investing billions in ultramodern, space age technology, if it's never going to be used?"

"God damn," David mourned, "since leaving the army, I've often appraised how the Falkland's War could have been ducked, leastways with regard to the pitched battles taking place. It occurred to me, if the security services had been allowed to arrange for a fatal accident to happen to Galtieri, producing a pause, it'd provide the opportunity for the negotiators to agree terms." Disconsolately pressing his lips together, he conceded, "but I suppose that's a bit too simple and idealistic."

"What you say, does have clout," Colin endorsed. "When it became compellingly clear in the mid-nineteen-thirties Hitler's intention was war and worldwide domination, some in the British Establishment wanted to arrange for him to have a fatal accident. However, a combination of fluffy politics and misconceived international law obstructed Baldwin then Chamberlin from authorising the essential agency. If allowed, World War II might never have happened."

"Such a solution could have been applied to multiple late twentieth century despots," Steve remarked, "counting Saddam Hussein and Ayatollah Khomeini. But rather than do that, the gutless politicians sacrifice hundreds of thousands, perhaps even millions of military and civilian lives, so they can be seen to be, or claim they are doing the right thing at the infernal UN to comply with international law."

"David," Glyn murmured, attracting his attention. "You use the word accident in place of assassination."

"Yes, in practice, assassination applies," he corroborated, "but arranged to resemble an accident, passable by all parties, and not resulting in stirring up the aggressors' followers to take revenge.

Such missions can easily be arranged and successfully executed by a combination of the security services and the SAS." Opening his hands in a substantiating motion he annexed, "Even if the aggressors build up a whirlpool, accusing the countries they hope to conquer of the act, nothing can be proved, and indubitably, the world's media take for granted conspiracy theorists will make the consequential case, but it has never resulted in the zeal for war."

"Goodness, this powwow really is a thunderclap," Bill noted. "In terms of far-ranging sequels and the shifting of history, we're delving into self-evident factors, possibly yielding very diverse fruits."

"For sure," Tom agreed. "It's disconcerting to conclude most twentieth century wars might have been circumvented, if the head serpent had been eliminated."

Taking in their tense gills, David grasped he had become the stimulus for his new friends straying into heavy duty territory. In a refulgent timbre, he encouraged, "Anyway, let's not get maudlin. I've come on this voyage to get away from all that. I'm confident in saying, all of you want the same."

Switching tack, he told the crew more about his life recipe post army. During their Med excursion, his colleagues were to find he frequently talked about dialectics and the concept of a fraction-less world, saying only whole numbers had real meaning.

"You can't get a little bit pregnant," he maintained. "Everything is binary. Yes, or no. You must choose a side, or select a position, and stick to it for anything to be achieved."

His boldness had led him to many bargaining victories and on occasion disasters, but there was no woolly-mindedness in his philosophy. Affirmative action was his god. Never making a politician, let alone a diplomat, he gauged their stock in trade to be half-truths, downright lies, and manipulation of reality, the sickening cant alien to his distinctive creed. Shot straight and true, David was the consummate antithesis, a non-deflecting arrow, always navigating in pursuit of unblemished argument and crystal-clear truth.

As with many athletes once possessing a Dionysian

physique, by the onset of his late-thirties, rich food and the plentiful grape had resulted in his solar plexus expanding and his derriere dropping. When furnished calorie-enriched food aboard Poseidon, often he was to jovially quip, 'I can resist anything but temptation.' Flexing his hands in a cosmetic insignia of self-denial, nine times out of ten, he then thrust out a hand clasping the goodie with relish and downing it in one. Difficult to accredit the transition from sleek, bronzed god to looming rugby ball pattern, he had the proof in the form of a photo taken in his final year with the British Army. A square jawed, spritely built David, replete with slim waist shone out from the photograph, his fellow crew members amazed by his former frame.

"I carry it to remind me," he told them that first evening, his kisser littered with irony.

Happily married for over twenty years with two children, when not embroiled in his events proponent occupation, David's family life soaked up most of his leisure time. Wanting to do a sea voyage for a long time, his empathetic wife had allotted him a three-month pass to fulfil his fantasy. While in the Med, she basked in Tuscany with their children and other family members.

When it came to his turn to spill the beans, Glyn told the ship's company he'd been ready for a stretched sea rendezvous for many years, the opportunity never arising due to household and business commitments.

Over six feet in height by his mid-teens and built like a surfboard, with long blond hair and clear blue eyes, by the time he arrived on Poseidon, his physique had thickened through diminished exercise, his hair was shorter, transformed into a salt and pepper-like tint, and his eyes had become clouded and slightly bloodshot. Long overdue a protracted holiday to recharge his batteries and recover his health, Glyn made it clear he intended to absorb sunrays and take in fresh air during daylight hours and chill out to music with a liberal intake of alcohol during the evenings.

"You told me you're in the software industry," Bill recalled. "How did it come about?"

"I only firmed up software as a career choice during A-Levels. Before that, I'd considered a number of possibilities."

"Butcher, baker, candlestick maker," Steve interposed, making the ship's company gleam.

"Yeah, not far off the mark," Glyn attested, pushing his friend's arm in a semaphore of camaraderie. "My compass finally turned in favour of a degree in computer sciences. It took me south from Lancaster where my parents still live to University College and employment with the computer systems giant Mariano Systems in Kent, where I still live."

Glyn went on to tell them, while on business for Mariano in Washington, he met his future wife Suzy. A Marilyn Monroe incarnate, vivacious and utterly stunning, she had been blessed with a mesmeric face and a statuesque, curvy body, with legs that went on forever. Her shock of shoulder-length, natural blonde wavy hair, large dazzling hazel eyes, high cheek bones and a Venus mouth merged to drop jaws with a single glance. When she glowed, or laughed, Glyn likened it to the sun suddenly ascending to full bloom. Though she could not have children, she meant so much to him, it became a non-issue, Glyn convinced he had been blessed beyond his wildest dreams, their chance meeting, a once in a lifetime opportunity to irrevocably plant happiness and contentment.

"She bewitched everyone, not just with her allure, but also by the sheer vivacity of her charisma. When we walked into a restaurant, people stopped eating to gaze at her film star looks." Dwelling, he qualified, "They experienced her Rebecca-like enchantment."

"As in Daphne Du Maurier's famous novel?" David suggested.

"Yes."

"She sounds fabulous, Glyn," Jeff complimented.

"Yes, and no," he cautioned, grimacing apprehensively. "A colleague once asked me, how I'd best describe Suzy. I responded, 'perfect', an accolade coming back to haunt me in later years, as she metamorphosed from immaculate goddess into full-blown lemming."

Suzy's practice manager job at Fields, a top firm of Harley Street lawyers, awarded her an excellent pay package, along with free first-class rail travel and a clothing allowance. Her boss had even authorised a free-of-charge apartment for Glyn and Suzy at Chelsea Cloisters. For a few years, they lived more in Chelsea than in Kent.

"Assuredly on her way to the top, all I could see ahead for Suzy was opportunity and clear water," he told the crew. "Everything lodged as fine and dandy for a very long time, then she began to get bored with the law firm role. I knew people at Saatchi & Saatchi, so I got her a meeting with a view to PR work, but no, it wasn't for her. Then ITN came into the reckoning, her elegance and eloquent tonality potentially making her an ideal TV presenter. She met with some ITN people I knew. They liked her, saying she fitted the bill, but once again, Suzy demurred. She wanted to find something under her own steam."

"Itchy feet combined with impetus," Tom put forward.

"If only," Glyn replied, his inflection sad.

During everyday colloquies, he never spoke about Suzy. But Steve had seeded the revelation trend, the other newcomers laying bare their life history short-comings. Glyn felt he should follow suit.

"Eventually, she left Fields and started to go off the rails with a string of over-optimistic privately funded business ventures. Makeup assessment was her weakness, something I had either missed, or glossed over during the early years. It became a fatal flaw. She got in deep with some shady scoundrels." Making a lamentable signal, he pronounced, "God had not made her perfect after all. Her driving motivation to run her own combine became inhibited by her inability to recognise skunk. It resulted in catastrophe after catastrophe."

"Not so fabulous then," Ed noted.

"No...but it took me a long time to admit it, though privately, I grappled with the foible way before events came to a head."

"You got into trouble then?" Bill tested.

"Yes, and as Steve will bear testament to, it became fractious."

Peering at their shipmates, Steve puckered his lips. "Yes, I saw what was happening."

"She'd introduce me to people and say, 'what's your opinion?'. When it comes to skunk, I can smell it at a thousand paces. If I told her not to touch them with a barge pole, she'd react badly, even worse, if she went ahead, and later I was proved right."

Glyn had shown more of his secret life in the space of a few minutes to strangers, than to most people he had revered for many years. But it felt right, the cleansing more beneficial than any fear of embarrassment.

"Her failed gambles put enormous strain on our marriage. I had to bail her out of several very tricky situations, some barely legal. Others were settled with a lot of disposable income, and at times, risk to my own life. She'd become like a lemming, irresistibly throwing herself off the cliff. It had to stop. However, pride stuck as a deadly sin beyond Suzy's bridle. When I announced I'd no longer bail her out, she felt affronted. Things went downhill after that, and heedless of her parents telling her to grow up and stop being selfish, her ego reigned supreme. Anyways, we parted, divorced, and she went back Stateside, her pride intact, but with the erudition it had destroyed us." Falling into more reflection, he confided, "usually, I only get to play the Nick Carraway type fictional personages, those auxiliary extras laden with narrating someone else's story. But in my own little passion play, I got to play Gatsby." He wrinkled his nose. "It's not a role I'd care to reprise."

Never really recovering from the incendiary chapter, for a long time Glyn envisioned himself to be less than ordinary, less than zero. There were other girls, mainly Suzy doubles, but he lasted totally smitten by the real deal, none of the clones making him float like she could. Transcending the physical became an involuntary norm. She had marked him for life, and in truth, the love was blind. Too young and too soft to handle ten-months his senior Suzy, later he derived she'd be too much for the Devil to handle, Scarlet O'Hara child's play in comparison.

"Now my only real love is Liverpool Football Club," Glyn affably admitted, bringing in levity to counter the awkwardness he sensed the crew felt for his dilemma. "My father began taking me to Anfield Road before I started at junior school. Even then, the sea had a fascination for me. Taking in Liverpool Bay from the docks and Southport, I could feel its calling, though I didn't dig what it inferred." Theorising they might not perceive the context, he elaborated. "Let me explain. We stood on the Kop, cheering on the mighty Reds. As the game unfolded and supporter zest rose, the tightly-packed-in Kop crowd moved, surging forwards and backwards like sea waves when Liverpool scored, everybody entangled in a human tide of exaltation. Regularly, I was lifted off my feet by the swell, bobbing about in an ocean of human turbulence, like being in the sea."

Often during the voyage, Poseidon's rolling locomotion reminded Glyn of the Kop. Gazing out from her beam, he pictured Kop faces and LFC banners in the Mediterranean's waves, their clarion calls hailing the Reds bouncing off swell peaks hitting the schooner's bows.

"After Mariano," Glyn apprised, "my career transitioned into mainstream software. Thereafter, my economic standing has been boosted to the grade whereby I don't have to sweat and toil anymore, but I still need the adrenalin rush I get from business success. Work is an aphrodisiac, an integral constituent to my life, keeping me going."

By 2009, like most English people, Glyn had tired of being screwed silly by New Labour and the PC zealots. Feeling chained, oppressed and in need of liberation, he craved sanctuary from their tick box, sanitised, regimented autocracy, where no room existed for non-linear solutions, and challenging insights were belittled and banned. Rife with spin, lies, deception, and worst of all, the rise of the mediocrity brought about by quotas and positive discrimination, the impending Orwellian cataclysm became insufferable. In President Blair's and then Führer Brown's kingdom, failure was rewarded, the treacherous guilty elevated to high office, and detractors hounded to the threshold of despair. Like Steve and his newcomer crewmates, Glyn had to get away from it, at least for a while.

Despite misgivings about the permanency of the nation, he

still needed professional life exhilaration, taking up his next assignment after the Med jaunt an absolute must.

~

Land proprietors hailing from Lincolnshire, Poseidon's owners and life-long friends, Jeff Tindle and Ed Swan, had been close since prep school, and were seriously rich. Albeit having what left-wing social commentators, perpetually wanting to reengineer Western society in a downwardly mobile slant, call a privileged bloodline, they possessed an aberrant and often unanticipated connection touchstone, facilitating them to talk to anybody, and not make them feel inferior by virtue of their wealth. To people unaware of their ancestry and breeding, they appeared to be just two ordinary Englishmen, getting their kicks sailing the Med and having a good time ashore.

Remarkably fit for a man in his mid-fifties, Jeff possessed the same physique and chiselled features associated with film legend Cary Grant, his constant suntan and weather-beaten appearance complementing the affect. To sustain a healthy weight, he trained himself to eat very little, making him fleet of foot about Poseidon's deck, and enabling quick movement up and down her rigging. A natural leader, congenial but assertive, and a brilliant seaman, he was always in control and command, never raising his voice and hardly ever showing aggression. Glyn assimilated the word 'cool' had been vastly overused in recent times to describe anything from cars to software, fashion models to football players, but it did apply to Jeff. Super-cool, he epitomised a heroic Hitchcock leading man brought to life.

With a rounder mush and a deeper complexion, Ed resembled a slightly rougher version of the same diamond. Stockier than Jeff, Glyn imagined bullets bounced off his strapping body. A superb motivator with a winning smile, the newcomers soon found Ed's infectious singularity helped them acclimatise to the demands of sailing Poseidon. Always managing to make the crew put in extraordinary efforts, particularly under adverse sea and weather conditions, they found themselves capable of things beyond their back-home notions. Taking life full-on without flinching, nothing frightened Ed. His temperate ascendancy dealt with any dispute, resolving torments and quenching concerns, but on occasion belligerence took hold, and he let fly with a visceral and scathing attack. Saleh would bring out his explosive side. Ed never abided work-shy freeloaders, and the Ethiopian drew his contempt.

Conversationally gregarious, but more essentially precision informative talkers, the seniors were even better listeners, possessing the hallmark of sprightly two-way communication, with no libido to be bossy or tyrannical ship captains. Inspiring through leadership and by setting example, they never required the newcomers to do any onboard charge they had not seen the seniors perform. Though exhibiting alternative attributes and methods to transact the same end-product, the new crew swiftly cultivated sincere respect for both seniors.

Estranged from their wives, and their full-grown children who had left home to pursue their own lives, for many a year, the seniors had conducted their loving cup linkages by proxy, sending gifts and birthday cards, rather than attending the event. Twice a year, the families got together for summit confabs in Lincolnshire, the Med, or the Caribbean where their other schooner, Poseidon 2, was moored in Montserrat, as Steve's Lloyds of London probe confirmed.

During their formative adult years, the seniors had rogered half the counties jet-set girls, but by age twenty-five they were ready to settle down. Both had married women from the South-East, not keen on the sea and more inclined to the pleasures of highbrow country life, mixed in with London fleshpots. Reluctantly, the wives participated in sailing endeavours, but neither matured a kinship with the sea. Their longings were Gascony in the summer and the Seychelles in winter, with regular trips to Bond Street and Harrods.

After the physical love waned, and the main task became bringing up the children, the men started to acquire wanderlust. With home and land-based pet projects only bequeathing fleeting amusement, the sea enticed more and more. So began their extended maritime history, up front mainly sailing competitions, then long sabbaticals.

Falling into a fatalism sphere, especially after their final offsprings left the nest, the wives consented to the flimsy domestic circumstances. Extremely well financed, they had many expensive pursuits to occupy them, even the occasional fling according to Ed. Tolerating their peccadilloes, the men never exacted the ultimate price be paid for their indiscretions. With no utility in divorce, the arrangement suited all parties, allowing the Tindle and Swann names to retain their traditional kudos amongst Lincolnshire's landowner fraternity.

As the newcomers got more familiar with the seniors, it became clear their sea life only endowed limited solace for lack of household success. They had become well-known with the sailing communities in the Med and the Caribbean, gaining respect for their seamanship, honesty and integrity. But in moments of confession, both told the crew something intimate, indicating marriage failure still plagued them. Apparently, the wives had adjudicated after twenty-five years of marriage their husbands were more in love with the sea, than they were with them.

Partially true, Jeff and Ed had been sailing since they could walk, a family tradition going back generations. Taking it from being a pleasurable hobby to virtually a lifestyle, the men had also been accused of extra-marital affairs, but that was simply grasping at imaginary straws. If anything, their love affair was with the sea.

~

Earmarking Poseidon's crew as disarming souls, several hipster-like, others judicious and sturdy, Glyn knew some had seen the rough end of the pineapple crash through their lives, whereas others had managed through careful decision making or by sheer luck to avoid the bear traps.

All the newcomers had gone through the same passing muster requirement with the seniors Steve and Glyn had been contingent on before being affirmed for Poseidon. They did not know how many candidates meeting with Jeff and Ed had subsequently been turned down. They never enquired, but Glyn hypothesised there must have been some form of template and checklist applicants were assessed against. Essentially, a credentials and temperament requirement, compliance signified they were robust enough to withstand a minimum three-months voyage, and embodied the necessary personal and social skills, plus the physical wherewithal, to form a strong, indivisible ships company.

During their baptising brand of introductions, it became clear the one thing all the newcomers conjointly had was they were driven people, Glyn electing it to be the critical component needed to be licensed for Poseidon, serendipity by selection.

Also detectable, like Steve, for ordinary apolitical Englishmen, they had grown to despise the New Labour Government, and the cartel cross-party politics it spawned to exploit the good nature of English people for ulterior ends, not to their advantage. Touching on the prickly controversy, Glyn speedily sussed a high calibre of resentment existed in his shipmates. It became a topic quite by chance, when Colin outlined how his local MP had been deselected for cooking his Parliamentary expense books, climaxing in a root and branch examination of English politics and politicians.

"The actual vacuum is not between New Labour and the opposition parties," Tom validated. "That is something fostered by spin doctors to give the perception opposition exists, and thereby we have choices. It's much more between a thriving, conceited metropolitan political class, mainly resident in the nuclear-free zone and PC paradise of Islington, and a largely disaffected nation, afflicted by collective conspiracy betrayal between the mainstream party machines."

"Categorically, I'd endorse your appraisal," Colin sanctioned. "My disgraced MP certainly got cross-party ten-four for his theft of taxpayer's money. But it's obvious the party system has collapsed from the inside and been replaced by this new cross-party ruling elite, a kind of protectionist guild interlacing what used to be demarcation zones, differentiating party doctrine, agenda and policy. By far and away at odds with the rest of society, this nouveau, self-righteous faction run the cartel exclusively for the benefit of those in the club circle."

"What are your interpretations, Jeff?" Glyn asked. "What do you see when you return to Blighty?"

"Well," He cast a hush-hush guise at the newcomers. "Ed and I spend so much time away from home, that we don't have the same feel for what's going on behind the scenes as you chaps. However, my impression is there's collusion between the Government and the opposition hierarchies, and party distinctions in place for at least a hundred years, have been forcibly melded into this…" Gawking at his sailing partner, he solicited, "what's it called, Ed?"

"Middle ground."

"Yes, middle ground, with anyone holding traditional opinions ostracised, decried and derided."

"*True*," Ed growled, his disgruntlement on the rise. "Long held party differences have been lost to this sterile centre foundation. It's just a meaningless and unintelligible hotchpotch of restricting tenets, contracted to confine originality and innovation to history." Eyeballing the new crew he queried, "That is about right, isn't it?"

"Yes," Steve positively applauded. "You both have a good understanding of what's happening back home. Daring schemes have been ruthlessly eliminated from the approval menu of public debate by the cult of modernisation. Nobody can define what modernisation is, but all politicos have embraced it, and talk about it relentlessly."

"What modernisation boils down to," Bill tendered, "is licensing a select band at the top of the political class to run England. Superficially, it's a kind of benign dictatorship, but beneath the cursory front, its strikes and falsehoods are just as severe as anything Stalin or Hitler could have cooked up." Rippling his brow, he prophesied, "It's the thin end of the wedge. Down line, and it might be only a few years away, the executive patriciate model will culminate in dire ramifications for our sovereignty, freedom and future."

"You're right, Bill," David agreed. "And have you recorded

how many times Brown and his lieutenants use key words like, 'new', 'modern', 'modernisation', 'reform', and the politicos' darling, 'inclusive', as a front to disguise the real betrayal under the covers?"

Betokening their agreement, both the seniors and the newcomers were reconciled to Blighty being dominated by duplicitous politicians for the foreseeable future.

"It just seems to me," Ed contended, "the convergence of cross-party themes, not inspirations mark you because they have intellectual currency, is frightening. As Bill says, it seems to form the increase in an ever-thickening wedge, inevitably terminating in a dictatorship."

"Hhmm, you do seem to have your finger on the pulse," Glyn vouched. "Your recalls are indeed symbolic of Blighty's political map."

"I don't mean a dictatorship we visualise to be of a Joe Stalin-type construction," Ed verified, "but something much more resultant from the soft indoctrination sell, with mechanisms to redress and go back withdrawn through subjective law at every paramount stage in the change process."

"You are definitely right on that score," Steve agreed. "If allowed to persevere, the Orwellian fate will happen, all civilians passively brain-washed into the privilege for some centric discipline; primarily the institution of expansive globalisation policies suiting the cross-party political cliques, as Glyn and I found when we delved into the Illuminati phenomenon." Frowning he carped, "It will allow them to guzzle on the taxpayer-funded gravy train until their trousers and skirts split."

"And hence, having a reciprocal identity and a shared focus," Glyn positioned, "who's going to stop them?"

As the Cadiz night sky deepened its translucent star array, the conference continued before they segued into preparation details for the next day's sail, Jeff and Ed going over indispensable fundamentals about Poseidon and sailing in the Med. In return for no charge levied for accommodation aboard Poseidon, the newcomers chipped into a provisioning pool to cover the cost of onboard consumables and berth duties, a settlement Jeff and Ed had been making for the last ten years. They liked meeting new people, but invariably crews were only allowed a single voyage.

For off-watch entertainment, the newcomers had brought DVDs and CDs to add to the senior's library. Among Jeff's film collection were *A Perfect Storm* and *White Squall*. Far too close to the real thing, the new crew never played these titles. They even shied away from *Moby Dick*. Always smiling when he saw them inspecting the DVDs, often Jeff mischievously appealed, 'Why don't you play *A Perfect Storm*?' making Glyn realise, there was a touch of the Peter Benchley created character Quint about Jeff.

7

EMBARKATION

Poseidon had been at sea for six weeks before entering Tunis harbour. Setting sail from Cadiz early April, she passed Cape Trafalgar and berthed at Barbate de Franco before Jeff steered the schooner on a due south vector for Tangiers.

Responsible for captaincy, navigation and communications, senior sailors Jeff and Ed each ran a crew watch, rotated every six hours whilst at sea. Badly in need of transformation recharge, soul cleansing, adventure, and the urge to transcend self-conscious self-hood, the newcomers performed required crewing duties with vim and enthusiasm. Flushed with suppositions of quest and images of Mediterranean delight, as Poseidon keeled over, they caught sight of the distant Dark Continent, igniting illuminations of faraway lands and unsettled seascapes, mythical cities and transcendental happenings. Directly, a surge of electricity ran through the new crew enlivening all their actions. Morale grew high and stayed high, an essential ingredient ensuring a happy and content ship's company.

Visibly effervescing with vitality, the newcomer's compulsions were very familiar to Jeff and Ed. A new crew is invariably an excited and willing crew, their objective to keep it that way throughout the voyage, making for good seamanship and camaraderie. During their decade-long stint in the Med, they had seen many new crews spellbound with fervour during their debut hours aboard their schooner, not gauging what sea trials lay ahead to test their mettle and eagerness. Often, green crews had to dig deep to meet the tests head on, but few flunked mastering their minds and bodies to successfully respond to the contest. Fellowship and absorption always imbued even the least adept sea novice with the will to succeed, and not let the ship's company down. Often, at the end of the voyage, they walked off Poseidon heads held high, distinguishing they had exceeded their perceived limits, the victory imbuing them with an improved readiness to deal with their regular lives back in Blighty.

After a while, though consistent, the buzz became secondary to the pleasures of sailing Poseidon, meaning maximising her speed under prevailing weather conditions. If done properly, it called for skill, dedication and teamwork, executed with a good heart, the selection etiquette identifying the prerequisites in successful crew applicants. Once aboard, the attributes needed to be refined into sailing skills, with pride of purpose attached to every assigned duty.

Their initial sail from Cadiz to Barbate de Franco took them into the fringes of the Atlantic, but on that day, the great ocean remained calm, misleading the newcomers into assuming the next day's sail to Tangiers abided the same alongside weather effects. They were wrong. Whereas hugging the Andalusian coastline under a potent westerly from the stern became bracing, turning Poseidon on a southerly tack meant exposing her starboard flank to the same wind, the narrow gap between Spain and Morocco acting as a venturi to magnify wind speed from the Atlantic through the Straits of Gibraltar and into the Med. Five nautical miles from the Spanish shore, the full collision of the westerly trying to thrust the sea currents back into the Mediterranean took hold. Tangled between the natural forces, Poseidon pitched over at thirty-five degrees from the vertical to port, the crew counterbalancing on starboard, the taxing baptism lasting for a further twenty-five nautical miles, until Poseidon drew some leeward cover from the oncoming north-west Africa landmass.

Tapping Ed's shoulder Colin bawled, "Is this typical?"

"No. This is the easy bit. It gets far more exacting later!"

A glint of wickedness in his eye, the fresh crew soon learnt the senior had a cutting sense of black humour. Though capable of premeditated assertiveness, should it be warranted, wisecracking Ed revelled in playfulness, the blacker and more satirical, the better.

Approaching Tangiers, Jeff called the harbour master and Poseidon made her way past the harbour's north wall, and thankfully for the newcomers, into calmer waters. A white-knuckle ride for them, nevertheless, they were ecstatic, the blood pulsing through their veins under adrenalin rush, making them conceive how fragile both the schooner and the crew were in the grip of such muscular elements.

Turning to Glyn, his lineaments still taut with engrossment, Steve groused, "That wasn't like sailing off Whitstable, was it?"

"Wanna go back home?" Glyn retorted, his tone petting a teasing quality.

Charged up with brio, Steve broke into a broad scintillation. "*No.*"

Going past Trafalgar, the wind had dropped as if paying respect to lost souls resultant from Nelson's famous victory, Poseidon's crew almost hearing the battle cries. Everybody logged it, though no comments were made during the event. If the sunken galleons had suddenly risen from their watery graves to liberate vanquished fighting men, letting them breathe again, the ship's company wouldn't have been surprised.

Sea birds circled the historic cape, an invisible potency evidently preventing their entry, whereas before entering and after leaving, because the schooner lay close to land, they followed her, yapping and squawking in the hope of locating sea food in her wake.

Finding wind, Poseidon picked up speed again.

"Something inexplicable happened back there," Glyn said to Steve, a zip of preponderance in his accent. "Something geographers and meteorologists might not be able to account for."

Perplexed, the intriguing comment made Steve face him with a quizzical aspect. "How do you mean?"

"Well." Licking his lips, he removed traces of sea spray. "Why should tranquillity suddenly arise creating a near-to doldrums upshot, then just as instantly fade, with forecast sea and wind *mise en scene* then resuming?"

Slowly breathing out, concurrently abandonment reflected in Steve's eyes. "I like the unexplained. It gives faith to the conviction there's something beyond science, making possible the assertion deities compel our weather."

"I surmise you're going to tell me, they can just as easily calm it, or make it a raging hurricane?"

"Correct," he asserted, staring back at the doldrums area. "Global warming is merely a man-made contrivance for climate change, convenient to the political programme." Tongue-in-cheek he contested, "It's really all down to the gods."

Beaming at Steve's impish deposition, Glyn also gazed sternwards, philosophising maybe some truth existed in what his friend had implied. Comprehending such noteworthy fortunes have the purity of mathematics, and were as incorruptible as the stars, he concluded they defied empirical science and logic. Patently, physical units of estimation defining their back-home Blighty world did not rule supreme elsewhere.

Getting used to secular world explanation being invalid in their new domain, disquieting irregularity became very attractive to the newcomer's taste for exploration. Sometimes life is tangibly real and painful. On other occasions, under artificial influences or propitious aesthetics, it can be ethereal, otherworldly. Hoping for the latter, and the voyage to be unlike their comparatively routine civilian worlds, they craved for something elevated above the tremulous norm, its finding perhaps among the tempestuous seascapes and crewing calls. There had to be something more to life, other than the awaited grind of servitude from the cradle to the grave. There had to be a counterbalance, a proportional reward apropos fulfilling at least one lifetime ambition, without wrecking normal lives.

As Poseidon left the eerie locale, appreciating the ship's company were transfixed between many worlds, some gratefully emblematic and allegorical, like the lighter side of Ken Russell's oeuvre, Glyn trusted for more of the same throughout the voyage. For them, the symmetry became Poseidon, an *affaire d'amour* with the sea, and the hope for a glimpse of nirvana, or something brand-new, memorable and life altering.

~

After docking at Tangiers Old Port, the seniors took the unseasoned crew to a chandler shop on the Avenue d'Espangne. Owned by a colourful kook come nonconformist named Hassan, to the rookies, he could have walked straight off the set of *Casablanca* after selling Humphrey Bogart some *bric-à-brac*. Buddies with Jeff and Ed for many years, he'd become attuned to their buying patterns. Immediately, traffic hit a brisk and plentiful beat, the seniors making multiple purchases to brace the voyage east along the North-African coastline.

A gifted musician, Hassan played violin in a Moroccan orchestra. They had seen Page & Plant when the ex-Zep duo visited Marrakech in 1994 to record stock for an album and film, Hassan proudly displaying a signed photograph of the rock legends behind his shop counter. Later in the day, when the crew returned to pick up their purchases, they found Hassan and some of his orchestra colleagues rehearsing a rendition of Zep's *tour de force*, *Kashmir*. Halfway through the number, more members arrived, spontaneously joining in with wind and tympani instruments. Assembling in front of the ensemble, motionless and enthralled by the captivating power of the performance, the ship's company took in the mystical peals.

"I can see why Page & Plant admire Moroccan musicians so much," Glyn praised.

Grinning at the felicitous comment, Jeff notified, "We'll be hearing a lot more North African music during this leg of the voyage. But Moroccan takes some beating."

After the earlier meeting with Hassan, the onshore contingent jumped into a couple of taxis, and headed to the old city, on the south side of the Avenue Moulay Ismail. Passing through the

European architectures of France and Spain, and along the tree-lined boulevards, they alighted at the Ecole Al Boughaz.

Proceeding on foot around the bazaars and artisan shops, the ship's company immersed themselves in local miracles and culture. Saturated in essence of pearl and the odour of fine-grade hashish, nicknamed kif in North Africa, the physical atmosphere was dense and murky. Crossing the threshold from walking through clean air into the syrupy, opaque concoction, it slowed down their travel, as if they were under the leverage of an imperceptible agent. Street entertainers with roguish displays, deeply lined by too many hours in the fierce sun, held court with adroit recitals of traditional Moroccan entertainment. Flamboyant jugglers played with fire and knives, narrowly avoiding the yellowy flame and the razor-sharp blade, their strange mannerisms suggesting lore of a secret ambiguity, their loose colourful garb lifting and falling with every expressive drive, augmenting the cyphering. Gliding in the Scheherazade-like entrapment, Glyn and his friends sucked on its aura. Witnessing one astonishing exhibition after another, it became intoxicating. As well as the dense hashish effluence, they were getting high on Moroccan distraction.

Sitting crossed legged, the kif users drew in the drug's releasing vapours through a pipe or *hookah*, its qualities transforming and liberating. Their senses modified and bent by the kif's hallucinatory property to transmogrify shape and visage, they stared at Poseidon's crew with whetted curiosity, like the Englishmen were aliens from another planet.

Laughing faintly at their inquisitiveness, Glyn remarked to Colin, "I half expect one of them to rise, and start telling us stories of Moroccan legend."

"Yes," he mumbled. "Wonderful looking beggars aren't they. Visions of desert inscrutability brought to life."

"I swear to god, that one just rose up," Bill claimed pointing to one kif user.

"No, Bill," Ed corrected. "It's just the hashish vapours messing with your mind. If we stay here long enough, they'll all be levitating."

Ed was right. The hashish fumes overwhelmed the crew's sensory systems. What normally registered as rectangular solid shape with identifiable colours, transfigured into a rhomboid form, casting a vast spectrum of hues.

Moving on, the Englishmen trekked further into the bazaar melee. Away from the kif envelopment, purer air and regular perspectives reigned again.

Drawing up close to Glyn as they walked along, Jeff professed, "What you were saying about Moroccan legend is not far from the truth."

"*Oh*," he reacted, surprised his observation had struck home. "In what way?"

"About six maybe seven years ago, when we were here, Hassan told us some Europeans had ended up going native with the kif users. They got totally enamoured on the pleasure promise." Noticing Glyn had taken on a staggered mien prompted by the detail, he elaborated, "You see, Europeans, in fact all foreigners, represent a selling opportunity. The kif pushers coax them in, then go to work, painting manifestations of how the drug will release them from all worldly bothers. There's a seduction subtext in the language they use. It hints the kif will emancipate the user, and he'll become confidant to some cryptic and ancient wisdom…Moroccan legend."

"I see. Ostensibly, that's the holy grail for inner space travellers."

"Well, in Tangiers, it's accepted street parlance in the hashish trade."

"In principle, we'd not condone hashish use back in Blighty, but here—" Resting, Glyn surveyed the surrealism. "Somehow, it seems to be in-keeping."

"Quite."

Further on down the rainbow, a multilingual tourist guide beguiled the crew's attention.

"Tangiers is an ancient Phoenician and Berber city founded by Carthaginian colonists in the fifth century BC," he recapped with pride. "It has a rich history of siege and occupation, their marks left in the manner of culture and architecture." Picking out various ancient edifices and landmarks in the foreground and background with an outstretched arm, the guide then articulated further. "Topmost, myth alleges Hercules slept in a cave a few miles outside Tangiers, before attempting one of his twelve labours."

Murmuring their amazement, his entourage earnestly wanted to hear more.

"Tangiers has been home to, and a refuge for, much religious diversity," he elucidated. "It was attributed international status by the European colonial powers in 1923, before attaining full independence in the nineteen-fifties. Since, it has become a major destination for wayfarers. The city is undergoing rapid development and modernisation. New edifices co-exist with traditional European and Islamic architectures, some with origins going back 2,000 years."

Resuming their expedition in the bazaars, the European quarter, and the modern trends, the ship's company left the guide still praising his city.

"The new buildings are fine," Steve qualified, "but I prefer the ancient ones and the old culture."

"Sure thing," Glyn backed. "We can get the modern back in Blighty. It's the spiritual and the obscure we are after here."

"You'll find most of the locals, principally in the bazaars and traditional areas will agree with you," Jeff attested. "Most we have met are dismayed the old world has become subjugated to creeping reconstruction. Every year, new buildings encroach further, swallowing up fully-fledged areas, once bastions of tradition and habitats for Berber ceremony."

As the crew sauntered through Tangiers, it was easy to see its citizens were not ready to solely live by the dictates of cognition alone, but more in combinations of dark and light stimuli, the juxtaposition making Glyn deduce Jeff was right. Many had eluded the paradigm shift into modernity, instead choosing a stand-in modulation to prolong centuries of cultural custom. Often treated with idolatrous reverence in twenty-first century Western Europe, modernity might give life the imperative, but not necessarily its meaning. A dizzying array of arcane alternatives held far more significance for the intrepid inner space voyager, than minimalist, some say charlatan art, the decadent subservience to materialism, and the crazed obsession by legislators for arbitrary conformity and obedience.

Heading the group, Ed verbalised to no one in particular, "It's said, if you are famous, you must have lived in or visited Tangiers."

"Quite right," Tom endorsed. "I did some research on Tangiers for my next work. Momentous signatures spending time here include Burroughs, Capote, Ginsberg and Matisse."

"Mmmm, what else do you know?" Ed sweated.

"Well, Tangiers has always been an impulse for popular culture. Burroughs *Naked Lunch* relates to some of his Tangiers dalliances, *Desolation Angels* by Jack Kerouac contains references to him and Burroughs living in Tangiers, and *The Thief's Journal* by Jean Genet, comprises the protagonist's experiments in negative morality held in Tangiers." After monitoring the pilgrim trail ahead, littered with aesthetics diligently absorbing a parade of cultural marvels, Tom advanced, "It seems Tangiers will always be a major draw for those tracking stimulation and release from conformity."

A few years previously, Glyn had briefly been in Tangiers with Suzy, his mind closed to ritual and romance on that occasion, its ambience not filtering into his consciousness. With his marriage in trouble, he'd entered an insular stage, Rimbaud and the enlightenment side-lined in favour of a pragmatic nostrum. A time for introspective reflection, figuratively applying the cleansing lash to his bare back, he no longer listened to the intriguing poetry of Patti Smith. Re-visiting grunge had taken her place in his self-imposed exile from vibrant radiance, the spectre of relationship failure superseding his ascetic nature, resulting in the need for high-energy music to replenish his will to go on.

Like the rest of the newcomers, with his psychic valve now lavishly open, Glyn hungered for the clear light of the revelation. They were searching for something sacred, something to justify their presence on a rock hurtling around the sun, something the Dali Lama had still not answered with assurance and limpidity.

Tangiers became the premier of a profusion of hypnotising places Poseidon's crew visited during the North African part of their voyage. Neatly spotlighting differences between the newcomer's regulated lives back in Blighty, and the free reign, no holds barred charge spelling daily life in North African ports, it sucked them in, excitement and invigoration enveloping them in esoteric *de rigueur*, its properties orgasmic and oceanic. After Tangiers, the unaccustomed newcomer's aspirational lifestyles seemed cathartic in comparison, a hollow monument without significant meaning. Some unforeseen form of symbiosis had happened, framing a divergent cadre of blueprints to be achieved. Something that became intuitively overt, the further they deepened their journey.

Apart from Jeff and Ed, none of the crew had any significant experience of North Africa. Sailing the Med and further afield for over twenty-five years, the seniors had gained a vast scholarship of its seaways and countries. They told the unconversant crew about their visits beyond North West Africa, into the eastern Mediterranean, the Red Sea, and the Indian Ocean. Imbuing them with worldliness and solace, the acquired collateral delineated essential facets for sailing Poseidon and managing the vagaries of North African port life.

Subjected to the Mediterranean zeitgeist resplendent at sea and onshore, the newcomer's quest would touch on chillingly convincing episodes, seminal eclogues, and a spiritual recognition of the sublime and the darkly haunting. Preconceptions though countless observed, not preparing them for many of the mind-blowing undertakings, irreversibly indenting their subsequent lives.

8

SAGES AND SEERS

Formed from awareness gained during their journey sailing east parallel to the North African coastline, the newcomer's high hopes for Tunis became fine-tuned. They had arrived at Cadiz with infatuations about the Arabian Med premised on depictions from film and the written word, their autcurism built on Rick's Café American apotheosis, T.E Lawrence's excursions into the Nafud desert, and the works of Albert Camus. Tangiers had not disappointed, Poseidon's new crew exiting the ancient city with amplified engrossment. Glyn wondered if what followed could continue the high.

Steadfastly refusing to say too much, the seniors insisted for maximum impact to be accomplished, the newcomers needed to let it happen without any prior edification of the dares to come.

"It's different for every crew," Ed told them. "We've been doing this a long time, but each voyage brings something unique, something from left field. It's what keeps the event vital, crisp." He stopped for a moment before emphasising his next word. "*Exciting.*"

"Yes, we've learnt the practice is better, if you just let it unfold," Jeff reinforced.

"Sounds a bit like an orgasm to me," Tom discriminated, smiling wickedly.

"Quite a good analogy," Jeff agreed. Unable to resist another sexual innuendo, he itemised, "You know what's coming, but it's slightly at variance every time."

Everybody laughed. True, sex could be singular on each practised occasion, and with different partners. Ergo, Glyn guessed every Poseidon voyage must be characterised by its own digest of episodes.

"Be patient," Jeff counselled, sensing the crew were still inquisitive. He gave them a hopeful gander. "I promise you won't be disappointed."

"You must get away from this European need to be told everything up front," Ed appended. Detecting metaphorical question marks over their heads resultant from the chastening remark, he clarified, "I mean immediate gratification, and the high pace of Blighty living. Just relax. This is going to be a slow burn. It will last. Unlike superficial headlines gone in seconds, this will be like a rich novel, not an ephemeral news report."

Restraining their natural fixations and trusting in the senior's advice, the newcomers knew they had to be submissive to the prescription. But after Tangiers they chomped at the bit, ravenous for the next amazing occurrence, their preconceptions already paling into insignificance as sketchy understatement, grossly underestimating the immediate punch North African life and sailing mighty Poseidon had on them. For mature grownups, used to managing complex business teasers back in Blighty, they found themselves reverse-engineered, time travelling back to their youth, when everything encountered shone with wonderment.

Uninterrupted throughout the voyage, the smack never ebbed, always something to drop jaws and remain embedded in memory forever.

After departing Tangiers, the senior's prophetic words came true almost immediately. Bottlenose dolphins escorted Poseidon off Malabata, and later, north of Ceuta, they saw a beaked whale off the coast, both sightings fitting out the tone for sea-based discovery.

Swimming a few yards from Poseidon's port and starboard bows for three to four nautical miles, the dolphins finally peeled away bearing south back to the coast. Viewing them through binoculars or a camcorder, revealed happiness in their bulbous but attractive faces, the scouting connecting the newcomers with nature, lifting their hearts and souls to new heights of contentment.

Communion with the wonderful sea creatures helped them to lose the self in subliminal cognizance, the pull enhanced by the polyrhythmic patterns of the waves pulsating with distracting imagery, before vanishing into soothing contours and feint misty light. Impossible to glance away, it became hypnotic, mesmerising. Only sea spray hitting the puss broke concentration, its salty fragrance driving the nostrils like adrenalin to recover the senses. Under such halcyon environs bow duty became an ethereal blessing, the aftermath shrouding the soul in a veil of mystique, washing out ugly memories, and replenishing the mind with zest and vibrancy. Like a rare gift or an epiphany moment, under its agency, the newcomers felt good to be alive. Proof positive of God, they fathomed his universe as a blaze of insurgent beauty. No drug could induce such a marvellous high.

Never failing to amaze them, Jeff and Ed tarried just as keen as the newcomers to come under the marine-mammals spell. Many times, they had snorkelled with dolphins in the Caribbean with their families.

"They just make you smile," Jeff said, grinning with pleasure. "An hour or so of playing with dolphins does more for the human condition, than any quack psychiatrist could ever mastermind."

For real, Glyn cogitated. They were a jovial crew, but when the dolphins adopted them, their smiles got even broader, the beaked whale also breeding a similar kindred distillation. With its course aimed at the Ligurian Sea breeding grounds north of Corsica, the whale's colossal four-ton, grey and light brown body, twelve-feet in length, and stabilised by a small dorsal fin to the rear, broke the surface at regular intervals, sending sprays of seawater skywards through its blowhole, the remarkable singularity making the newcomers gape in awe, the primacy of nature far more recondite than anything manmade.

On a near-to immaculate day, with the wind strong enough to propel Poseidon along at twelve knots, and the sea surface calm with only a slight swell, Steve came on deck, settling himself against the fore staysail rigging. With the sun in the 14:00 hours position, its intense radiation baked the structure he leaned against. Closing his eyes beneath a flawless sapphire sky, he let the sea jingles and booms and boat agitation roll over him. Later, he told his comrades, he had dropped off for a while, and imagined he had dreamt about the dolphins mixed in with white horses. In fact, only a momentary release from volition, to Steve it seemed to go on for hours.

"I dreamed I was soaring like an eagle," he enthused, still taken aback by the phenomenon.

"It's quite routine to fall into a semi-sleep onboard," Ed certified. "Above all, when the rigours of civvy life have melted away, and the mind is free to ramble."

"I can see that, but this came without lucid publication, like treacle seeping inconspicuously from a jar imprisoning everything in its path. It just took hold, without me realising."

"In smaller craft, as opposed to ocean going vessels," Jeff instructed, "people get light-headed by sea motion far more easily. After the first time, you assume you'll spot it creeping up again. But no, we all get mugged without recognising it. That is, until we come out of the other side."

"Don't worry, Steve," Ed entreated. "It usually only happens when relaxing off-watch. If you're expansively occupied with a sailing initiative, the influence is unlikely."

As Ed forecasted, when off-watch, similar on-the-edge-of-hibernation participation became the province of the ship's company throughout the voyage.

Happening to Glyn off the coast of Mostaghanem, in his aphrodisiac semi-sleep, a Delphic nymph rose from a transparent mosaic beneath the sea. Gone in seconds, it left him unsure if sleep had happened. More likely, he dosed on the threshold, kept there by the wind and rocking boat movement. Nonetheless, the intimacy was indicative that the Med was cleansing his mind of Blighty distractions and alarms. *Instead of playing societal predestination games,* he pondered, *I should have done this voyage long ago.* In that moment of eye-opening clarity, he wanted the wind to drop, and Poseidon to be marooned forever.

~

Sailors can be a superstitious lot, burdened by unsubstantiated myths and old wives' tales. They carry doom-laden delusions of disaster with them like a Jeremiah's bible, the slightest deviation from plan reeling them in assumed misfortune. Poseidon's crew met such a salty old sea dog in Ceuta. They never did catch his name properly, but he did make a lasting impression on them.

From what they gathered, he hailed from Corsica, possessed some Arab blood in his ancestry, and had been on the Earth for eighty-six years, sailing the Med for over seventy of them. He and his much younger wife, his third by all account, and many of their extended family, owned a hotel in the Avenue de Lisboa, a location conscripted by tourists in downtown Ceuta. Taking lunch at the hotel resulted in the Englishmen striking up a conversation with him.

Because of multiple frailties, he told them he did not sail much anymore, but his mind abided sane, and he had a weather-beaten disposition giving substance to his stories.

One sea folklore stood out, because it betrayed his reluctance to subscribe to coherence, inexplicably conveying him into faintheartedness.

"I joined the Free French Forces during World War II," he proudly recalled. "They operated from Corsica. One day, with other comrades, I was ordered to join a fishing fleet at Propriana on the west side of the island. We were ordered to destroy German patrol boats, intercepting and scuppering Free French Marine Corps sorties. We planned to use the fishing fleet as cover to get within a mile of the anchored patrol boats at Cargese. Then under cover of darkness, scuba dive to the target, and lay magnetic charges. Under timer constraint, they were primed to explode hours later, long after the fishing fleet had gone. The raid went per plan, but when the convoy was returning to Propriana, a storm blew up turning into a nasty squall. Many of the small fishing boats went down with most of their hands drowned, including my comrades." Wringing his hands, he fostered a grievous demeanour. "For many years after the catastrophe, the area of the disaster was sidestepped by the Propriana fishermen."

Attaching realism to the dispatch, his facial expression transferred quirkiness, making the ship's company sympathetic to his remembrance. Sometime after the war ended, the salty dog entered the daunting zone, sailing from Ajaccio to Propriana at night.

"I swore I heard the cries' of drowning men," he maintained. "But it was a whale making the eerie weeps and bleats. Although I accepted they were of marine mammal origin, I couldn't get the drowned seamen's screams out of my mind. Afterwards, every time I went to sea and heard whale moans; effigies of the drowned men materialised." Delaying his monologue, his already sullen expression turned serious. "Consequently, I've become a very cautious sailor, ducking bad weather and night sailing when the sea is other than calm." Shaking his head, he solemnly chimed, "At times, even in calm and clement weather, I feel I am cursed. Sometimes, I deem those drowned on that mission from long ago, want me to go the same way. When I hear whales calling to each other, my authenticity aptitude is nullified, and I concoct it is my ex-comrades calling to me through the whale singings to join them."

A disquieting tale, but one not uncommon to seasoned sailors like Jeff and Ed, it left the newcomers with an abundance of intensified awareness befitting sailing protocol to obviate disaster.

"We all recall road accidents, and most of us survive them, but the sea is an unforgiving mistress," Ed heeded as they left the hotel. "When haphazard maritime events happen, often survival is remote. Tragedy is the norm."

Onboard Poseidon, the seniors told the newcomers about other tragic reports they had heard over the years happening in the Med and the Caribbean, equalling the salty old sea dog's memoir.

"As a comparative factor, road accidents outstrip air and sea accidents by at least 500,000 to one," Jeff enumerated. "The odds of dying in an air crash is eleven-million to one. However, the prospect of coming to a premature end, primarily at sea, has always been one of the worst imaginable fates."

Despite striving for the new, none of the novices relished death by drowning.

On the fiasco front, Jeff came to grief during a Fastnet race when his Bermuda sloop capsized, and he had to be rescued. Ruin befell Ed in the Caribbean, when he ploughed into an underwater reef at dusk, rendering his yacht un-sailable. Neither mishap life threatening, under a more turbulent sea climate or sailing circumstances, they could have been. Happening when the doughty sailors were in their devil-may-care twenties, took more risks, and were still learning sea craft, nothing major had happened since.

"Even adhering to the rules of good seamanship does not make the articulate sailor immune from calamity," Jeff advised. "If you sail for long enough, the laws of probability dictate some sort of misadventure is inevitable. The trick is to minimise risk by training for the unpredictable." Focusing on the mainsail masthead, as if it evoked past alarming incidents, he announced, "Periodically during the voyage, we'll run simulated emergency procedures, as part of being prepared for any eventuality."

"I've flown over two million air miles in the past seventeen years," Glyn recalled, mulling over Jeff's probability model. "If this rate of air travel is prolonged, then statistically, I have a far greater chance of meeting my end in an air crash, than either on the road, in the water, or through natural causes."

Ogling the sea indifferently and not expecting a reply, Jeff broached, "Do you know what the difference is between air and sea accidents?"

"Go on."

"In the sea, at least you have a chance, and can practice for survival. In a passenger aeroplane, survival is virtually non-existent."

Smiling weakly, Glyn knew what he said to be true, fatalism unavoidable. To do his job, he needed to tour throughout Europe and beyond by air. On the basis there are calculated risks in many jobs, long ago, he had resigned himself to the chance of an air accident occurring.

Later in the voyage, the newcomers saw squarely how merciless the sea could be to those venturing into its realm, unprepared.

~

Both capable of rudimentary Arabic repartee, the skill enabled Jeff and Ed to assess Arab confrontations with due diligence, and thereby when to stay and when to go. Fused on the fundamental asset, their guidance played a crucial role in some of the newcomer's early onshore encounters.

"Don't be taken in by an amiable smile and a welcoming gesture," Jeff instructed them as the cardinal engagement directive. "Weigh up the situation before making a decision or becoming involved. And remember, never get boxed into a corner. Plan for escape before you start."

Learning from early bitter interactions not to trust anybody inhabiting Mediterranean ports, notably in North Africa until they had proved themselves, the seniors had retained an initial reserved detachment with itinerants and outlanders. Hassan in Tangiers fixed the gold standard, encounters benchmarked by the seniors against his credentials. Smart Arab sellers knew they pitted their wits against adept minds, conducting a transaction with integrity, essential to effectuate a successful sale. Moreover, Jeff and Ed were well-built six-footers, with a physical presence meaning business, should the need arise. Arab worldly, unflappable and friendly but firm, they knew how to conduct the game without being snared into sticky predicaments. Ashore, the newcomers felt safe with them, chiefly in remote places, such as in minor ports with casual custom officials, having little regard for the formal code.

Not altering in millennia, the smaller, largely, fishing and agriculture-based communities represented North African existence at its most rudimentary, lifestyle prevailing uniform in function without any colouration from outside authority. Like an English country village untouched by the vagaries pronounced by the government in metropolitan London, for these out of the way collectives, ambition beyond the next meal was an anathema. If visitor prophecy embodied a profound knowledge of Omar Khayyam and Kahlil Gibran, disappointment followed, Arabic enlightenment light years away from their monochromatic lives. Locals appraised such highbrow pursuits to be the domain of city intellectuals. Persisting as it had done for centuries, their primary objective remained survival from one year to the next. A full-time job, they had no opportunity to explore beyond, and no need. They prayed for good health, good crops and good fishing, everything else becoming fashioned from these basics. When the minaret called the faithful, the fishing and the farming stopped, and the praying began, born more out of pragmatism for good fortune rather than blind conviction.

Such a condensed description applied to most of rural North Africa, El Jebha, a quiet approaching monastic, rundown, Moroccan backwater, typical. Drawn there by its imposing coastal geographies, Poseidon's crew strolled around its streets in search of fables and folklore, the prosaic town about as far removed from the cultural ecstasy of Tangiers as could be anticipated. Scrutinising them like they were spacemen from another planet, the residents, particularly the imams, narrow mopes betrayed disdain, their irritation tangible. If anyone did attempt communication with the strangers, they were quickly admonished.

Converging on the ship's company, a teenage boy made the traditional Arab greeting, saying, "*as-salamu alaykum*," meaning, the peace be upon you.

Twinkling, Jeff reciprocated, exchanging a few Arabic words before a woman rushed the boy away, scolding him with rancour.

"What did she say?" Glyn enquired.

"Oh, the boy's mother is chastising him for talking to us," Jeff clarified. "She said, the imam would come for him, if he didn't stop. It's why she took him away."

Anguished by the boy's quandary, the crew gaped at him, their sorrow plain as his mother continued to berate him. Having extended the olive branch, his tilt at friendship had been met with rebuke from his own kind.

"It's not like India, Tibet and Nepal," Colin remarked, "where the Hindu and Buddhist illumination coexists with abject poverty. No shamans, seers or saddhus here."

"No, but you'll get used to it," Jeff apprised. "There are no blissful, benevolent gods like Shiva or Krishna to guide you through the maze either." Shooting a slightly sarcastic gawp at Colin, he warned, "Here, and it applies to most of the Arab world, there are only sombre Islamic earthbound officials, regulating every rumination and action."

"Unequivocally true," Ed endorsed. "But these people mean us no harm. It's just, they seldom see foreigners like us, and they're afraid of the imams. Out-of-the-way places like El Jebha contrast markedly with the bustling Arab cities. To gauge this world you've entered, you need to see the sticks as well as the highlights like Tangiers. It's all part of your North African education."

"Yes, we haven't been in El Jebha for at least eight years, but nothing has changed," Jeff added. "There's no tourism here, so the people are not attuned to commerce and European savvy. All they see, is the occasional boat in the harbour like Poseidon. Strangers are surveyed with suspicion, especially when they look as we do and dress so radically different from them."

Making progress, the shore party absorbed the rustic and agrarian atmosphere, assimilating it in the context of Tangiers. Whereas in the celebrated Moroccan city they were relaxed, trying without success to blend into the juxtaposed environment of El Jebha, they received more heat from the locals, Jeff and Ed constantly primed to forestall troublesome antagonisms.

"Oh, by the way, don't photograph them," Jeff told everyone. "They believe you are stealing their soul."

That one Glyn knew about. One of his early merchandising trips for Mariano included a week in Israel. During the Sabbath, he drove to Jericho, taking photos of the ancient town from a nearby hill. Espying a Palestinian woman with a donkey, he started to frame her, but before he could snap the shutter, she threw a stone at him, shook her fist and shouted. Later, he found out as Jeff said, Muslims believed being photographed stole their soul.

∿

Home to Muslim fanatics, the larger towns and cities offered scope for optimising consonance by striking fear into the followers. Enforcing an uncompromising gospel, pivotal on pain of autocratic obedience, with no room for unfettered cogitation, the verboten act discerned as blasphemy, the zealots ensured complete control over all dealings. Describing Allah and Mohammed as gentle, understanding and welcoming, the Koran paints a quixotic picture, but the earthly implementation of Islam for over 1300 years by its proponents, the mullahs and the imams, and thereby its benefactors, was harsh, austere and uncharitable. Breeding intolerance of other religions and secular societies, it castigated, imprisoned, and even killed its own followers having only marginally strayed from the prescribed path. Encouraging its disciples to be foot soldiers, willing to kill others and die for the cause, Islam navigated a course of world domination and the eradication of all other religions and secular associations, not to mention democracy, its modern incarnation becoming much more than problematical to Western leaderships from the mid-nineteen-seventies onwards. In practice, Muslim fundamentalists were a bigger menace to the world than any of the despots preceding their rise.

Western interventionism, whether philanthropic or with an ulterior motive, only exacerbated the ruckus, resulting in more and more rabid bigots flocking to al-Qaeda, Hamas and the

Muslim Brotherhood. Self-evidence must apply, Glyn and the rest of the crew computed. If Christian country fought Christian country as in WWI and II, the winner aimed at peace, and the achievement of social and economic stability, the underlying universal godhead and often intercultural commonality between victor and vanquished nailing down ceaseless binding with the preservation of civilisation. England had warred with France for centuries but having too much conjointly to let the discord be everlasting, most English people admired and felt kinship with the French and vice versa. To apply this precept when Christian defeated Muslim, like in Iraq and Afghanistan was the worst kind of wishful and irresponsible hard-headedness. As soon as Western troops left, Iraq could plunge into tortured anarchy, and inevitably the Taliban rule Afghanistan, neither outcome palatable to Western minds brought up on ethical principles, fairness, justice and other Christian virtues. But like oil and water, they simply do not mix, and never did, no matter how much legislation is enacted to harmonise vastly opposing cultures and religions by compulsion and coercion.

Discussing the obvious deficiencies on their return to Poseidon, the Englishmen tried to comprehend the Muslim duality.

"It's preposterous to ordain Western Christian democracy and probity on Muslims," David argued, exhibiting after-signs of frustration post the El Jebha excursion.

"Yes, but why?" Tom questioned.

"*Why*," he retorted, astonished Tom should canvass a qualification. "Because Islam is mechanised on the fulcrum, those ruling and purporting to have a direct connection with Allah and Mohammed know best."

Appending to the treatise, Glyn acknowledged, "David has a valid gist. It's a massive con on ordinary Muslims, but how do 'Western Christian infidels' win over the Muslim masses?" Grimacing, he glanced back at the harbour path leading to the town centre. "This might appear defeatist, but we have to accept the Christian West with its consumerism and full freedoms aspiration, will never take pride of place over Islam. Surely what we witnessed in El Jebha corroborates the sentiment."

"Perfectly correct," Jeff ratified. "The egotistical mullahs, imams and other Muslim clerics might lose their ascendency, and thereby their power and importance." Gawking back at El Jebha, he murmured, "That, they will never allow."

"It's none of our business anyway," Bill argued, his innuendo pragmatic. "If security from terrorism is genuinely the West's torment, then the *quid pro quo* should be expulsion of all Muslims from Europe and America, in exchange for the West abandoning the Middle East to its own affairs without intervention."

Blithely nodding in agreement, the ships company knew the no-nonsense and necessary step was always too much for the lily-livered federalists in Blighty and the EU to enact. Like most Europeans, Poseidon's crew could see politicians keeping their heads firmly planted in the sand, even when Bosnia style war broke out all over Western Europe, spelling the end for 4,000 years of advancement and a return to the dark ages.

Back in downtown El Jebha, apart from minaret duties, the locals didn't give a damn about Muslim fundamentalism. Evaluated to be a perverse luxury beyond their feudal lives, they reflected the world attitude, amounting to an actualisation that the uncontainable political classes, whether they were New Labour PC prudes or wicked Muslim clerics, only saw their self-proclaimed diktats slavishly adhered to in densely populated urban and metropolitan domains. In out of the way rural communities, scant regard was paid to such injurious dictators.

Between the nadir and zenith of the sun's arc, sunsets and sunrises could be anodyne at sea, the newcomers often spellbound by its magnesium light producing a collage of seminal beauty in unguarded eyes. Sometimes when the lens momentarily caught the sun, psychologically energised creatures inhabiting the remoter recesses of the mind were revealed, like a fleeting glimpse of a petrifying phantom. Though transient, the watchers did not crave the experience. Part of the release from their decades of pent-up legacy afflictions, it happened as the mind cleared, allowing not only pleasant distraction, but also the odd lurking incubus to distil into consciousness.

On the outbound leg of the trek across the Mediterranean, Poseidon headed east, mainly on a track within a hundred nautical miles off the North African coastline, the rising sun invariably breaking on her bows, producing a beckoning horizon beyond mescaline induced vision. Putting Glyn in mind of the spiritually and aesthetically minded romantic poets, Coleridge and Keats, and Western writers Hesse and Baudelaire, drawn to the East for edification, he tried to conjure up what they had experienced and how it had bled transcendence into their work. Like for those visionaries, with the *Tibetan Book of the Dead* at their side, the newcomers were shrinking in agony from the clear light of the void, but for them it was from their back-home world. Afloat on the gently lapping waves, they were stoned by serenity, immaculate and pervasive in its reckoning.

As day broke through the distant sheen, those on inner space hitchhiker relief journeyed further into spectral epiphanies, the warming sun stimulating skin pores into relaxation, and melting the early morning chill. Towering to its midday acme in a cloudless aqua sky, the on-watch bathed in its amorphous relaxing rays, their perspiration feeling like liquid poetry, dripping as honey from their tongues and flesh. Needing its luxuriant grip more than they accredited, only later did the turning point dawn upon them, the portal leading away from back home regularity into a fathomless Mediterranean mashup of abstract felicity.

Though the period from dawn to late afternoon provided memorable absolution, the early evening to twilight was the unsurpassable paradigm to indulge in the dreamy, escapist world, the sinking sun set against the western horizon creating the most advantageous sketch to lose the self in a utopian array of luminescent colours, the backdrop beyond Turner's fabulous palette.

Sometimes, low hanging cloud blurred the boundaries between Earth and the Cosmos, but on a clear night, the Mediterranean astral plane shone with an immeasurable cosmorama of geometrical constellations, its apparent remoteness vanishing in seconds. Dwarfing the Earth, its vastness made the crew's self-made world insignificant and lacklustre in comparison. Always magnificent, Glyn rated the untainted cradle of the heavens as the best free-of-charge planetarium happening to be had anywhere, or at any time.

Responding to previous crew demands, the seniors had installed a telescope on Poseidon. Bringing the full majesty of the heavens into stunning focus, spectators witnessed the omnipresent Crab Nebula, raging in its mesmeric and implacable supernova remnant. Notionally static, Polaris the North Star aligned with the Earth as the heavens rotated about it, giving superficial truth to the ancient's perception, the Earth was the centre of the universe. Because backcloth light did not fade the phenomenon like in cities, millions of stars could be seen, even by the naked eye. Listening to Pink Floyd's *More* and *Meddle* albums or *The Planets* by Holst, whilst staring aghast at the spectacle, magnified the sensory elation. As the subconscious became illuminated during stargazing, the music's haunting cadence helped suggest something obscure, beyond the clear-cut visual delight.

"*Hey*, Steve," Glyn called whilst on-watch during one such light show. "Is this spectacular quenching the flames of dissolution?"

Taking stock of the heavens, his friend commended, "This is like Disneyland for adults. I can't recollect the last time I felt so relaxed. Now I can understand why the seniors spend most of their time in the Med and the Caribbean."

"It's got to be a life enhancer."

"No doubt. I've come across so many rich people, wasting their lives on plastic pursuits adding nothing to their wellbeing. Conversely, Jeff and Ed have worked out how to use their wealth to both maximise life wisdom, and hang on adjacent to, and largely detached from, all the PC pap happening back home."

"Yep, the more we see of the Med's phantasmagorical attractions, the more I'm convinced its meditative-like affect is not only a life amplifier, it is also a life preserver."

"Mmmm, maybe even a life stretcher. We could all live to be a hundred if we stayed here."

With the telepathic tap amply open, the night sky surged over manmade inconveniences and limitations, fact and convention sidelined. Stellar transcendental and termagant charged, it became intoxicating, a grandiose and transporting vehicle, uncontested. Entranced under the night's ubiquitous spell, Glyn and Steve were emancipated renegades bolting from the twilight zone. Out on the vastness of the unbounded sea, and between the firmament and the endless threshold of expanding space, they were no longer lost in myopic and insular societal dictated meanderings. As they sojourned through the desolate Med, the near appeared as seductive as the far, the empyrean regions speaking to them in refined dynamics. Paralysed and delirious in moonstruck awe, they were alone beneath the plumbless mysteries of the heavens, reflecting on the pathos of human isolation. Like grandmasters in search of the bodhisattva, they perceived the universe was truly wonderful, only recent man spoiling it.

Occasionally, a blip arose on Poseidon's radar display denoting another vessel lay near her track. If the vessel got within one nautical mile, radio contact made definite they were not on a collision course. Apart from that, the night arena was only disturbed by the staccato creaking of masts yielding to the wind, and a soft flushing caw from the stern, as the schooner cut through the sea. With waves of searing luminosity washing over the on-watch, it became easy to fall into a deep malaise, but then deck duty beckoned, and at least one eye returned to be sailing task driven.

~

Back in Cadiz, Colin registered two rifles locked in a wooden casing affixed to the wall of Poseidon's radio room. 'What are these used for?' he asked the seniors. 'To discourage pirates,' Ed replied. Laughing, the newcomers assumed the comeback to be typical Ed black humour, cogitating no more about it.

However, off the Algerian coast opposite Ghazaouet, on-watch at the stern, Bill and David saw a motorised vessel fast-approaching Poseidon from the south-west. Alerting Jeff, he hurriedly climbed the mainsail mast, and fastened onto the craft through powerful binoculars. Adjudging the emerging intruder could be manned by pirates, necessitating full defensive provisions to counter the adversity, without delay he descended to the deck. Summoning the off watch, both rifles were then unlocked and loaded by the seniors. Stationing themselves in the stern, rifles at the ready, Jeff and Ed scrutinised the craft bearing down on them. On-watch, Tom monitored Poseidon's auto-tiller keeping her on track, the rest of the crew positioned themselves aft on the steering well deck, surveying from her starboard flank.

Coming from shore, the craft had ten men aboard, all armed with swords and daggers. Although under full sail and making twelve knots, the motorised vessel was rapidly catching Poseidon.

At 150 yards, Jeff and Ed opened fire above the heads of the oncoming raiders. Residing true and steady on course, the attacker accelerated, its occupants undoubtedly serious about their intentions. At one hundred yards, they released a second volley. Still nothing, the inbound persisting to test Poseidon's steadfastness. At fifty yards, the mark became its bows, bits of plastic flying upwards, as lead punctured the hull of the incomer. They finally took evasive action, turning sharply to starboard whilst waving their fists and knives furiously and swearing in Arabic, before reversing back to shore.

During the few minutes the pirates confronted Poseidon, the newcomers stood transfixed, unable to speak or move. Having seen it all before, Jeff and Ed knew if faced with gunfire, the pirates would relent. As the raider sped away from their quarry, the newcomers emerged out of their deadpan immersion. *Who'd have believed it back in Blighty*, Glyn conjectured, *pirates in the twenty-first century?*

"God damn Arab brigands," Ed angrily snapped, beholding the aggressors speeding away.

Marking the newcomers had become tense and vexed by the staggering interlude, Jeff pleaded, "Relax gentlemen, they won't be coming back."

Offering further comfort, he told them such encounters were recurrent in recent times, and seasoned Med sailors carried firearms on their boats to act as both a deterrent, and a last line of defence.

"But, but..." Bill gabbled, his incredulity manifest. "They could have killed us."

"No," Ed replied. "If they had been really serious, they'd have used guns."

"They were just testing us," Jeff assured in a calm, matter-of-fact modulation, mannered to neutralise disquiet and restore normality. "It was just posturing. They wanted to see if they could bluff us into a premature surrender."

More of the Quint persona, Glyn mused.

On reaching Oran, Jeff reported the altercation to customs officials, with the full expectation they'd apply little to no resource to hunt down the pirates. All along the North African coast, the beadledom had no interest in such encounters, and even less in instituting preventive procedures.

By then, the new crew were blasé about the circumstance, the incident becoming a source of much amusement and simulated role play throughout the remainder of the voyage. On return to Mighty Blighty, they became mindful of how rampant piracy had become off the North and East African coastlines, something known by few Europeans, and not publicised by the EU on political and commercial grounds.

∾

Many vessels Poseidon's crew saw off the North African coast were barely seaworthy. Used by fishermen venturing no more than a few nautical miles off-shore, the most frequent sight became single-sail, wooden boats with narrow keels making them inherently unstable. Just about practical under calm sea conditions, when the barometer needle edged from fair to change, signalling rough weather, these elemental craft became death traps, the fishermen speedily backtracking to shore before catastrophe happened. At the opposite end of the spectrum, cargo carriers, oil tankers and other large vessels were treated with due diligence. Epitomising a significant menace to sailing craft, these monsters could mow down even a mid-sized schooner like Poseidon without even noticing, hence, her radar remained constantly operational. Supplementing the radar picture, if a vessel got within half a nautical mile, the radar system automatically enunciated an audible warning through the on-deck and below deck mounted speakers, the alarm explicitly essential at night and under foggy conditions.

During their second night sail, Poseidon tracked fifty nautical miles due north off the Algerian coastal town Saida on a heading of eighty degrees, radar indicating three vessels off her port bow, on bearings between forty to seventy degrees. Not an unusual occurrence, the Med ceaselessly flowed with a procession of commercial, private and military vessels. Even so, a watchful eye had to be kept on the traffic. Two of the targets decoded as small to medium-sized craft, probably local cargo carriers about four nautical miles away. The third, a much larger vessel, on a near-to reciprocal course with Poseidon, ten nautical miles away from her position, ascribed a much more significant obstacle to evade, but nothing to be panicked about. Five minutes later, one of the medium-sized craft passed Poseidon's stern, half a nautical mile away from her location, as did the second a few minutes later, the on-watch not physically seeing them, but radar confirmed their track and placement.

Closing swiftly on Poseidon, it left the third larger vessel as a possible hazard, the on-watch knowing they'd soon have the take avoiding measures. When radar signaled Poseidon was five nautical miles from target three, on-watch captain Ed initiated watchman practice, counting sending Glyn to the bows. With daybreak coming up, and the eastern sky beginning to lighten and glow orange yellow, he scanned the horizon off the port bow with binoculars. Adjusting the focal length and becoming accustomed to the prevailing light, he saw a very large silhouette on the horizon.

"What can you see?" Ed bellowed from his captain's post in the steering well.

"Something really big," Glyn shouted back. "But I can't make out its features yet. Wait—" Straining his eyes, he picked out a control tower on the body shape's starboard side.

"Come on back," Ed hailed.

Retreating to the steering well, Glyn speculated, "You might deem this fanciful, but I believe we have an aircraft carrier bearing down on us."

With Colin on steering detail, Ed turned to Steve and Glyn. "Whose turn is it to climb the mainsail mast?"

Grinning, Steve attested, "Mine."

Stepping frontward he took the binoculars from Glyn and climbed the mast.

After inspecting the vista ahead to bows port side, he called down. "Whatever it is, it's huge, and yes, Glyn could be right. It has the contours of an aircraft carrier."

Immediately, Ed went to the radio room and made a ship-to-ship call.

"Vessel vectoring on 255 degrees off my port side, this is the sailing schooner Poseidon on eighty degree track, four nautical miles from your position. Please identify yourself and confirm your heading."

Turning out to be the Italian aircraft carrier Giuseppe Garibaldi making its way to the mouth of the Med, Ed elected for evasive measures knowing large ships create gargantuan stern wash. Poseidon's radar designated she made twenty-five knots, equating with a hefty wash swell containing a prodigious ration of dynamic energy spelling peril for Poseidon. To better ride the wash coming their way, Ed directed Colin to update track to a 150 degrees vector for a few minutes, then resume on eighty degrees.

Coming within one-third of a nautical mile of Poseidon, the irrepressible and unstoppable leviathan carved its way through the sea. From the schooner's low attitude on the water, she came across as enormous. Apart from an EH 101 helicopter marooned on an emergency readiness point, aft of the control tower, all her aircraft were below the flight deck. With minimal human resources observable going about their deck duties, she had the hallmark of a ghost ship, but Poseidon's crew knew within her vast maze of command and control centres, hundreds of men occupied themselves in the seven by twenty-four-hour business of a man of war.

Returning to the deck, Steve joined the on-watch in the steering well. For safety considerations, and to also afford them a chance to see the aircraft carrier, Ed roused the off watch. After battening down hatches, stowing loose gear and securing lines, the ship's company then prepared for the wash wave running at their port side. As the Giuseppe Garibaldi passed, Poseidon's crew waved, those on her flight deck reciprocating the token.

Now her flank could be seen clearly, they began to rank the aircraft carrier's scale. 10,000-ton displacement, 600 feet in length, and her deck one hundred feet above her Plimsoll line, she towered over Poseidon, and like the potent and almighty heavens enrapturing the crew nightly, dwarfed the schooner's lowly presence. Her battleship grey assemblage garnered long-range and early-warning radar, ensuring she had seen the schooner well before her bulk dominated Poseidon's radar.

Less than fifty seconds behind her travel, the wash wave converged on Poseidon. Taking the helm from Colin, Ed turned Poseidon, so her bows took the wave first, knowing even for a medium-sized schooner it was best not to take any chances. Bedevilled by both apprehension and contrarily exhilaration by the imminent event, the newcomers held onto the steering well stern rail, bracing themselves.

Ed told them, twenty years previously he and Jeff had not done this manoeuvre when they were passing an oil tanker, again on a reciprocal track.

"When the wash wave hit our boat," he recalled, "one of our crew was thrown overboard by the impact. The instance has made us treat large vessels with renewed respect, and plan accordingly to minimise wash-wave jolt."

As the aircraft carrier's wash wave closed in, Poseidon's crew comprehended its spine-tingling proportions looming up in front of them. Well over eight feet at its peak, with a width of at least eighty yards, it reminded Glyn of a tsunami. When it collided with the bows, the crew experienced the shock back in the stern, Poseidon soaring up with the wallop, then falling forward ploughing through the trough of the wash. After the primary wave, the peak height lessened with each succeeding smaller wash wave hitting Poseidon's bows. When the peaks diminished, and the wash waves faded away, Ed reverted track to eighty degrees, relinquishing the helm back to Colin. Watching the Giuseppe Garibaldi journey on behind their port flank, she gave a blast on her foghorn in appreciation of Poseidon's courtesy.

"If the sea had been rough, caused by adverse weather," Ed notified, "we'd have turned away from the aircraft carrier as soon as possible, so to avert an even bigger wash wave."

"Better to be safe than sorry," Jeff cautioned with a knowledgeable grimace.

"Ed," Steve prompted, "you didn't say what happened to the guy thrown overboard."

"Oh…he drowned," Ed assigned, his enunciation deadpan, his expression festooning into a wicked smirk.

Whilst in the Sidi El Houari district of Oran, the crew met a merchant whose family once owned a large fertile estate bordering Lac de Telamine to the east of the city. The land had been in his family for at least six generations, but under his father's stewardship, lethargy and indolence set in. Instead of managing the land holdings and re-investing rent revenues to improve the estate, the family squandered money on misguided, failing ventures or frivolous pursuits. Climatically, the family owed taxes they couldn't pay. One of the tenant farmers made a bid for the estate, inclusive of the family home. Crestfallen, the merchant's father had no choice but to sell, pay the outstanding taxes, and move significantly down the socio-economic ladder. In turn, the farmer buying the estate also failed, because he knew nothing beyond farming. Consecutively, he sold the estate at a knock-down price to city hall.

After moving on, the ship's company talked about the merchant's ills on the veranda of a Sidi El Hamri street café.

"It's just like Chekov's *The Cherry Orchard*," Tom alleged.

"You mean," Glyn posed, "in the shape of social change?"

"Yes. You'll recollect the play is centred on an aristocratic Russian family boomeranging to their estate including a large cherry orchard, just before it must be auctioned to pay the mortgage. When furnished with options to save the estate, the family procrastinates. The play ends with the estate sold to the *nouveau riche* son of a former serf. In the final scene, the aristocrats leave to the crashes and creeks of the cherry orchard being cut down. The story is deliberately allegorical, framing themes of cultural futility, both of the aristocracy to maintain its status, and the upwardly mobile bourgeoisie to find meaning in its newfound materialism."

"Ah, I see what you mean," Glyn certified. "I suppose since recorded history was inaugurated, the merchant's socio-economic heritage in Oran reflects the adjustment determinants at work around the globe."

"Very true," Colin supported. "It seems every empire, every oligarchy, and every self-made combine, is eventually doomed to failure and destruction by the decadent descendants of the highly-motivated originators launching the enterprise."

Joining the discussion, Ed added, "The merchant's tale is a smaller yardstick example of what happened to the British Empire, and it's unwrapping is still ongoing."

"How?" Steve enquired.

"Without doubt," Ed proposed, "England is being dismantled from within by the current bunch of double-dealing buffoons occupying the corridors of power in Westminster." Stepping to the veranda's edge, he then turned, pinpointing his comrades, a mournful lour spreading across his countenance.

"England could end up like the merchant's family, bankrupt of assets, tradition, character, and the will to uphold its heritage."

"You're right," Colin concurred. "Most oligarchies fail because they're defeated by external warring factions, like the Visigoths and Huns invading the Holy Roman Empire. But defeat for England is being engineered from within by traitorous politicians, and charlatan immigrants gaining political sway, then imposing their will on the English. In the end, it will amount to the same dismal end, and a gigantic leap towards the ever-impending apocalypse."

Collectively, the crew pondered Colin's valuation of the manipulation in play back in Blighty. But now wasn't the time to articulate about how to mount a revolution to depose the traitors and the interlopers. In the Med, the newcomers were on sabbatical from the dissonance leading to disharmony devouring their country. If they were ever going to do anything about it, they needed to conserve the cleansing benefits of the voyage, recharge to full potential, then address the issue on their return.

Sauntering side by side with Colin and Ed along narrow streets in Algiers, Glyn became enthralled by the sight of the Casbah and lesser buildings neighbouring it in the distance. Ahead of them by some quarter mile, the other crew members neared the fortified citadel, a district founded on the ruins of old Icosium, and now a small city built on a hill running down to the Med. Already Algiers had the newcomers in slack-jawed awe. Offering tantalising attractions to antiquity hungry Europeans, here was yet another great North African city, rich in architecture and glowing with history and Arab culture.

"Ed, have you distinguished many shifts in the nature of North African ports over the past ten years?" Glyn enquired.

"Well, let me see," he began, tilting his head skywards and rubbing his chin as precursors to his reply. "In the sort of vicissitudes to the population demographic and the nature of Arab societies? Absolutely nothing. It's been like this for decades, and in some cases centuries. Arabs make up at least ninety-seven percent of all the North African countries, and they don't like outsiders, as you saw in El Jebha. The prospect of sharing Arab land is alien to them. It's always been that way. They don't want their way of life diluted by foreigners. Hence, they've always been, and will always be, the dominant majority. To protect Arab civilisation, culture and traditions, without them being tarnished, outsiders are not allowed advocacy or power."

"Every nation wants that fundamental," Colin interjected.

"Quite," Ed agreed. "And most North African Arabs have little appetite for Muslim world domination espoused by Abu Hamza and other extremist Muslim clerics in Europe and the Middle-East." Stopping, he scowled, as if about to make a bombshell comment. Colin and Glyn turned to face him. "You see, most of those extremists are not Arabs. They are Pakistanis or negro Africans. Arabs get tarnished with the same brush. They don't like it, because it's insulting that Westerners can't see Arabs are a different race to Pakistanis and negroes. And, in the main, they don't like Pakistanis or negroes, because they cause trouble in the Middle East and want to feed on Arab wealth." Narrowing his eyes at Glyn, he asked, "Does that answer the enigma?"

"It does. I anticipated what you describe. I've travelled to five continents, and the one thing I've found to be common, whether in Thailand, Chile, South Africa or any points in between, is the fundamental desire nations have to safeguard land ownership, customs and tradition, exclusively for their own kind. That's what makes up the individual nations and has deep-rooted them down the centuries."

"Perfectly true and understandable," Colin spelt out. "Pity it's been watered down as a political prerequisite in Europe."

"How do you mean?"

"Ed's review got me thinking. Until recent times, it was as he described in every country, but now, Western Europe is swamped by colonists, principally economic migrants and asylum seekers. Therewithal, Western societies have been misshapen, and re-directed down paths completely alien to us. We feel like strangers in our own country because foreigners have superimposed their religions, their customs, and worst of all, their demands on us, to the extent whereby our towns and cities have become unrecognisable to what they were just a few decades ago."

"Hhmm," Ed mumbled, sliding an astute smile at his companions. "There's no concept of asylum here. Even thirty years ago, people arriving from other parts of Africa vanished, never to be heard of again. But more recently, making them comply with the Convention on Human Rights, the EU insists that North African governments return invaders to where they came from. They must even allow migrant workers, though they don't like it. At the very most, it is tolerated in return for European trade, but it's a fine balance. Often Sub-Saharans are beaten, even killed, when they take jobs away from Arabs. The Arab authorities know their people won't stand for it, because the migrants represent the thin end of the wedge. They're afraid that if they are too relaxed, it will be taken as a sign of feebleness, and more and more will come, leading to internal strife." Pausing, he then reproved, "*Remember*, this is a highly volatile part of the world. Change at the top through revolution can happen very quickly."

"For sure," Colin backed. "I get the distinct impression Poseidon's crew are accepted as passing tourists, but beyond that..." Pressing his lips together, his demeanour became guarded. "We're not welcome."

"You have to understand," Ed pressed, "as far as the Arabs are concerned, Allah gave them this land. Its fine for European contractors to aid petroleum exploration and production, but that apart, only a handful of foreigners are admitted from anywhere, and few Europeans stayed after the North African Arab countries gained full independence." Lingering, his eye became caught by the remaining ship's company waving to the three stragglers from the distant Casbah. Acknowledging them with a reciprocal gesture, he then carried on. "Yes, there are legacy European buildings and businesses, and even a few European government systems have been part-adopted. Howbeit, in the main, the Arab nations have not reformed since the seventh century. That's right isn't it, Colin?"

"Affirmative, Captain."

"They're hierarchal, homogeneous societies, with no latitude for the principles of commonwealth and congress beyond their own kind," Ed professed. "Hence the constancy and the consistency." Sensing a contradiction coming from Glyn, he cast a neutralising glance at him. "Oh, revolutions perennially come and go, as do their dictators, but the bedrock, the underlying elements making up Arab society remain undiminished. We condemn their intolerance of anything other than Islam, but they regard our liberal regimes to be weak and easily corrupted and exploited by outsiders."

"Yes, put like that, and with the knowledge of what's happening back in Blighty," Glyn ventured, "maybe they've got it right."

Walking on at a brisker pace, the debate evolved.

"What are your impressions of England, when you are back home, Ed?" Colin petitioned.

Perturbed about the request, Ed halted again. Clearing his throat, he then cased about to make sure their conversation remained private. "I'll give you the uncensored response." Gathering his thoughts, he outlined, "For me, the England I grew up in doesn't exist anymore. Doesn't even feel like England anymore. It's more like some kind of sociologists' experiment, designed to see if hundreds of different races, religions and cultures can co-exist without civil war breaking out. Last year, when I was back in Blighty with the family, I had to go to Geneva for a few days on business. Coming back through Heathrow passport control, there wasn't a single English person doing passport checks. They were all black or Asian, wearing turbans, burqas and niqabs. Didn't feel like coming into England, felt more like a Third World country."

"Ed, Heathrow has been like that since 1997," Glyn specified. "I've heard that comment on numerous occasions, mainly from taken-aback foreigners visiting Blighty. Passport control is their first impression of England, her introductory shop window if you like. What they're expecting, is pretty blonde girls, Beefeaters and

Rule Britannia, not a vanguard of enforced, PC, social reengineering."

"Hhmm, hardly an equitable state of affairs, is it?" Ed burbled. Searching his memory for more impressions, he itemised, "Lincolnshire is much the same as it's always been, but if you go into any of the Midland's cities, or London, the only minority group you see are the endangered English. It's just not right. Jeff and I often wonder what it will be like for our children over the next ten years, and their children beyond that. Quite frankly, I'm very concerned, and it seems that if you enter into the subject back home, the do-gooder, liberal-elitist brigade accuse you of racism." Waggling a warning finger, he vehemently got into his stride. "Let me tell you, Glyn, if any of the North African cities you have been so impressed with, were faced with a mass infiltration of Europeans, riots would break out followed by bloody civil war." Drawing up close to him, he lamented, "So why should England be destroyed, just to appease these do-gooders? Tell me that?"

"Oh, the usual reasons," Colin offered, before Glyn could speak. "Lassitude, laziness, and lack of moral fibre by the indigenous population. Dread of being branded and ostracised. Fear of the consequences for breaking discordant EU imposed Race Relations and Human Rights Laws." Breathing out heavily, dismay covered his features. Twisting back to face Ed and Glyn, he stopped them in their tracks. "It's not new you know. In the nineteen-thirties, Baldwin's Government turned a blind eye to Hitler and most English people had their heads in the sand. They ignored the problem, hoping it'd go away. Only Churchill and a small coalition of other like-minded people spoke out about the Nazis', and the threat to England."

"Yes, that's right," Ed granted. "The only difference today is, there are no Churchillian-like politicians protesting about the invasion of England. No one from any of the major parties is willing to speak out, for fear of being shunned, and their political careers heading south. Patriotism is dead, and that will enable the hordes to destroy Blighty."

"*Wake up* England," Glyn ironically pined. "Wake up."

Persevering with their walk to the Casbah, they felt depressed, even complicit in the treachery, because they too were taking no action.

~

Sometimes it became dangerous to reflect and allow the mind to roam wildly in the past, dragging up unsettling demons and running over tragedies and injustices. Glyn's maxim became 'best to try and keep it engrossed in the present and less torturous memories'.

Life aboard Poseidon largely accomplished this aim for him and the other newcomers. New physical environs coupled with sustaining the mental application required for crewing duties and companion camaraderie, plainly made a significant modification to their *modus vivendi*, resulting in something wonderful happening. Liberated from Blighty societal conformity, the ship's company felt a huge burden had been lifted, something that had progressively enlarged and been stored up since birth. The simplicity of their adopted sailing lifestyle equalled the regime of primitive peoples living on remote islands, untouched by the demands of modernity in all its soul-destroying and caustic states. It begged the question, was so-called advanced Western civilisation and the drive for material gain and status, the best way to conduct life?

Extra to the release from their back-home lives, Glyn contemplated, under propitious terms it was beneficial and healthy to lose the steady-state, conscious self, derange the senses and dive deep into nothingness. Generally, it is assumed drugs are needed for the purpose, but meditation works just as well, and with no residual baggage.

Occasionally when off-watch, with the sea calm and the sun setting in the Western sky, its full orange ball attenuated enough to allow surveillance without being blinded, Glyn sat cross-legged on the deck, holding his arms out in the *I Ching* lotus position and losing himself in the magnificence of his surroundings. The further from the coast, the purer the ozone. Slowly breathing in its therapeutic vapours expanded the ecstasy. No Pink Floyd accompaniment needed here, just the waves, the boat movement, and that centre of the solar system.

Nonetheless, dependent on the state of mind, sometimes it became impossible to enact the meditation without something soporific and sense drenching. If it was Glyn's turn to select music, he went for blissing out to the mesmerising sounds of Quintessence, the band's fused jazz and rock creations blended with Eastern mysticism, forging the ideal accompaniment for inner space travel. Some religions prescribe a repeated cycle of frenzy and calm to approach paradise as per the *Bhagavad-Gita*. Perfect for the intended purpose, Quintessence augmented and intensified the trance-like state. Their sublime music rose and fell in peaks and troughs, bringing the listener within fingering range of the face of God. Release came on reaching the summit, its Elysian plateau dauntless and everlasting, the place visited by Baudelaire and Hesse, the trick being to persist the euphoria through grip of the meditation. Sometimes others joined in the ritual, and communally, they wandered in the pale insignificance of obscurity, that place where the mind becomes expurgated and free from colour, like in Blake's famous concept.

In one micro-universe, a deep, pulsating wave fixed Glyn from across the horizon, it's curvature effectively frame-frozen in the camera eye before it could crash down decimating beach life. Designed to test intellectual agility, his wave eyed him with an air of superiority, dictating the games they'd play, its menu offering hedonistic emergence and other forms of distraction. They talked of life, of death, claimed knowledge of cryptic things, pretended a solution to the eschatological riddle, and got lost in the cosy world of soft symbols. Anything for escape, anything for release, anything for a momentary glimpse of nirvana, as the slender slit through Blake's doors fluttered further open.

Through the portal, secular Fabian strategies were cast away. *Babylon calling*, he considered. Probably yes, because in the release and flight to silky emblems, fragility led to the predictable exposition, meaning, if his concentration flagged, Glyn's wave disappeared. Fixing his attentiveness on the transitory object, he absorbed its magnetic fascination, letting it envelop his psyche. *Ad initio*, the diversion manifested itself as a nascent revolution fought with pride and passion, the revolt akin to an altruistic, pure and beautiful woman. But soon those high principles decayed, collapsed and withered, the revolution mutating into a crude whore, the adages of innocence ravaged by the nauseating mob.

So as with revolution, retreat to Blake's world appeared calm, omniscient and infinite, displaying transcendence and acknowledging anything open to hypothesis within its compass bounds. But in trying to lay a tangible hold on that world, when Glyn gazed at his wave, he fancied it laughed at him, and paralysed by notions of the ultimate revelation and the fear of the Boatman's hand on his shoulder, return to profane reality became pre-destined. With the hypnotic trance broken, his wave no longer appeared frame frozen in time, beach life safe. It always moved, only in Glyn's meditative state, he chose not to see it. Passing overhead, his wave was really a stealth fighter in disguise, but invisible to the conscious mind.

~

With the bravura of Algiers fading from view behind Poseidon's starboard flank, off-watch Steve and Glyn took in the vast seascape to the west at sunset. After five weeks in the North African Mediterranean, their minds and souls had largely been purged from back home horrors, refreshment shining through. A new sense of optimism about the future seemed possible. Only a few months earlier, Glyn's mind-set had been rigidly disciplined with professional objectives and dealing with daily quandaries. Now having the scope for other considerations, he started to examine things stored in memory, awaiting scrutiny from years ago.

"You know what Ed and Jeff were saying about the voyage being more like a novel then a news report?" Glyn posed.

"Yep."

"It grabbed my attention."

"About the voyage?"

"Incontestably that, but amongst a surfeit of other things, what I've also been reading in recent years." Stepping to one side of the foresail mast to address Steve head-on, he stated, "It strikes me that every modern novel I read is the same."

"In what way?"

"Well, *hah*," As if suddenly recognising the blindingly obvious, he grinned. "Everything is laid out up front on page one, or the plot becomes conclusively transparent in the opening pages. Beyond that, it's a verification exercise, with the remainder leaving little to the imagination. The art of the mystique has been lost."

"You mean—" Steve halted to make sure he had the correct interpretation. "The novelists are treading exactly the same path?"

"I suppose I do."

Consumed in reflection, he gaped at the horizon. Dusk hot on her tails, the sun had all but vanished, leaving the sky awash with a temperate, warm glow as the day god bid goodnight to Poseidon. Facing Glyn, he submitted, "I'm tempted to say, if modern writers could see what we are beholding right now, it still wouldn't inspire them to elevate their game, raise the bar, or at the very least, emulate the great writers of the past."

"So you agree?"

Esteeming his friend had snagged him in a contentious issue, Steve voiced, "I do, and writers like Faulkner and E. M. Foster might find it very difficult to get established today."

"Undoubtedly, but why?"

"Lowest common denominator."

"You mean, modern books are written and edited, so as to appeal to mass markets, and the really good stuff never sees the light of day?"

"I do. Judy used to tell me, she'd get stick from her publishing house, if her script editing left too much meat on the bone, and the plot wasn't unclad quickly enough. She'd been given instructions, an acceptance template if you like, that the work had to fit into. It made stories extremely staccato, with no depth. Do you understand what she meant?"

Glyn nodded.

"She said, most sagas banged along the surface, never diving deep to see the possibilities beneath the prominent, or unmasking the kind of secondary subplots and creature idiosyncrasies making the work of say Virginia Woolf so fascinating."

"Just the facts, as Joe Friday never-endingly insisted?"

"Precisely, only this was not a police report. It was intended to be art, not pulp fiction to be filed under product."

"So, if I understand you correctly, Judy confirmed authors were not allowed to introduce rich sub-plots and effect colourisation?"

"You've got it."

Dwelling on Judy's rigid template discipline for a moment, Glyn certified, "I see what she meant, but I do like for example Bukowski, because to quote Ed, it provides immediate gratification. But I suppose, his works are more like a comic than a classic novel. There's no profundity, opulence or splendour in the text. It's just a fast flow diary of his sexual conquests and his struggles working for the US Postal Service. I have four Bukowski books, but have only read them once, whereas, I go back to *The Fountainhead* and *Sophie's Choice* every year, discovering something new."

"For me, its Hammett's *The Maltese Falcon*, and my front-runner, *The Man with the Golden Arm*."

"Nelson Algren?"

"Yeah. I prefer *Golden Arm* to his seminal considered work, *Walk on the Wild Side*."

Whilst snagging the inspiring panorama, the friends eulogised about more authors, tabling what they found moving in their work, or alternatively what constituted the abysmal. Finally, the sun waned, cerulean blue turned dark then black as night cloaked Poseidon. Slipping through the Med, straight and true on-course, her sails billowing, and her superstructure keeled over at ten degrees to the vertical catching the prevailing wind, to Glyn and Steve she translated into a paragon of purity, virtuous and imperial. So accustomed to her dynamic movement, they barely registered her steady, regular pitching from bows to stern as she made passage.

"You know Liam Walsh?" Glyn prompted.

"I *do*," Steve replied. "He's a prize-winning twat, and that's a generous assessment. Haven't seen him in years. He got the hint that his preaching was not admired at the sailing club."

"Yes…well, erm." Glyn broke off, chuckling at Steve's vociferous appraisal. "Five years ago, he recommended *Vernon God Little* to me. He told me it was like a modern-day version of *On the Road*. When I read the Kerouac in my youth, I drained every enthralling page, whereas the DBC Pierre I found hard going." Gyrating his head, he criticised, "It never really projected a cohesive, compelling story, yet remarkably it won the 2003 Booker Prize."

"Doesn't surprise me that Walsh liked it," Steve blasted. "He always *did* slavishly follow the in-crowd, though I doubt if you pumped him, 'What is its particular excellence?' he could make a rational reply. The bloke has never had an original conception in his entire life. *Tosser*."

"You never did like Liam, did you?"

"Couldn't stand him. He used to come down to the sailing club spouting his trendy, lefty, PC bullshit. Despicable, jumped-up, little turd." Magnifying his intonation, he rasped, "Do you know, he kept a photo of Blair in his wallet? Typical middle-class, rich, socialist, do as I say, not as I do, toady bastard."

"I conjectured you were going to say, 'Not a lot of people know that'."

"Michael Caine?"

"Yeah."

Steve cut a smile. "*Yikes*, even Cainey would find Walsh repulsive, 'Oh yes'."

Trying to bring brevity back to the discussion, Glyn wisecracked, "Don't sugar coat it, Steve, tell me what you really think."

Laughing, he gauged energy spent on castigating the dubious Walsh was wasteful. "You're right, he's not worth the steam off my tea, as they say in Manchester."

Caught up in the biting humour they both chortled.

"Anyway, Walsh is not the point," Glyn gushed. "Why did Pierre get the Booker Prize?"

"Ohh," Steve pressed his lips together forming a judgemental mannerism. "Fashion, nepotism, industry politics. The usual, 'I'm in with the in crowd' narcissistic crap. Judy told me, they worship the drab, the mondaying and the ordinary, so long as it complies with the agenda, and drags everything down to the lowest common denominator. Most of what her company published was lightweight, chick-lit, Mills & Boon type stuff, devoured by pulp romance lovers. She tried to find the new du Maurier, or even a Susan Hill, but any new writer straying into original conviction, quickly became rejected."

"I can see that. But what I'm driving at, is the sheer banality of it." Wavering, he tried to find a cohesive finish to nail the assertion. "It's as if it's been designed to be soporific, guaranteed to solve insomnia, never to explore, always to comply. I'm not saying the Pierre was without some value, more the case, surely there were better works out there in 2003?"

"Probably. Most of what I've read over the past ten years has cured my insomnia. Judy certainly found it tedious." Grimacing at the troubled remembrance, he snapped, "But as you know, that's another story."

Aware Judy's infidelity was still a sore point, Glyn got the conversation back on track. "I suppose it's like the post-modernism art model is bound to ultra-minimalism," he proposed. "Turner and Blake proponents seen as heretics by today's in vogue fashionistas. But the same status quo elevates Tracey Emin to god's gift. That I don't understand."

"Ah, well, she's a fully paid-up member of New Labour," Steve chided. "That opens many doors to mediocrities and the downwardly talented."

Smiling at the scathing truism, Glyn applauded, "I just love your caustic, undiplomatic humour. It's very fortifying. Please don't ever change, Steve."

"Well, I hate the way that Blighty has drifted into mediocrity."

"Yes, regrettably, standards have declined. I suppose in reality, there are no standards anymore, only levels of political correctness."

"President Blair and Führer Brown have bred a blank generation, dull and easily amused," Steve asserted, his retort punctuated with scowling bitterness. "So, I suppose publishing houses cater for this dim-witted flock. That's the explication to your problematical issue, Glyn."

Troubled by the explanation, he grilled, "Do you adjudge that's sad, disturbing…even sinister?"

"I do, but what can be done about it?" Steve quizzed. "It's all wrapped up and enshrined in the PC creed. It's the cancer both running and ruining England."

Materialising in Glyn's mind, the bothersome conversation he and Steve had before leaving England incited circumspection. "*Hey,*" he hollered. "Don't forget our agreement to make Blair and Brown a strictly verboten subject?"

"Hhmm," Steve uttered, nodding in agreement.

"We joined Poseidon to get away from all that tosh back in Blighty."

"Yes, we did," he admitted. "Won't happen again."

Staring ahead they clocked the horizon, now unperceivable between the dark sky and even darker sea. Hardly touching the surface Poseidon glided, her giant multi-mast sails full without flapping and trimmed for maximum speed, the auto-tiller pilot holding her track true. Choosing to immerse themselves in the escapism of inner space travel to cleanse the revulsion plaguing Blighty, Glyn and Steve began meditating.

Glyn wished he hadn't addressed Steve on the modern novelists' issue, not intending it to run into the Blair and Brown domain and destroying all the soul cleansing they had accomplished to date. Making a mental note to be subject matter prudent for the remainder of the voyage with Steve, he descended through the rumination barrier, and into the calming aura of the introspective life force.

~

Sometimes dawn greeted the schooner with early morning fog, as distinct from translucent and wispy mist. Sea fog, or frets as Essex seafarers call it, appears dense and unfathomable because the sea surface tends to flatness. Unlike in cities, there are no objects to give darker background, and thereby assess distance. Hence under fog-bound sailing environs, radar coupled with faultless navigation is essential to ensure safety.

Poseidon neared Port de Bejaia under such conditions, darkness receding in favour of the new dawn, but dense fog masking off the rising sun. Strewn with perilous underwater rocks off the high cliff's coastline to the north and west of Bejaia, like at Lizard Point Cornwall the hazard necessitated Poseidon to sail three nautical miles to the north along a secure arcing track into the port. Slipping through the murky dimness, her course became progressively amended from 110 degrees to 190, and finally 280, the fluctuating heading strategy intended to take the schooner through the harbour entrance and into port, with minimum risk. Responding to Poseidon's identification radio call, the Port de Bejaia harbour master advised extreme caution to be taken during her passage.

Along the route transition on a course of 160 degrees, twelve small blips appeared on radar two nautical miles from Poseidon's position off her starboard bow. Experience told the crew to expect a small fishing fleet soon crossing their path. At one nautical mile from the potential hazard, the on-watch operated the foghorn, lowered all sails apart from the fore-jib and fore-staysail, and fired up the twin diesels to allow for agile manoeuvring when the convoy emerged from the masking fog bank. Because reverberation is dispersed in fog, they knew the fishermen might have difficulty adjudging Poseidon's position, and more essentially, the size of their approaching craft.

Like clockwork, the watch had been changed at 06:00, but the off watch remained on deck, keen to be part of the unfolding encounter. Handing the captaincy over to Jeff, Ed apprised him *vis-à-vis* the traffic and Poseidon's point on track, before taking a position on the bows with a loud hailer. Sounded every twenty seconds, Ed supplemented the schooner's foghorn with warning calls pertaining to their position and direction. Radar indicated the task force were imminent. Sure enough, like phantoms materialising from enchantment, they came gently rocking into view, fifty yards from Poseidon's bows, some rowing their small sail craft, others tugging on sail controls trying to find a breeze to propel them along. Holding course as the diminutive craft passed her to port and starboard, their crews looked both inquisitive and more than a little relieved collision had been bypassed. With Poseidon half a nautical mile from the harbour entrance, radar showed more traffic emerging from port heading out into the Mediterranean, and inbound traffic building in the port's channel astern of the schooner, the ship's company hearing their fog horns and occasional shouts aimed at the out-going fishing fleet.

Cautiously proceeding onward, a large ketch emerged from the fog on a near to parallel outbound reciprocal heading with Poseidon, the schooner's crew calling good morning to the ketch crew, and exchanging a few further words as she skimmed past, evidently en route to Palma in the Balearics.

Minutes later, they saw the harbour entrance. Its east and west walls, 1100 feet apart, displayed on the radar and the GPS repeater, but the stone constructions eluded direct vision through the fog bank. Even as Poseidon passed right of mid-centre through the entrance, the Englishmen barely made out the walls.

After docking, it became manifest the fog had also shrouded the entire harbour area, making it impossible to see buildings and other vessels, other than as speckled outlines.

Estimating the fine margins between disaster and survival at sea for those venturing out in craft far too small for the intended purpose, Glyn realised it must be a daily call faced with nerve by their occupants. Some people gamble on the odds, just to see if they can be beaten, but for fishermen, the drive came through necessity. Without their catch, their families starved.

Swivelling about, Glyn faced Steve. "Can you recollect those times when we risked going out on the North Sea at Whitstable, conscious that sailing was highly risky?"

"I can. What about them?"

"Knowing what we know now, do you deem it was foolhardy?"

Recoiling, Steve enquired, "What brought this on, Glyn?"

"Oh, just the recognition that for some people, it's a daily risk, not done to test mettle, but for fundamental economic reasons."

"You mean, the fishermen?"

"Yes."

"It's just a different scene," Steve countered. "They do it because they are here. We sail off Whitstable in inclement weather for adrenalin rush. Both are just tests. That's all."

"I suppose you're right," Glyn yielded. "But since we've been in the Med, my perspective has become enlarged. I can see things clearly here, whereas back in Blighty they'd have remained sightless." Hesitating, he then conceded, "I'm not quite sure what I'm trying to say, Steve, other than this cross-over we have all come to recognise, has made me acutely sensitive to how other people have to live their lives."

"Don't beat yourself up, Glyn," Jeff reproached, nabbing the back end of the conversation. "Out here, we are free to receive a glut of sensory images and mental agitations. Back home, they don't touch us. Your mind is liberating itself from all the rubbish and crap thrown at it by contemporary life in England. It's being used for its intended purpose; to pick feeds from body sensors and make interpretations as opposed to judgements. The latter is the currency used in your back-home life. We're just passing through North Africa like time travellers, unable to affect anything. We discover what is going on, but as outsiders, value judgements have no place for us here. This altruistic feeling you have, happens to us all, even Ed. Unless you are a soulless android, it's incredibly difficult not to pick up on things here, that perhaps people back home are only vaguely aware off through newspapers and TV pictures."

"I appreciate that," Glyn accepted, "only, how do you deal with it?"

"You don't," Jeff directed. "We are merely observers in this often-bizarre world. We have no influence, and no standing.

Thereby, we have no choice but to evaluate what goes on in the vicinity dispassionately. Some of the things we see here are truly wonderful, well beyond European premises, but no society is without incongruity. As Steve said, those fishermen go out into the Med in their flimsy craft because they must. They've been doing it for centuries. They know the risks, but every day, out they will go."

Several hours later the sun finally broke through the haze while the crew serviced Poseidon. At last they were able to see Fort Sidi Abdelkader on the quayside road, and further back, rising up the slopes of Yemma Gouraya, a mix of ancient and modern structures.

Not the last time Poseidon negotiated fog during the voyage, the Port de Bejaia action forewarned the newcomers what to expect in terms of risk and the potential for tragedy.

"How on Earth do those fishing boats navigate in dense fog?" Bill posed as he finished stowing away deck swabbing gear.

"They feel their way," Ed enlightened. "It's down to a lifetime of familiarity with these waters. It's the same for every fishing fleet along the North African coastline."

"It's also born out of necessity," Jeff detailed, facing Glyn and recalling their earlier conversation. "If they don't fish, they can't trade. Then they can't feed their families and pay the bills."

"Must call for a great deal of skill and knowledge," David put forward.

"Oh, for a fact," Ed confirmed. "Not everyone can simply jump into a small fishing boat and negotiate the Med. Many have tried, but few have succeeded and lived to tell the tale."

Less than a week later, those words proved to be prophetic.

At Port de Bejaia the newcomers had to make a collective decision connected to the extent of the voyage. Two choices were tabled by the seniors. A three-months sail having them beginning the trek back to Europe when they reached Tunis. Alternatively, a five-months sail allowed for circumnavigation of the Med, taking them to the coasts of Libya, Egypt, Israel and Beirut, before heading west to Cyprus, Rhodes and other Greek islands, then on to the foot of Italy and Sicily, where the three-months sail route picked up.

After much soul searching, because of commitments back in Blighty, the newcomers elected for the three-month option.

9

PREPARING TO EXECUTE ALLAH'S WILL

During the flight from Addis Ababa to Tunis-Carthage International Airport, Saleh resolved to make his act altogether watertight by assuming a measured and composed persona in front of the Tunis Muslim fundamentalists. To pull off a breakout during the next stage of his mission preparation, he must show he had ice in his veins, demonstrate allegiance to the cause, and dedication to his delegated task to their complete satisfaction.

Massood had warned him in advance, the Tunisian authorities were on constant watch for Muslim terrorists, and accordingly, the Tunis fundamentalists appointed a far more rigid discipline in the execution of the operational agenda than anything he had undergone in Nazret. Well-nigh operating on a war footing, and to avoid their HQ being raided by armed forces, the Tunis fundamentalists employed sophisticated maximum-security procedures and tactics to ensure they blended in with regular Tunisian life, undetected by the police and the government's anti-terrorist squads of agents working underground. Proven worldwide, the methodology empowered Muslim terrorists to operate virtually under the noses of government law enforcement agencies, both in Islamic countries and the West. To make sure their endeavours could be conducted without suspicions arising from ordinary Tunisian citizens in the area they were located, a strict routine had to be adhered to by all participants in the enterprise, harsh treatment metered out to anyone even suspected of duplicity. Those caught in the act of betrayal summarily executed.

Because of the stringent security model the terrorists adopted, Saleh still had no idea about the nature of his mission, other participants, its enactment zone, and the how to accomplish the attack. All the same, he guessed the carry out to be somewhere in Western Europe.

On arrival in Tunis, he made his way to the Hraïria district to seek out his contacts. So as to seamlessly blend in with locals, they were holed up in a nondescript house amongst a myriad of lookalike abodes, in the densely packed artisan and craftsmen part of the area.

With the Tunisian economy at breaking point, it could not resource any more unproductive overhead. Consequently, the Government tasked the police and border patrol to bring illegal immigration from the Sub-Sahara under restraint and reverse the trend. Moreover, the EU put pressure on North African governments to end illegal immigration from their shores into Southern Europe. Most of all, the secular driven Tunisian Government were concerned about Muslim fundamentalism and insurrection from within. Beyond official frontier posts, their homeland security was easily breached, making it simple for infiltrators intent on making trouble to enter the country from the Sahara. Nominally having little knowledge about the identities of the fundamentalists and their secret location, they did however know dissident Muslims were recruited from the Sub-Saharan countries. Ergo, when suspicious documents were identified at an official entry station, they allowed the suspect to go through in the hope of leading them to the fundamentalists. Unbeknown to Saleh, the Tunisian passport control authority had picked up an irregularity in his documentation.

Having been told by Massood to watch out for police following him, Saleh sensed a gumshoe on his tail as soon as he left Carthage International Airport. Managing to lose his follower in the Ezzouhour district, he then made haste to find his contacts. Already, he contemplated, his security had been compromised, heightening his sense of survival and instinct to hone his play-acting skills.

~

Under directives from the Muslim Brotherhood, leader Khalis Hammad bin Qureshi bin Basara put together the Tunis fundamentalist troop. A fellow Syrian like Massood, he came from a good family, but rejected their passive brand of Islamism, instead opting for and wholeheartedly embracing radical Muslim fundamentalism. Still in his early teens, Basara had been recruited by a Muslim Brotherhood scout after being detained by the Syrian Police for anti-establishment activities.

Taking his delegated position very seriously, he abstained from the pleasures of the flesh, and governed his entire life as a model Muslim. Truly believing in the axiomatic right for Islamic doctrines to be applied worldwide, he sided with the notion that other religions and secular societies should be eradicated by force. Like all Muslim fundamentalists, he was an Islamic fascist, unfeeling, remorseless, and unremitting in the drive for world domination. To Basara, tolerance of non-Muslims equated with weakness, diluting the resolve and effort needed to accomplish their goal. Instrumental in many Muslim terrorist atrocities, and proud to be responsible for the deaths of thousands of Christians throughout Europe and Asia, he typified a faction of cruel and barbarous Islamic sadists, present on the Earth since the sixth century.

Intolerant of disloyalty, Basara executed suspected informers with a passion, his gleaming scimitar severing heads on a very regular basis, his brutal, overbearing and unyielding nature, coupled with the unbridled belief that he did Allah's work, insulated him from any feelings of regret or lament for his actions. His heartbeat never rose above normal when he coldly applied the blade, going back to whatever task had been interrupted by the unfortunate victim, while his cohorts disposed of the severed head and its carcass. Like all sadists, he grew to enjoy decapitator duty, feeling that the more people he executed, the stronger he became, affording him to go down fighting to the last, should the Tunisian authorities assail and defeat the fundamentalists. Imperturbable of his glorification in heaven, he vowed never to be captured alive.

Beyond the concept of peaceful negotiation, like his fellow Islamic terrorists, he saw any attempts by the West to agree settlements as fragility to be exploited. Indubitably, the only everlasting solution the West had to end the age-old conflict was to fight fire with fire, expel all Muslims from the West, kill all Muslim terrorists worldwide without trial, and finally put an end to 1400 years of bloody conflict. Albeit, Basara knew the West did not have the stomach for the necessary action, beneficially enabling Muslim terrorism to persist forever. Like all the senior-level Muslim terrorist elite, he went about his work cocksure timid and gutless Western politicians would sooner see their own cities bombed and their own people murdered than take the required step.

His mission in Tunis concentrated on training foot-soldiers to discharge Allah's will, as he zealously called it. In practice, that meant brain-washing easy-to-fool, young Muslim men and sometimes women, into carrying out terrorist atrocities as human bombs, or being part of a larger circle for mass destruction.

Designed to send a message to governments and citizens at large, Muslim fundamentalists had no hesitation making the ultimate sacrifice in the cause of Islam, human bombs expressly a major worldwide problem. Auxiliary to Western targets, human bomb attacks were summarily carried out in Israel, and secular-governed Muslim countries outlawing fundamentalism such as Egypt and Tunisia. Creating fear in the masses that human bombers could strike anywhere and at any time became their objective, al-Qaeda propaganda sowing the seed the only way to prevent the resultant carnage was insurrection from within to overthrow the secular ruling elite.

In the case of Israel, it meant full surrender and withdraw from what Muslims considered to be Palestinian territory. Embracing the intransigent policy, Western, liberal, Muslim apologists conveniently forgot it amounted to ethnic cleansing, a purge apparently unacceptable to them in Bosnia, but perfectly alright in Israel, and Pakistan.

Orchestrated attacks on the West designed to hit major institutions and strategic targets, as the world had witnessed in the nine-eleven and seven-seven atrocities, took military style planning and execution. Refined and well-organised means at the terrorist executive tier, plus cohesive operational and logistics skills at the middle level, accomplished the intended impact of bludgeoning governments into capitulating to Muslim demands. Withal, to cover the costs of terrorist operations, the executive's main thrust centred on raising capital from powerful and rich Muslim patrons, and even rogue governments such as Iran.

Discernibly, the latest incarnation of the ancient radical blocs was not like the ragbag collection of disorganised and woeful protestors often seen on Western television screens rampaging through London or Paris, demanding special rights and privileges for Muslims. To terrorists, it merely equalled noise, but noise that could generate keystone sponsorship for radical solutions, explicitly among the naive young. Comparatively speaking, Muslim terrorist organisations bore all the hallmarks of a sophisticated and regimented international army, often exceeding the capabilities of Western military and counterintelligence forces. Coupled with Western, liberal-dominated, politically correct rumination resulting in institutionalising Islamic tolerance, the capacity determined why the West was losing the battle with Muslim terrorists. Openly waging war on the Christian West, the aggressor knew the Western political classes pretended the atrocities were committed by a few lunatics, when in stark contrast, under the covers tens of millions of Muslim immigrants abetted the terrorist action. Shamefully, the politicos did nothing to condemn it, let alone terminate it.

Attempts by the West at containment were never going to work. Reality dictated an outright, no-holds-barred assault using the full military might of NATO was required to eradicate all Muslim terrorist organisations worldwide. But impotence and procrastination by double-dealing politicians and a growing legion of fifth columnist Muslim sympathisers infiltrating core

Western and Christian establishments, ensured ever-present Muslim terrorism increased year on year.

Though rejecting the material world, nevertheless, Muslim terrorists utilised computer and telecommunications technologies as part of their organisational model, and even as a conduit to enact terrorist actions, many Muslim followers recruited for their I.T and communications skills to complement the central corps of bombs and WMD constructors and deliverers. Overlaid by a cohesive operational management structure, the technocrats and field agents formed the bulk of the terrorist army. Demanded by the executive layer, middle managers developed the strategies, tactics and plans to implement the radical Muslim doctrine worldwide by force and coercion.

Patronised by financial benefactors, including Muslim billionaires and 'axis of evil' countries, Muslim terrorist organisations flourished. Whereas the IRA played the old country card act with American Catholics, whilst strutting the clubs and bars of the major East coast cities like Boston and New York to beg the odd dollar here and there, Muslim terrorist fund raisers operated on levels far higher up in the social stratum. Principally consisting prominent Middle Eastern, Pakistani and African businessmen and landowners, their targets contributed hundreds of millions in multiple currencies, washed through the world's more dubious banking systems into private accounts to bankroll the cause. Secondary to the probable contributions made by Iran, other rogue states such as North Korea saw it as in their interests to fund Muslim terrorism against a perceived common enemy, the Western democracies.

Though Western governments never admitted they were losing the war on Muslim terrorism, recognition became flagrant to their indigenous populations, the sheer numbers of Muslims participating in terrorist dealings overwhelming Western security forces. Only through inter-government cooperation, and the use of superior surveillance technologies were they able to hang on to the shirttails of the enemy. Parity remained a distant peak never accomplished, let alone getting ahead off in the game. British and American counterintelligence agencies told their masters, containment never worked, but lenient harnessed Western governments shied away from doing the necessary, fearing accusations of racism, and breaking the human rights laws they had imposed on their indigenous citizens without consent, and paradoxically, not sanctioned in Muslim countries. Putting more pressure on the security services, the fractured political stance made it even easier for Muslim terrorists to enact their atrocity campaigns, cognizant if caught, exploitation of the pliant European Court of Human Rights to hold up extradition to countries where the crimes took place, ensured their recurrent freedom from justice. Abysmally, after arrest, many known Muslim terrorists simply went through the law court debacle, coming out free through lack of substantiated evidence to convict them.

Preaching hate and Islamic fundamentalism from his Finsbury Park mosque, known al-Qaeda member Iman Abu Hamza managed to evade extradition from England to stand trial in the United States for over six years. Every time the Home Office made a move to rid him from British shores, scurrilous human rights lawyers played the race and human rights cards in British law courts run by liberal-elitist judges, getting them to grant his right to stay in the UK at the taxpayers' expense. Claiming over two-million pounds in welfare benefits, his extended family lived the life of Riley, his lawyer fees amounting to over one-million pounds, also picked up by the British taxpayer. Typical of the barrage of Muslim clerics left by Western authorities to go about their daily poison spreading, Hamza laughed at their sickly liberalism, using its precepts to garner more impressionable young Muslims into the rank and file of hard-line terrorism.

Contrasting sharply with the ripe-for-exploitation Western regimes, Saudi Arabia, Egypt and Syria adopted a no-nonsense discipline. Employing zero tolerance against Muslim fundamentalists, if Muslim terrorists were killed during anti-terrorist operations, just as the terrorists expected to kill their victims, their taskmasters in the terrorist hierarchy had no complaints about the like-for-like justice measured out to them.

Not playing by the same rules of engagement, the USA, the UK and other European governments were utterly ineffective in stemming and reversing the Muslim terrorism tide. Containment policies and the due process of liberal law gave further advantages to Muslim terrorists, making them sneer at and despise the Western Achilles' heel even more. Though demonstrating aggressors with worldwide domination ambitions had to be mercilessly hunted down with the full might of military force and eradicated, history was ignored by the Western powers, knowing if the Allies had steered the gently, gently tact with Hitler, World War II might have gone on for decades, procrastination resulting in even more people losing their lives. Highly publicised, the generals knew how to end Muslim terrorism for good, but as usual, feeble and traitorous politicians, particularly in Westminster, spurred on by their self-interested agendas, watered down the necessary solution to the pinnacle of banality. As Western citizens became more and more frightened and frustrated with their governments' water-weak response, and capitulation to the blueprints of radical Islam, Muslim terrorism got stronger and stronger.

A beneficiary of Western complacency and appeasement, Basara's resolve for worldwide Islamification intensified with every successful atrocity carried out in Europe. Like all field commanders in the employ of the Muslim Brotherhood and al-Qaeda, he knew if he could dominate his foot soldiers to the summit of delivering and exploding the bomb or WMD, there was little chance of advance detection by Western intelligence agencies. Clubbing together, Muslim terrorist organisations laid substitute trails, counterfeit sorties, and most importantly, the dissemination of fabricated intel, ending with Western security forces chasing their own tails, taking excursions down blind alleys, and making incorrect conclusions regarding terrorist targets. Mixed within the camouflage of falsehoods were the real missions, intended to maximise death and destruction.

Many terrorist field commanders, Basara amongst their number, had argued for the use of tactical-nuclear and germ warfare devices, not caring in the least the blooming outgrowths of such weapons spread much farther afield from the epicentre of their blast. Unlike the politician-like terrorist executive layer, Basara and his fellow officers were fully indoctrinated and pre-programmed soldiers, purely motivated to deal out wide-ranging mayhem, without reservation or concern for its consequences. In effect, field commanders and their expendable human resources provided the battering ram to diminish Western resolve, in preparation for Western leaders requesting concession talks with the Muslim terrorist executive. In Basara's mind, that was the end game, the zenith at which Islamification of the entire world could be institutionalised, the terrorist executive donning diplomat's clothing, and telling the World's peoples, they were now to be governed by Muslim clerics and overlords, and subjected to Sharia Law without redress.

Basara longed for that glorious day, but if he got cut down during its making, he deemed his sacrifice to be necessary and worthwhile.

~

When Saleh arrived, Basara made it very clear he wanted the Ethiopian's clear-cut loyalty in all things. Unlike the relative softness of Mullah Massood back in Nazret, the Tunis Muslim fundamentalists were harsh, exacted blind obedience, and did not brook any dissent or defiance, Basara emphatically stating anyone failing to carry out their orders or betraying them, resulted in the offender being hunted down, and summarily executed.

Quickly evaluating he needed to use all his crafty and calculating powers to induce them into his sincerity, superficially, Saleh went along with their scheme.

Assessing Saleh, Basara's principle responsibility spun around judging if he was made of the right stuff required for a real mission, or whether he lacked the necessary self-sacrificing credential, and thereby only suitable to be allotted a dummy mission, acting as a decoy to the real deal. Suspicious of anyone joining their league, Basara set Saleh dependability tasks. Drawing upon his devious nature to ensure success, he completed the tests to the headman's satisfaction. Remarkably, Basara did not spot Saleh's sly roguishness in any of their early interactions, the Ethiopian's ability to remain believable overriding his innate fear of being found wanting in his fidelity to the cause. Amazed by his abilities to mask off his true intent, his confidence grew to the grade whereby he believed he had the Tunis fundamentalists in the palm of his hand. Subjected to further indoctrination, Basara instructed him, the duty of all true believers was to bring down the West and rid the world of non-Muslims. Responding, Saleh made all the right noises, finally taking any lingering doubt away and convincing Basara of his faithfulness to the cause.

Then without warning, Basara became suspicious about Saleh, weighing his wholehearted dedication was too good to be true.

"You are a very clever man," he declared to Saleh, his tenor deliberate.

"*What?*" the Ethiopian bleated, taken aback by the suddenness of the remark.

"I said," he duplicated, staring deep into Salch's eyes, way past the pupil layer, and into his mind and soul, "you are a very clever man."

Grimacing, still not sure if Basara issued a compliment or a criticism brought about by suspicion, he uttered, "I don't know what you mean."

Receding and smiling thinly, Basara informed, "We have dealt with many Sub-Saharans coming through our ranks on their way to doing Allah's work." Examining Saleh's face, he posed, "I wonder how well you'd stand up to torture, and whether you have the bravery and nerve to take your own life, if you were captured."

"I'd never betray my brothers," Saleh blurted, feeling the need to make a positive retort. "And if I was caught, I'd take my own life."

"Mmmm," Basara murmured, pondering. "I wonder."

"What have I done wrong?" Saleh bawled; his air purposely impassioned but etched with a sliver of concern. "Why are you questioning me like this?"

"You are a little too good to be true. Narrowing his eyes, Basara studied Saleh's face more deeply. "Yes, we demand consummate obedience to the cause, but you, you are like a robot, a machine we programme to do our bidding, executing everything without tangible pleasure, and with meticulous adherence." Pointing his finger in a jabbing action at the new recruit, he contested in a menacing timbre, "That is just too good to be entirely true."

"I don't know what you are getting at," Saleh protested. "I do everything you demand of me." Ceasing the rebuff, the dauntless side of his nature he normally displayed to Basara became overtaken by annoyance and burgeoning fear. "*What is it* you expect of me?" he pressed, his voice rising above its normal pitch. "*What is it* I have done?"

"Nothing," Basara calmly answered. "But I have a feeling that you are not as next to perfect, as you seem."

"I cannot help the way I am," Saleh defended, sweat droplets forming on his brow, "or the way you perceive me."

"I might be wrong," Basara conceded, turning away from him, "but I will be keeping an eye on you." Refacing him, the Ethiopian took the full force of his recriminating look. "Be warned," he coldly whooped. "If you try to trick us, or fail to measure up to our callings, your family will never see you again."

Saleh didn't reply. Sitting down amongst the other fundamentalist novices, he tried to recede into himself, Basara continuing to knit brows at him probing for signs of faithlessness and betrayal.

During the next few days, Saleh felt Basara's eyes on him every time he turned around. Wise to displaying compliance without hesitation became paramount to survive the final part of the mission training, before being let loose to make his departure to Europe, he strode to gain his mentor's approval. Passing all the tests given to him by Basara and other seasoned fundamentalists with flying colours, made the headman reflect he had misjudged the Ethiopian and been unnecessarily hard on him. Using all his guile and cunning to persuade Basara and his proxies he was prepared for whatever task lay ahead, they finally anointed Saleh with praise, saying he met all the requirements. Soon he'd be on his way.

Privately, Saleh had no intention whatsoever of becoming a martyr. Whilst creating the illusion of a dedicated disciple of Allah, ready to make the ultimate sacrifice, in parallel, he prepared his bolt to Europe.

Satisfied Saleh could be trusted, Basara finally told him Holland was his ultimate destination, to take part in a bombing campaign, a revenge mission for what Muslims considered to be an insulting portrayal of the Prophet Mohammed by a national newspaper.

Indifferent to political correctness, the publication ran a series of stories about how Christians were being systematically persecuted and fitted up for anti-Islamic crimes in Pakistan and Bangladesh by pious Muslim clerics, claiming to be acting in accordance with the Koran and the teachings of Mohammed. Markedly juxtaposed with how so-called ethnic and religious minorities were treated in the West, the paper alleged the EU's race relations laws were superimposed on native Europeans to accommodate the likes of bolshie, devious Muslims, but no such quid pro quo equivalent existed in Muslim countries for Christians. Symbiotic to already anti-Muslim resentment by Christian and secular organisations in Holland and other Western European countries, angry about Muslim terrorist atrocities, correspondingly the factual account also ignited widespread condemnation and protests by Muslim immigrants outside the newspaper's offices.

Though an extremely serious matter Western governments should address, they turned a convenient blind eye to the treatment of Christians in Muslim dominated countries, yet again burying their heads in the sand, and afraid of offending Muslims living in their own backyards. Consequently, Blair and Brown, and a whole raft of EU country leaders were portrayed by the Dutch newspaper as duplicitous, mendacious hypocrites in cartoons accompanying the text, and Mohammed depicted as a nefarious oligarch, rubbing his hands with glee after master-minding their seditious treachery.

Enraging Muslims worldwide, it gave the lie to the notion that only Muslim radicals and extremists were intolerant of any criticism of their belief system. In practice, virtually all Muslims, especially those from Yemen through to Pakistan, were just one step away from becoming willing participants in the jihad. More horrifying, rogue Muslim clerics operating in Western Europe stoked up the flames of hostility courtesy of exploiting EU Human Rights Laws, blatantly preaching hate of all non-Muslims and encouraging impressionable young Muslims to become jihadist warriors.

Ignoring the obvious marshalling of Muslim forces aimed against the West, EU politicians stood firm in their conviction, given time, Muslims could be assimilated and harmonised into Christian and secular society. Knowing full well that oil and water never mix, the naive, dishonest and disloyal rhetoric only served to amplify the West's lethargy, strengthening Muslim drive for the Islamification of Europe and beyond.

Disturbed by the hostile reaction, Holland's indigenous citizens knew it'd only be a matter of time before Muslim jihadists took their vengeance out on the Dutch newspaper.

"You will take the ferry from Tunis to Salerno in Italy," Basara told Saleh. "From there, you will make your way to Paris via Lyon by train. There, you will be met by the local Muslim Brotherhood, and maybe al-Qaeda. They will give you orders about your part in a revenge attack on the Dutch newspaper that blasphemed against the prophet Mohammed."

"Can you tell me the contact's name in Paris?" Saleh enquired.

"No need. They will watch out for you at Gare de Lyon rail station."

"What will they ask me to do?"

Basara glared at the Ethiopian. "Whatever the Brotherhood instructs you to do, *you will do it.* Is that clear?"

"Yes," Saleh meekly replied. "And after Paris?"

"Whatever you are told to do, it will happen in

Amsterdam," Basara staunchly trilled, his eyes bulging. Unusual for him, the field commander then became less grave, the severity of his speech tone lightening. "I shouldn't do this, but this is your debut, so I will reveal some of what is going to happen."

"I'd appreciate that," Saleh gibbered, shaking slightly.

"Once you have been given your instructions in Paris, you will meet up with the operational team in Amsterdam. The leader of that team will assign you tasks to be completed."

"You mean, plant a bomb in the newspaper premises?"

"Whatever method of revenge is chosen, it is justified," Basara insisted, peering intensely at the novice again. "We must send a message to the world that Muslims will not tolerate even the slightest blasphemy of Islamic icons."

Notwithstanding the need to sustain his devotion act, Saleh could not help but hang his head low.

"You are supposing a lot of people will be killed and injured?"

Appreciating the gravity of the heinous act, Saleh gaped at the taskmaster blankly, mouth half-open, eyes expanded to their extremities.

"These Christian infidels deserve death," Basara trumpeted. "They have mocked Mohammed, and they are part of a much wider regime opposing Muslim fundamentalism."

Saleh knew what that meant. They did not want to be ruled by Muslims and live under Sharia law, but he did not debate Basara's callous justification for the intended atrocity.

"Examples *must* be made," Basara hissed, his undivided persona enlivened with zest, the blood vessels standing out over his temples. "Muslims everywhere, need to see the Brotherhood is taking revenge, not only for the insult to Mohammed, but for all our defeats at the hands of Christians going back over a thousand years." Removing his sword from its scabbard and thrusting it aloft, he then snarled, "*Death* to all Christians," his enraptured disciples following suit repeating the cry. Grasping Saleh's right shoulder with his free hand, Basara proclaimed, "You will be our instrument. You will be part of our glorious revenge before you enter paradise." Leaving the field commander panting and red-faced with hate, the ominous outburst came as a shock to the would-be bomber.

For the first time since arriving in Tunis, Saleh truly understood Basara was a cold-blooded fanatic, having no hesitation in killing Christians and secular non-believers, if they did not submit to the will of the radical Islamic clerics.

Gulping before resuming a solid stance, he asked, "When do I leave for Salerno?"

"Tomorrow morning, and be aware, Saleh—" As on previous occasions, Basara bore deep into the Ethiopian's eyes, and inwards into his mind and soul. "You will be watched all the way to Paris. You will never see your shadow, but he will be there, ready to take action should you falter."

Finishing the investiture, Basara gave him fictitious Algerian travel documents in the name of Younes Faudel Merak, money for the journey, and a selection of European clothing Saleh packed into his suitcase, to be changed into on arrival in Salerno, the fundamentalists knowing when moving through European societies it was best not to draw unnecessary attention to themselves by wearing traditional Arab attire.

Taking in the gravity of the dilemma he had thrust upon himself, Saleh went to his place of rest. Dawning on him he only had a few hours to make his escape, or Paris awaited him with no opportunity to flee, he called on all his cunning and devious talents to extricate himself from the fray. Deducing to make a successful flight, he needed more money and ancillary European clothing, he plotted to raid a cash box Basara kept hidden behind a loose brick in a wall of the house, and the anteroom used to house a stash of European clothing.

When the house quietened, he felt safe to make his move. Edging his way to the room containing the hidden cashbox, he removed most of its contents, and moved on to purloin a second set of European clothes, stuffing them into his suitcase. Then in the dead of night, he stepped over the sleeping fundamentalists, crept out of the house, past a dosing guard, and made his way through central Tunis, down to the shipping area of La Goulette Port, on the south shores of Lac de Tunis.

Using the forged documentation in the name of Younes Faudel Merak and the stolen money, he planned to acquire passage to either Sardinia, Sicily or Malta. Once in European territory, he'd tell the authorities he was from a minority sect being persecuted by the Ethiopian Government, claim asylum seeker status, and eventually end up in England.

10

SEARCHING FOR PASSAGE

Conscious if he took a scheduled ferry from Tunis, Basara could track him through the synthetic name on his fake passport, instead, Saleh chose to seek a berth from a local commercial shipping company, maybe even offering his services as a deckhand.

Knowing the Hraïria district house always stirred at 5:30 a.m., in preparation for the opening prayers of the day, Saleh figured they'd quickly establish he had fled, Basara reasoning he had been treacherous, and immediately sending out resources to bring him back for judgement and punishment. That meant death on the razor-sharp edge of his blade. He also foresaw Basara checking the cashbox, noting how much money had been taken, and determining Saleh's conduits for his getaway. Working out Saleh did not go to the airport, the fallacious travel documentation permitting the Brotherhood to trace him, for the same reason, he'd realise it also negated a listed ferry gateway to freedom.

Putting himself in Basara's shoes, Saleh saw the headman concluding the escapee had two more options. Either go south across the Sahara to Ethiopia, an unlikely course of action because it needed a Bedouin guide, the land-based journey fraught with danger, or try for transit to Europe through commercial shipping. Saleh saw Basara nominating the latter.

At daybreak, La Goulette Port began to come alive with the hustle and bustle of shipping industry, stevedores and dock labourers going about their business loading goods on to small and medium sized vessels, while their crews readied the ship to get underway. After surveying the readying activities, Saleh made his move. Approaching several crews along the quayside combing for passage, each time they told him no openings for passengers, or for crewing, were available. Trying further down towards Lac Sud de Tunis, yielded the same result. One crewman instructed him to book transportation in advance at the shipping office or contact the shipping line general manager about becoming a crew member. Not bargaining for officialdom, Saleh had assumed small shipping companies to be free from protocol. Knocked back by the actuality, he grasped his plan might not be so easy to execute. If he applied for transit or crew status, it involved paperwork, in turn meaning he could be traced.

About to attempt to become a stowaway, out of the corner of his eye he thought he saw one of the Hraïria district house occupants on the quayside. Ducking down behind freight containers, he cautiously took another peek. Sure enough, he identified Jabar, one of Basara's most trusted lieutenants. Then he clocked Rafik and Wassim, two of the staunchest Muslim fundamentalists in Basara's band of brothers. Resolving there must be others in the La Goulette Port area also tracking him, and probably Basara had assigned further packs to seek out their quarry in other parts of the commercial shipping port, he had to think fast. Whilst considering his plight, he kept low to preclude detection, his precarious position digging deep into his psyche.

Sensing quietness, he slowly lifted his head up, scanning about. When no one faced in his direction, he dived inside a warehouse and climbed onto a stack of freight boxes high above ground level. From his vantage point, he watched Rafik and Wassim 300 yards away down the quayside talking to longshoremen and crews, probably giving them his description, and asking if they'd seen him. Some must have replied in the affirmative, his pursuers heading in his direction, inquiring with those involved in the ship loading workflow.

About to move to a more secure hiding place, suddenly the large doors to the warehouse were rolled shut, Saleh hearing a lock being turned to secure the building. Peeping out of a window presenting a panorama over the docks to the channel leading to the Gulf de Tunis, Saleh saw Rafik and Wassim busy with their search. Then from the opposite side of the quay, Zoheir and Tarek, two more of Basara's henchmen, came into view and began talking to Rafik and Wassim, Saleh rationalising they must have come from the Port de Rades area, adjacent to La Goulette. Upholding his earlier conclusion *vis-à-vis* the Muslim fundamentalists were out in force, investigating all possible breakout avenues he might use, Saleh prepared himself for an extended stay in his refuge. Also joining them, Saleh heard the muffled hubbub of Jabar issuing orders where to hunt next for the Ethiopian.

When his five assailants moved off back in the direction of central Tunis, the fugitive held his position, determining not to leave the warehouse until the heat lessened.

During the day, he considered his alternatives. Those pursuing him had probably given both his real and false names to the quayside workers they talked to, possibly saying he was a thief they were pursuing. Assuming word spread throughout the commercial shipping area, even if he applied for passage or crew status, he might be given away to his shadows. His situation looked more and more untenable.

Broadening far and wide, the Muslim fundamentalists search web intensified in dimensions. Supplemental to core activists like the Basara combine, there were legions of sympathisers in all Muslim States and in the Western countries they had colonised, the Muslim Brotherhood and al-Qaeda differentiating not all Muslims had to be members of fundamentalist units for them to wage jihad. When necessary, this massive lower layer of believers could be called upon to do low grade tasks on their behalf, including monitoring for a traitor to the cause, such as Saleh. Aware of the network scale, the runaway presumed some of the docks workers his pursuers had talked to, must be partisan to the drive for a worldwide Muslim state. They'd be keeping an eye out for him.

With the admission in mind, Saleh determined early the next morning when the warehouse opened, he'd sneak out and try to become a stowaway aboard one of the commercial shipping vessels. Several times during the day, the warehouse re-opened for more freight to be loaded on to vessels, or to store inbound goods. Maintaining his position high above the activity, he listened, trying to pick up any words from the workers indicating they were searching for him.

At dusk, the warehouse doors were rolled shut for a final time, Saleh settling down for the night. Additional to the money and clothes, he had also purloined some food. With quietness reigning over the commercial docks area, he ate his meagre rations to the rumble of waves crashing down on the Port de Rades beach, less than 400 yards away. Filling him with optimism, he derived, on the other end of the waves lay Europe, a warm inner glow coming over him. Smiling to himself, he cogitated, in a few days he'd be in Sardinia, Sicily or Malta, or if lucky, the European mainland of Italy, France or Spain.

After many hours of tossing and turning, he drifted into an uneasy sleep, his dreams brimming with macabre logos proclaiming his fate, and images of Basara slicing off his head. When the squeaky noise of the warehouse doors rolling back invigorated his senses early the next morning, he awoke startled, momentarily forgetting his fix. Still dark, he heard the gruff voices of stevedores discussing the workload ahead and bitching about their employers. Wondering if they'd speak his real or false name, he crept towards them from his interim haven spot. If that occurred, it was proof positive the Muslim fundamentalist's worker ants had been marshalled in the drive to find him.

After a few moments, the shore workers began the business of loading freight from the warehouse onto wagons, their bitty conversations free of reference to the absconder. Other workers then pushed the loaded conveyances the short distance to the quayside for shipboard uploading. Saleh saw his opportunity to become a stowaway. When the stevedores left the warehouse, he took out a European jacket from his suitcase, put it over his traditional Arab garb, descended from his elevated post, then hid in one of the wagons, pulling some soft packaging over him and making sure his suitcase remained hidden. Moments later, he felt it being moved to the quayside. When the wagon came to an abrupt halt, he waited until the clatter made by the worker's footsteps faded away, then emerged from his hideaway, browsing in the direction of the vessel being loaded by the longshoreman and its crew. Out of their line of sight, he climbed down from the wagon with his suitcase, moved forward and stepped onto the gangplank of the vessel, his head crouched down to aid his anonymity. Albeit, in his preoccupation to keep an eye on loading proceedings, he had failed to see a man at the top of the gangplank onboard the vessel.

"*Hey*," the man shouted, "what do you want?" making the Ethiopian freeze and the focus of those loading the vessel drawn to the gangplank.

"Hey, *you*," hollered the man again, moving down the gangplank. "What are you up to?"

Inventing on the hop, Saleh burbled, "Is this the Midnight Blue?"

"The Midnight Blue," the man parroted, stepping further down and fixing Saleh suspiciously. "No, this is the Autumn Moon." Frowning, he bellowed, "What shipping line is the Midnight Blue with?"

"The er...the," Saleh began.

Before he could reply any further, one of the stevedores hailed, "Hey, what's your name?"

Saleh fell totally silent.

"I bet that's him," gabbed the same stevedore. "That's the man Rafik is trying to find. He's a thief."

As the longshoremen began to move in Saleh's direction, he leapt off the gangplank onto the quayside and began to run.

Charging after him, the reverberation thud of the workers footwear on the quayside echoed in Saleh's ears. One of them caught up with him, taking a swing on the run to bring the Ethiopian down. Misdirected, the intended blow caught Saleh's upper arm and neck, making him lose his grip on his suitcase. Tumbling down, his pursuer tripped over it and fell, empowering Saleh to increase his speed.

Turning the corner of a warehouse further up the quayside, he saw a large waste disposal container. Opening its lid, he climbed inside. Seconds later, he heard the cries of the chasing pack, their clamour peaking as they passed his hiding place, then diminishing to a fading hum as they sped on. Discerning they'd quickly calculate he'd taken shelter when they couldn't find him, he clambered out of the container, headed down an alley, and re-concealed himself behind some stacked crates at the entrance to another warehouse, yet to be opened for business. With his heart pounding, occasionally he caught the shouts of his pursuers, still in the act of finding their quarry. When the racket died away, he assumed they'd given up the hunt and returned to the Autumn Moon. He also anticipated the man mentioning Rafik's name getting word to him, they had spotted the thief. Doubtless if he stayed in the La Goulette Port area, it'd only be a matter of time before Basara's men caught him.

Reconciling it was safe to move, he circled around the back of the warehouses, and made his way to the Port de Rades main road, leading to a bridge over a manmade channel in Lac de Tunis. On the bridge, he squinted to his right at the quayside area in the near distance, the men chasing him busily back at work loading the Autumn Moon. On the north side of the bridge, he asked a passer-by for directions to the Carthage commercial docks area on the Mediterranean shoreline. Another area used by both Tunisian and European shipping companies, and thereby probably being monitored by Basara's foot soldiers, he had to risk reconnoitering the locale as a possible thoroughfare for fleeing to Europe.

With the sun rising over the Gulf de Tunis, Saleh moved quickly through the Khereddine district, then into the heart of Carthage before heading to the docks area.

Crouching down behind a goods trailer parked on the access road leading to the docks, he saw a series of suitable vessels along the quayside, all in the process of making ready to embark. Still possessing the fake documentation and money, he'd try to buy passage, or failing that, go for the stowaway routine. Just about to make his move, he saw a couple of faces he appraised he might know and ducked down behind the trailer again, before slowly bobbing his head up. Straining his vision, he recognised Safa and Akeem, two more members of the fundamentalist's ring. Deliberating Basara had all his alternates covered, and more Brotherhood followers dawdled alongside the Carthage docks area in pursuit of him, he had to make a quick decision.

With daylight flowering, he reckoned if he made his move to one of the quayside vessels, he'd be identified and caught. Determining he had to go into hiding until nightfall, then conjure up another scheme for bolting to Europe, he turned, rapidly walked to the nearby old market area of Carthage in El Kram and laid down under a stall.

At mid-morning, when the market trade had matured into full swing, with hundreds of people engrossed in buying and selling goods, he carefully withdrew from his hiding place, unseen by the stall owner, and joined the throng. After buying food from a street seller and hungrily wolfing it down, he then settled down cross-legged amongst the kif users, his head bowed low adding to his intended invisibility.

Blind as to what to do next, by pure chance, he overheard a conversation between two men on the periphery of his position, talking about a marina at Sidi Bou Said, the next district north of Carthage, and only a few miles from his present position. Judging by their palaver, the two men were part of a smuggler gang, intending to sell illegally shipped goods in the Carthage market, before returning to Sidi Bou Said. Immediately, Saleh pictured their trade might provide a vent for his escapade, money being the smugglers only driver.

Following them across the market, discreetly concealing himself behind stalls and shoppers, Saleh made sure they did not see him monitoring them. Meeting a third party, the threesome went into a small café, leaving the Ethiopian hanging around the stalls, pretending to be shopping whilst waiting for them to re-emerge. Constantly on watch for familiar faces, Saleh saw none.

Concluding Basara must have all his resources scrutinising the docks areas for him, rather than the inner districts such as the Carthage market, he felt more secure. For all that, as his resolve to leave Tunis by sea escalated, he remained vigilant.

Emerging from the café, the two men appeared very pleased with themselves. Saleh guessed whatever had gone down must have been a good bargain for both buyer and seller. Heading north through the market, the Ethiopian followed the smugglers at a safe distance, allaying discovery of his presence. Passing the Carthage Amphitheatre and Le Phénix de Carthage, before heading for the Rue du Maroc taking them into the centre of Sidi Bou Said, the two men stayed oblivious to their follower. Walking along Saleh mentally noted significant landmarks, should he need to return to Carthage. As the route cornered the nearby coastline, he knew he'd have to be extra careful. Thorough in all his dealings, Basara would have resources covering all the defector's sea absconding pathways.

Eventually, the contrabandists entered a small house neighbouring the Galerie Ammar Farhat, making Saleh deem he had lost his chance to waylay them. Giving him sight of the house, he hunkered down in a nearby alley, patiently waiting until late afternoon when the two men reappeared, heading to the shoreline through a park area containing the Centre des Musiques Arabes et Méditerranéennes, Saleh following. Talking in small councils, a large crowd of people milled about outside the centre. Pivotal on the twangs and peals emanating from its interior, Saleh adjudged a musical event was about to get underway. Briefly losing his targets as they surged through the crowd, he quickened his pace, reengaging them as they emerged into clear space. Allowing them to join the road on the far side of the park, he then charged after them. Reaching a vantage summit on the road, ahead he saw a marina. Concluding it to be their destination, he knew he had to make his move before they entered the confines of the marina quayside, just in case Basara had it staked out.

Rushing headlong, he hailed, "Excuse me."

Freezing in their tracks, the smugglers immediately deduced

the Tunis police were upon them. Guardedly swivelling around to see Saleh, immediately they knew their worst fears were misplaced. Glancing at each other, they then eagle-eyed Saleh, but said nothing as he advanced upon them.

"Excuse me," Saleh replicated in a more relaxed tone.

"Yes," acknowledged one of the men. "What is it?"

Intending to go for a measured stratagem, instead Saleh ended up becoming flustered, blurting out, "You might be able to help me."

"Help you?" repeated the same man, glaring sternly.

"Yes. I'm seeking passage to a European port."

Having been accosted in the past by others seeking covert transportation, the two men bedded perceptive expressions, mindful they now had primacy over the confrontation.

"What makes you anticipate we can help you?" enquired the second man, his body language stiff and hard-core as he spoke.

"I er," Saleh stuttered in a faltering lilt, unsure how his unsolicited address might unfold.

Glowering, the first man yapped, "*Yes.*"

"I—" Saleh began, before licking his dry lips. "I saw you in the Carthage market, I thought you might—"

Before he could go any further, the second man grabbed his jacket lapel, dragging the Ethiopian to him. "You were in the market?"

"Yes."

"What did you see?"

"Nothing...I saw nothing."

"Then *why* did you follow us?" quizzed the first man.

"I, I...I have money," Saleh gibbered, arching his head away from the second man's face and pouting.

Slightly releasing his grip, the second man flicked his head at his associate.

"What do you want from us?" babbled the first man.

"I think you might be able to help me get to Europe."

"Why?" the second man exacted, retightening his clutch on the Ethiopian.

Deciding to come clean, Saleh revealed, "Because you are smugglers."

Alarmed, the two men scoured the foreground then behind Saleh, assuming they were the subject of an entrapment sting, police officers suddenly emerging from nowhere to descend upon them.

"Who are you?" blared the first man.

"I'm *not* with the Tunis police, if that's what you suppose. I'm a refugee from Ethiopia, intent on making a new life in England."

Laughing out loud at the docile declaration, the two men found renewed confidence. Issuing Saleh a condescending leer, the second man released his grip, sure they were dealing with someone not wishing to compromise their illegal activities.

"A poor refugee," the first man mocked, "from Ethiopia?"

"Yes."

Taking up the interrogation in an equally dismissive tone, the second man probed, "Where did a poor refugee from Ethiopia get money from?"

Glimpsing at each other again, they grinned knowing whatever Saleh formulated, it'd be a lie.

"I, I erm…" Saleh started before falling silent.

"Huh, no matter," the second man snapped out. "How much have you got?"

Still having his wits about him, Saleh parried, "How much do you want to get me to a European port?"

"You have travel documentation?" pushed the first man.

"Yes."

Again, the smugglers exchanged insightful deportments.

"Come with us to the Sidi Bou Said Marina," bid the first man. "We might be able to help you."

"I can't go any further," Saleh yelped. "I'm being pursued, and those after me might have watchers at the marina." Hesitating, he opened his hands in a pleading gesture. "I need a place to hide up before nightfall. It will be safer under cover of darkness to go to the marina."

Breaking into whispers, the two men kept a shady eye on Saleh. Recognising a watershed moment, he felt totally alone in the world, whatever the two men decided either having him irretrievably falling off its edge or fulfilling his ambition.

"Alright," expressed the second man, his manner casual, even encouraging. "We have a place for you to hide until dusk. Come with us."

Feeling more assured, Saleh walked back to the park with the smugglers.

"What is the name you are travelling under?" pressured the first man.

"Younes Faudel Merak."

"*Hah*!" exclaimed the second man, tittering. "Do you know the name Faudel means honest?"

Staring back blankly at him Saleh resided mute, distinguishing honesty and he rarely if ever fitted in the same glove.

"That's not your real name, is it?" the first man knowingly posed.

"No."

"Okay," he favourably responded. "It is not an issue."

"What do I call you?" Saleh enquired.

"I am Jamel," the first man answered, "and this is Azzam."

"Where are you taking me?"

"There is an outbuilding adjacent to the music centre," Jamel explained. "We will hide you there."

Inside the outbuilding, Jamel and Azzam told Saleh they had availability to a motorised sailing vessel leaving the next morning for Cagliari, Sardinia. Before Saleh stepped aboard the vessel, its captain needed to see his travel documentation, and required an upfront payment of 10,000 dinars. Baulking at the price, the escapee tabled a much lower digit for the service. Adamantly refusing to budge on the number, Jamel and Azzam made it clear no reduction in the asking price was possible. Fathoming he had no other way out, Saleh handed over the 10,000 from the stash he had stolen, plus his made-up documents, including the Algerian passport Basara had given him in the name of Younes Faudel Merak.

"We will be back for you this evening at eight," Azzam advised.

"I haven't a watch," Saleh highlighted.

Signifying to the far side of the outbuilding, Azzam enunciated, "You see that window?"

"Yes."

"You can see the clock on the side of the music building wall from that window. It is illuminated at night."

Before departing, Azzam and Jamel said they'd make the arrangement with the motorised sailing vessel captain for the Ethiopian's passage, and he should not leave his place of sanctuary until they returned.

As the hours passed, Saleh visualised himself boldly walking into a Cagliari police station to claim asylum seeker status. After that, England and his free-loader lifestyle awaited.

Darkness began to descend. Stepping in front of the window, he gazed out at the music building clock reading 7:45pm. Envisioning Azzam and Jamel returning to collect him, he felt sanguine. Howbeit, the appointed rendezvous time came and went, his benefactors not showing. Saleh's mind started to race. Had the police detained them? Had they been caught by the Muslim fundamentalists, or worst of all, scarpered with his travel documents and money? By 8:30pm, he could wait no longer.

Leaving the outbuilding, he made his way across the park, over the adjoining road, and headed for the Sidi Bou Said Marina. Just short of its entrance, he saw an indistinct mélange of figures in the murky distance. Keeping low he went ahead, dodging in and out between motor and sailing vessels up on the quayside pending hull maintenance. Through the dimness and within forty yards of the gathering, he picked out Azzam and Jamel, Basara and six other Muslim fundamentalists encircling them, making his heart leap into his mouth. Not quite able to hear the dialogue, he judged by the smugglers body language they were bartering with Basara.

While Saleh trusted his apparent rescuers to fulfil their end of the deal, they had no intention of delivering transit to Sardinia.

At the marina, Azzam and Jamel made enquiries appropriate

to an Ethiopian refugee-fugitive, finding out someone probably going under the name Younes Faudel Merak was wanted by a clique of Muslim fundamentalists for theft. After stashing Saleh's documentation and the 10,000 dinars back at the house neighbouring the Galerie Ammar Farhat, they then sent word through a third party to the Muslim fundamentalists, saying they might know the whereabouts of the man wanted for theft. Though in no way sympathetic to the radical Muslim cause, the two petty criminals saw a further opportunity to make more money out of Saleh's misfortune.

Now they were haggling with Basara about a price to be paid to betray his hideout. Saleh knew Basara brooked little defiance. It came as no surprise when the field commander ordered his men to beat the scamps and hold razor sharp blades to their throats. Immediately, Azzam and Jamel relented, both pointing in the direction of the Centre des Musiques Arabes et Méditerranéennes, before being pushed in the theatre's direction by Basara's men. Crouching down behind a mid-sized motor cruiser to conceal himself, Saleh watched as the group passed the maintenance area, ruminating once Basara discovered he was not where Azzam and Jamel had left him, the rascal's lives would soon be over.

When they'd faded from sight, the Ethiopian moved silently back to the marina entrance, ogling both ways along the road as if in search of inspiration. With his documentation gone and surrendering a quarter of the stolen money, he had no idea what to do next, but something inside told him to head back south to central Tunis.

11

ESCAPISM AND BEYOND

Happily for Glyn, Poseidon provided many opportunities for escapism. Supernumerary to the distractions offered by sunsets and the stars, the general movement of the boat made it easy for the crew to drift-off and explore the deeper recesses of the mind, finding what had been waiting to alight under suitably releasing stimulus. Shore visits also presented the occasional astounding and succulent nugget.

Before the ship's company met the Oran merchant whose family once owned an estate at Lac de Telamine, they witnessed a religious rite outside the Mosque of Hassan Basha. Whilst listening to frenzied music played by an accompanying wind, string and tympani octet, participants danced into an irresistible trance, a liberal consumption of Algerian kif helping ferment the effect.

Sharing his impressions with them, the crew got talking with a local onlooker. Witnessing the sacrament many times, he couched once a participant's mind had been freed from its anchorage, visionary release followed, its purpose religious, along the lines of achieving oneness with the deity.

When the ceremonial took hold, Glyn noticed both the dancers and musicians developed a detached transcendence deportment about them, initial calm poise turning to shaking convulsion as the dynamic matured.

"How long does the trance last?" he murmured.

"For as long as the musicians play," the local stated.

"Have you participated?" he enquired, gesturing at the ritual players.

"Yes, many times."

Gaping at the rite, his curiosity barely concealed, Colin excitedly pressed, "Did you see the face of God?"

"That, and many other things," articulated the local.

His keenness growing, Colin moved onwards. "Do you think they'd let me join in?"

Amazed by the petition, the local stood back taking in Colin. "Are you a believer?"

"Not exactly."

Grimacing, the local quivered his head. "Then no."

Intervening, Jeff ushered Colin aside. "It's best you don't get involved. This chap is being as diplomatic as he can be. The amenity is for Moors and Berbers only."

Overhearing, the local annunciated, "Your friend is right, best just to spectate."

Frustrated, Colin sucked in air sharply. Resigned to non-participation, he regained his usual calm indicating his acceptance to the local.

With the dancers fuelled on kif, the trance progressed as the musicians played, their skill, to produce diminuendo, so as to slowly bring the venturers back to actuality. Abrupt stopping of the music could result in an adverse reaction, sending the dancers screaming as the idyllic state avalanched into sensibility. Dawning on Glyn the custom was an Arabic form of escapism, respected by believers and bystanders alike, he nodded in appreciation.

All the same, the city mullahs had outlawed the practice, participants employing others to keep tabs on the authorities. Despite the vigilance, sometimes the religious police intervened, broke up the rite, and the avalanche strike ensued. Beguiled by the positive aspects of the observance, trance seekers deemed it to be a worthwhile risk.

Dissecting deeper, Glyn perceived the crew were never going to come close to that kind of escapism pleasure. Apart from alcohol, no drugs capable of delivering, enhancing and accelerating the desired meditative state were allowed on Poseidon. Like for Glyn, those studying Buddhism and the teachings of the *Bhagavad-Gita* were convinced long-standing meditation coupled with near starvation could generate and realise the same result. Subsuming themselves in the ultimate revelation by crossing the threshold and reaching out to Hesse's *Brahmin Siddhartha*, pure enlightenment distilled upon them. Often discussed when off-watch on Poseidon, principally at sunset when a profound transitional state existed between day and evening, propitious for such deliberation, the juxtaposition sustained their fascination.

By far the most proficient at accomplishing an enigmatic state through meditation, Colin's desire to see the face of God drove his dedication, though as for all of them, the starvation element directed at deranging the senses further was beyond him. Sea air produced ravenous appetites, the smell of cooked food coming from the galley just too hard to resist.

Submissive to the limitation, in place of the ultimate revelation, they found other mediums for intellectual and physical escapism.

~

Some people Glyn knew back in Blighty were extremely complex, or at least the modern world produced unnecessary complexity in them, leading to extreme mood swings verging on the schizophrenic.

One girl from his past firmly alleged all men were bad, and not to be trusted, even when the voicing was demonstrated not to be true. Seemingly obliterating her enterprises, she also believed the entire world opposed her, the tilt at paranoia cementing her melancholia.

Take her away from her blinkered environment, and she blossomed, her innate femininity shining through. Laughing and dancing with joy, she became human, escapism liberating her from self-imposed shackles. Left to stew in her mushrooming delusions, her arcane demons dominated and destroyed, leaving her hollow and unfulfilled. Not a happy ending, as Glyn later discovered, heading for the abyss, her dark side overpowered and ruled her psyche, making her nasty and obnoxious.

Once, a perfect white angel, capable of flight through imagination, after the demons took hold, she became caged and chained in her self-made insular universe, a streak of pure evil overriding her otherwise gentle nature. Hurtling into the spin doctor's maelstrom, a victim of PC socialisation, and only capable of uttering 'Newspeak'-like responses from the 'Ministry of Truth' to any issue or proposition, escapism became impossible for her. One of the new liberal elite's re-programmed androids, she lost all sense of reality, her frontal lobes under tightly connected remote-control by the metropolitan media at large.

Growing up, Glyn chronicled his parents showed consistent behaviour when dealing with all matters, including himself. Their cheerful carriage delineated by confidence and dignity represented a microcosm of society, England at the national level stable and even in terms of personality and tone. A unifying thread ran throughout the country connecting everybody. Whether rich or poor, all were English. Back then, people were much happier than the twenty-first century's dystopia mixed breeds. Little of the played-up angst constantly bombarding TV screens under the Blair-Brown reign, or lurid newspaper headlines driving people to the brink of suicide interfered with their lives.

England was still England, replete with football in the winter and cricket in the summer, fantastic music from the Fab Four, holidays in St. Ives and the Dales, country pubs without piped music or gaming machines, and most essentially, freedom of cogitation and action. Admired, even mimicked by much of the outside world, Englishness and nationwide attributes were taken for granted.

Escapism became an easy exercise, the English verging on it relentlessly through existentialism, and experimentation in the arts, industry and commerce. Thresholds were vigorously blurred between reality and the Holy Grail just out of reach, but with a little invention blooming into the attainable. In those terms, historians gauged English society to be in a golden age, the renaissance liberated as an antidote to the austerity of the inaugural post-WWII years. Everyone wanted it from Harold Macmillan to John Harvey-Jones, Mary Quant to John Lennon. Every walk of life, endeavour and appetite found an entrepreneurial and innovative voice to push barriers into new territories, symbol of the supersonic jet age Concorde an instantly recognisable motif worldwide, the flagship proclaiming a pioneering Shangri-La. Anything was possible, the nation inspired, political correctness decades away from invention.

Those freedoms creating the new renaissance were gone in Glyn's current world. Imperceptibly, people had been disciplined into regulated, template-defined cognitive processes, designed to preclude unique ideas and action. Surging through England like a Nazi Panzer division, the reformation hungrily depleted any asseveration aimed at free thought, excellence and high standards. Concurrently birthing the rise of the mediocrity in all walks of life, the Blair-Brown totalitarian ideal, sanctioned for ulterior reasons by the Illuminati, denied the possibilities by demanding outright and unequivocal conformity to their imposed status quo, made categorical by subjective law. Original brainwork challenged the oligarchy and thereby had to be eradicated by mass indoctrination through the BBC and partially State-funded Channel 4, plus manipulation of the paper and internet news media. Everyone must be a roundhead, cavaliers banned, escapism frowned upon. Albeit condemned as non-conformist, escapism uncovered gaping loopholes exposing the absurdity of the PC doctrine. Consequently, it had to be outlawed and those advocating or practising its disciplines, marginalised by denial to the media to present their view, or ostracised as anti-PC heretics by an army of PC-inflamed zealots.

The more Glyn experienced modern Blighty life with the people he knew, the more they altered and ultimately disappointed. Consumed with a life-style set often unwittingly absorbed from modern society at large, they became sterile and impotent, individuality sucked out of them and replaced by a cloned substitute, blandly elevating its hand in salute and uttering the required words in response to tick box, homogenised and brutally imposed New Labour and EU diktats.

Once happy go lucky in outlook, they adopted acumens given to them by loaded TV soaps and politicised newsreaders, or worse still, hectoring government spin doctors. Outwardly incapable of adjudicating for themselves, they worried about their health, their diet, their hairstyle, their golf swing, their career, what their wife or girlfriend said or didn't say, and a host of other irrelevancies and nonsense. Wringing their hands, they contemplated what to say and what not to say, so as not to offend certain factions made holy cows by the Government and the media. They even agonised over what to wear, how they must behave, and what acceptable understandings to hold about every blessed issue under the sun. Like in *Invasion of the Body Snatchers*, they had been taken over, their minds subjugated to someone else's will. Perfectly regular people devoured by external forces, unable to resist like in a nomadic Kafkaesque nightmare, they made Woody Allen's paranoia look normal.

Escapism for them had been deleted from their options menu.

Typical of the psychosis, one of Glyn's younger work colleagues sought his guidance on a girlfriend problem, what he described, not unusual in the burgeoning boyfriend-girlfriend relationship context. Attempting to make light of a trivial issue, Glyn put a hand on his colleague's shoulder, and tongue in cheek voiced, 'You have to understand, women are not like normal people.' Laughing, his colleague suddenly realised the problem he described was not so bad after all. In fact, it did not exist. Like many modern people, he simply over-analysed and fretted over a perfectly normal occurrence. Intentionally promoting politicised subliminal messages, he had seen the cast of soap operas act that way, and understood from TV pundits it was quite normal, even expected.

How on Earth, Glyn ruminated, had it got to the degree whereby they were all candidates for the psychiatrists' couch, their inevitable visit brought on by neurotic and dysfunctional brain waves? So commonplace, he rationalised it must truly be institutionalised and societal driven by the media, advertisers, and the infernal, interfering nanny-state Government.

Wrestling *ad infinitum* with the irrationalities back in Blighty, Glyn and Steve saw no end to the tawdry campaign to impose the Illuminati's New World Order autocracy, replete with its global, liberal-elitist puissance, the wedge ever-thickening. Constantly shocked by its impact on people they had known for most of their adult lives, but reconciled to the detrimental outcome enduring until the dictatorial PC fascists could be overthrown and eradicated, they soldiered on in the hope a Churchillian-like messiah might rise, and reclaim England for ordinary English people again.

Only then could escapism be restored to the options menu.

∽

Being a naturally theatrical bunch, Poseidon's crew spontaneously acted out scenes from *Lawrence of Arabia* or performed the *Sheik of Araby* aboard the schooner whilst wearing Arab garb acquired in Tangiers and Ceuta, the enactment producing no end of hilarity and impulsive behaviour, all in the name of escapism.

Much to the consternation of both Berbers and Europeans alike, Poseidon entered port at Melilla with her crew reprising Wilson, Keppel and Betty's Sand Dance, replete in Arab dress.

Passing a moored-up catamaran, its astonished crew became frozen in mid-action performing deck cleaning duties at the spectacle onboard Poseidon.

"We have exotic merchandise for sale, the finest silks and satins," Ed shouted. "Women can also be arranged for a moderate fee."

From Ed's accent, the catamaran crew discerned they were English, and responded with orders for burnous, djellaba, kaftan and thwarb, all traditional North African Arab garments. Poseidon even had one request for a voluptuous courtesan. Accommodating the buyer, Tom did his best rendition of the sought goods, both crews bursting into laughter at his antics.

Conducted with good nature, the encounter began to seal a cordial, bi-lateral association.

After Poseidon berthed at the Gerencia Territorial del Catastro del Melilla harbour, the Englishmen met the catamaran crew on the quayside. Typical for sailors of European origin, the rendezvous facilitated immediate camaraderie between the crews. Independent of where they hailed from, their undivided European identity made for comradeship, storytelling and communistic social occasions. Though the seniors and the newcomers invariably got kicks out of their interactions with North Africans, sometimes it became a blessed relief to talk to someone from their home continent.

Of Spanish and Portuguese origin, the cat's crew had embarked from Almeria where the craft was registered, their buccaneer-like ascendency and peculiarities typified by an assortment of roguish beards, reminding Glyn of seventeenth century pirates Blackbeard and Henry Morgan. Her captain, Armando Castillo Rodriguez, told Poseidon's crew they had hit upon a very punishing crossing, the cat at sea for sixteen hours the previous day to cover the 130 nautical mile sail.

"As it invariably does in this part of the Med," Armando emphasised, "the prevailing westerly wind made us take up a southerly vector to improve speed, before we picked up shelter from the Bou Mahroud peninsula, and tacked about a south-west-west heading to enter Melilla harbour."

Arriving close to exhaustion, they berthed then made straight for La Muralla on the Mirador de Florentina, desperately in need of sustenance and refreshment.

"It's a really good restaurant," acclaimed one of the cat crew during the combined quayside confabulation. "We've been using it for years."

Always one for making new acquaintances, Jeff advocated, "Why don't we all get together for dinner this evening?"

"Yes, why don't we," Armando endorsed. "We could do with some entertainment.

"The La Muralla?" Jeff suggested, also familiar with the famous, high-grade Spanish bistro.

Turning to his crew, Armando broke into a brief discourse in Spanish. Addressing Jeff again with a fulsome smile, he cordially consigned, "Though La Muralla is excellent, you'll enjoy El Caracol Moderno II even more."

Jeff cast a quizzical mien at Ed. "We don't know that one, do we?"

"No, it's new to me." Ed swaying his head in accord.

"You will not be disappointed," Armando persuaded, his mischievous grin implying past pleasure of the venue could enthral Poseidon's crew.

"Can you give us directions?" Jeff requested.

"It's situated at the intersection of Calle de Poeta Salvador Rueda and Calle de Mendez Nunez. You can't miss it."

"*Oh*," Ed exclaimed. "Has it got a Spanish flag flying in its forecourt?"

"Yes, that's right."

"Ahh," Jeff muttered. "Indeed, we do know where it is. Mmmm—" Grinning at Armando, he tendered, "We've often talked about using that restaurant, then nominated a conservative selection and gone for the better known La Muralla."

"Right. Well, here's a chance for you to see what makes it exceptional," Armando promoted.

Though the European colonials had long departed North Africa, a few cultural outposts were perpetuated, El Caracol Moderno II amongst them becoming an oasis for lovers of high-calibre Spanish cuisine and a magnet for those craving temporary escapisms from Arab culture.

Entering the restaurant in the evening, Jeff and Ed immediately discriminated between what made El Caracol Moderno II different from La Muralla. Though both were ornately decorated in the traditional Spanish style, the dynamic of El Caracol Moderno II had been aggrandised with Castilian dancers and a small acoustic orchestra, creating a rarefied atmosphere reminiscent of early nineteen-thirties Iberian chic and sophistication.

"Oh, a floor show," Ed whooped, brightly radiating as the entertainment materialised. "This is good."

"Unusual in this part of the world," Jeff noted. Swivelling on his heels to hail the newcomers, he blared above the background din, "This is going to be one of the dining highlights of your Med journey."

"*Jeff*," they heard Armando shout, gesturing at them. "Over here."

Shaking the Spaniard's hand, Jeff praised, "Wow, you were right, Armando. This is very much at variance with the La Muralla, but in a highly cultivated way."

"Yes, as you can see from its clientele, it holds attraction for both locals and foreigners."

Taking ganders into the restaurant's depths, Poseidon's crew watched Europeans and rich Arabs enjoying the lively entertainment as they wolfed down Spanish *haute* cuisine dishes.

"Come my friends," Armando urged, "I have arranged for a table to take all of us."

Stepping into the central diners' area, the Englishmen reacquainted themselves with the cat's Spanish and Portuguese contingent. Complemented by the invigorating atmosphere created by the floor show imbuing them with nostalgia and yearning for the past, the two ship's companies gorged themselves silly on Spanish food and wine. Never ebbing, the entertainment constantly drip-fed them with divinations of long ago La Mancha, *Don Quixote*, and Columbus setting sail for the New World from Palos de la Frontera. In that instant, they were no longer in North Africa. They had been supplanted into a Seville backwater, their minds transported to a traditional Andalusian backdrop. If they stepped outside, they envisaged greetings from conquistadors and gypsy queens. A breakpoint moment of pure escapism from their North African space-time coordinates, it fired their imaginations with fantasies about the faraway Iberian Peninsula, and its vivid history and heritage.

Using the occasion to discuss their respective voyages to date with their opposite numbers, Poseidon's crew heard what Armando and his compatriots had been up to. Defined by sparky interchanges, bellyache inducing seafaring yarns, and several unsuccessful cracks at consuming wine directly from a carafe, as

Jeff predicted, the night became one of the most memorable highlights of the ecumenical pilgrimage. Joking the Englishmen were not wearing their Arab gear, the Iberians asked about the promised Arab clothing for sale, and more essentially, the voluptuous woman?

Mimicking the Humphrey Bogart character Rick from the film *Casablanca*, Steve grilled Armando. "*Who are you really, where did you come from, and where are you going?*"

"Ahh," Armando jubilantly replied, "our new-found friend is a film buff. I too can quote or misquote lines from *Casablanca*." Cracking, he slapped Steve on the shoulder as a mark of nouveau comradeship then said, "I will not couch my reply in geographical location appellations, but more in the metaphysical sense."

"Now you're talking our language," Glyn heralded.

"You too are inner space travellers?"

"Since joining Poseidon," he pronounced, pride evident in his vocalisation, "we've all become pioneers in that domain."

"Good," the Spaniard lauded, "it's the only place to be. My Arab friends often tell me, we Westerners have little aptitude when it comes to truly testing the metaphysical. But I've been browsing that space for many years. It dispenses the antidote to the stark reality and the disappointments of the physical world."

"Can you share some of your acmes with us?" Glyn nudged.

"Of course, it's my pleasure."

Recalling a plethora of his marvellous and surprising inner-space wayfaring jaunts, Armando had Poseidon's crew enthralled. Accumulating them since his first voyage over two-score years earlier, some were drug induced from his nascent sailing period, Arabs showing him the delights of kif, and how it released the argonaut into mind exploration. Since meeting a Nepalese girl, versed in the art of Buddhism and the role of mantras for effectuating oneness with the great deity, he had meditated daily, and married her.

"Even in rough seas," he appointed, "I can find a place off-watch to lose myself in the practice. Many of my crew also follow the doctrine."

"Not gone the whole hog, and shaved your head then?" Ed spotted.

"No," he corroborated. "Though I love my religion, I am far too vain to shave off my hair. Facial and head hair is traditional in Iberian culture. They upgrade a man's gravitas, defining him, and giving him some individuality."

"I couldn't agree with you more," Steve supported. Since Cadiz, he had not been near a razor, his normal clean-shaven front becoming supplemented with a beard and moustache. "I might just keep my full set, when we return to Blighty," he declared, playing with his David Bellamy-like facial expansions.

Not the only newcomer to go native, the last time any of them had visited a barber or stood close to a razor was back in England. Nobody had counselled, they let their hair grow or foster facial fuzz. It just seemed to be another unsaid collective factor, a vehicle for self-expression beyond them in their civvy worlds, the unopposed need for compliance resulting in clean-shaven faces and shortish hair being essential constituents of their business uniform. Going through their rebellious hair period long ago, Jeff and Ed fully understood the newcomers need to remove conventional shackles, if they were going to find something within them, they knew did not exist back in Blighty. Facial hair growing became an emblem of the covet, a defiant statement designating they were in search mode, no longer restricted by compartmentalisation.

"As well as an adventure, this sea trek you are on is a voyage of internal discovery," Armando advanced. "Without back-home distractions, it's easier to find time for meditation. It might be difficult, but when you're England bound, keep up your search for inner space wandering." Taking in Poseidon's crew, he assimilated their glow. "I can see you are a happy crew. Don't let it lapse when you rejoin your professions and loved ones. That's my advice."

Acknowledging in full agreement, the newcomers fathomed their pursuance of escapism, something they distinguished to be unattainable in the Republic of Blair and Brown, had become an integral part of their sabbatical. Resolving to extend hunting the blissful quarry down, ravenously feeding on its fruitful loins, they'd take enough of the liberating nectar back with them to substantiate the habit on return to Blighty.

A joyous bunch, the cat crew added new dimensions to the newcomer's depictions of the Med sailing community. Everyone agreed if their paths crossed again, the cat crew would dress in the style of Napoleon Bonaparte and Marie Antoinette, if the Englishmen reprised their Arab garb, and Tom impersonated a voluptuous woman. Roaring with laughter at the prospect, the two crews parted on a high note.

~

Another regular Poseidon pastime providing escapism for the crew centred on acted out role play, the ship's company tabling names of famous people thrown into a hat, each of them then taking potluck, dipping into the receptacle for a headliner to be impersonated.

To enrich the display, twenty-four hours were allowed for show preparation and prop evolution. Invariably performed on return from dinner ashore towards the witching hour, the crew copiously relaxed after loose intoxication and thereby were confident of providing good humour, if not precision entertainment, the theatre mutating into a mix of alter ego exhibition and exaggerated grandeur. During the session, points were awarded for performance and the proficiency to gain audience participation, leading to prizes donated by Jeff and Ed, usually more alcohol.

Steve had drawn the role of Henry V, 'Henry Vee', as he called it under the influence of North African beer. Before the show, he emulated chain mail from spent tin cans, telling his audience to use their ingenuity concerning the prop. Whilst reciting lines from the Shakespearean play in his best Lawrence Olivier lilt, he thrust a sword purchased in Algiers above his head for dramatic punch, and to encourage onlooker assistance.

Starting into *Once more into the breach, dear friends, once more*, his comrades began ad-libbing on Henry's famous speech.

Stiffen the sinews, summon up the blood became 'stiffen up the main brace, summon up the supper', followed by impersonations of sea sickness. *Sheathed their swords for lack of argument* rolled out as, 'Sheathed their manhood for want of opportunity'. Falling about laughing as Steve resolutely carried on impervious to their japes, his passion play ended with *Follow your spirit and upon this charge*, the ships company rallying and chiming in with, *Cry God for Harry, England and St. George* followed by further malformed repeats of 'Cry God for aunt Sally, Johnnie Walker and more cheddar cheese'.

Triumphing, Steve walked away with the night's prize, without any of them upstaging him, his escapism complete and compulsive on account of crew cooperation, and thereby a shared high.

～

People play many parts on the stage of life, adapting into the various roles to be played; mother, father, child, student, worker, manager *et al.* Learning the maxim early in life, Glyn also witnessed people transformed dependent on who they were with and their footing with the other person, or within a corps.

While at university, he ran with both the rugby crowd and the wine club, the only person in the former also a member of the latter, the way he conducted himself in the fellowship of rugby players very different to when making an informed appraisal, more a guess, pertaining to the attributes of a *Chateau neuf du Pape*. Most of his contemporaries computed the two denominations to be mutually exclusive. In their stereotypical mind-sets, rugby union players were boisterous, brusque, heavy-set, flag of St. George waving, no-nonsense alpha males, downing gallons of beer and rogering anything that moved. Conversely, wine connoisseurs were sophisticated, slight-set even effeminate, high-pitched voice academics, conducting an insular bibliomaniacs life, and plausibly, clandestine MI5 agents. Fervently disagreeing, Glyn stipulated neither interpretation held intercontinental validity; a free spirit could come to rest on any pursuit furnishing some form of exploit or illumination, and any demarcation was a sign of erecting artificial barriers. Tending to the pseudo-intellectual, few undergraduates had an opposing retort to his insight.

Digging deeper into the ingrained outlook, Glyn reckoned it sad, especially for the university set, such diverse distractions were envisioned to be contradictory. For most undergraduates, belonging to the one bevy automatically ordained a veto on the second pack. At the time he mused, as people matured, such narrow-minded understandings dissipated, enabling inclusivity for a wide variety of vastly different activity divisions. By the time he climbed aboard Poseidon, he still loitered disappointed, escapism for the insular improbable, even if they had Einstein comparable I.Qs.

Of the same mind as himself on this issue, at the double, Glyn and Steve enumerated their new-found shipmates were also cut from the same bedrock. Each had multiple diversions, confounding most people owing to their diversity and unrelated connection from one pastime to the next. None had affinity to any of the mainstream canons and popular modernist philosophies. Like Glyn, they were all disciples of Bob Dylan's don't-follow-leaders ethic, borderline anarchists refusing to fly someone else's flag, oblivious of the colour or cause. Non-conformity of cognition and turn-down of the ruling media broadcast message in most things, a virtual bible decree to them. The more they were told to uphold the world protocol standpoint, the more they rebelled against it. Espousing the indisputable opposite to show they never condoned and conformed to diktats considered alien to their sensibilities, and against their country's best interests, they resided outside the pen containing neatly indoctrinated sheep.

∾

One evening while off-watch in Poseidon's saloon, Glyn and Steve talked about their escapism journals, and the concept of misjudging people hinged on assumption.

"Jim Powell, a friend of mine from back home in Lancaster," Glyn began to explain, "used to sit in the George & Dragon with his girlfriend, studying people coming into the riverside pub. Contingent on the car they showed up in and their garb, Jim and his girl made rudimentary estimations *vis-à-vis* the pigeon's socio-economic rank, and what they did for a living. Sometimes they tested their theories by initiating a powwow with the patsies over a few drinks."

"I imagine they mostly got the results wrong," Steve ascribed.

"Quite. Often, they discovered their earlier assumptions were radically off beam. However, it was a splendid social experiment, so I indulged in the pastime with my girl of the time, plus Jim and his."

"Were your classifications any better?"

"No, but what intrigued me, was the wide variance coming from four assessors relating to the people we evaluated, and subsequently befriended. Sometimes, we told them we had tried to calculate their societal eminence, based on car type and dress code. It often produced hilarious results and stimulating conversation for both spectators and targets. However, the crux and quintessentially the lesson learnt was, don't assume temperament traits and assumptions of wealth or lack of it, grounded on prime glimmerings or dress sense."

"Hhmm, I can see your line of determination. Some people aspire to retreat from that constant mantle, and cast aside social fetters."

"Yep, quite right. Anyway, it was one of my early excursions into escapism."

"You know, we all assume an aura and a part," Steve upheld, as if the deposition troubled him. "And even a dialect quality with a role, or a responsibility commensurate with the undertaking. Here on Poseidon, we have a certain dress criterion, a specific word set, and a community model essential for life onboard. Without it, we couldn't function. It's paramount, even natural, but it does serve to mask off a person's real self...you never quite know who you are dealing with."

"Oh yes, assuredly you're right on that score," he concurred. "I can offer something else grounding the opinion."

"Go on."

"My sales director's baseline stance is affected to instil belief and confidence in both the sales team and our customers. To accomplish those twin goals, my accentuation is measured, calm, but with a touch of authority, and my uniform comprises a tailored suit, plain shirt, conservative tie and black shoes, the infallible tools needed to participate in the game. However, beneath the veneer, I'm an entirely multifarious person, but I'm not alone." Waggling an outstretched finger, he conjectured, "I'd wager the description applies to most people."

"I agree about the overt chicanery. It was the same for me at Ove Arup & Partners. But on a related subject, to be frank, I found the executive dress formula stultifying. When I'm not in front of clients, I much prefer the more casual attire my assistant MD role allows at the family construction firm. But I'll admit, both are uniforms, dress adages we assume to befit the role we play."

"We wear uniforms all the time," Glyn asserted. "But most people live transparently to the compliance. Jeans and a t-shirt are just as much a uniform, as a suit. It's all about creating a predictable identity, allowing entry into any assortment. We gauge what is befitting founded on the undisputed convention, and dress accordingly."

While examining his latest artefact purchases from the bazaars, Colin had been half-listening to their repartee. Pausing his inspection, he piped up, "What do you mean by, uniform?"

"Hah, if you're going to join in," Glyn proposed, "we might as well get comfortable."

Sitting at the saloon table, the threesome opened a case of *San Miguel* from the fridge, sipping on the beer throughout their debate. "If I'm going to see Jeff Beck at the Royal Albert Hall," Glyn justified, "my accent becomes West London, I'm all wedged-up with wonga, have a Doctor Feelgood attitude, and my garb resembles Iggy Pop's. It's just role play...savvy?"

"Me savvy," Colin joked, assuming a mock-uninformed manner, his pithy humour making his companions grin.

"We get into character, and uniform," Glyn elaborated, "often without crystallising the vicissitudes we make to accommodate the situation, just like here on Poseidon, or in the office, or at a social event."

Getting in tune with the polemic, Colin caught on. "You're saying, we subconsciously assume the requisite for whatever role we play, be it professional or domestic."

"The lights gone on," Steve mirthfully teased.

"I'm not usually so slow on the uptake. It's just, I've never arbitrated this line of reasoning before."

"Forget it," Glyn coaxed, "we all have blind spots. I have more than most."

"So, is what I said correct in the context of the proposition?"

"Yes, Colin, but contrary to the discernible artfulness, even duplicity, I daresay dressing attuned to role play is normal and healthy. It gives variety to life and enriches a person's persona."

"It's also escapism," Steve postulated. "Why go to the movies intent upon experiencing escapism, when you can have a far better time achieving it through your own endeavours. Far better to be a player, than merely an observer."

"Absolutely right," Glyn ratified. "Can you see the real me?" he broached. "Businessman, or wannabe rock impresario. Is there any difference, apart from the uniform?"

"I suppose it won't surprise you," Colin began, "if I say, when I worked at the Lord Chancellor's Office, a strict dress byword regime prevailed."

"Plainly," Steve sponsored, "the civil servant archetype is one of the most recognisable tokens of the Establishment."

"When it became clear I didn't fit into their mentality, and had already made provision to leave, one day I strolled in to the office in let's just call it, more casual garb."

"Holy crap, I bet that went down like a lead balloon," Glyn drawled.

"Oh, nothing was expressed, at least not directly to me. The civil service does not deign to make remarks about non-conformance. They simply scowl and send the culprit to Coventry. I did it to wind them up and stick two fingers up to the elite."

Wrinkling his nose at the review, Steve asked, "But what's your point, Colin?"

"My point is, although they knew I could do the job, and do it well, rebellion against the status quo was the crime. How dare I not fit into their regulations and covenant, an unforgivable sin. Conversely, those poor at their jobs, but strictly conforming to the traditional dress statute, required comportment and *de facto* thoughts, could bugger the permanent secretary of state, and still only receive a mild rebuke."

"I suppose, we shouldn't be surprised," Glyn sanctioned. "More than ever, acceptance is not pivotal on talent or capability, but on convention and kowtowing to the dominant caliphate. The trick is to cosmetically follow the instruction but be non-conformist in spirit."

"Like your hero Churchill?" Steve summarised.

"Superb example. Churchill worked the system as per any other politician, but he staunchly refused to approve laws built on naivety and blind faith."

"Unconditionally true," Colin attested. "He bravely took the taunts and condemnations from Baldwin's Conservative Government in the nineteen-thirties, when he spoke out in Parliament about the rise of Hitler. Few took any heed, but painstakingly Churchill was proved right. He could easily have towed the appeasement party-line, gone for a quiet life, and feasibly been awarded a post in Baldwin's cabinet, but Winston had a keen moral compass, trumping party policy. In that respect, he epitomised the archetypal non-conformist."

Exchanging more escapism-type rhetoric, the three companions talked further about famous non-conformists, typically Oscar Wilde and Bertrand Russell, before the theme cascaded back into amassed instances of escapism.

"When Suzy and I lived at Chelsea Cloisters, we often went to Christie's on the Old Brompton Road to watch the auctions," Glyn recollected. "Paintings were sold for astronomical prices.

One day, I decided to have some fun and up the ante. An early William Holman Hunt was on the roster. Far from his best work, nonetheless, avid collectors were out in large numbers, keen to acquire the work."

"Of all the Pre-Raphaelite artists, Hunt is my treasure," Colin commended. "His product is virtually photogenic *ad modum* accuracy and the faculty to capture feel and mood."

"Quite. Suzy and I stood at the back of the auction room. With the sale in play for a few minutes, the bid had reached eighty-thousand pounds. Without warning and keeping a very straight face, I waved my catalogue betokening an offer of eighty-five thousand pounds."

"Oh, yes," Steve interrupted, a wicked grin etched into his lineaments. "I remember Judy saying Suzy told her about the incident. You'll like this, Colin."

Cheerily, Glyn persevered. "Near to fainting, Suzy gaped at me, her mouth cracking involuntarily in astonishment. She grabbed my arm, admonishing, 'What are you doing?' 'Buying a painting, darling,' I replied. Rooted to the spot, she became visibly shocked, lost for words. The auction continued, ninety-five thousand, a hundred-thousand, all the way to a hundred and twenty-five thousand pounds, Suzy barely breathing and on the verge of collapsing. Finally, the Hunt went for one-hundred and sixty-five thousand pounds with me dropping out at one-hundred and forty thousand pounds, much to my wife's relief."

"I'm all for testing the boundaries of bluff," Colin specified, "but it could have crippled you financially."

"Ahh, wait until you hear the finale," Steve gushed.

"She dragged me away into one of the empty anti-rooms," Glyn reprised. "'Are you mad?' she reprimanded. Smiling, I counselled her to relax. You see, ascertaining the reserve price in advance, I'd been role playing, my financial footing always secure, my final bid five-thousand pounds short of the one-hundred and forty-five thousand pound reserve price."

"So, am I right in concluding," Colin shared, "it was just another exercise in escapism?"

"Unequivocally. However, that little episode cost me a dig in the ribs and an expensive dinner at Barbarella's in South Kensington. Suzy had her pound of flesh for my escapism, but it was worth it. The Benzedrine-like rush during the sale, phenomenal, escapism at its finest. That lampoon made me twig why people bet on the stock market, or gamble on the gee-gees. Most of the pleasure is in the taking part, the winning or losing purely bi-products."

"You know, delving more into this role play phenomena," Steve began, "it strikes me, people long-lasting exactly the same in the mould of disposition and tact to any pigeonhole or under any circumstance, tend to verge on the dull to boring, their constancy of volition negating any intemperate possibility. For them, the *bête noire* of showing another side, whether it be comic, controversial or dark, is just too risky to allow."

"Quite," Glyn guaranteed. "Allow me to give you a personal illustration." Taking a pull on his *San Miguel* he then outlined, "A really straight person I once worked with, failed to see how sales-types could be extremely professional during working hours, and uninhibited barnstormers after work, fooling with each other and having light-hearted fun. I told him, it was down to role play, and the sales team were just letting off steam and relaxing by assuming other sides of their identities." Quivering his brow, he then exhaled noisily. "But no, he didn't get it. It didn't compute in his ultra-regulated and societal acclimatised mind."

⁓

Dependent on the activity, Glyn showed multiple personalities or characterisations on non-business occasions. It did not mean he tended to schizophrenia. On the contrary, he perched amply in control of the adopted role, able to turn it on and off, at will. Often, he did it for devilment, to see how far he could go, without someone working out he was joshing around.

Sometimes known to introduce himself at parties as either Daryl Van Horne or Dante Gabriel Rosetti, not once had anybody howled, 'You *must* be kidding.' Remarkably, he got, 'How you doing, Daryl?' or 'Do I call you Dante or Gabriel?'

Enduringly astonished the people he met apparently had no understanding of either late twentieth century American film, or the nineteenth century Pre-Raphaelites, he brazened it out, explicitly the latter incarnation with a very bad Italian accent, though Rosetti was English through and through. To his amazement, people believed him to be an Italian. Up front chancing they were being polite, the sheer number of times he transformed into Daryl or Dante mode without query, made him re-evaluate and conclude many modern people had an extremely narrow bandwidth of erudition.

Growing to detest the rebuke, 'It was before my time', a phrase constantly trotted out by people with no imagination or bent to research anything prior to their birth date, and apropos restricting their vernacular content to the dull and the mind-numbing, he found himself addled by their failing. Arguing just about every event in the Earth's history happened over tens of millions of years, 'before your time', why should that hinder 'you' being curious about the vast epochs of life happening before 'you' were born?

Ripening up the charade, Glyn went into Daryl or Dante mode with Suzy, or later, some other girl without prompting them, just to see if they acted in a complementary role to underpin the deception. Often Suzy gave her husband a sideways stare, moderately careening her head from side-to-side, then launched into her role with, 'You've not met my husband, Daryl'. She then whispered to him, 'You should have been an actor', Glyn replying, 'I am…but we all are'.

Used to counter the tedium of everyday repetitive life, for Glyn, the light whimsical ruse equated with harmless escapism. Having an extremely short threshold of boredom, as he had told the chairman of the software firm he had left before joining Poseidon, he freely admitted to others, it was one of his many failings.

Having a strong awareness to accommodate people, he even updated his modulation to something germane, making them feel comfortable in his circle. Telling Suzy, it was an attribute selected from his sales toolkit, the appliance brought universal inclusion to social junctures. But most likely, the underlining vindication, as Suzy insisted, lay in the fact he was an actor. 'Maybe all people are actors, but few are conscious of their own performance', he told her. 'Do they conceive they are indulging in escapism?'

Often, Glyn discussed the conundrum with friends, ending the assertion with, 'Think about it'.

12

SPYING ON POSEIDON

After witnessing the rendezvous between smugglers Azzam and Jamel and Basara and his men at the Sidi Bou Said Marina, Saleh fled back to the Carthage old market area. When the group did not find him in the Centre des Musiques Arabes et Méditerranéennes annex, doubtless he surmised, Basara assessed the smugglers had lied to con them out of a finder's fee, not bargaining to be frog-marched back to the crib to test the veracity of their claim. At best, Basara might have adjudged he had already boarded a vessel heading for a European port. Alternatively, he'd keep his flunkies on a watching brief, in case the Ethiopian still hid amongst the endless street sub-enclaves of Tunis.

Not taking any chances, over the following days Saleh kept a low profile only emerging once a day from the hidey-hole he had earlier found, to buy food from the market stall traders.

Extraneous to the Dutch terrorist operation, Saleh knew the Tunis Muslim fundamentalists were involved in a number of other incendiary activities, Basara unable to dedicate all his lieutenants to ferreting out their miscreant for more than a week, without taking heat from his taskmasters in the Muslim Brotherhood executive. Knowing Basara's suspicions about his infidelity to the radical cause were proven, the Ethiopian never intending to carry out the Amsterdam revenge attack, the headman would also suss out he could never buttonhole Tunisian officialdom, telling them about the intended atrocity, the Ethiopian associated by implication. Muslim Brotherhood propriety bonded Saleh knew very little about the Amsterdam attack anyway, and irrevocably, no contact names had been given to him. Optimistically, Saleh gambled Basara conceded he was not a threat to the mission if he stayed out of the clutches of the Tunisian police and made it to Europe as a bogus asylum seeker. However, if detained and sweated, Basara's band of brothers were at risk. In that event, he foresaw through fundamentalist champions in the Tunisian administration and the police force, word speedily leaking back to the Hraïria district, Basara moving the operational unit to a pre-planned fallback location before they came for him.

A full week after he narrowly made his exit from Basara's grasp, Saleh bet it might be safe for him to resume his dash for Europe. But what to do next? Without travel documents, paid transportation aboard a local commercial vessel was impossible. Alarmingly, his brief interlude with the Tunisian smugglers made him reckon a clandestine exodus could be just as risky.

Incontrovertibly, he conceptualised his only plausible pipeline for entry into a Southern European port centred on buying passage on a private European motor cruiser or sailing vessel. Mindful Tunis formed part of the round-trip voyage for European chancers and pleasure aspirants, setting off from Spain, France and Italy for a North African Mediterranean romp, he elected to explore the realisable channel. Having no allegiance to Muslim fundamentalism, potentially they allotted a promising means to him, without Basara getting to know about it.

All he had to do was find a crew onshore and transact the barter whilst at the same time evading both his pursuers and the police. After they scrambled to follow him from Carthage International Airport the day he arrived in Tunis, he knew Tunisian Passport Control must still have him on their radar. He also forecast Basara contacting sympathisers in the Tunis police force, directing them to be on guard for Saleh, and deliver him into the hands of the Muslim Fundamentalists, should he come into their realm.

Summarising his strategy, the Ethiopian perceived in exchange for money, he'd find a European crew he could persuade to take pity on his plight and willing to risk Tunisian customs officials finding him aboard during departure procedures. Avoiding discovery by concealing him in a hiding place unlikely to be inspected, thus bonding his security, he estimated large cruisers and multi-mast sailing vessels to be prodigious enough to equip such a possibility.

Confident Basara had reduced the number of subordinates searching for him, Saleh ventured out of the market area hurrying over to Carthage Harbour, one of several docking points used by European private sea-going craft in the uppermost Tunis area. Petitioning a few crews on the north side of the quay provisioning their craft, on each occasion he was given short shrift. Unable to produce any travel documents, everybody he talked to eyed him doubtfully, alert undercover police agents nosed the locale for illegal trafficking.

Walking the circular harbour's length to its south side, he tried his luck with several boats, again finding no one wanting to take the risk, not even when endowed with all his money. Eventually, he stumbled on a French crew fluent in English. They told him there might be a chance to take passage aboard their brigantine, and he should come back at three, when their captain came aboard from a commerce meeting in central Carthage. Returning to the comparative safety of the market, he holed up in his hideaway. Overjoyed to at last be in reach of his goal, as the meeting time hastened, he made his way to the harbour early, wanting to show willingness.

Passing the Lycée Carthage Byrsa whistling to himself, he suddenly froze. Ahead on the quayside road, he saw a police car parked by the side of the brigantine, two uniformed policemen questioning the crew on its main deck. Immediately, he adjudicated the brigantine's crew had informed the authorities about his illegal agenda, the police awaiting his arrival to arrest him. Licking his lips to find moisture, he monitored the activity again, then some people slightly further up the road beyond the brigantine bagged his eye. Aided by Jabar, Rafik and Wassim, Basara stood behind a goods trolley, surreptitiously eyeballing the brigantine. Saleh speculated Muslim fundamentalist sympathisers in the police must have informed Basara, they had received notification about a man hounding for conveyance to Europe without travel documentation.

Though over 300 yards away, Basara and his followers immediately picked up on Saleh, moving swiftly towards him. Catching his breath, the Ethiopian turned and took flight. Once Basara and his detachment passed the police car, they sped after their quarry. Running for his life, Saleh headed back down La Goulette Road past Carthage Salammbo, and along Avenue Farhat Hached. Occasionally mugging back to see the pursuers on his tail, he disappeared into a dense crowd in the old market area and rebounded to his den.

Breathless and dry-mouthed, he checked the melee for his stalkers. Less than a few minutes behind him, he expected to see them stomping through the market, asking people if they had seen him. After a while, without espying any of them, he guessed they'd not seen his endmost destination and were flailing about seeking to reengage him without success. Assuming they either capped he had found an undetectable hiding place in the market or passed through it making for central Tunis or back to the Sidi-Bou-Said area, he relaxed. By the early evening, with the market starting to downturn for closure, Basara and his cohorts were still not to be seen. Deciding to take no chances, their quarry appointed to stay in his hidey-hole until the next day.

Auditing what had happened, and appraising his choices were fast becoming reduced from slim to none, he knew it only to be a matter of time before the combination of Basara's fraternity of followers and police sympathisers seized him. Deciding to move to the south-side of Lac de Tunis before daybreak and try for transit with the European vessels docking at the Tunis Marina, he settled down for the night.

～

As the new day dawned, Saleh stood by a row of chandler shops, spying on an array of European motor-cruisers and multi-mast sailing vessels at the Tunis Marina. Already, many of their crews were making ready to depart, Saleh grasping the need to make his move to barter passage before the Tunis Harbour Authority, went through customs departure routine, permitting the craft to leave. Still keeping a careful watch out for Basara's men and the police, he crept frontward to the nearest vessel, a forty-feet at the Plimsoll line ketch, propositioning the man he assumed to be overseeing the embarkation preparation. Reacting badly, the man swore at the Ethiopian and gestured for him to go away. Backing off to his former scrutinising retreat, Saleh waited a while, then roamed down the quayside, out of sight of the ketch crew, and made his request for admission to the crew of a large catamaran. Waving his cash in front of the seamen, he was given inconsiderate treatment, and vehemently told to clear off, other crews making leaving preparations attracted by the fracas over by the catamaran.

Once again retiring back behind the row of chandler shops, heedful he had exposed his hand, he determined further sorties to departing moored-up vessels to be fruitless. Instead, he waited for a fresh batch of vessels to arrive. This time, in place of making his appeal on the quayside, he'd follow a crew into Tunis, calculating they'd either be shopping for supplies or sight-seeing, before returning to their craft. When the opportunity arose, he'd make his play for buying carriage to Europe. Alternatively, if the tactic still flopped, he'd go for the stowaway selection.

By mid-morning, a new armada of motorised and sailing vessels began arriving at Tunis Marina. Beholding them from his bulwark, Saleh weighed up possible dupes that might yield to his plan.

When a large brigantine arrived, Saleh chirped up, rating it had plenty of possible lairs for a stowaway. After an hour of patient vigilance, he saw the brigantine crew leave their vessel making for central Tunis. Following them, they went into the Carlton Hotel for a coffee before going on to the Bardo Museum, Saleh only a few steps behind. Though unquestionably a good place to make his play, a policeman stood on guard outside the museum entrance doorway. Not wanting to risk being challenged for identification before entering, he revised his blueprint and doubled back to the brigantine, deducing with the crew away, it consigned an ideal opportunity for him to stow away aboard. His secondary scheme also came to nought. Back by the chandler shops, he catalogued a skeleton crew had been left behind on the brigantine. On deck, they performed sundry duties or relaxed, pending the return of their comrades, rendering the stowaway contrivance null and void.

Another hour passed without any new arrivals, then a midsized ketch docked, Saleh adjudging from its crew's chitchat they were Greeks. Unsure of them also speaking English, he nominated an approach to be too wearisome and dicey.

Frustrated by the lack of a solid opportunity, he slid down the wall of the chandler shop he hid behind, burying his head in his hands. Deriving the folly of his ways, culminating in his expulsion from the Dire Dawa camp, and his subsequent white-knuckle rides in Nazret and Tunis, he wished he had behaved himself, and never set out on his foolhardy expedition to find the easy life.

Later, after an indeterminate time awash with self regrets, he lifted his head. Gawking at the gently lapping waves on Lac de Tunis, the Ethiopian spotted a schooner displaying the Flag of St. George on its mainsail masthead, making for the Tunis Marina. Concluding the sailing vessel must be crewed by Englishmen, he moved slowly away from the chandler shops area and along the quayside, straining to achieve a nondescript status passing transparently through the marina.

As the schooner docked, he logged the name Poseidon embossed on her gleaming white superstructure. Hearing the crew speaking whilst mooring the schooner, indeed confirmed they were English. Backtracking to his former crib, Saleh kept an eye on the Englishmen making ready to receive Tunis customs officials.

Later, after completion of formalities, the crew prepared to leave the schooner. Counting eight crew members during the docking travail, having locked the schooner cabin, Saleh clocked the same number left the vessel, heading due west into central Tunis.

Following them at a discrete distance, he blended in with the crowd, but never lost sight of his targets.

13

INTO THE TUNIS NIGHT

After all the mind-blowing escapades the ship's company had experienced from Tangiers to Port de Bejaia, Poseidon finally trekked in the Golfe de Tunis, ready to enter the bustling city of Tunis via the port of Halq al Wadi, and a sea gate canal connecting Lac de Tunis to the Mediterranean.

Arriving Spring Bank Holiday Monday, Tunis basked in bright sunlight driving the air temperature to eighty degrees Fahrenheit, nine degrees above the seasonal average. Back on Easter Day when they set sail from Cadiz, the temperature at sea struggled to reach sixty degrees Fahrenheit. At Tangiers it rose a few degrees, but by mid-April when Poseidon docked in Oran, it had become a skin warming seventy-two degrees Fahrenheit.

Electric heaters plus the heat generated from close cabin quarters and a kitchen constantly delivering hot food promised a warm environment below deck. At night, a contradictory reign prevailed on deck, the temperature plunging to as low as fifty degrees Fahrenheit, dependent on wind direction and sea swell, making thermals and waterproofs an out-and-out necessity. Unmistakably, night was not a time to lose concentration and slip overboard, the shock of hitting cold water could result in cramps and inevitably hypothermia, and ominously, sailors associated night-time with the most unforgiving circumstances for attempting rescue. Unless the person in the water was kept in view whilst the craft doubled back on track, they could be quickly lost. As cramp took hold, it incapacitated the unfortunate's ability to draw attention by calling for help.

At three nautical miles from the canal entrance, Jeff radioed the Tunis harbourmaster, requesting permission for the schooner to enter the harbour. Well known to the person on the receiving end of the transmission, Jeff used friendly and humorous banter as part of the palaver. Whereas rules were for guidance in North Africa, contrastingly, South European ports obligated a strict radio transmission etiquette. Finishing with a flourish, the senior then requested Bill to steer a south, south-east course, the action turning Poseidon into a mellow off-shore breeze, final electric-winch, sail-trimming performed by Tom and David.

With less than a quarter nautical mile to the sea gate canal, the on-watch smartly brought down the schooner's vast sails and stowed them, leaving her under diesel-drive for the final stage of manoeuvring.

Returning with their plentiful bags, local fishermen were also inbound to Halq al Wadi, the unmistakable smell of bluefin tuna, razorfish and sea bass filling the air. Predictably, their enterprise attracted pied avocets, black winged stilts and various members of the gull family, the birds swooping down on the flotilla, feeding on scraps resultant from pre-quayside fish sorting. As Poseidon slid through the canal entrance, more fishermen going about their business and casual onlookers on the quayside took in the glistening schooner, her crew extending waves and a few shouts of 'mrhba', hello in Arabic. Some responded in kind, others carried on with their labours oblivious to the new arrival. Having seen many vessels like Poseidon filled with European hotspurs and filibusters, the Englishmen were on no account exceptional to their acquaintance.

Witnessing the emerging city from Lake Tunis became a remarkable watershed for the newcomers. Creating an illusionary evaluation, it hinted the nearer they meandered, the larger the city became, Poseidon conclusively enveloped and swamped before reaching the western shore.

Balancing his mass against the foresail mast, Steve declared from his bows haven, "Wow, this is something else."

Just behind him, Glyn complimented, "It looks even better than Algiers."

Further back, Colin leaned against the mainmast salivating at the extraordinary panorama, a foreseen reaction for the self-professed history scholar. Elevating his camcorder to eye level, he began filming, then speaking to no one in particular spouted insight from his pre-Poseidon research.

"In 1270, Tunis was briefly taken by Louis IX of France, hoping to convert the Hafsid to Christianity. He easily appropriated Carthage, but died of dysentery before the walls of Tunis, and his army was forced out." Lingering to ingest more of the cyclorama, he then chronicled further, Steve and Glyn listening intensely. "At the same time, propelled by the Moors' re-conquest of Spain, the first Andalusian Muslims and Jews arrived in Tunis. They became axiomatic to its economic prosperity, and the expansion of intellectual life in the Hafsid capital."

Wondering if the conquerors were similarly inspired by the marvel of Tunis as they crossed the lake, Glyn became riveted as the grandeur and scale of the city came into clear focus.

Proceeding carefully through the nautical traffic Poseidon crossed the lake, the remainder of her crew also glaciated in dazed admiration of the pageant ahead of them. In the distance, the usual array of multi-mast, sail vessels and power-cruisers signifying the sailing community came into view. Ten minutes later, they made land.

Docking and embarkation drills had been run many times since departing Cadiz. Each member of the two, four-man watches had a specific job to perform, the responsibilities rotated to bestow maximum expertise for sailing mighty Poseidon. Deck hand, galley, cleaning and maintenance, navigation under the senior's supervision, and the much-treasured steering duty, became the work domain for the newcomers. Only Jeff and Ed were qualified to make ship-to-shore and ship-to-ship radio calls, although the newcomers were given tuition on emergency May-Day procedures. As Poseidon's beam was brought parallel with their assigned berth, Tom and David leapt ashore securing her fore and aft, whilst Bill turned off her twin diesels and switched off her array of radar and navigation instruments.

Finalising docking at the Tunis Marina, Poseidon's crew awaited customs inspection. Often, North African customs officers performed their duties with scant regard for decorum, as the ship's company noted in El Jebha, but because of EU political pressures, Tunis customs procedures were a serious happening. When the officials arrived, Poseidon and her crew were subject to the full rigour, nothing precipitous or objectionable, more like they did their jobs with vigour, tempered by courtesy and narrow smiles. It had been the same in Algiers, only in Tunis, rather than French, the leading officer spoke English immediately. Examining for contraband, drugs and human cargo, they pried into every nook and cranny, the process mirrored on embarkation, only with more emphasis on human cargo.

Captivated by the location, while the officials did their work, the ship's company stood on-deck finding their bearings. Stalking the vista from every angle, they took in its depth like nourishment, licking their lips as if tasting nectar, their inquisitive feeding lost on passers-by.

"You know, Tunis really is a fascinating city," Colin extolled, still engrossed in camcorder capture. "It seems to exude a milieu of both the present and the past." Swivelling to lecture Glyn and Steve, an enthralled show emerged on his face. "It's possibly named after the Phoenician goddess, Tanith, and in recent times, has been twinned with many great cities worldwide, counting Paris, Rome and Rio de Janeiro." Gazing into the backdrop again, he proclaimed, "Believe me chaps, this is going to be wonderful."

"Yes, Colin is right," Jeff approved. "If you were impressed by what you've seen so far, you'll find Tunis is the *crème de la crème* of North African cities."

Intrinsically mysterious, even romantic, Tunis had been a source inspiration for Arabic and Western writers and artists for over 2,000 years, its quixotic atmosphere drawing in the visitor like a seductive siren. As if through magnetism, the newcomers discriminated an immediate pull, the allurement of the invisible fury sucking them onward, making the invitation, planting the curiosity seed. From their quayside perspective, they witnessed the city's buzz and aura, merchants going about their daily transactional routines, cutting shady deals in the hubbub of street cafes, tourists gawping at a myriad of stupefying antiquity, and the nonstop bustle of motorised vehicles competing for road supremacy with horse and donkey drawn barrows, traditional modes of Arab transport.

Built on a steep hillside running down to Lake Tunis and a narrow strip of land known as the Séjoumi, the city resembled an overarching amphitheatre, its soaring buildings' the stalls and the circles, and Lac de Tunis its stage. Standing proud, the epitome of an immovable object, the Tunis Dome fashioned the isthmus between the two major geographical cusps. Since ancient times it formed a natural bridge, and thereby the epicentre of Trans African Highway One, heading west to Algeria, and east to Libya then south into the Sahara.

Long ago, the Séjoumi had become the starting site for Bedouin tribes, ships of the desert, ceaselessly navigating between remote water wells, and visits to Tunis where they bartered and traded goods and services. Sustaining the tradition, Saharan Arabs still used the facility to marshal their camel trains, before setting out along the highway and dissolving into the vastness of the desert.

Clocking the newcomers were impressed, Ed expressed, "Wait till we get to the medina. It will really stagger you."

"Unequivocally," Jeff agreed. "The old medina of Tunis lies at the centre of the modern European architecture influenced city centre. It is truly wonderful. If memory serves, it was classified UNESCO World Heritage status in 1979."

Before Jeff could go on, having already genned-up on the medina as part of his earlier study, Colin took over the eulogy. "It contains hundreds of monuments, palaces, mosques and mausoleums, dating from the Almohad and the Hafsid periods," he enumerated, as if addressing an archaeology class. "Scholars have been pouring over it for at least three centuries. It is virtually unique in Islamic architectural history."

"What's your take on the economy, Colin?" Glyn enquired.

"Oh, it's fairly standard for this part of the world. The Tunis economy is based on textiles, carpets, olive oil and tourism, but the country at large depends on agriculture and fishing."

"Don't forget to tell them about Hannibal," Jeff prompted.

"Right. North of here, are the remnants of the ancient and world-renowned city of Carthage. Its importance is pivotal to the Punic Wars, Hannibal and the Carthaginian Empire." Spying for Jeff's approval, he then supplemented his explanation. "After Hannibal, it became a centre for commerce beyond the confines of the Med, and a place of major patronage and authority, though this ancient history denotes little to the Arabs occupying Tunis since the seventh century."

Absorbing the street life enacted in front of them, the crew snickered at the resourceful goings-on of various colourful doyens, intent on commercial dealings with local customers and excursionists. After many weeks of unfolding green phenomena, the newcomer's sensitivity had become attuned to the customs and cultural differences separating North African from European norms, each subtle nuance becoming a source of fascination. So frequent, they no longer monitored Arabic affairs and converted to a European interpretation. Cogitating in Arabic terms, they participated as inclusive players, spirited to find more to satisfy their cravings, and metaphorically attiring themselves in T.E Lawrence's Beni Wejh sheriff robes to aid blending in, the magnificence of Tunis further cementing their studious appreciation.

Little did they know an unexpected encounter hid around the corner, ready to alight upon them. Something they did not yen for, it'd be thrust upon them, and rapidly develop into a significant occurrence for all concerned.

～

With customs formalities finalised, the crew showered, changed into shore clothes, locked the boat and headed off. Their foremost memorable prospect became the central tree-lined promenade

Avenue Habib Bourguiba, the Tunisian Champs-Elysees, named after the inaugural president of Tunisia. Dominating the avenue, art deco and art nouveau colonial era architectures, the National Theatre and St-Vincent-de-Paul Cathedral held pride of place, their overbearing proportions in sharp contrast to the smaller, older structures. One of the busiest commercial streets in Tunis, Avenue Habib Bourguiba housed an abundance of cafés, popularised by locals and trippers alike to socialise at and talk relentlessly.

With their every step revealing something to astound, they advanced through the matrix of modern streets known as the Ville Nouveau, passing the Theatre Municipal de Tunis and the Maison Doree Hotel, before turning north-east to enter the medina centre. Coming the other way, they saw another European contingent.

Waving, Ed then grabbed Jeff's arm. "Well bugger me with a fish fork, it's Martin Driscoll."

Turning to his front, Jeff spotted Martin waving back at them. Raising an arm in recognition, Jeff broke into laughter as Martin approached.

"What on Earth are you reprobates doing here?" Martin trilled, embracing the seniors. Readying a garish dial, he wisecracked, "Ed, you old bastard, how the devil are you?"

"I'm fine, Martin, good to see you again, you old seadog."

"And you, Admiral Jeff," Martin cooed, "still showing the Med locals how to sail a schooner properly?"

"As ever, Martin, as ever," Jeff modestly acknowledged, his warm physiognomy indicating to the newcomers the stranger held a special attachment to the seniors.

"So as I said," Martin reiterated, "what brings you to Tunis?"

"Oh, just reconnoitering for buried treasure and ladies of the night," Ed jested.

Chuckling heartily at the pun, the three old friends took each other in, slaps on backs and more toothy grins following.

First meeting the seniors in the Gulf of Aqaba when his schooner Endeavour anchored off Ras El Barqa, Jeff and Ed had seen her as Poseidon sailed north, north-east up the gulf. Making radio contact, they reciprocated a few servilities, culminating with Martin inviting Poseidon's crew aboard. With the grape flowing freely, friendships were forged.

"Is Holly with you?" Jeff enquired.

"Yes, she's back on Endeavour with family members," Martin verified. "Oh, by the way—" He turned to his companions. "These are my nephews, Nigel and Francis."

Reciprocating, Jeff took the opportunity to introduce the latest Poseidon crew. Swapping a few courteous words, they all shook hands with Martin and his nephews.

"Where are you headed?" Ed enquired. "Oh, never mind," he hurriedly followed, "let's have a drink."

"Ah," Martin replied, glittering with fellowship and laying a friendly hand on Ed's shoulder, "we're on return from Tel Aviv, heading for Toulon via Sardinia. We're doing a night sail, so we should be in Cagliari by mid-afternoon tomorrow. I'd love to have a session with you guys, but Endeavour is sailing at 17:00 hours, and there's lots more preparation to do, so unfortunately, we can't."

"Pity," Ed groaned.

"Next time, hey," Martin decidedly advocated. "In the meantime, what have you guys been up to?"

After brushing over the tour schedule, Jeff told Martin about the pirate encounter off Ghazaouet.

Not shocking him, the Endeavour also carried firearms, Martin using them to ward-off unwanted advances from Arab pirates, just as the seniors had done.

"You know," Martin sternly retorted, "despite how much we report these incidents to customs officials, they seem not to take a blind bit of notice. One day, some unsuspecting Med novice is going to get a big surprise, even killed, if it hasn't happened already. I'd wager if it had, the authorities have hushed it up, for fear of losing the tourist trade."

Agreeing, the seniors prescribed robust vigilance was the only deterrent, the three friends then talking further about their respective voyages. Seeking the newcomer's impressions of the Med and North Africa, they responded to Martin with positive appraisals, not far from gushing about discoveries to date, their obvious joy not surprising him.

"When I incipiently trod the steps you are now taking," Martin recalled, "I too became amazed, but let me counsel some caution. As I told Nigel and Francis, it's their introductory trip around the Med as well, be attentive, don't assume anything, and always be wary. Foreigners have few rights in Arab society. It's not like Piccadilly Circus. You can't hail a policeman if you're in trouble. Enjoy yourselves but be watchful." Turning to the seniors, he affixed, "I'm sure Jeff and Ed agree."

"Yes," Jeff concurred. "We've given them the bible of do's and don'ts, and so far, they've not got a bloody nose."

More banter and storytelling ensued between the three senior sailors, the newcomers and Martin's nephews amused by cases recounted from the past. With time pressing, Martin peeked at his watch, reluctantly he and his nephews had to return to Endeavour.

"Glad to see you chaps again, but we must go, or Holly will have my wedding tackle for supper."

With that he bid them farewell and started off.

"Give our love to Holly," Ed shouted. "Oh, and mind your wedding tackle."

Twisting about Martin hoisted an indebted arm. "See you soon."

Melting into the crowd melee with Nigel and Francis, Poseidon's crew waved them off.

Furthering their trek through the medina, Glyn caught up with Jeff. "You and Ed seem to have a pretty good homogeneity with Martin."

"Yes, we've known him for over ten years. He's the type you can rely on if you're in trouble."

"He certainly didn't seem like a shrinking violet."

"No, Martin is solid bedrock, dependable, and…an excellent companion. He's one of the very few people we could entrust Poseidon to, knowing he'd treat her, as one of his own."

"Doesn't surprise me. He came across as being someone you and Ed naturally gravitate to."

"Mmmm." Smirking with pride, Jeff shared, "I'll tell you a little story. It paints a thumbnail picture about Martin's integrity, and why we revere him so highly."

"Go on."

"Back in 2001, we were in Saint-Tropez with Martin and other schooner owners for a mini regatta. He led the three-day event by a few points after day two. On the final day, his major competitor got ahead of Endeavour, but his boat capsized going about a turning buoy. Instead of ploughing on to the finishing post, Martin heaved to, and gave assistance to the stranded boat. When Poseidon came upon the rescue, and Ed heaved to, Martin shouted Endeavour had it bottled up, and we should go for the finishing line, allowing Poseidon to take the blue ribbon from way back in the field."

"A selfless act then?"

"Quite," Jeff confirmed, his mien unusually self-conscious. "Afterwards, Ed and I felt so bad we won the trophy by default, we begged the organisers to award the blue ribbon to Endeavour, because she had won the most races, and for Martin's altruistic act. Huh—" Glowing, he gyrated his head. "Martin had none of it. He testified Poseidon had won fairly and squarely, and he'd only heaved to because the first rule of the sea dictates the nearest craft to a stricken vessel must assist. It's true, but Ed and I knew, under race proprieties and within the confines of the Golfe de Saint-Tropez, no one would have admonished Endeavour for not stopping. But that's Martin for you. He really is a top-drawer act, one of the very best."

"I'm sure we all gauged he is held in high esteem by you guys."

"As I say," Jeff replicated, "Martin Driscoll really is one hell of a guy. We'd all do well to come anywhere close to the way he conducts his life."

Jeff's characterisation of Martin, chiefly the sacrifice he made denying him the winners' prize at Saint-Tropez, made Glyn meditate. Back in Blighty, in the main, everyone he knew, including Steve and himself, seemed self-possessed with what was best for them. Blair and Brown always banged on about the caring, sharing, inclusive society they had allegedly created, but it had resulted in the polarised opposite, people preoccupied by their own well-being, looking after number one. He also recalled a time from long ago, when he knew people capable of noble and charitable acts, but now, the philanthropic capacity never surfaced in them. Maybe he was once capable of such benevolence. What had happened in more recent times, to make people exclusively self-serving?

Remembering a disturbing give-and-take with a work colleague, a few years prior to Poseidon, the colleague had the opportunity to help someone out of a tricky situation but turned his back on the person. Canvassing why he had not done something, the colleague told Glyn, he used to comfort people, but recently it had become interpreted as weakness to be fleeced time and again. Because of this, his once egalitarian colleague favoured a dispassionate sentiment, scornful of how England had lapsed into a downward spiral, making people cry wolf far too often.

Wrestling with the root cause behind the depredating cynicism, Glyn revisited a discussion he had with Steve, regarding the devastating downside of the Blair-Brown administration on the English. They had determined it turned open-minded, kind and generous people into insular pessimists, skeptical about all aspects of life, and doubting unconditional honesty and probity existed any longer in England.

Somehow expats living their lives in the Med, had managed to exclude becoming stung by the debilitating nettle, accounts of people like Martin Driscoll far outstripping reports of Englishmen gone bad.

～

A magnet for holidaymakers from across the world, the Tunis medina district contained a network of covered streets known as souks, the dense morass of alleys and pathways saturated in intense scents and colours. Brimming with craft shops and stalls, their artisan owners busily churned out leather, plastic, tin and the finest filigree goods, whilst others took care of business transactions. Consummating the scene, traditional fast-food emporiums enticed passers-by with exotic dishes.

"Classic Persian bazaar street-sell mixed in with Western retailing devices to suck in willing rovers," Glyn quipped.

"Yes, like Whitstable market on a Sunday morning," Steve eulogised.

"Just goes to show the universal acquiescence to mercantilism. It cuts across all cultures and religions and has been doing so since man learnt to trade goods for currency, thousands of years ago."

Industriously moving into its midst, the ship's company came upon an array of illusory riches. Typical, a rare and precious artefact, recently discovered in the ruins of Carthage, according to the seller, could be theirs for a bargain 10,000 Tunisian dinar, about four-hundred pounds. Knowing the far-fetched claims to be totally untrue, it still lodged as fun driving the price down, mindful if the item was indeed an ancient gem, not found long ago by the Tunis Department of Archaeology, it'd be priceless.

Many replicas mirroring the fourth century BC when the Berbers founded Tunis, and from the second century BC when the Romans destroyed Carthage and Augustus rebuilt Tunis, were on sale.

"It seems this city's historical heritage," Steve began, "never fails to feed barterers with captivating ideas *vis-à-vis* marketable trophies for antiquity bidders."

"Perfectly true," Ed granted. "But the truism can be applied worldwide."

"*Ahh*," Colin blurted, betokening a metal slave-powered galley replica embossed with phony precious stones. "Here is something relatively new. It profiles the eighth century AD, when the Arabs used Tunis as a naval base for their dominion over the Western Mediterranean." Abandoning his valuation, he dialled his comrades. "Those slaves were European captives from Greece and Italy."

Later, David unearthed a reasonably-priced ornate vase,

allegedly from the sixteenth century Hafsid period. "What do you guys think of this?"

Apart from Colin, none of them could provide a reliable estimation. Chancing the eighteenth century Husseinites dynasty as its origin, rather than the earlier Hafsid period, but most likely, an early twentieth century re-production, he advised against a purchase on grounds of blatant deception. Suddenly, they were all casting opinions, half in fun, half to bring the review to a swift conclusion. Seeing through the Mickey take, his good nature indulging their exertions to show expertise accompanied by put-on masterful masks, Colin rested his chin on his left hand, his right hand buttressing his left elbow, and grinned at his shipmate's misinformed calculations, clearly reciprocating the Mickey-take.

Earlier in the voyage, it emerged Colin had a penchant for antiquity. Twenty years prior to Poseidon, he had visited Crete in search of Atlantis, and got bitten by the archaeology bug. He visualised North Africa expanding his antiquity canon, a secondary factor in his dream to be accepted for Poseidon. Buying several items in city bazaars, they acted as components for a physical diary providing material for future scholarly studies, rather than as trinkets to be flaunted.

In a cheerful and genial way, the ship's company were playful with each crew member's own area of excellence. Cadiz had broken down initial barriers, and in a trice promoted trust and friendship, the on-going playfulness further enhancing camaraderie. Encouraged by the seniors, it nurtured the good teamwork essential for sailing Poseidon.

Wrapping up the satirical debate, Colin propounded, "You know, the past is not necessarily fixed or unalterable. Its facts are rediscovered by every succeeding civilisation, its values reassessed, and its meanings redefined in the context of present-day tastes and preconceptions." Dissecting David's projected purchase again, his erudite countenance implied he should treat his verdict with reverence. "This vase is merely a twentieth century interpretation of a previous dynasty."

"You mean it's a fake?" David ventured.

"Indeed."

No one queried the finality of the judgement. Slightly self-conscious he nearly got duped, David replaced the vase. Exchanging jeers, like they were high-school students out on the time-watch trail, the crew laughed then moved on.

Beyond the superficial commercial realm, the medina's infrastructure astonished the newcomers. They had become used to the awe-inspiring prospects of traditional Arab architecture found in North African cities, but the Tunis medina stood head and shoulders above other medina sites. Whether by chance or by design, at every turn they made, the creators had managed to arrange its architecture in such a way that one splendid extravaganza uncovered itself after the other. Finding themselves entranced, their gaze firmly planted on the roof and dome lines of the constructs, they inadvertently stumbled over streetsellers' produce and bumped into people.

As usual, Tom the babe magnet found himself the centre of attraction to both girl wayfarers and local fillies alike. In Hassan's Tangiers chandler shop, a couple of cuties had put the glad eye on him, comparable things also happening in Melilla, Oran and Algiers. Not biting on any occasion, he left his companions curious but respecting his standpoint. Remarkably for a serial husband with a long and distinguished bed-notch career, he always managed to extricate himself from their tentacles, without being stand-offish.

Like the rest of the newcomers Tom had allowed his hair to grow, effectively morphing into a Spartan warrior of Homer's creation, and by Tunis sported a full moustache and beard supplementing his handsomeness. Barely concealing their enthralment, even in the hallowed Tunis medina the ladies flirted with him, persisting with requests for him to talk to them. Duly obliging, Tom told them he was sailing the Med with friends, and girls were strictly out of bounds. Marking the rest of the crew, he appended veracity to his elucidation.

"Not going for more conquests, Tom," Glyn gabbed without any connotation of censure.

"No. Though I said in Cadiz I'd protract basking in the

fleshpots, I had second thoughts during the crossing from Spain to Morocco." Narrowing his eyes, he almost blushed. "You might call it an epiphany moment, but I decided on a tenure of sexual abstinence whilst in the Med."

"Oh, you do surprise me. Why?" Recoiling, he qualified, "You're not becoming a monk, are you?"

"*Hah*! no," he countered, breaking into laughter. "When we were all making disclosures about our personal lives, regrets, foibles and shortcomings in Cadiz, it made me realise compared to some, I've been very fortunate in my life. I've not always valued the asset or treated the fairer-sex properly." Embarrassed by the announcement, he stopped walking, his phiz navel gazing. "Having only just met you guys, I didn't have the confidence to say the session had influenced me. Later, I lay awake in my bunk, pondering about some of the inappropriate advantages I'd taken with women over the years, knowing I could always move on to the next one, if it got too much for them. After hearing your story and those from the others, I figured on the romance front, I'd been living a charmed life." Quivering his head like an errant church goer in the confessional, he guaranteed, "I'm not like that in business, Glyn. I'm like the rest of you, hard-working and professional, but ever since my schooldays I've found it easy to attract girls. It just became a natural part of my adult maturation, but—" Unsure how to pitch his exposition in creditable terms, he paused. "The other thing springing to mind over the past year or so, are children. I signified if children do come along, it'd bring out a different side of me?"

"Indeed, you did."

"Well…Jesus—" He grinned. "I'll be forty this October, and I don't want to be an old man by the time my children reach adulthood. Trudie is ten years younger than me and wants children. I hope it's not too late to make the change and commit myself to her for life. I've been sending her postcards from the ports we've docked at for the past six weeks, and I've called her a couple of times from hotel restaurants."

"You, er—" He winced. "Told her about your epiphany moment?"

"Hell's teeth! She didn't believe me up front, but after a call I made from Port de Bejaia, she's softening. I'm positive I've convinced her that when I get back home there'll be no more horsing about." With an aura of strong credo enveloping him, he conveyed, "I'm going to make a go of it with Trudie…if she'll have me. The cruise is providing a proving ground to see if I've got the discipline to resist female seduction. Besides, the rest of you have got me hooked on this meditation kick." Stepping off again, Glyn followed suit. "Does that make any sense?"

"Assuredly," he okayed beaming broadly. "I'm so pleased for you, Tom. I really hope it works out for you and Trudie."

"Well—" assuming a sober demeanour, he divulged, "this fidelity lark is brand new territory for me. I have to get some practice in before returning home. If I can do it here where there is nothing to hold me back, then I'm damned sure I can keep it up in Blighty."

"You'll have to lose the facial fuzz and trim the locks, if you want to avoid the ladies coming on to you."

"Yeah. Until the voyage, I've always been clean shaven and kept my hair well in hand. It has surprised me how much more my adopted Med guise has amplified the ladies' fascination. Good god—" He grinned. "If I'd known that twenty years ago, I'd have grown a full-set then."

"So, are you going to keep the Med look, as you call it?"

"I'm surmising it could pave the way with Trudie, if she saw me the way I am now. I can always go back to being clean shaven, if she doesn't like the fuzz."

"Somehow," Glyn persuaded, "you'll succeed either way."

Tom's candid intention and subsequent resolution delighted him. A further incontestable sign the Med voyage positively afflicted all the newcomers, in Tom's case it meant a calling card signalling an end to his dalliances.

Progressing their medina pilgrimage, the newcomers were amazed by the legacy accommodations, arsenals, and armouries from the reign of the Ottoman Empire. Undoubtedly palatial apropos form and environs, the Tunis medina lasted as the crown jewel of their tour, arguably bequeathing the best examples of over ten centuries of Arab construction to be found anywhere in North Africa. Whereas they considered Tangiers to be exciting, Ceuta, Melilla and Oran mystical, and Algiers enchanting, Tunis and its medina were simply breathtaking.

With their thirst for Arabic culture and architecture quenched, the ship's company backtracked to a cosmopolitan cafe in the heart of the Avenue Moncef Bey, then on to a second, on the Avenue Habib Bourguiba. Sitting outside drinking beer, Poseidon's crew gazed at the shimmering mirages over Lake Tunis, late afternoon turning into a typically soft, balmy south Mediterranean backcloth, the still-hungry gulls and stilts silhouetted against the sun as it descended into the western horizon.

Going inside the coffee house, inevitably, they got talking with other Europeans and locals. One waiter told them he had been an extra on the film, *The English Patient*, shot in Tunis studios and the Tunisian desert. Another was an out of work stage actor, and a member of the Étoile du Nord, a combine performing plays at the Theatre Municipal de Tunis. Part-time symphony player with the National Theatre of Tunisia, a third waiter briefed the crew on the history of Tunisian music. After hearing their English accents, several well-dressed Arab merchants absorbed them in courteous parleys about commerce, globalisation and various international affairs. Ubiquitous in its appeal, bestowing comfort and a stimulating ambience, Poseidon's crew could have got lost in the coffee house's high-brow, cerebration-provoking atmosphere for days without coming up for air. Participating in group and one-on-one confabs, they found the Tunisian intellectual-set easy to talk to, and keen to understand the Englishmen's imprints of North Africa, specifically their city.

Whilst the various discourses seasoned, ebbing and flowing as more participants joined in, suddenly Bill rotated around from the gathering, spying at the café door.

Riveting Ed's eye, he notified, "Do you know, I've got this strange feeling we're being followed."

Gimbal-eyed by the palpable paranoia, Ed reciprocated, "Oh. What makes you say that?"

"I had the same sensation when we were talking to Martin and his nephews, divining someone spied on us, and then later as we walked the medina, I got this distinct portent someone trailed us."

"It's just a flight of fancy, Bill," Jeff expounded, alerted by the conversation makeup. "The locals will be watching us all the time, some out of curiosity, some because they want to sell us something."

Turning his diligence to the crowd inside the café, Bill polled the area for familiar mugs. Registering none, he conceded, "I guess you're right. Sorry, must be just my imagination."

Moving on to the Hotel du Lac for a traditional Tunisian dinner, the crew feasted on mouth-watering calamari, lamb in saffron and coriander spices, baklava and asida, all washed down with *Sidi Brahim* red. Strong coffee finished the meal before they retired to the equanimity of the Tunisian evening. Imparting refuge away from the hum of the dining room, they found a terrace garden on the Avenue Mohammed V side of the hotel. Exhausted after the day's exertions but very content, they ordered more drinks before falling into ritzy chairs and couches, the night's endless star array sparkling above them, the moon lustrous like a magnificent pearl.

Peeping skywards, Glyn breathed out a gratified sigh. "The *Arabian Nights* are our oyster," he acclaimed, gesticulating upwards, his companions following the bearing and fixing their sight on the firmament above.

"I could go on doing this forever," Steve attested, snuggling down in his seat like a satisfied cat.

Budding exultant kissers, Jeff and Ed smiled at Steve's not unforeseen ambition.

"It is intoxicating, and it doesn't get any better than this," Jeff joyfully hailed. "Perhaps now, you begin to dig why we've been voyaging the Med for…what is it, Ed?

"Twelve years. It's as we told you after Tangiers. Just let it happen, and you will not be disappointed."

Stretching arms and legs, the ship's company sank into the night, glad to relax after the two-and-a-half-day sail from Port de Bejaia to Tunis.

～

Beating against a stiff headwind and a ten-foot swell off Bizerte in the night put Poseidon half a day behind schedule en route to Tunis. For safety compensations, the sails were lowered in favour of the storm jib, and the schooner tacked on a replicated north, north-east and south, south-east heading for eight hours.

The sixth of twelve overnight sails attained during the round voyage trip, it proved to be a test of mettle as well as sailing proficiency. Just like the Straits of Gibraltar baptism, the pirates' stunner and the Giuseppe Garibaldi encounter, the adverse weather severely examined the new crew's resolve. For the seniors, rough weather spelt challenge to evaluate their seamanship skills. Conversely, it became a physical and mental endurance trial for the newcomers.

On a wet deck with the boat pitching from stern to bow, it's all too easy to slip overboard. For deck duties during the storm, cable ties secured to the masts and other key points on the upper works nailed down if someone did slip, they were safe from going over.

During a particularly arduous watch, Steve went forward to the bows tying himself to the fore staysail mast before re-tying rigging worked loose by constant sea wave battering, the sheer concussion of waves breaking on the bows making him slip. Moments earlier, Ed said after going below for a radio check to leave the flailing rigging to him. Seeing the ramshackle gear worsening, Steve took the initiative. When the senior re-emerged, he immediately dashed to assist Steve. Struggling to jointly command the tiller keeping Poseidon on track, from their steering well deck station, Colin and Glyn saw the precarious position of their on-watch mates. Just about to call the off-watch for backing, Ed signalled the loosened rigging had been successfully retied, he and Steve reversing to the steering well, drenched and cold.

Later, when off-watch and hugging cups of hot tea, Glyn praised Steve. "That was an incredibly daring thing you did. Ed was going to perform the task, so why didn't you wait?"

"A spur of the moment conviction," he admitted. "I could see if the gear wasn't stowed pronto, the fore jib and stay sails might have come loose from their sheathings."

"He's right," Ed ratified, joining them. "If those sails had come loose and started to drag in the water, it could have destabilised the boat. Anything could have happened thereafter." Tapping Glyn's pal on the shoulder, Ed congratulated, "You did the right thing, Steve. Well done."

"It was as simple as that then?" Glyn gabbled, still taken aback by the audacious action.

"Yes. I knew it had to be done. I couldn't have done it at the beginning of our Med eucharist, but now I've got a feel for Poseidon, I felt confident enough to at least try."

"*Try!*" Ed exclaimed, his cadence strengthening. "My friend, you succeeded, and to misquote from *Blackadder*, as a reward, you are welcome to have carnal knowledge of my sister, anytime you like."

Typical Ed, in the midst of reviewing a potential crisis, he always found room for a tension-relieving joke.

On reflection, Glyn knew he should not have been surprised, Steve's natural drive to test himself undeterred by the danger, still a big motivator in his life. *What a guy*, he mentally revered, proud to be his friend.

Operational wise, Poseidon ran four six-hour watches, every twenty-four hours. Below deck, the off-watch prepared food for the all-inclusive ships company, while the on-watch performed sailing duties. The trick for those below deck was to catch some sleep between food preparation and other domestic duties. Under tranquil sailing, the cadre functioned well, the crew nourishing themselves with sustenance for the evaluation and the adrenaline-rush excitement of sailing Poseidon. A team activity, they were reliant on each other for the smooth running of the schooner and their combined safety. Not wanting to let the side down, often efforts were made above and beyond the call of duty.

Storm conditions characterised the meridian yardstick, the unpredictability of how the sea reacted to a low depression always needing careful judgement and decision making, construing the best sailing preference. Even with the increased stability ascribed by downing the mainsails, storm brokers acting against each other could conspire to make capsizing a distinct possibility. Running head-on into the wind minimised the unnerving likelihood, but it resulted in a stationary fix, or incongruously, going backwards on track, hence the compromise tacking tactic under the storm jib.

As dawn ripened, the wind quelled calming the sea, Poseidon resuming on course under full sail. More exhausted due to sleep deprivation than physical activity, by noon, the sea-sailing newcomers were spent. With the Med placid again, Jeff allowed both watches to sleep until six in the evening, with him and Ed on deck duty, and Poseidon on auto-tiller. Having crossed swords with Neptune and prevailed, when Jeff called the first night watch to resume crewing duties, they came on deck refreshed, eager to reengage, and standing just a little bit taller, the Bizerte storm not the last time during the voyage the crew's spirit, will to perform and teamwork were stress tested.

With the newcomers reinvigorated and high on anticipations of Tunis, the following morning mighty Poseidon entered the Golfe de Tunis.

～

"I can't conceive we're at the midpoint of the voyage," Bill noted, still bewitched by the lightshow scintillating above the Hotel du Lac. "It only seems like yesterday we shipped out from Cadiz."

"Yes," Glyn endorsed. "Maybe we should have gone for the five-months voyage jolly, after all."

All the newcomers smiled, not smiles of satisfaction, but ones of regret. Deliberating, it struck them in another six weeks they'd be back in Blighty. Not an enticing prospect. Like Steve and Glyn, the others had little time for Brown's new world order, PC republic, not relishing their reacquaintance with his regimented, restrictive, and often treacherous oligarchy.

"What's the schedule for the inbound leg?" David enquired.

"Well," Jeff began, raising himself up in his seat. "Tomorrow, we head for Sicily, then the foot of Italy, the east side of Sardinia, Monte Cristo, Monte Carlo, Barcelona, and other ports of call, before returning to Cadiz."

"Does it embrace Toulon, Montpellier and other gems along the Cote d'Azur?" Tom quizzed.

"Yes. Nice, Cannes and Port Vendres."

"Good. Gives me another chance to practice my French again. I'm contemplating setting my new story in France."

"*France!*" Glyn exclaimed. "That's surprising. You've been querying our conceptions of North Africa for the past six weeks. We all presumed you'd enact your story here."

"I had originally planned it as you say, but lately, I've been mulling over transferring the Poseidon backdrop into a Marseilles context, at least in part. It depends how the homeward voyage pans out, what escapades we have in Southern Europe, and what play-actors and neo-auteurs we might meet."

"I can appreciate your rationale, Tom," Steve accredited, "but why France?"

"I want to individualise the story, set it apart from normal prospectuses. My defence is, if I make Poseidon's crew French, the tale coming from an Englishman will put an unfamiliar but intriguing slant on it."

"Captain's Jacque and Emile instead of Jeff and Ed," Glyn nominated.

"For sure. I've found writing is a fluid art form. The place you begin from, might not necessarily be the place you return to, because the novel is like a living, growing organism. You have the kernel of an idea, but when composing, the undertaking takes on a life of its own, going off tangentially, unwrapping fortuitous possibilities. Leastways, that's what it's like for me."

"You mean, you interpolate the story?" Bill articulated.

"Yes. You see, unlike a fiction, story-boarded from start to finish and then fleshed out and deepened, I'm going for at least a part-biographical and factual delineation."

"To blend the two aspects together?" Glyn asserted.

"Definitely."

"Huh, you'd have enjoyed a chin-wag with my ex-wife, Judy," Steve retorted. "As a manuscript reviewer, one of the tenets she explored for in notionally fiction works was some foundation in fact. She designated, in the main real life stories are infinitely more plausible and captivating than pure fiction."

"That's precisely what I'm trying for."

"Well, Tom," Jeff interposed, "when this masterwork is published, you must send a copy to all of us. Decidedly, we'd all like to know how our actual selves become translated into your fictional debutantes."

"Of course, Jeff, my pleasure."

"Changing the palaver slightly," Colin guided, his tone spiced with relish. "The French part of the voyage will also give us a chance to sample some Provence-Alpes-Cote d'Azur cuisine."

"And some proper cheese," David augmented. "Much as I like North African food, their goat's cheese gets very samey."

"Well, this time tomorrow night, we'll be tucking into classic Italian," Jeff apprised. "At least the regional Sicilian variation."

"Which neatly turns us to an organic axiom pertaining to the next stage of the voyage," Ed authoritatively inserted, making the newcomers eye him intensely. "We'll be sailing in a prevailing northerly direction all the way to Monte Carlo. With either an easterly or westerly wind, it means Poseidon will be tacking more than you've experienced to date." Goggling around the crew, a climate of presage emanated from his entire being. "This section will be more testing on energy reserves. If we get into a days' tacking, trust me, when you come off watch, you'll feel the burn as athletes say."

"Yes, starting tomorrow," Jeff directed, "your seamanship will be taken to a higher echelon of endurance. So—" He squinted soothingly. "Make the most of relaxing this evening. Until we reach France, you might feel less inclined to party, because the sailing will be a lot more exhausting."

"You mean," Glyn advanced, "like Armando and his crew underwent, sailing from Almeria to Melilla?"

"Exactly right."

"Bring it on," Steve happily urged, clapping his hands and rubbing his palms together.

"Yes, bring it on," the rest of the newcomers chimed in.

Radiating with satisfaction, Jeff and Ed swapped glances, genuinely pleased the crew retained objectivity and motivation.

Gleaming wickedly, Ed established, "I'll remind you of that comment, Steve, when we're beating against a westerly off Messina or Capo Comino, Sardinia."

Grinning back, the newcomers virtually purred with contentment. Secretly, they had crossed over, their back-home lives no longer dominating their minds. Craving eternal release from nine-to-five regularity, and the humdrum of what they now recognised to be conformity prison and tax-payer slavery, the Med had permeated their psyches, driving on the desire to be tried further. Once accusing Suzy of lemming-like behaviour, Glyn fathomed regardless of the one-time only adventure justification, he and the other newcomers were taking the same devil-may-care attitude, casting aside risk and ignoring fatalism, their only objective, the pleasures of sailing and experiencing new people and places. Instead of returning to Blighty, they harboured aspirations about calling their loved ones to join them, buying their own schooner, and withstanding the vitalising, pulse-escalating lifestyle, the Med offered.

During the evenings of shore visits, the ship's company invariably discussed the next day's sail in terms of re-provisioning Poseidon and performing crew assigned upkeep services, encompassing watch rotors, plus rough navigational and timing details.

"So, Admiral Jeff," Glyn enquired, using Martin Driscoll's

nom de plume to salute the senior. "About Sicily, what's our course?"

"Well, some caution is required here. We must be careful to navigate away from submerged wrecks off Capo Feto before the final track to Marsala. Over many centuries, this cape has become a graveyard for napping sailors, unaware a large, submerged reef spelt doom for their ballgame."

Several years before the latest voyage, Poseidon sailed off Capo Feto in high summer, the seniors deciding to put on wet suits and use scuba-diving equipment to explore the graveyard.

"Even a few feet below the surface," Jeff recounted, "it became tenable to see a large array of vessels, ranging from clippers to steamers having their last moments opposite Capo Feto. Clipper masts and steamer funnels were still erect and thrusting up, barely twenty feet beneath the surface."

"For boats with a deep draft," Ed warned, "unequivocally, they present a hazard. In rough weather, with the sea pitching in the vertical axis, both the reef and the graveyard come close to the keel of a passing craft. Virtually all the sunken vessels are shown on charts, but underwater currents shift the wreckage, making the area even more chancy."

"As we descended further," Jeff continued, "more wreckage debris became unveiled, the reef implacable like solid granite, no vessel capable of surviving a collision with the ambusher. We swam down to the nearest wreck. Initially, we surmised we'd discovered a multi-mast clipper, but closer inspection disclosed it had been a steamship with sails, including roughly ninety feet of deck length and a draft of perhaps twenty-five feet to its keel. Making graceful aerobatic manoeuvres, shoals of damselfish, black tailed wrasse and picarel swam through gaping holes in its broken hull. At the stern, a white spotted octopus had made its home between the reef and the softer seabed."

"In one respect," Ed portrayed, "the drama of an underwater graveyard generated regret and sympathy for the lost sailors." Dwelling, solemnity consumed him. "This is Neptune's kingdom. He rules supreme, only giving his victims to Hades once he's finished his pleasures."

After making Neptune's acquaintance in the Bizerte storm, the newcomers connected with the senior's portrayal. Already they were visioning out Capo Feto, making inner deliberation estimating its ruination potency, and thereby how to minimise the risk it posed to Poseidon's safe passage.

"From a different perspective," Ed went on to tell them, "viewed with an artistic eye, the Capo Feto aftermath was still active and being worked on by the sea, producing a kind of compulsive ballet motion. Caused as a consequence of sea currents rushing over the reef, and in their wake producing swirls and eddies, the slow inescapable movement of the wrecks resulted in the dynamic performance. But monitoring the subsea entertainment, we became heedful many of the masts were still robust enough to broach a pitfall to a midsize schooner, like Poseidon. After, we elected to embolden this area on the chart, so as to alert us for future sailing off the cape."

"There are many other infamous wreck makers in the Med," Jeff notified, "but Capo Feto is the only one we've seen up close."

"After the diving discovery, we gave a wide berth to all wreck areas," Ed justified. "It's the axiomatic vindication why we took such a long, convoluted arc into Port de Bejaia."

"Yes," Jeff tagged on, "Bejaia's rocky coast is also a harassing beacon for wreck bait."

Further discussing the Capo Feto shipwreck area, and the next day's sail to Sicily, the crew were unmindful someone spied on them from the balcony, leading down to the terrace garden at the Hotel du Lac.

Bill had been right *vis-à-vis* his suspicions they were being followed. Saleh was about to enter their lives.

14

COLONEL NASSAR

After the Ethiopian's frantic bolt from the Hotel du Lac, the police took Poseidon's crew to the main police station on Avenue de Carthage. Following certification of their European citizenship, the front desk officer said the chief of police wanted to question them about the escapee. Escorting the Englishmen to a bleak, nondescript interview room, only enlivened by a photograph of Tunisian President, Ben Ali, hanging from a wall behind a desk, and a ceiling installed, low-wattage electric bulb providing meagre light, the officer then collected their passports and left. Awaiting the chief's arrival with trepidation and in silence, the newcomers especially began to feel the heat of the exasperating happening snagging them in its web.

Squeaking on its hinges, the door to the room opened and two policemen entered, the lead officer holding their passports and introducing himself as Colonel Rafiq Nadim Nassar, Chief of Police for the greater Tunis zone, with special responsibility for border security. Removing a peaked cap, he laid it on the desk, along with his swagger stick, the instruments of orderliness indicating a military temperament and the glow of undisputed authority, exertion of his rank unnecessary to command respect from his police team, and the full cooperation of detainees. His smart, well-pressed, beige uniform, tailored to produce a perfect fit, crisp white shirt, dark tie, and shiny black shoes completed the vibe of absolute dominion.

"I won't bore you with my full name, it takes too long to say," he imparted, his voice mild, composed, the pithy comment making the ship's company titter.

Sitting down at the desk, he outlined the relevance of the inquiry, his codebook paradigm accent making his spoken English flawless, flowing without edge and building bridges with the suspects falling into his domain, his tall physique and natural elegance attaching gravitas to his station in life. Later, the Englishmen found out he had hit his mid-fifties earlier in the year, but Nassar appeared much younger, and very fit. From his clean-shaven face, it could be deduced he tended more to a terrestrial rather than Muslim doctrine, his light skin evincing probable Circassian ancestry, and thereby other religious creed feasibilities commensurate with a secular leaning.

As he talked, his physiognomy persisted sincere, his crystal-clear eyes heartening truth. An ethical mouth far from lies, suggested his commission came about through the wholehearted consent of the police executive, administration corruption rife throughout Africa not a factor in his appointment.

Making many enemies in the political orb for his resolute angle on integrity undaunted by doctrinaire pressures, nonetheless, Nassar's masters knew him to be loyal. Decorated many times throughout his career, he could be relied upon to perform his duties with professionalism, gaining respect from friends and foes alike.

Concluding his introductory review, he rested his forearms on the leather backed arms of the chair, his body language assuming a sanguine karma. Appraising his interviewees, he leaned across the desk, making initial mental judgments and noting their comportments. Having initiated buzz sessions on many occasions, he'd cultivated the art of sensing miscreants premised on body language. Knowing the suspects were nervous, beyond that he adjudged them to be tourists, accidentally hooked up in a local oddity. Most likely, they were good productive citizens of their own country, and thereby in principle to be trusted, but the latitude had to be gauged for validity.

Holding their passports like a deck of playing cards formed into a fan arrangement, he began ascertaining validation and travel history. Each time he got to a passport photo, his head jerked up and scanned the gathering. When his eyes made a physical equal, he keyed the name into a desktop computer, humming away on the desk. Like most people in such situations, the crew became fidgety in their seats, ruminating, imagining, uncertain of their standing, the initial relaxation generated when Nassar introduced himself giving way to presupposed imminent inquisition. Even Jeff and Ed's customary cool wilted, their complexions pastie, pensive, troubled.

"Glyn Gregory Sumner," Nassar impassively articulated.

"Yes," Glyn acknowledged.

Nassar searched around his features but said nothing.

"Steven William Fleming."

Arcing his head up, Steve anchored his stare on the Colonel. "That's me."

Reacting, Nassar narrowed his eyes, but again stayed tight-lipped.

"Edward Paul Swan."

Uplifting a hand, Ed cracked a calculated puss in recognition.

Making more keystrokes, Nassar then enquired, "Have you previously been in Tunis?"

"If memory serves, this is the seventh time."

"Yes, we have you on record," Nassar confirmed. "What is the purpose of this visit?"

As if foreshadowing judgment day looming, Ed's eyes widened. Going for definiteness in his speech, he summarised, "Jeff and I own a schooner. Once a year, we sail the Mediterranean with a crew from England, something we've been doing for many years…" Whilst Ed made his explanation, Nassar inspected their passports again, reverifying names against passport control records. "…We start from Cadiz, sailing south to hug the North African coastline, then either head for the eastern Mediterranean, or return north through—"

Before he could go further, Nassar held up an interrupting hand. "Jeffery Daniel Tindle," he tattled, scrutinising the ship's company.

"I'm Tindle," Jeff verified.

"You too, have been to Tunis before?"

"Yes, the same as for Ed."

"Mmmm, you are also in our records." Pinpointing Jeff and Ed, he evaluated them as if he might have seen them before. After making a few more keystrokes, he queried, "Do you own the schooner Poseidon?"

"We do," Jeff authenticated.

"Yes, we have her in our records as well." Whilst reading the customs dossier on his computer screen, he shuffled back in his chair making it swivel slowly from side-to-side, the stir denoting his immersion in cogitation. "Our customs officers report the Poseidon has docked in Tunis seven times. They say you are cooperative, and contraband has never been found aboard your vessel." Delaying, he guardedly extended, "Or human cargo." Ceasing swivelling, he leaned forward again, staring intensely at the seniors. "We must be very careful. Other Europeans on our radar are smugglers, but the Poseidon has a clean bill of health."

Hoping direct eyeball contact might engender further credence, Jeff and Ed peered straight back at the Chief of Police.

"Sorry, Mister Swan," Nassar apologised, leaning back. "I interrupted you. What are you doing in Tunis this time?"

His silky enunciation provoked the need for a careful response, Ed giving a synopsis of the voyage to date, plus their syllabus for the homeward bound trip. Seemingly easy going with the explication, Nassar jotted down the odd note, then finalised the passport verses person identification ritual with the remainder of the crew, each of them trying to exhibit a show of verity.

"We have to tread carefully with foreigners," Nassar firmly announced. "Sometimes, like you, they come across as trustworthy, but turn out to be criminals, so we have to table these direct investigations." His intonation softening, he pleaded, "Please, do not be disturbed or offended. It is normal police practice."

In defiance of the dictum, Poseidon's crew tarried apprehensive, signposts assuming something more sinister to come written into facial patterns. Resting his forearms on the desk in a neutral bearing, Nassar cocked his head to one side, glinting slightly to convey solace.

"Relax gentlemen," he requested. "We dispensed with torture long ago."

Exceeding Ed's black humour, the throwaway notification released the tension. Flip-flopping glances, the ship's company broke into shallow laughter.

Proficient in interrogation technique, Nassar exhibited an easy, relaxed, even consultative manner, at least with Europeans, to gain the information he sought. If the crew were not innocents, Glyn chewed it onerous to figure how he might conduct the fishing expedition. They were receiving the lighter shade of his method, but no doubt under mismatched circumstances, he could be very unyielding on defendants, and those nabbed in unlawful acts.

Later, Steve told Glyn, during the grilling he wondered what contrivances and contraptions lay down in the basement, used to wheedle out truth and information from those steadfastly refusing to cooperate. Contrary to the Colonel's reassurances, similar preoccupations also crossed Glyn's mind.

Before the Med enterprise, both had suppositions about the friendly English country bobby being emblematic of the unabbreviated police service in Blighty. Unlikely even those cornered red-handed suffered injury through savagery or psychological third-degree techniques. But when it came to foreign police, their visualisations turned to grim scenes of torture and excruciating pain, the further from Europe they ventured, the more they assumed sadistic procedures took place. Certainly, in North Africa, there were no guarantees how foreigners are treated, even less by way of compliance with international ordinances and obligations. Howbeit, Steve and Glyn arbitrating assumptions regarding Blighty law enforcers to be fair and impartial, and all foreign police bureaus used intimidation and violence as their main weapons, oversimplified the reality.

Largely formed from childhood film and television viewing, their disparate depictions comprised of two antagonistic poles, Humphrey Bogart, hard but fair, and Conrad Veidt, a pernicious torturer of the innocent. Equally, Russell Crowe invariably played the brave but flawed good guy, and James Cromwell, the calculating oppressor. Invariably portrayed as honourable and righteous, British security services' operatives never abused the nasty people they caught. Conversely, the Gestapo, the KGB and Third World spooks enjoyed the prospect of beating their prisoners senseless, or filling their veins with truth serum, independent of guilt or innocence. And when it came to foreign police, the crazed and brutal antics of Chinese, African and Arab inquisitors, with their evil personas and sadistic enjoyment eye glee, left an indelible imprint of terror.

Carrying the attachments in their subconscious, under Nassar's gaze they reoccurred, generating oracles of unbearable torture, their worst nightmares possibly becoming real. Though unlikely, the Chief hypothetically too much of a gentleman to suddenly mutate into the raging tormentor, associated with fictional tyrants Colonel Saito and O'Brien, there was always the unexpected, as they'd found with Saleh. In contempt of meticulous care and planning, the unanticipated can come crashing through barriers, fixing its prey square-on, and saying, deal with me.

"Once more," Nassar petitioned, "to certify I have the story right. Will you please tell me why you are in Tunis?" Browsing the ship's company, he solicited, "Who will speak for you?"

Turning their attention to Jeff, as usual, his natural leadership credentials had already primed him to assume accountability. Testifying there were no ulterior reasons for their presence, he told Nassar about their business, the Mediterranean voyage to date, and how they came to be in Tunis.

"I see," Nassar credited. "So, you and your crew are all English, and of good stock and intention. Yes?"

"To be sure."

"Where are you headed when you leave Tunis?"

"Marsala, Sicily."

Brooding, Nassar gawked deep into Jeff's eyes, leaving the plaintiffs undecided as to whether he'd bought their story in its totality. Varying tack, he reclined back in his chair assuming a straightforward disposition. "Tell me what happened this evening?"

Again, Jeff led the recollection, the rest of the crew subsequently joining in with comments about how Saleh had occupied them on the Hotel du Lac garden terrace, and what then took place.

"So," Nassar responded, "the fugitive, Saleh bin Tariq bin Khalid Al-Asfour, wanted you to take him to Sicily?"

"Affirmative, Colonel," Jeff replied.

"And from there, he'd go on to England as a synthetic asylum seeker?"

Taking in his companions before answering, Jeff justified, "So we prophesied."

"Hhmm." Pondering, he distilled a resigned veneer. "It sounds very familiar."

More cross-examination followed from the Chief of Police. As the evening's events were recounted, the officer entering the interview room with Nassar, stood behind him making copious notes. Unlike Nassar candidly giving them the benefit of doubt, the second officer scowled abrasively at Poseidon's crew. Netting their eye on him, he returned a jarring, unforgiving glare, making them deduce he did not like foreigners. Hinged on his facial hair embracing a long beard, Glyn knew he must be a staunch Muslim, detesting all non-believers, principally European Christians. Undoubtedly if this officer had been at the helm, the Englishmen could have found themselves in Steve's imagined basement torture chamber.

Rising up at the end of their transmission, Nassar glowered at Poseidon's crew like a headmaster admonishing errant schoolboys. "Is that all?" he tested, his resonance brusque and disappointed, as if he hoped for more.

Nodding, they supplemented with a few yeses.

Screwing up his eyes as if only partially crediting them, Nassar muttered something in Arabic to the supporting officer.

Issuing a final damning sneer at the Englishmen, the officer then left the room.

Alone with Colonel Nassar, as the room settled into a galvanising silence, the crew felt vulnerable and anxious. Bottling the stillness, well-versed it made his captives feel vague about their surety, Nassar tapped their stack of passports on the desktop, the stirring intensifying their qualm. Taking a deep breath and exhaling slowly, he studied them, then lowered his eyes.

Sleuthing their apprehension, he avouched, "I see you were alarmed by my colleague."

Embarrassed by the remark, they had not appreciated while telling their story, Nassar clocked them squinting at the other officer. Raising his eyes again, he cast a comforting frontage at his detainees.

"You should not be perturbed by Lieutenant Shamoun. He dislikes everybody, not just foreign infidels, as he calls them. He will not bother you."

Loosening up, some sensed they were perspiring, others sighed, glad Shamoun no longer surveyed them with his arresting x-ray vision.

After informing Poseidon's crew the Department of Immigration and Border Protection had Saleh on record, certifying his identification by comparing his bogus passport photograph against Ethiopian government records, revealing his true name, Nassar alerted the fly-by-night should not be underestimated. Abundantly aware he had entered Tunisia on a forged passport and under a false name, the police also knew about his connections with a subversive Muslim fundamentalist junta in Tunis.

Stressing the Saleh affair was not at all unique, he told them he had to deal with identical ordeals virtually every day. With his meagre *aides-de-camp*, he struggled to regulate the fictitious asylum seeker stumper, and its knock-on implications for Tunisia, and beyond. Having listened to the interviewees illustrations of the Ethiopian, the possibility Saleh had been groomed for a

Muslim terrorist atrocity engrossed him far more than his illegal label.

"Two brigands were found in the Sidi Bou Said district with their throats cut," he relayed on without the slightest hint of emotion, the sudden remark making the ship's company recoil.

They had reckoned Saleh was desperate, but never hypothesised him to be involved in murder.

"We raided their house," Nassar went on, "finding travel documents in the name of Younes Faudel Merak, and 10,000 dinar. We derived your friend Saleh might have once owned the documents and the money, or more probably, they were given to him by Muslim fundamentalists." Hesitating, as if not altogether self-satisfied, he qualified, "We're piecing together a composite of Saleh's endeavours in Tunis. Known radical mullah Mayhar bin Ishak bin Massood sent him from Addis Ababa to join the local Muslim fundamentalists. They gave him his instructions and the new passport, presumably to wayfare to Europe and fulfil an act of terrorism. We know this same confederacy is scouring the city to find Saleh, possibly because he got cold feet about becoming a terrorist, and—" Nassar flicked his eyes from side to side, the action further condemning the Ethiopian. "He could have stolen money from them to fund his getaway."

"It explains his nervousness at the Hotel du Lac," Ed proposed. "But—" Stroking his chin dismissively, he grew a doubting mask. "I can't see Saleh having the stomach to kill anyone. Oh, he was full of aggravated bluster, but it was brought on by annoyance when we refused to take him to Sicily."

"You might be right," Nassar conceded. "But someone killed those brigands."

"Maybe the Muslim fundamentalists?" Jeff submitted.

"Maybe, but you should realise this Saleh affair is not simple." Sitting up, he regarded them with a reproving inclination. "Are you absolutely certain you did not see this man before the Hotel du Lac?"

Momentarily, the crew's calculations swung back to Bill's feeling they were being followed at the Avenue Habib Bourguiba café. Making an instinctive ogle at Bill, Jeff signified to keep quiet. Nodding his head slightly, Bill indicated he wouldn't volunteer the awareness, not chancing where it might lead.

A chorus of no's were murmured to Colonel Nassar.

"Perhaps earlier in the day?" he fervently protracted.

Rubbernecking at each other, they then generated blankness in return.

"He might have spotted you on the Tunis Marina quayside," Nassar pushed, "followed you to the medina, then to the Avenue Moncef Bey, the Avenue Habib Bourguiba, and finally the Hotel du Lac."

Again, they all exuded vacancy, Bill protecting his minor secret.

Accustomed to Arab traders following them around the markets and bazaars, agitating to sell them their wares, the crew wouldn't have registered anyone exclusively eye-catching. If Saleh had picked them up on the quayside or in the medina, apart from Bill's feeling, it was unlikely any of the ship's company had noticed the Ethiopian blending into the background, indistinguishable in the Arab crowd.

Concentrating on his police drivers, Nassar informed, "You see, we must try to establish his contacts. Any information is useful." Lingering momentarily, a probing posture covered his mien. "Once again, what were your thoughts about Saleh?" then more strenuously, "what are his plots?"

Corresponding as best they could, they reiterated that mouthy Saleh had a massive chip on his shoulder, but it was unlikely he had ever been a confederate in terrorist activities. Professedly, given his constitution, under the right motivations, he could commit a terrorist abomination. However, they rated it much more the case, the Ethiopian masqueraded as a crafty good-for-nothing, using the fundamentalists and the good nature of Europeans to sew up his goal to get to England, and live the lush life.

Conditionally agreeing, Nassar appended a pragmatic adjunct to the assessment, saying as much harm could be perfected by insurgents stirring up mayhem, as direct terrorism. Saleh certainly fell into that category.

Every night, from a hundred-mile stretch of the Tunisian coastline, between fifty to 200 Sub-Saharan phony asylum seekers attempt to cross the Med to Sicily and Malta, he told them. Operating in tandem with customs, the police were under enormous pressure from President Ben Ali to avert the exodus, but the tax bore as unworkable. Combined army-police shore patrols were heavily outnumbered, their efforts resulting in few captures, the same situation existing in Morocco, Libya, Egypt and Algeria. Pelting shady illegals with stones, locals encouraged them to go back home, but very few did. Instead, they elected to tough it out in Tunis, or try for Europe.

"Many strive to buy transportation, like your friend Saleh," Nassar wryly posted. "If that fails, they form divisions and either buy an old fishing boat or steal one from Halq al Wadi. Unrealistically overcrowded, the boats often sink with all occupants drowned, or they perish if a storm blows up in the Med. Gracelessly, they're hoping for rescue from the Sicilian or Maltese Coast Guard. Huh—" His physiognomy darkened. "The first rung on the freeloader ladder. Those making land, boldly walk into the nearest police station and claim asylum. Because of the EU Human Rights Act, the police are obliged to accept them. I have police friends in both Palermo and Valletta, and these pretenders spoil our otherwise very good nexus." Keenly boring at the crew, he forewarned, "It's a monsoon in the making, and it hasn't hit its peak yet. God knows how many more will come, but mark my words, if nothing is done to reverse the trend, Europe will be swamped. The monsoon will turn into a tsunami of human scum, a locust-like swarm forming an unstoppable beachhead, devouring your wealth and resources. Your social and welfare systems will be overwhelmed. Your crime rate will soar, and your women will be raped. And it won't be just ersatz asylum seekers and opportunist economic migrants. Terrorists will hide amongst their number. They will bomb your cities and commit atrocities on a grand scale."

Sullen, his frustration boiling, Nassar stalked around the dimly lit room occasionally peeping out of the window, apparently snooping for suspicious persons on the Avenue de

Carthage. Resenting economic migrants and asylum seekers, he had become bitter about the never-ending deluge. With his hands tied by politics, it meant too many of his deputies became channelled into a thankless activity, rather than the proverbial Tunisian citizen wish of enacting law and order and apprehending local criminals.

"It gets more foreboding every year," he told them. "The army is also responsible for homeland security. They've advised what to do, but the President won't let them." As if anticipating a reproach, he rifled the crew's quizzical expressions, then drove an accusing finger at them, complaining, "You foreigners have some very high and mighty ethical rites, contradictory to dealing with the asylum seeker quandary." Flowering infuriation escaped poise, his face contorted by anger. "The army has told the President, the only way to cease the influx is to make some examples, and ensure the operation is publicised in the Sub-Saharan zone. It's a well-supported solution in the public domain."

"Do you mean," Glyn began before vacillating, "shoot them?"

Remembering the interchange, he had with Colin and Ed back in Algiers, when they discussed asylum seekers entering North Africa from the south, Glyn eagle-eyed Ed. Lowering his head slightly in response, demonstrated he had already made the connection.

Stemming from Glyn's pointed brain-twister, gloom nestled on Nassar's contours. Sitting down, again he thrust the accusing finger frontwards bolstering his defamatory attack. "It's easy for you to be shocked, but if something rudimentary is not done soon, not only Tunisia, all of North Africa will be swamped. Our populations are small compared to the Sub-Saharan belt. It is simply a matter of numbers." Briefly tarrying, the finger dropped. "Your own General Gordon was defeated and killed at Khartoum by the Dervish," he reminded them, his modulation slipping into a lower timbre. "Not because they were better fighters, but by sheer volume of numbers. If the migration reaches critical mass, the army will be helpless to stop them. They will then invade Europe." Up came the finger again, his pronunciation back to potent. "And you too, will be powerless to stop them, unless we are allowed to act." Frowning at the Englishmen, a cheerless slant spread across his mug. "It is judgment and moral supremacy that defeats us," he argued. "We set ourselves a code of ethics to abide by, which others see as weakness to be exploited."

～

Finishing his education in France and England, Nassar gained a significant comprehension of their societies, cultures and histories. Whilst in England he took the opportunity to explore the Lakelands and the Peak District, their rich greenness and spectacular panoramas moving the poet in him. Writing to his parents in expressive terms, he waxed lyrical about the beauty of Northern England, and how he had never seen such dramatic sights in the Aures and Atlas mountain ranges of Tunisia. Chronicling people he met in out-of-the-way places like Coniston and Derwent, he described their lifestyles and regional sub-cultures at length, his undertakings resulting in an expressive fondness for Blighty, notably the desolate and stunning Cumbria countryside. Unbeknown to Poseidon's crew, the harvested findings generated the capital contemplation as to why he awarded the Englishmen magnanimity pertinent to the Saleh affair.

An enthusiastic Anglophile, he had mastered English at an early age, also speaking fluent French, as well as Arabic. Albeit, holding an unfluctuating affinity of belonging to Tunisia, his primary love reposed as his own country and his family. During his lifetime, Nassar had seen Tunisia stabilise and progress under strong but benevolent political leadership, a far cry from the abject repair the country found itself in post WWII. Solid trading links and political alliances had been formed with Europe and other North African countries. Prosperity became available to those prepared to work hard, and in general, relative freedoms were good for a Muslim state.

Rubbing shoulders with senior government officials and ministers, his family advanced up the social ladder. He took his wife to their functions and celebrations, attended formal ceremonies, and represented Tunisia in inter-policing conferences with other North African and European forces. But in spite of making valuable contributions to Tunisia, like a spider paring a fly, the enemies he had made picked away at his accomplishments. Those intent on bending the rules, opposed his fastidious stance on honesty and fair play, facets amplified by his Anglophile nature. Transforming into their nemesis, he hid little of his contempt for their underhand methods used to gain influence and eminence. Though at length, the scoundrels bought their way into the national sphere of authority, he still had the respect of his superiors at the Ministry of Justice, and invariably they rubberstamped his high-minded *corpus juris* and sagacity for public service. Firmly discriminating his way ultimately prevailing over the carpetbaggers and political tricksters, intent on bleeding the State dry, his adversaries did not scare Nassar. Debunking their duplicity, he foresaw the people demanding swift retribution. Yet with all the positivity, nagging dreads still plagued him about the future.

Whilst in England for a second time in the mid-nineteen-seventies, he read Priest's *Fugue for a Darkening Island*. At the time, he quantified as fanciful the author's spectre describing a near-future dystopia, unrelenting in its grisly intensity about the swamping of Europe by black Africans. But sheer practical experience over the past fifteen years had changed his mind, Priest's prediction faithfully becoming reality. Cognizant with the limitations of a small country like Tunisia to reverse the trend, it agitated him. He worried about the impact on his family, his country, and even England.

～

"So, Colonel," Steve prodded. "You do mean shoot them."

Displaying daggers at the ship's company, he hissed, "Yes."

"What's preventing the army from acting?" Ed enquired.

Fuming, a disparaging sulk spread across his dial. "Your *damned* European Union," he spat out. Conscious he must maintain restraint in front of the Englishmen, he took a moment to compose himself. "You Europeans are such hypocrites," he coldly pronounced. "You complain about predatory economic migrants and sham asylum seekers, but throw your hands up in horror, if we make recommendations as to how it can be reduced." Wavering, he squinted. "Even stopped."

Annoyed not with his interviewees, but with the headache he had to manage, his natural calm evaporated. Out of his seat again, he paced slowly across the room in front of them, hands clasped behind his back, caught collared between the need for constraint and the proclivity to be extremely frank. Occasionally turning, he weighed their reactions. Apart from minor signs of incredulity, none came, Poseidon's crew bewildered as to how to respond in a way Nassar premeditated.

Ramming home the reality check, he whined, "The EU compels us to do everything attainable to immobilise asylum seekers getting to Europe, but paradoxically, they tie our hands by insisting we respect their Human Rights Laws. Such dichotomies are impossible to manage. If we get serious about repelling the interlopers from the south by shooting a few of them, the EU will terminate our trade with Europe." Ceasing his pacing, he twisted around beetle-browed. "It's what the Americans call Catch Twenty-Two."

Nassar's disheartening appraisal stung to the core, the ship's company inwardly empathising with his predicament. As usual, EU politicians had their heads in the sand, buried in the political correctness they had created. Clarity identified if the human tide of economic migrants and asylum seekers, fraudulent or otherwise, was not thwarted, indeed it'd reach critical mass, North Africa swamped, with Europe next.

No winners could emerge from the bedlam created, and indubitably, no welfare benefits utopia for the invading hoards to milk dry, those networks along with crucial institutions and commerce, destroyed forever by the gross engorgement. Refusing to swallow the aliens imposed upon them by the high and mighty EU, many clued-up observers foretold of indigenous populations undertaking Bosnia-style civil war across Europe, irretrievably fracturing country economies.

Dismayingly, with homeland security breached, under instructions from al-Qaeda, Muslim extremists could run riot, maybe even detonating a nuclear device or enacting germ warfare. Eventually, Europe's indigenous peoples would wrestle hegemony from Brussels and Strasburg, the invaders dragooned back through race wars, but the damage, irreparable. All combatants would lose, regression back to primeval times inevitable, 3,000 years of European development wiped out forever, the offspring the same as the spinoffs of global thermonuclear war.

Glyn presumed the probable conflict must have been played out as a virtual war game by the EU many times over. Yet still intransigence, stubborn political correctness, and far too many left-wing political agendas throughout Western Europe meant the result might become reality, a ticking time bomb the EU concealed from its enforced citizens, making its draconian legacies everlasting.

Speculating there must be a 'Plan B' involving an enlightened syndicate dissecting the catastrophic rattrap behind the official formality in Brussels and even New York, he further envisaged the trust being commanded to foster a different solution, other than guilt-trip incentivised, ineffective and corrupt international aid to give Third World economic migrants and asylum seekers far better advantages in their own backyards.

Behind his rage, Saleh showed intelligence, seeing the swamping of Europe by blacks and others was not sustainable. Instead of the infiltrator becoming Western in outlook, the opposite could happen, Europe reflecting the chaos and barbarity of black Africa. *What's the profit in that PC absurdity*, Glyn deliberated?

Later in the voyage, after digesting events in Tunis, the crew discussed some plausible solutions, conceivably sellable to all parties. But in front of Nassar, a benign resolution eluded them. Taking in his prediction, in their minds they saw a gargantuan human tidal wave hammering the Kent coastline, the breakers at Whitstable broken like frail matchsticks in its wake, and further up the beach, the Anglo young mown down and trampled underfoot by the uncontrollable flood, Priest's dystopia demon substantiated. Unanimously, the scale of the crisis and its indisputable disastrous sequel, if not inhibited, acted to constrict the crew's rational cognizance.

"What happens to those illegals you nab, Colonel?" Glyn sought.

Nassar grimaced. "Law breakers are imprisoned for a long time, convicted terrorists, hung." Pausing, he audited the Englishmen for retroaction, their rebuttals minimal with only half-gestured acknowledgments. "Other illegals are detained at a holding camp on the Séjoumi. From there, Bedouin contractors take them back to their own domiciles along Trans African Highway One, questing for further costs compensation from their families and often their governments. The Bedouin treat the illegals harshly. It is the only deterrence we are allowed."

"What do you mean by harshly?" David enquired.

"The Sub-Saharans know the Bedouin despise them. These ships of the desert appraise them to be cockroaches and vermin, contributing nothing and feeding off the endeavours of others. Thus, they take foremost delight in the repatriating process. During the journey, the illegals might lose an arm, a leg, or worse. When they leave here, thank God, it is no longer our problem."

His last words peppered with venom, a leer returned to Nassar's lineaments, Poseidon's crew startled by the vicious denunciation, unanticipated from a clearly erudite man. Still, if they walked in his shoes, the luxury of hypocrisy might not be at their disposal.

Composing himself, Nassar clasped his hands behind his back, his body carriage and eye inflections constraining the detainees to appreciate his pickle with empathy.

"I have wrestled with my conscience regarding this enigma and have even prayed for guidance. I gape at my sons, wondering what is in store for them over the next twenty years, and later, my grandchildren. I argue with my daughter about the issue and my wife tries to calm us, but my daughter is alert to the threat from the Sub-

Saharans. My wife talks to the wives of other senior police officers and ministry officials about the subject. Some used to argue Sub-Saharan Muslims should be welcomed, but their number has dwindled. Even the more liberal in government circles no longer talk about accepting economic migrants and asylum seekers from the south. Everybody recognises it is a very serious perplexity for Tunisia."

Mopping his brow, the stinging admission resulting in perspiration, suddenly he appeared spent.

"When you return to England, tell as many people as you can what you have witnessed in Tunis." Upgrading his intonation, he entreated, "*Tell them* about this contentious subject. *Tell* your politicians. *Tell* the press. Make them understand the reality. Make them understand, it is *they* causing the hindrance, not us. Make them understand measures must be taken *now*, or it will not only be North Africa that is swamped, it will be the undivided European continent as well."

Thumping his hand down on the desk to emphasise his vexation made the crew jump, the vibration echoing as he sat back down. With his head bent down at an acute angle, so he could not see their phizogs, Nassar beseeched, "And now, gentlemen, I have duties to see to."

Waving a dismissive hand, he flagged he did not intend to indulge the Englishmen further. With his hackles aggravated, they twigged their lingering attendance might only lead to further recriminations germane to European hypocrisy.

A few nervous seconds passed before Jeff took the lead. "Well, if that's all, Colonel Nassar, we'll make a move."

"Yes...it is best," Nassar slowly approved, his mind placed elsewhere.

Sticky and stiff from being unremittingly seated, the Englishmen got up to leave.

"One final point," Nassar voiced, resolutely fixing them, his prosecuting eyes penetrating their flesh, as if with a sword tip. "If you do happen-on your friend Saleh again, you will inform us, won't you?"

"We will, Colonel," Jeff assured.

After returning their passports, his piercing eyes never left them as they slowly filed out of the interrogation room.

Back on the Avenue de Carthage, Poseidon's crew saw Nassar spying on them from his window observation den. Evidently still under suspicion, they headed back to the Tunis Marina, the hardship over, or so they imagined.

15

MAJID'S CRUISER

During the trek, Glyn posed to Jeff and Ed, "That wasn't new for you guys, was it."

Unusually reticent to reply, the seniors clocked each other awkwardly.

"Tell them," said Ed.

"We've had comparable interactions," Jeff informed the newcomers, "but fortunately not with the Tunisian Police. Nine years ago, in Port Said, customs found a stowaway in a storage room in Poseidon's bows. Unbeknown to us, he had got aboard while we were provisioning and servicing the boat. The Egyptian police took some persuading we were unwitting of his occupancy. Then in 2005, we made a mistake with a Bulgarian passenger. Accosting us in Benghazi when we were going on to Crete, he spoke excellent English and came across as trustworthy. We told him he'd have to sleep in the saloon during the three-day sail to Heraklion, but he okayed the imposition. We'd taken the odd paying passenger occasionally, and he seemed alright. However, when the Libyan customs came for embarkation oversee, incontrovertibly they knew the Bulgarian, found hashish in his suitcase and arrested him. Again, we had to talk our way out of that one. After much effort, the Libyans esteemed we didn't know the Bulgarian before the nab, and were ignorant about the hashish. Since then, we don't take human cargo under any circumstances."

"So that's why you were both a little strained," Tom chimed in.

"Yes. Luckily, North African police departments and customs organisations seldom share information. It's why Colonel Nassar abided heedless of those events."

"Even Jeff and I, have our limits for staying ice cool, you know," Ed dryly declared.

Astounded, the newcomers made no comment. No point. They were taking the plunge when they climbed aboard Poseidon at Cadiz. Unequivocally, the bold stroke had delivered, but over the past few hours, not in the form they envisioned.

Down on the marina quayside, the ship's company ran into Majid Hamzah bin Najimy bin al Fakhoury, one of the Tunisian moguls they met in the café on the Avenue Habib Bourguiba. A medium built man with a dimpled chin, flashing deep brown eyes, and dressed in smart European clothing, he had talked to Poseidon's crew about dealings and sailing, his bubbly and sociable charm leaving a lasting impression.

"I arrived at the Hotel du Lac, when you were being taken away by the police," he told them. "Is anything wrong? Are you alright?"

Taking turns, they précised the events of the last few hours, sometimes Majid acting alarmed at what he heard, sometimes relieved and non-judgmental, specially about their reluctance to extend Saleh passage to Sicily.

"You were quite right to deny this Ethiopian access to your boat. We are plagued by these fiends. If you had agreed to take him, you might have got into hot water with customs, and then the police." Backing away from them, he leaked, "Europeans can be jailed in Tunisia. Be warned."

Reacting to the uncompromising advice, Jeff pressed his lips together. "Yes, Colonel Nassar made that quite clear."

Aroused by the happenstance, Majid beckoned them to come closer. "Please," he besought, before terminating to browse their characteristics, still taut after the taxing police station endurance. "Come back to my cruiser, and we will talk more. It's not safe here. You never know who is lurking or listening. It's moored only a few minutes from here. Come."

As usual, everyone trained on Jeff to take the reins. Answering Majid in the affirmative, he nodded indicating for the crew to follow the dapper Tunisian businessman. As they turned the next corner, Majid rested to acclaim his cruiser; a twin-engine, sea going vessel, thirty feet at the Plimsoll line, constructed in burnished, white-coated aluminium and highly polished deck metalwork and woodwork.

"She can accommodate six passengers with ease," he proudly told them.

Onboard, a man dressed in traditional Arab garb acknowledged Majid. Forging ahead, their host bartered a few words with the large, imposing man, then ushered Poseidon's crew aboard. Eyeing them dubiously, the man then left, stationing himself on the quayside.

"Jibran will keep watch for us," Majid guaranteed. "He has been with my family for many years, and I trust him implicitly."

Beneath deck level in the stern, Majid and his guests went down a few steps to enter a sumptuous saloon. Oozing opulence, it made the Englishman comprehend their host must be one of the cities more successful magnates.

"Can I offer you some refreshment?"

Desperately needing liquid after the exertions of the Colonel Nassar coming together, the crew requested Tunisian beer, Majid opting for orange juice.

"Occasionally, I try to be a good Muslim," he certified, beaming graciously at his guests. "Your good health, gentlemen," he toasted raising his glass.

"And yours," Jeff reciprocated.

Extending their legs out whilst seated on luxurious built-in benches and a few equally plush chairs, Poseidon's crew relaxed, happy to be away from the police station. While Majid played mine-host, they intermeshed complementary smiles and polite words with him.

"You must have done well for yourself, to own such a grand motor cruiser," Ed flattered taking in the saloon.

"Mmmm, let me tell you about myself," Majid wrote back, brimming with pride.

Taking a position stage-centre, he proceeded to trace his family name going back five generations. A well-known community leader at the turn of the twentieth century and a grain merchant by trade, his great, great grandfather contributed milling and wholesale flour services between the local farming community and retail outlets. Diversifying into exporting a wide range of Tunisian products to other African countries, the Middle East and Europe, his great grandfather expanded the business, then his grandfather and father grew the combine, annexing imports, mainly from southern Europe. Recently retiring, his aging father left the running of the Fakhoury Empire to Majid. Concluding his review, he proudly showed his guests photographs of his family, principally his wife and children.

"God has blessed me," he proclaimed, grinning widely with satisfaction.

Warming to their host, the ship's company began to feel human again.

Indisputably wealthy, possibly even more so than the seniors, nonetheless, his gentility and body language unveiled a successful entrepreneur, never pre-judging and tarrying neutral in search of new capers. By embodying a friendly, interpersonal style, his countenance seemingly always tender, even affectionate, it became easy to see why the family proprietorship resided safe under his tenure.

"I do like talking to Europeans," he told them. "It gives me a chance to practice my English or French."

Like Colonel Nassar, Majid had been part-educated in France and England, speaking both languages fluently. Founded on a combination of traditional Arab mixed in with European agents, he projected a perceptive, eloquent deportment. Though content with Tunisian life, he still needed to complement it with English and French culture. Travelling in Europe, he liked to dress in a Saville Row suit, wear a homburg at a jaunty angle, peruse *The Times* or *Le Figaro*, dine at The Ivy or L'Arpege, visit the National Gallery or the Louvre, and play the horses at Ascot and Longchamp. Descartes, Zola and Waugh were his reading passion, but his front runner author lodged without precedence as Graham Greene.

Given the opportunity, Majid possessed a vivid imagination, often placing himself in the role of a Greene character, his pets being Holly Martins from *The Third Man* and *Our Man in Havana* main protagonist James Wormold, the escapism adjoining flair and vitality to his nature. Often, he reprised Greene character impersonations on social occasions for the amusement of his guests. Conversely, when the real world impinged uninvited on his business and household life, he found conserving the cool of a Greene hero unyielding to consistently pull off. Notwithstanding his high status coupled with his outgoing personality, he quickly lapsed into panic.

Soon Poseidon's crew were to see the self-admitted shortcoming played out before them.

Very familiar with Colonel Nassar, Majid filled-in his guests *vis-à-vis* the Chief of Police, some of the Colonel's angles they witnessed at the police station explained permitting them to assimilate his motivations, explicitly his liking for England, and prodigy for impending catastrophe.

"How do you know all this?" David probed.

"Nassar is a public figure, often in the society pages of the Tunis press with his family and other dignitaries. We in the commercial community have close ties with the Government, but we do try to keep adjacent from the police."

"For a man in his early forties," Glyn applauded, "he's done very well for himself."

"Oh, the Colonel is much older," Majid accredited. "He displays youthful features, but he is in his mid-fifties."

"He must work out and have few vices."

"By all accounts, he runs every day, and has a reputation for self-denial. He's a good man, but don't suppose he is incapable of ruthlessness, even brutality, should it be predestined by circumstances." Frowning, Majid conveyed, "He does have a menacing streak in his armoury."

"Now why do you say that?" Jeff ticketed, throwing him a bowled-over pout.

"Because my friend," he began, leaning headlong in his chair. "I too, have met Colonel Nassar…officially, only under a different footing to yours."

"You mean, you've been in trouble with the police?" Bill jabbed.

"Regrettably, yes." Candidly flexing his hands, he divulged, "I won't pretend my transactions are always squeaky clean. No wheeler dealer can claim such piety in this part of the world. But I regulate how far to go without incurring molestation from the law."

"So, what happened, Majid?" Ed pressed.

"*Ah*, goodness me," he retorted, shaking his head as if he should have known better. "Customs found some stowaways in one of my shipping vessels…so-called asylum seekers, like your Saleh. Because I'm the owner, I was summoned to Central Police Headquarters. Like you, I found the Colonel to be courteous, but because I'm Tunisian, I was dealt a stern warning. Nassar told me, if future customs inspections found anything on any of my vessels, even mildly contravening the law, I'd be fined and possibly imprisoned." Halting momentarily as if conjuring up the trial again, he shrugged his shoulders and winced. "By all that's holy, he phrased it in such a pleasant way, I almost felt sympathy for him. However—" Gaping out of the saloon window at Jibran, he then acquired his guests again, reengaging in a hushed tone. "Since then, I have told crews I will be conducting random governance before customs arrive. If they find anyone aboard, the stowaways have been disposed of before my possible arrival. But —" Again he goggled out of the saloon window, as if unsure of his own security and well-being. "I have been told by a business friend I am being followed by the police."

"Is that why you keep on gawking out of the window?" Glyn grilled.

"Yes, you can't be too careful."

"When did this incident happen?" Jeff enquired.

"Oh, let me see…about four weeks ago."

"And the police still have you under surveillance?"

"My friend is very well informed. He has a relative employed in the police administration centre who sweeps reports for my name. Just last week, I was told this person had seen my name. It implies the police still have an interest in my operations, so I assume, yes, I am followed." Leaning frontwards, he briefed, "Be aware, the Colonel could have dispatched someone to keep an eye on your activities."

Discussing their similar examinations further, both parties determined the best way forward was to espouse a vigilant frame of mind. Saying Poseidon's crew would remain on police radar until they left Tunis, Majid emphasised the carry out to be a typical routine after an interrogation, and they should not be unduly distressed.

"It's a question of being seen to be doing the expected thing," advised the bigwig.

"How do you mean?" asked Tom.

"There are EU observers based in Tunis superintending how we deal with illegals and terrorists. The President doesn't like their interference but knows because Europe has become our major trading partner, Tunisia must play ball." Squinting, he fired off a shaky regard at his guests. "That is the right phrase, isn't it?"

"Yes indeed, Majid," Jeff endorsed, attracting Ed with a hand gesture, their harrowing escapades in Port Said and Benghazi coming to mind. "We are aware if illegals are uncovered on foreign vessels as stowaways, the owners can be levied a hefty find, even imprisonment."

"And," Majid cautioned, opening his hands in a sympathetic gesture, "their boat can be impounded, even permanently confiscated. But, let me tell you, the same punishment can also be metered out to a Tunisian national. This is why I have embraced a careful *modus operandi* since being carpeted by Nassar."

Still acutely worried about the possibility of further stowaway mishaps, Majid told the Englishmen more about his ancestry to qualify his magnified concern.

Instituting a long-standing reputation as good citizens over many decades, the Fakhoury family had gained local kudos. His grandfather had a term as Mayor of Tunis in the nineteen-thirties, and his father like Majid possessed Tunis Chamber of Commerce credentials. Essential for business proprietary, both were also benevolent contributors to Red Crescent. Albeit, a family history of civic allegiance did not make Majid immune from police investigation and supervision. More alarmingly, any scandal resultant from him being convicted of smuggling, damaged the family name and thereby Fakhoury commercial connections. Doubtless, Glyn deduced, he had taken the Colonel's admonishing very seriously.

To the Englishmen's surprise, Majid's clement accent deviated. Buttonholing them with a vexed temperament, he exposed, "There is another consideration for me, gentlemen. I freely confess I am an imperfect Muslim, but I do try. You see—" Hesitating, he took a sip of orange juice. "My religion teaches observance of the law. There are texts implying a deep lineage between the soul and God's judgment. It's what Christians call Last Judgment Theology."

Unfamiliar with the guidelines, they drew a blank from most of Poseidon's crew.

Seeing his companion's lack of comprehension, Colin intervened to delineate the phrase. "It means, religious ideologies about the soul, in its relationship to death, judgement and heaven and hell."

Surprised by the lucidity of the definition, Majid upstretched his eyebrows. "Yes, sounds right." Moving into their midst, contrition afflicted him. "So, you will understand for both physical and spiritual reasons, I wish for no more showdowns with Nassar." Dawdling for a moment, he then prescribed, "I'd advise you to ensure your schooner is clean."

With the unlimited police episode making for heightened watchfulness, Jeff and Ed imparted their assurances to the grandee.

"Good, I'm glad you agree," he responded. "I'd also advise…"

Before he could go further, Jibran engrossed his master's eye.

"Excuse me for a moment, gentlemen."

As Majid talked to Jibran on the quayside, Poseidon's crew watched through the saloon windows. Distinctly agitated, the merchant lifted his arms in what they perceived to be a disconcerted stamp before inspecting the quayside back and forth.

"Something going on there," David broached. "That big Arab fella has seen something."

"Yes," Tom notarised, "I wonder what little drama is about to unfold."

Minutes later, both master and servant returned to the cruiser, Jibran staying in the stern keeping watch.

"What is it?" Ed trilled, as Majid re-entered the saloon.

"Jibran has seen a man, possibly a policeman, spying on us from over by those closed chandler shops." Denoting out of a saloon window at the single-story buildings, the Englishmen spied in the given direction. "The polarity is—" Wavering, he gazed at Poseidon's crew. "Is he spying on you, or me?"

Moving to a window, Steve strained out towards the chandlers. "I can't see anyone."

"No, presumably, he is hiding in the shadows," Majid conjectured, "knowing Jibran had spotted him."

"Is he a uniformed policeman?" Jeff challenged.

"No. The police use plain clothes for undercover functions."

"So he's in Arab attire?"

"No, European I think."

"Are you sure?"

"*Jibran*," Majid pealed.

Entering the saloon, Majid talked to the big Arab in Arabic, then bid him to revisit his vigil.

"Ah…" Majid hesitantly began, "it seems he is wearing conventional Arab dress with a European jacket."

Poseidon's crew gaped at each other in amazement.

"Rings very much with the way Saleh was dressed," Glyn designated.

Alarmed, Majid blurted, "*what!*"

"Yes, Saleh was wearing what you describe," Jeff enunciated. Musing about the ramifications if it turned out to be the Ethiopian, his expression soured.

Screwing up his eyes, Majid glared over at the chandlers again, attempting to locate whoever skulked in the shadows. "If it is your Saleh, he must have followed you to the police station… and then here." Tensing up, Majid's lineaments became a legion of incrimination. "He must still picture you might take him to Sicily. This Saleh of yours is very persistent."

"Might not be him," Tom guessed. "Difficult to see how he could be pursuing us, when he must know the police are still after him."

"A good point, Tom," Ed okayed, turning to scrutinise the chandler shops. "We need to find out who really is out there."

Concurring with Ed, Majid then traded more words with Jibran, his servant leaving the cruiser and walking briskly across the quayside.

"Jibran will make out like he is going into the city," Majid told them. "But he will circle around and try to see more clearly who is watching us."

After ten fractious minutes for those aboard the cruiser, Jibran returned. Updating his master on the quayside, with bated breath Poseidon's crew studied them talking. Re-joining them, a mystified badge breached Majid's face, magnifying everyone's keenness to learn about what they were about to confront.

"It seems there are two watchers in the shadows," he enumerated, "about fifty yards apart. It appears neither is wise to the other's presence, but both are monitoring my cruiser."

Unbridled supposition broke out amongst Poseidon's crew.

"Let's be logical about this," David petitioned, his army training coming to the fore drawing their focus. Moving about the saloon, he gathered his brainwaves. "There are two potentialities. One, the two spectators are both policemen. Or two, one is a policeman and the other is possibly Saleh." Ogling the seniors, he warranted, "Saleh was not stupid and undeniably, scared of the police. On that basis, the two onlookers could both be policemen. The riddle is, are they both spying on Majid, or is only one, and the other is spying on us…and maybe, just maybe, they are unaware of each other's existence out by the chandler shops."

"I see your logic, David," Jeff muttered. "But until we identify the bystanders, we cannot establish an action plan."

"There is another possibility," Glyn suggested. "Saleh's strong desire to escape to Europe might have fuelled his preparedness to prolong trying for Poseidon, meaning he is out there, and the other beholder is a policeman, holding vigil on either Majid or us."

"And neither is alive to the other's actuality," David distinguished, completing the adjudication.

"We can either tough it out here until daybreak," Glyn recommended, "when both kibitzers will either make a move, or recede back into the city, or better still, smoke one or both of them out now."

"Yes, Glyn is right," Bill laid down. "I don't relish being here in the morning, and still not conversant with what we must stand up to."

So convoluted, the enigma had the rest of the Englishmen analysing the various permutations for a few seconds.

Retaining black humour even under hard-nosed conditions, Ed jeered, "thank you for clarifying the puzzle, gentlemen. Irrefutably, we're now thoroughly savvy with our deadlock. Sir Humphrey Appleby couldn't have put it better!"

Howbeit the surmised serious state of affairs, Poseidon's crew chuckled. Previous North African skirmishes had imbued them with a devil-may-care, invulnerable resolve to handle any poser embroiling them. Somehow, they'd get through it, though inwardly, they anticipated more white-knuckle rides until they departed Tunis.

Still lost in oppressive reverberations and inattentive to the humour, Majid eulogised, "I cannot fault your dissection of the impasse…but what should we do?"

Further group discussion took place, but before they decided anything, Jibran came back into the saloon, murmuring into Majid's ear.

"Gentlemen, it seems events have overtaken us," Majid announced. "One of the watchmen is making his way to my cruiser."

Goggling out of the saloon windows, everyone strained to see who approached. As the shape emerged from semi-darkness it became clear the inbound was indeed Saleh.

"What should we do?" Majid nervously bleated, his agitation increasing.

"Let him aboard," David advocated. "We have to assume neither of the two pathfinders was hip to the other's occurrence, and if the second more distant figure is a policeman, he is unmindful of Saleh's predicament."

"Everything is binary, hey?" Glyn quipped.

"What?" David exclaimed.

"It's what you said back in Cadiz. Is it what's fuelling your cerebration processes now?"

"Yes, it is, Glyn. Saleh must be allowed aboard. If the second explorer is a policeman and unacquainted Saleh is wanted, he will assume there is an additional guest coming onboard the cruiser. We can then reassess the perplexity and decide what to do."

All signified their approval, Majid instructing Jibran to go back onto the quayside and bring Saleh aboard.

Beckoning him to hurry, Jibran growled something snappy in Arabic. Double-checking the Ethiopian making his last few nervous steps, Glyn concluded whatever the big Arab aforementioned, it made Saleh move nimbly to the cruiser. Taking him by the upper arm, Jibran brought him aboard, and down into the saloon, submitting him like a sacrifice to his master. Nodding for Jibran to release their unwanted guest, Majid stared at him as if he represented a jinx. Scowling and hissing at Saleh, the big Arab then went top-side, assuming his ever-attentive vigil.

Bedraggled but composed, Saleh stood in the saloon doorway mooning at Poseidon's crew with immense presumption.

"So, we meet again," he footnoted, forcing a smile, and gesticulating his relief to the Englishmen.

"Saleh, I'd not be flippant, if I were you," Jeff sternly counselled. "We made it very clear, we can't take you to Sicily. After the police chased you at the Hotel du Lac, that little fling should have brought you to your senses to be heading back south to Ethiopia by now."

"The option did cross my mind, but Muslim fundamentalists are after me for theft, and for not carrying out their decrees." With a melancholy attitude, he let his hands drop. "They'd be able to trace me."

"So, you *were* involved in a terrorist activity?" Glyn asserted.

Dipping his head, he divulged, "They wanted me to join a Muslim Brotherhood sect to commit a terrorist act in Holland." He ogled up. "But I couldn't go along with it, so I knew they'd pursue me."

"*Holland!*" Majid exclaimed, grimacing anxiously and stepping towards Saleh.

"Yes."

"Oohh...God." Slumping down in a chair, his exhaustive being racked with regret, he disclosed, "A terrorist atrocity was reported on Tunisian national television this evening. Twenty-eight people were killed and over seventy injured when a bomb exploded in the offices of a Dutch newspaper." Staring blankly at the Ethiopian, his incredulity deepened. "You were to be involved in that?"

"Yes...I was to have taken part."

Ashamed someone from his religion could be tangled up in such a heinous act, Majid's head fell. His heart filling with acrimonious foreboding, he became unable to say anything more.

"I worked out the Muslim fundamentalists could use their networks in Ethiopia to find and kill me," Saleh further explained. "If the police capture me, I'll be deported back to Ethiopia." Assuming a timid disposition, he bug-eyed Poseidon's crew, the frail demeanour they noted in the Hotel du Lac garden terrace resurrected uncloaking his flimsy and brittle nature. "My only option is Sicily," he whimpered.

Fixing them imploringly with frantic eyes, his visage welled up with uncertainty, his shoulders sloping even more than at their earlier meeting. Shuddering uncontrollably, not far from terminal collapse, what little dignity occupied his psyche deserted him. With his volatile anger dispelled, his persona resembled that of a desolate street urchin, reliant on charity for survival. Once again, the Englishmen began to empathise with Saleh's conundrum. Though they knew the Ethiopian was capable of the most vulgar and disparaging condemnation of everything non-Muslim, his unconcealed vulnerability and helplessness made it delicate to reject him in his hour of need. Even the encumbered Majid put away self-centeredness and censure of the Ethiopian's fundamentalist association, showing some distress for Saleh's dilemma.

"The chasing police could not catch me," he triumphantly told them. "I knew they'd take you for questioning, so I hid in an alley outside the police station, waiting for you to be released. Then I followed you to the quayside."

"Yes," Ed malevolently grouched. "We tallied that out when we saw you in the shadow of the chandler shops."

Forming a huddle, Poseidon's crew discussed the befuddlement. Fired by their compassionate commiseration for the man on the run, they went around the buoy again, telling Saleh even if they allowed him onboard Poseidon, custom officers could easily find him when they inspected her for stowaways. Not bothering to emphasise the impact of that discovery on the crew, at any rate, Saleh knew it to be self-evident. They told him Colonel Nassar had been tasked with apprehending illegals and relentlessly pursuing transients, making it hopeless for him to gain transit to Sicily from any boat registered at the Tunis Harbour Authority.

"Every vessel is combed on arrival and before departure by customs," Ed informed. "We have been subject to their rigour on many occasions. Believe me, they'd find you."

"I'm afraid it's not on, Saleh," Jeff backed. "Surely, you can see that?"

"Yes...yes of course," he settled, the tang of resignation resonating in his pipes, savage reality distilling on false optimism.

Wilting, he collapsed down holding his head in both hands, muttering something about he should have listened to his mother.

Despite his earlier diatribe against them at the Hotel du Lac, Poseidon's crew felt very bad about the Ethiopian's jam. They wanted to do something to defend him, but what?

Sensing his guests softening, Majid's initial magnanimity for the absconder waned. Rising, he assertively announced, "There is another head-scratcher." Peering at Saleh, he raised an accusing finger, reminding Glyn and his comrades of how Nassar did the same thing earlier in the evening. "You were not the only voyeur spying on my cruiser."

Saleh's mouth opened in surprise at the stark admission, his madcap glare familiar to Poseidon's crew returning. Slithering back up, he took a step back, his mien apprehensive and crabby. Comprehending he had underestimated how much heat his irresponsibility had brought on Poseidon's crew, he wrung his hands and hopped from foot to foot, just as he did in the hotel terrace garden.

"There is a second clocker out there by the chandler shops," Majid assigned. "He must have seen you come onboard. Almost certainly, he is a policeman."

Not bothering to verify his own under-surveillance status, or that Nassar might have despatched someone to keep an eye on the Englishmen, he gave the distinct imprint the second patroller pursued Saleh. Scenting no further moves were available to the runaway, Poseidon's crew did not attribute a clarification. By coming aboard Majid's cruiser, he had boxed himself in, reducing his alternatives even further.

Reconciled they were going to extricate themselves from the quandary, the Englishmen's consideration decayed. Without a word spoken, they knew Salah had to go. Before any of them became prescriptive, Jibran entered the saloon again, whispering in his master's ear.

His eyes bulging to their extremities, Majid blurted, "The second peeper is on the move. He's *coming* this way."

Updating his classification, David modified, "If I was wrong, and it is a policeman cognizant with Saleh, he has probably been waiting for him to come onboard, so he can nab us all in the act."

"Here he comes," Steve broadcast, drawing everyone's attention, including Saleh's.

Gawking out of the saloon windows, they all marked the bod on the quayside nearing the cruiser.

Holding his breath momentarily, the Ethiopian stopped hopping, realising he was interwoven in a spider's web of his own making.

When the second personage hit fifty yards from the cruiser, those onboard enumerated he moved with a cocksure, purposeful stride, the click of leather soles on the quayside top tinkling as he advanced. Dressed in a light European style suit, with a white shirt and dark necktie, he projected the epitome of an imagined secret policeman stalking his prey. Sensing the cruiser occupants were ascertaining his progress, his movement quickened. Too late for Saleh to decamp out of the stern, and back onto the quay.

Alarmed, Majid turned to Saleh. "I am sorry, but you must leave. I cannot take the risk." Hastily surveying the saloon, he related, "There is a door along the cabin corridor leading onto the bows. You can slip onto the next cruiser and escape." Aiming the briefest of glances at the second unwelcome caller forging across the quayside, he then drawled, "Here, I will take you," heedful to get the dodger of his cruiser before the second watcher saw him and before Saleh could procrastinate.

Throwing a glimpse of finality back at Poseidon's crew, Saleh followed him down the corridor. They said nothing. There was nothing more to be said.

Less than thirty seconds later, they heard the second phantom demanding entry onto the cruiser, Jibran's physical presence neutralised by his unambiguous jurisdiction.

Conceding the unknown-someone was about to blag his way in, uninvited, Majid rushed back to the saloon, quivering and mumbling prayers. Grounded on his tonality, unmistakably, the second shadow had authority and was coming aboard, his insistence non-negotiable. Not waiting for permission, he descended the stern stairwell and entered the saloon, customary Arab servility sidelined.

Under the saloon lights, Majid and his guests took in the intruder. Tall, smartly groomed, with a thin moustache and well-trimmed sideburns, they ranked him to be in his early thirties. Stylish in his carriage, confident and in charge, he possessed gravitas even before speaking.

Taking in Majid and Poseidon's crew, his eyes then traversed about the saloon. Turning, he barked something in Arabic, and Jibran joined them. Closing the double-doors, as if sealing the threshold between the stairwell and the saloon to lock everybody in, the erudite man then silently walked about perusing the saloon's occupants. Peeved by his probe, regardless they stayed silent. Turning his audit to the corridor running to the bows, he drew a gun from his jacket-concealed holster then searched each of the berths, heads, storage spaces and galley for other occupants, before returning to the saloon.

Eyeing the incumbents with suspicion, he replaced his gun and walked into their midst as if prying for incriminating evidence. Ripening uneasy physiognomies, uncertain of what the stranger intended, tension grew, Glyn having reveries of a repeat Colonel Nassar chapter, the new spectre posing an even greater curse to their continued freedom.

Lighting up a small cheroot, the trespasser delved for their approval. "I hope you don't mind me smoking," he heralded, his vocalisation dismissive of any criticism.

No one's lips moved.

"My name is Lieutenant Zarif bin Siddiq bin Al-Ramiz," he informed, desisting to let the introduction sink in. "Colonel Nassar ordered me to keep an eye on the crew of the Poseidon and guarantee they didn't get into any more nettles." A sadistic locution spread across his kisser, his semi-open mouth flaunting perfect white teeth. Evidently enjoying the disquiet, it solidified the merciless impression his suspects had formed about him.

Without doubt, Glyn discriminated, Ramiz would take pleasure in quizzing them. "Can I see your passports?" he requested.

Moving amongst Poseidon's crew, Ramiz perused photos against their owner's faces, in the same way the Chief of Police had done, then proceeded with rudimentary queries, his English clipped in the Arabic fashion, but his command, impeccable. Approaching the two Tunisians, he solicited their identity cards, Glyn logging he did not ask Majid to confirm his identification. In fact, he barely clocked him. Opening a second round of interrogation, in a heartbeat he shifted effortlessly from Arabic into English, depending on whom he interrogated, Glyn adducing, here was yet another expansively educated Tunisian, conceivably finishing his schooling in Europe.

His no-nonsense, straightforward manner hinted Ramiz might be an old hand at this kind of police work, managing the situation with undiminished paramountcy and aplomb. One man acting alone with ten implied recidivists, he loitered untouchable, unassailably safe, those under his authority not presenting any problem to him.

Finally, he moored his accusative train on Majid. Propped up against a saloon roof pillar, and discernibly shaking, he had gone ashen with dread, blood draining from his countenance through notions of presupposed consequence.

"You are the owner of this craft?" Ramiz tabled.

"Ye...yes," Majid stuttered.

"I see. And how do you come to know these Englishmen?"

Majid accounted for when they had met at the Avenue Habib Bourguiba café, how he came to be at the Hotel du Lac when the Englishmen were taken by the police, and quite by chance how he had run into them on the marina quayside.

Whilst he spoke, Ramiz strolled up and down the saloon, picking up various high-priced items to examine, and occasionally glimpsing back at the cruiser owner, as he listened. Unsure if Ramiz was aware of his brush with Nassar, Majid's faltering voice became reduced to little more than a hiss, the notion of meeting the Chief of Police again stinging him like a knife in the ribs. Although Majid's recollections were authentic,

Glyn knew his diminished speech could cast doubt on the veracity of the exegesis. Notwithstanding, if the policeman did find it unconvincing, he kept it to himself.

"I see," Ramiz credited, his back to Majid but the sheer vibe he emitted preserving the strict facade. "Tell me...is there anybody else aboard your cruiser?"

"*No*," the jumpy businessman snappily shot back.

Replacing the item he studied, Ramiz slowly riveted Majid, the eagerness of his reply stimulating reservation.

"Are you sure?"

Wilting under the unrelenting pressure, no reply came from the twitchy host. Frozen to the spot, unable to form words, Majid's mouth refused to kick into action, his tongue as dry as straw.

"You see," Ramiz enlightened, "I saw someone come aboard about fifteen minutes ago." Twisting his head, he locked onto the Englishmen with an icy stare, before verifying, "A black, Sub-Saharan Muslim, wearing a European jacket."

Again, silence prevailed amongst his captives, the physical atmosphere becoming dense, an imaginary fog forming to mask off latent truth, Poseidon's crew totally in Majid's hands.

Spluttering to compile a decisive comeback, at length Majid stammered, "Ah...yes, there was another person...someone trying to sell us goods from the medina bazaar." Coughing, he cleared his throat of tension. "He has gone," he stipulated, his tenor sanguine hoping to engender credence.

"I didn't see him leave."

"Oh, he left through the bows and went on to the next cruiser."

Positioning himself directly in front of Majid and emanating menace, Ramiz plumbed for truth in his jittery puss. "Unquestionably?" he tested.

"Yes," Majid corroborated in as irrefutable a verbalisation as he could muster.

Turning to Poseidon's crew, Ramiz queried, "And you Englishmen can attest to this?"

They all nodded or rendered 'yes' in full agreement.

Still unconvinced, Ramiz moved on to entreat Jeff.

"Mister Tindle, you are the leader of this ensemble. Are you positive no one else is onboard this vessel?"

"Yes, I'm sure," he replied, his accent thick with certainty.

"Because as you know," Ramiz reprimanded scanning the Englishmen, "you and your friends are already under suspicion regarding the fugitive, Saleh bin Tariq bin Khalid Al-Asfour." Dallying, he let the assertion take root. "It'd be a grave mistake to become involved in some other folly beyond the law," the sinister silkiness of the threat crystallising on the Englishmen's hyperactive sensibilities.

Perceiving Ramiz undoubtedly knew the alleged seller from the medina bazaar was Saleh, they tried to convey dumbfoundment, but with guilt stupefying them, anxiety grew as the knot strained taut, breaking point not far away. Mindful he had brought them to the brink of collapse, Ramiz eased his austere body language to be flexible and goggled at them, a call for relaxation in its inflection.

"So…you all met at the café," he detailed, in a softer timbre, "then at the Hotel du Lac, and later on the quayside?"

"I actually saw them being taken away by the police at the Hotel du Lac," Majid corrected, assuming the Lieutenant's small inaccuracy was a ruse to trick him.

"Quite." Cogitating, Ramiz eyeballed the Englishmen again, his scrutiny fruiting nothing concerning his suspicions. "Do you have anything else to tell me?" he prospected, his tone soliciting truth.

Offering little riposte, they either blanked him, or made shallow attempts to distance themselves from the inquisitor's gloat by clearing their throats or fidgeting subconsciously whilst shaking their heads in the negative.

Finishing his cheroot, much to Majid's hidden annoyance, Ramiz extinguished the stub in a petite, onyx sweet tray. Shooting a cutting glower at the Englishmen, he slowly oscillated his head, weighing them up to estimate how much further they could be pushed.

"Do you know what I believe?" he announced. "I believe the

person who has now left…was in fact Saleh. He followed you to the quayside and waited for an opportunity to resume his plea to be taken to Sicily."

Taken aback by the reference to Sicily, Poseidon's crew were staggered.

Marking their shock, Ramiz popeyed wickedly. "Oh yes, while you were talking to Colonel Nassar, I listened via an intercom in an adjacent room. I heard the full extent of your story."

Saying nothing in recognition, instead the Englishmen traded discerning gleams, appreciating an obvious police ploy. If they'd been alert, instead of fearful in the interrogation room, the gambit should have occurred to them.

Replenishing tack for a moment, Ramiz conveyed almost cordially, "Incidentally, the Colonel and I have no secrets. You see…he is my uncle."

Coming as no surprise, common attributes between Ramiz and Nassar with respect to physique, deportment and assumed schooling were identifiable. Swapping ganders, Poseidon's crew subliminally constructed the cosy kinship used in the wily, if not cunning deception.

Resuming his challenge to their illumination, Ramiz pushed, "Now, who is going to tell me the truth? It will come out eventually."

Lamping their aspects, cocksure of rejoinders, none came, his charges stiff with inertia and silence.

"Very well," he tersely rebuked, "let me tell you what I divine happened." Making himself comfortable in a luxury swivel chair, he reviewed, "The fugitive came aboard the cruiser. You were disinclined to throw him off right away because you knew someone else surveyed the cruiser. Oh yes…" He turned to supplicate Majid. "…I saw your employee, Jibran, or is he your servant, when he was recceing, I understand that's the term you English use, the chandler shops. You told Saleh about what happened at the police station. You made it clear to him, even if you allowed him on the Poseidon, customs would find him. Then your sentry saw me coming, so you abruptly got Saleh off the cruiser." Swinging the chair about sharply, he digested the Englishmen, then in a persuasive articulation, adjudicated, "That is correct…isn't it?"

Again, nobody uttered a single word.

Getting up, Ramiz eyed Majid. "Plausibly, you are surmising I am oblivious about your own upset with customs a few weeks ago…but I'm not." Sneering, he displayed a bellicose reckoning. "Oh yes, I know all about you, Majid Hamzah bin Najimy bin al Fakhoury."

Verging on exhaustion with abstractions of another scathing instalment with Colonel Nassar, Majid visibly crumpled, leaving the Englishmen either sat or stood transfixed, scarcely breathing.

Sensing Majid's re-aroused discomfort, Ramiz blandished, "Calm yourself, you have been proclaimed clean…well, clean enough, shall we say."

Relieved, blood oozed back into the Chief Executive's face.

Pinpointing Jeff, Ramiz granted, "I will put your meeting with Majid down to coincidence. You have been unfortunate Saleh resurfaced again, and Majid was only thoughtful for your welfare." Grinning, his hubris in overdrive, he qualified, "However—" Resting momentarily, he heightened the tension, his sneer broadening. "You should really have told me the truth about what happened here this evening."

With that, he bid them goodnight, and departed the cruiser.

～

"Break out the brandy, Majid," Ed implored.

"Yes, I will join you," he riposted, clasping his hands together and tilting his head heavenwards. "Forgive me, Allah."

Reviewing the confrontation, Poseidon's crew initially evaluated it as another close shave with the Tunisian police, but then distinguished Ramiz fully knew the score long before he stepped onto the cruiser. In a perverse way, he'd been having fun at their expense. Bored with conventional policing duties, they fathomed it was the way he got his kicks. On reflection, Glyn determined the distinction to be academic, the colossal charade enacted for visceral amusement still dispensed more inquiries than it answered, principally, was the ordeal over?

With the brandy purging their discomfort, jagged nerves relaxed, brows were mopped, and sinews stretched out. Signs of upbeat normality reappeared.

"What about Saleh?" Glyn prompted.

"Oh…" Majid skittishly safeguarded, "I'd forgotten about him."

"Where did he go?"

"He slipped over the side onto the next cruiser, then made for the west wall of the marina. It's not far. His timing was impeccable. Ramiz couldn't have seen him leave."

"What will he do now, Majid?" Steve catechized, guessing like the rest of them, Saleh's prerogatives were fast running out.

Entirely in control again, the cruiser owner sauntered around the saloon constructing a supposition. "Arguably, he will head to Halq al Wadi, and try to bribe a fisherman to take him to Sicily. Failing that, he'll gang up with other bogus asylum seekers, and steal a fishing boat. They do it all the time." After taking a long satisfying pull on his brandy, he gushed, "I must confess, I am glad he has gone."

Deliberating on Majid's rebuttal, ostensibly, Poseidon's crew knew a fishing boat was Saleh's best chance, though founded on their recent sea experiences, it could be no picnic, above all for a novice sailor out on the unpredictable Med.

Finishing their conversation with Majid on a lighter note, they made their farewells and headed for Poseidon.

16

BACK ON POSEIDON

Before retiring, the ship's company mutually agreed to let discourse on the Ethiopian cataclysm and its subsequent repercussions drop. In the morning, they'd service and re-provision Poseidon for sailing to Marsala, 115 nautical miles north east of Tunis. Under full sail, the forecast prevailing wind from the Sahara would drive the schooner at an average speed of twelve knots, equating to a ten-hour trip. If they cleared the Lac de Tunis canal by 09:00, Poseidon could berth in Marsala Harbour before dusk.

Substantiating the need to show leadership and buttress crew motivation after their traumatic caper, Jeff tutored, "By late tomorrow evening, we'll be in a restaurant off the Lungomare Mediterraneo. Tonight's affair will have wafted away and been put into perspective, and the return voyage through the North-West Med will become central to your brainwork." Lingering, he took in the newcomer's exhausted demeanours. "Get a good night's sleep, and we'll begin again tomorrow."

However, expressing the sentiment intelligently, *au courant* beneath the gloss, he knew the Saleh affair had impregnated the crew and they'd be experiencing a plethora of mixed emotions after hearing Colonel Nassar's spurious asylum seeker critique, its juxtaposition with Saleh's plight exacting to classify for even the worldliest of men. Without doubt, his and Ed's job as ship's captains had become ratcheted up in the shape of preserving the crew's self-esteem and keeping spirits high.

Recalling the seniors had seen other happenings in both the Med and the Caribbean equalling and even surpassing the evening's events, apropos imperilment to life and limb, Jeff mentally reassessed the occurrences. Whilst in Montego Bay, the Poseidon 2 crew were held at gunpoint by Rastafarians and nearly robbed until police intervened. After docking in Port Sudan, they got word Nubian rioters were setting light to Western holdings. Defending speedily, they cast off as flaming torches were thrown at Poseidon. But these were relatively ephemeral moments, nimbly appraised and managed without any major jolt to crew psyches and sensibilities, whereas an enduring intensity over many hours differentiated the Saleh affair, digging deep into survival instincts, whilst simultaneously challenging moral code adages.

Reflecting more, Jeff understood Poseidon's crew to be good men, straight and true. Though empathetic towards the Ethiopian, all the same, what was going on back in Blighty in the context of the systematic invasion of their country by bogus asylum seekers and opportunist economic migrants was impossible to ignore. Grasping contradictory to his prudent words, those counter burdens plagued the crew, to what extent they might materialise as trying dilemmas was indeterminate, he and Ed needing to be vigilant, monitor for anguish and spontaneously nip it in the bud, or the rest of the voyage could be unsettling.

Expanding the concern, he knew a schooner is a very confined place for eight people to co-exist having ambivalent issues and feelings of guilt, invalid though they might be. For sure, he resolved it was essential to defuse fluster and torments swiftly, or the wanderlust could lapse into onboard conflict. Indubitably, he did not want their unwanted showdown with a hyped-up fugitive to defocus the ship's company, spoiling inter-crew relationships, jeopardising camaraderie, and thereby stirring Poseidon's smooth running.

Having also detected the newcomers had been hit hard, in the privacy of their cabin Ed shared his worries pertaining to upshot, the seniors mutually deciding on a regime of positivity to reboot morale. Though very confident their crew had the quintessential backbone to deal with what had happened, nevertheless, they'd not make assumptions. Hidden feelings and attitudes not expressed were counterproductive to required sea-sailing operational disciplines, resulting in mistakes putting Poseidon and the entire crew at risk. Only happy crews made good and effective crews, their happiness resultant from contentment and a tranquil mind. They had that prior to Tunis. It had to be recovered *tout de suite*.

In spite of Jeff's rousing words, the night was restless for the newcomers. Entering the twilight zone, they had found it to contain zoo creatures beyond the bounds of their back-home Blighty lives. Up close and personal with unforgiving reality had brought them into a domain they had previously only seen in B-movies. No matter how much refreshment was symbolically applied to the mouth, a peppery tang roosted in the saliva persisting the event's features, leaving a pungent taste of sickliness and a permanent trace on memory. Whilst shadowing placid adventure, they'd inadvertently stumbled on bleak realism, melting their boyhood Scheherazade depictions and driving home lugubrious misgivings about their quest.

Finding the unexpected encounter profound, Glyn compared it to some hairy moments he'd undergone whilst on business in Quito, Karachi, and even some parts of New York, but the Saleh happenstance was so intimate and heart-rendering, its aftermath fluttered above and beyond anything he could originate from private memoirs. True, he did not want Blighty swamped with immigrants, but the picture of Saleh ending his days prematurely also appalled him, the dichotomy unfathomable and beyond temperate resolution.

Incontrovertibly versed in scrapes, the most testing when

Suzy got into dire straits with the near-to criminal fraternity, the Saleh clash made him recollect the incident.

Whilst he was Stateside dealing for Mariano, she had a traffic accident, crashing her brand-new Suzuki jeep into a public road sign. Foolishly, she took the damaged car to a less than reputable garage to have it fixed, the garage owners wanting to charge her a fortune for their services. Failing that, they schemed to keep the jeep, witting she could not use her insurance provider because she had left the contretemps zone before the police arrived. Having Suzy over a barrel, no amount of business savvy diplomacy from Glyn made them relent. Calling on a Camden Town Irish Mafia contact to lean on the scoundrels, a quid pro quo price had to be paid in the bargain. In return for recovering the jeep and putting life-long frighteners on the scurvy garage owners, the Irish Mafia required Glyn to do a courier job for them. Accepting, they gave him a package for consignment to a Marseilles location. He could only hypothesise what it contained, and though at the extremities of his nerve, his love for Suzy drove him on, the delivery role passing without incident or interception from French customs, Glyn glad Suzy had been extricated from her calamity, and vowing never to let her screw-up again.

Lying in his bunk knowing cabin-mate Steve was also brooding about what had happened and correlating it against his own background, Glyn contrasted and compared the Ethiopian affair with Marseilles and less minor intricacies he had to disentangle in the past. Concluding the Tunis affair was totally about a third party, whose antics led to the ship's company coming under the authorities' microscope, his humanity for Saleh waned. They were innocents in the whole, damned, tricky gambol, but still got garnered and tangled in his intricate deception.

"Are you awake, Steve?"

"Yes."

"Do you think it's over?"

"No."

"Nor do I."

～

Next morning, a beaming Ed clanged Poseidon's bell then went around the cabins mustering the crew for chowtime. Ravenously wolfing down a splendid English breakfast prepared by Jeff, the early morning sea breeze whetted appetites and promoted light waffle. Afterwards, they went to work on their assigned jobs, servicing and re-provisioning Poseidon. By 08:00, replenished with consumables, and made clean, she glistened ready for embarkation. Radioing customs earlier, at 08:15 Jeff welcomed them aboard the schooner. First auditing crew credentials, they then began inspecting the vessel for contraband, and stowaways.

Absorbed by the customs officers and their departure protocol, the Englishmen did not notice a black Mercedes with tinted windows draw-up on the quayside. Alighting from the front passenger seat, Lieutenant Ramiz waved a stiff hand at the customs officials and boarded Poseidon.

"Good morning, gentlemen."

Responding to his presence, the crew moped at each other, uncertainty growing, pulses starting to quicken.

Sunglasses had been added to his smart attire. In outright command again, he cast a suspicious eye over the ship's company, his slightly upturned mouth designating he sought more pleasure at their expense before commencing on the day's tedious police duties. *Is there going to be a final sting in the tail?* Glyn rationally balloted.

Distracted again by the clink of the Mercedes back door opening, Colonel Nassar got out and stood before Poseidon's crew on the quayside, hands clasped behind his back holding his swagger stick, his peaked cap shielding his eyes from the sun. In daylight, their inquisitor came through as more statuesque and sphinx-like, his indisputable high station drawing glances from passers-by. Entranced by the spectacle, some dwelt but were hurriedly moved on by the Mercedes driver and one other officer.

Externally, Nassar showed no signs of replicating the savour of friendliness and courtesy afforded them during his initial introduction the previous evening, the crew's pulse rates taking a further upward step in response, making temples throb and jugular veins stand out. Reasoning Saleh was still on the loose and Nassar under strengthening pressure to apprehend him, Glyn determined the police had discovered a link between the Dutch newspaper Muslim terrorist barbarity and the Tunis-based fundamentalists. Conscious Saleh had some form of interdependence with the fundamentalist order, perhaps he reposed as their best chance of capturing the terrorists, hence the operator behind the Colonel's stiffness and implacable body language.

Finishing the customs admin pendency, Jeff was signing the departure declaration when he heard Ramiz speaking. Tramping back to the stern well, he acknowledged the Chief of Police.

"Good morning, Colonel Nassar."

"Mister Tindle," he reciprocated in a measured intonation.

Jeff continued sternward.

"Can we help you, Lieutenant Ramiz?" he calmly enquired, signifying all was well with the customs process.

"You are about to get under way?"

"Yes, we're completing customs declaration for departure."

"Hhmmm…and you have not seen your friend Saleh, again?"

Exhibiting he still fished for intel, he swung his sunglasses between his fingers, so they came to rest on his shoulder. Jeff had to be careful. The previous night, they never admitted Saleh was aboard Majid's cruiser.

"Not since the Hotel du Lac."

Smirking narrowly, Ramiz emanated the clear-cut seal he did not buy into the reply. "I see."

Whilst pondering his next move, he swivelled on his heels to glimpse Colonel Nassar, then turned back to eyeball Jeff. "Mister Tindle, if you ever return to Tunis, be very careful who you make friends with." Stealing a second flash at his uncle, Nassar lingered resolutely still, observing from his quayside retreat, as if meditating on the fate of their quarry. "I don't recommend another interview with Colonel Nassar. He might not be so understanding, if anything unfortunate were to happen again."

Nourishing fortitude, Jeff did not reply.

Entrenched in total supremacy, Ramiz nonchalantly ambled down to the bows, the customs officer at the helm saluting as he approached. Clustered in the stern, Poseidon's crew watched them exchange a few words, Ramiz double-checking the exodus routine, hunting for if customs had found anything. Congregating around Jeff and Ed, their adopted safety blankets, the newcomer's mouths dried up with apprehension, worried stamps forming on pastie faces. *Is Ramiz going to hold up our sailing*, Glyn surmised, *possibly not even allowing exit?* Though only a few minutes passed, his dialogue with the customs official seemed to go on for hours before the Lieutenant backtracked to the stern well.

"Customs say your boat is clean," he notified browsing their dismayed expressions. Wittingly taking an elongated pause, the tension became unbearable. "Do not forget my warning." Returning the sunglasses to shade his eyes he announced, "You are free to leave. Good day, gentlemen."

Jeff lifted a hand in affirmation, the rest of the crew starting to come down from unease, sweat glistening off fretful phizogs, sighs coming between breathing.

"Mister Tindle," Colonel Nassar snapped, gaping placidly beyond Poseidon to a distant vessel crossing Lac de Tunis. "If you do see Saleh again, remember those two brigands with cut throats. We might fail to find the escapee, but the Muslim fundamentalists will have no pity for anyone they find with him. Be warned."

Pinpointing Jeff with an overwhelming lour, he then took in the remainder of the crew, his penetrating bore making them wince or spy away.

Confirming the inspection formalities were faultless, the customs officials joined the police contingent ashore. Firing up her diesels, the on-watch then cast off, David beginning to steer Poseidon across the lake, as a customs officer noted their time of departure and destination.

Lighting up a cheroot, Lieutenant Ramiz surveyed them for a minute, then climbed back into the Mercedes. Maintaining his watch on the schooner as if about to call it back, Colonel Nassar exacerbated the crew's concern. Finally, he scoured the quayside area, as if half expecting Saleh to emerge from a hiding place, dive into the lake, and swim for Poseidon. Issuing the Englishmen a last narrow-eyed pout, he then joined his colleagues in the Mercedes, the ship's company scrutinising from the stern as the limousine disappeared back into the city.

Turning to address Jeff, Ed excreted tangible signs of displeasure. "Next time we are in Tunis, if anybody even acting remotely suspicious comes within ten feet of us, I will shoot them."

Whilst Jeff glimmered at the pithy proclamation, the rest of the crew shared a few salutary comments, mainly the language of relief. Blanched from anxiety, their pulse rates decreased to normal, the call of the sea beckoning them to make haste and rid themselves of bothersome aggravation.

As Poseidon crossed Lac de Tunis, their weariness became rekindled after Steve suggested if Ramiz still played games, the harbour patrol could detain them. Quasi kismet, not far from the canal entry, a harbour patrol launch materialised, awakening in Glyn the final scene from *Midnight Express*, when Billy Hayes absconds from a Turkish hell-hole prison, only to see a police vehicle coming his way. Instructing David to keep Poseidon on a steady vector, Jeff eyed the launch with circumspection. Any deviation from track might alert the harbour patrol, making them suspicious of the schooner's gauche liveliness. As the motor launch neared, mouths became dry again, nervousness reappearing. They began to concoct the worst, envisioning the harbour patrol slowing and hailing them to heave too. Instead, she slipped past, her crew immersed in duties, barely clocking the outgoing schooner. As the Englishmen watched the patrol boat head to Tunis Marina, her wake caressed Poseidon.

At 09:15, Poseidon cleared the canal and slid into the Golfe de Tunis. At last, they were free. After hoisting the mainsail, the on-watch raised the five supporting sails, set course to fifty degrees, and turned off the diesels. With some sail-trimming, the schooner accelerated to ten knots. Verifying the radar repeater and the depth finder functions were operational, David then engaged the auto-tiller, Poseidon advancing under steady-state sailing, the on-watch assuming monitoring duties.

Standing in the steering well, the crew *in toto* silently gazed back at Tunis, the newcomers deep in rumination about the events of the last twenty-four hours and wondering if they'd ever visit the city again. Setting out in pursuit of more bluefin tuna, razorfish and sea bass, Halq al Wadi fishermen spied impassively at Poseidon as she cut through their ranks, pied avocets, black winged stilts and gulls hovering relentlessly over their tiny, single-sail craft, in the hope of finding scraps. Diving down on the fishing fleet, the ship's company heard their wails and squawks when they spotted food.

With Poseidon's thermometer still registering a healthy eighty degrees Fahrenheit, and her barometer 1030 millimetres, it signalled another beautiful morning in the Med.

What on Earth could be wrong in the world on a day like this, Glyn proposed to himself?

17

CLEAR BLUE WATER AND CLEAR MINDS

Seeping out of them like slow-moving lava, the Englishmen's pent-up trepidation lessened as they rubbernecked back at serene Tunis, the stimulus almost advocating the previous evening had never happened.

"Maybe it's all been an illusion," Glyn deliberated to Steve, "a stargaze, the kind of inducement bred in a Dennis Potter play, or a film noir movie starring Humphrey Bogart. It simply doesn't seem veritable." Shaking his head, he weighed the tenuous commotions. Had they really crossed swords in an unexpected encounter with an Ethiopian fake economic migrant? Had they been taken to police headquarters for inquisition by Colonel Nassar, and then played cat and mouse with Lieutenant Ramiz aboard Majid's cruiser?

In Cadiz, the newcomers had been glowing with visions of unflinching flights of fancy, but none of them could have envisaged last night's mini opera.

Reprising the unappetising review, Glyn satirically posed, "Maybe we could sell the book and screen rights back in Blighty."

"Well, Tom must have enough material now for a raft of novels about our Med expedition."

"Yeah." Readying an incredulous mien, he theorised, "If someone from Whitstable Sailing Club, told us they had the kind of sticky adversity we went through yesterday, can you see us believing them?"

"Probably not. It's just too improbable to be real. Back home, you and I are far too grounded in actuality to believe such a story."

"Yes, that's my belief. But out here, I wonder for example, if we were to recount the quirk to Hassan in Tangiers, the old seadog we met in Ceuta, or Martin Driscoll, how they'd react?"

Considering for a moment, Steve replied, "They'd believe us. It's the difference between the regularity of Blighty, and the unpredictable nature of North Africa. Our astonishing episode could never have happened in Whitstable, but I'm willing to bet, it might just as easily have happened in Algiers or Oran."

As the friends gawked back at Tunis, the odd phrase or comment began to meander back into Glyn's mind. 'If I don't get out of Tunis, I will be killed', 'Oh, I actually came by plane from Addis Ababa', 'It is judgment and moral supremacy that defeats us', 'Your damned European Union', and, 'We are plagued by these fiends'. In his mind's eye, he could still see Saleh's forlorn gawp when his guard slipped and he confessed his real rationality at the Hotel du Lac, Colonel Nassar pacing the interrogation room as he grilled Poseidon's crew, the splash of alarm on Majid's face when they told him about the police station, and the resigned sulk of fatalism washing over Saleh as he fled from his cruiser. With so many conflicting and contradictory images swirling about his mind, again Glyn became torn between benevolence for Saleh, and the prospect of Europe being swamped, resulting in the distinct possibility of Bosnia-style war breaking out.

For a moment, he wished he had never set foot on Poseidon. Rather the voyage should have been enjoyed through virtual reality, the power of suggestion producing the placebo outcome. But then sober mindedness prevailed. Putting himself in a risky environment, he knew it more likely the accidental might happen, and some of it might be X-rated.

Many years before Poseidon, a friend of Glyn's and his family had tired of the monotony yielded by European and American package holidays. They wanted something more exciting, more left field. Satisfying their yearning, they went to Borneo on a jungle holiday. Thirty feet above ground level, part of the junket encompassed traversing from tree to tree via rope walkways. During one trek, a walkway gave way in front of them. After hanging on to the faltering rope for a few moments, four people fell to the ground. As the friend and his family witnessed the horrifying catastrophe, the walkway they stood on also began to give way. Frantically hurrying back in the opposite direction, their hearts pounding furiously, they made it to the safety of a secure tree terminus. Though two of the fallers were killed, and the other two seriously injured, the tour operator assured the holidaymakers such mishaps were very uncommon. Nonetheless, a formidable cross to bear colouring their holiday, it made an indelible imprint on their minds. The following year they returned to package holidays.

His friend's square off and that of Poseidon's crew in Tunis were events far more likely Glyn deduced, if you place yourself in the interdictor zone. It's the price sometimes paid for curiosity and restlessness.

Conserving their ceremony, the ship's company gaped sternward until the bird coos' and the prospect of the fisherman expired, Glyn left wondering if the others were privately reflecting on the previous day's events, contemplating Saleh's whereabouts, and musing if he'd make it to Blighty.

"*Stop it,*" Steve demanded.

"Stop what?"

"I know what you're imagining. We must move on, Glyn. It's history now."

Giving his friend a cursory glance, Glyn then ogled back for a final time, but Tunis had retreated over the horizon.

~

As Poseidon ploughed through the Med, someone put the Rolling Stones *Sticky Fingers* on the CD player and ramped up the volume, Mick 'n' Keef giving it large, the crew joining in to

Wild Horses, Sister Morphine and the rest of the album. Recalibrating their minds, their sudden burst into Western rock culture allowed them to resume the aura they had before Tunis. Howbeit, instead of intrepid adventurers, they just wanted to be neo-rock 'n' rollers for a while, singing into hypothetical microphones and playing air guitar. Running through them like electricity, the Stone's music purged their core from the remnants of yesterday's ghastly dread, bringing them back to their roots and planting their feet firmly on solid familiarity.

Prior to docking at Algiers, and over two weeks before Tunis, it was David's birthday. To mark the event, he had been given carte blanche over music choice, selecting Wagner's *Ride of the Valkyries* and *Spartacus* by Khachaturian. 'We're going to have some real music today,' David avowed tongue-in-cheek. 'No rock and jazz rubbish on my birthday.' Particularly appropriate, *Spartacus* fitted seamlessly into Poseidon's motion as she glided through the sea, making their trajectory feel more like flying than sailing, every cadence of the music, wave-like and soothing.

Though the theme turned to the current sail to Marsala, the sway persisted the same, imbuing the crew with an auspice for belonging, and rejuvenating their fervency for discovery. With the sun blazing down in a cerulean sky, the pulse-quickening music of the Rolling Stones hit the spot. Unlike with *Spartacus*, Poseidon did not fly, on this occasion, she became a fairground roller-coaster, amplifying the crew's gyrating movements in praise of the World's greatest rock 'n' roll band.

Colloquially known as the 'Stolling Bones', they had been functioning for over forty years, Mick and the boys still putting the hook in and taking some beating. Though dallying with New-Wave and Grunge, nothing prolonged Glyn's everlasting craving like the Stones could engender. When his fascination dipped with the latest genre entrant, invariably he reached for the Stones masterpiece albums, *Let it Bleed* or *Beggar's Banquet*, long ago commissioning if he ever wrote an autobiography it'd be entitled, 'Growing up with the Rolling Stones'.

As the morning unfolded, Poseidon moved into clear blue water, no other vessels in sight or on radar, apart from an oil tanker en route from the Middle East to somewhere in Europe, six nautical miles from their bearing, and vectoring away from the schooner's trajectory.

At noon, with the sun directly overhead scorching her deck, Poseidon cast no shadows to port or starboard. Lunch followed an hour later, then the on-watch converted to Ed, Steve, Colin and Glyn, the last on steering detail. Finding their GPS position to be a point off track, Ed told Glyn to uncouple the auto-tiller, and reset course to forty-seven degrees compass bearing. As he began the correction, Steve and Colin adjusted the sails to accomplish maximum speed, meaning no flapping with the prevailing wind. Once Poseidon steadied on track, Glyn reengaged the auto-tiller.

"You boys are really beginning to get the hang of this," Ed complimented, overseeing the action approvingly. "That was as good as it gets."

Inwardly purring with satisfaction, the on-watch felt a sense of achievement.

Glyn turned to Steve. "Glad we came?"

Parrying, he beamed back at his friend. No words necessary.

After rock music had purged their minds of Tunis bothers, and their bellies were full, Poseidon's crew basked in warmth and security again. Time to be playful and resume their pre-Tunis persona. Whilst the on-watch occupied themselves in humorous banter, the off-watch roll-played the pirates' anomaly yet again for entertainment. David had bought a pirate's hat, eye patch and sundry paraphernalia in Oran, the props used to annex further authenticity to the enactment, each player providing a convincing complementary performance. Then going into his quick-fire, joke telling routine, Colin lambasted his lawyer profession, the others gleefully joining in, Glyn making his contributions from the tiller. Sea shanties aficionados, the seniors encouraged the newcomers to join in when one of them suddenly broke into *Sailors Hornpipe*, *Blood Red Roses* or *Dogger Bank*. On this occasion, *Pump Shanty* became the rum tale they sang. Accompanying the shanty, the ship's company made their best impersonations of Long John Silver, Captain Flint and other blaggards from Stevenson's *Treasure Island*. Ending in raucous laughter with bodies strewn about the deck, the theatrical rendition enhanced their appreciation of normality.

With gaiety at its peak intensity, Tom gave an impassioned if not humorous appraisal about the limitations of the *Heinlick manoeuvre*; something he had tried on his myriad of wives and girlfriends, not always successfully, the crew staring in amazement at his thrusting projections concomitant with the tale.

"What did he just say?" trilled a perplexed Bill, still caught up with the seniors in remnants of the sea shanty. "What manoeuvre?"

"Oh, he's speaking fluent gibberish," Ed flippantly assessed.

Enduring with Bill recounting witty anecdotes from his time at ICL, and Tom confessing to more domestic ineptitude, the amusement subsided when Ed called the on-watch to crewing duties, and the off-watch retired below for sundry directives. Recovering their humour, like before Tunis, the ship's company felt normal again, stress-free and ready for more sprightly odysseys.

❧

After tending to sailing-duties, the on-watch supervised Poseidon's path whilst launching into a colloquy about the age of leisure, something forecast in the early nineteen-seventies, and scheduled to happen in the nineteen-nineties, but it never came about.

"The premise made for eye-opening reading," Steve avouched. "According to the scientists, gathering automation could relieve man of the soul-destroying toil needed on production lines, exploration platforms, in mines and in offices."

"For sure," Glyn endorsed. "It was also indexed to subsume all those tedious human-performed jobs done in the service and logistics industries, and at home, with robots performing virtually all work-related assignments. The applications, well—" He shrugged his shoulders. "They must have seemed limitless to those scientists, and the blessings universal."

"Wow, they'd have been a boon for us. We could have done this Med trip far earlier in our lives."

"And on a regular basis, not what we conjectured to be a once-in-a-lifetime jaunt, as we are doing now."

Hearing his companions opening remarks as he came back on deck, Tom joined the debate, his engineering background involving him in many automation initiatives. "In my early Aston Martin career, the prospect of driverless motor vehicles, pilotless aircraft and crewless ships became a distinct possibility."

"You're talking about automation?" Bill enquired, also joining his companions on the steering well deck.

"We are," Glyn confirmed. "Do you have any input?"

Book-marking the copy of *Heart of Darkness* he had been · reading in the saloon, Bill laid it on the steering well shelf. "Well gents, I agree those early pioneers did say our every whim and pleasure could be catered for through automation. Plus, and this is something often sidelined, the automation revolution massively uplifted GDP."

"*Oh*," Steve exclaimed. "Why's that, Bill the brain?"

"Because it drove up efficiency and increased productivity. Still does. And here's the positive for the nation at large—instead of adopting the labour ethic until sixty-five—people were to be free to enlist in leisure activities, supplement their education, or delve into domains previously unattainable because of work-time constraints. To my mind, that was the real value."

"Unequivocally," Tom applauded, "and like most people, I eagerly awaited inheriting this age of leisure, but it never came. Instead, the inflated GDP resulting in more tax revenue was not released by the Treasury to fund alternative lifestyles for UK citizens." Fixing a spot on the horizon, a grim affectation covered his features. "No, those relieved of vocation through automation rollout, a euphemism for made redundant, found they were perpetually stalking for alternative utilisation to prop their baseline lifestyles. It happened to a lot of people I know in manufacturing."

"Yes, since the early nineteen-eighties" Steve asserted, "automation has been responsible for more mass unemployment in the West, than any undreamt-of economic downturn, natural disaster, or war. Decidedly, the unstoppable spread of automation through robotics and I.T, has made some people extremely rich, but the corollary is, millions have had their lives ruined forever by its consequences." Dithering, he lowered his voice to impart sobriety. "Skilled people, proud of their trade, and used to working five-day week minimums, have been re-trained for jobs in the service industries on much lower incomes. I'm not persuaded that it represents progress."

"Comprehensively right," Glyn agreed. "Try telling a redundant machinist, miner or technician, that after three decades of productive and respected work effort, there are opportunities at Starbucks, a newly created tourism office, or becoming a health & safety officer, and they can still feel the same pride of purpose, they experienced in their previous occupations." Turning to Bill, he lamented, "You know, we in the IT industry are largely to blame for enabling global automation, and thereby generating its adverse by-products."

"Quite right, Glyn, however, what those well-meaning scientists didn't take into account was the political instrument."

"What do you mean by that, Bill?" Ed quizzed, marginal to the discussion, but the steely articulation connoting his attunement to its concord.

"I mean, in a developed country such as England, the automation versus expanded GDP argument only works on the basis, the population rests constant and there is very little unproductive fat on the social bone gobbling capital without contribution."

"Ah, okay. Sounds like efficiency optimisation."

"Yes. In the computation of a modern combine strategy or business model, resource efficiency optimisation of skills and assets is the precept making the inviolate thing work. Those scientists prescribed the same creed be applied nationally."

Producing a flurry of bewildered feedback from the rest of them, Bill's farsighted asseveration dug deep into why the leisure age never came about, and what happened to the incremental GDP and taxes created through automation.

Recognising he had fashioned a puzzle, Bill clarified, "If England's population had lasted at its 1970 approximate thirty-six-million, then the positive paybacks of extensive I.T-empowered automation could genuinely have created an infinitely sustainable and enlarging GDP."

"So, the age of leisure should have been achieved?" Ed pressed.

"Absolutely, the utopian ambition should have arrived by the mid-nineteen-nineties, perennially growing, and with improvements in the millennium."

"So, what happened to prevent it?" Glyn tested.

"Well, examining Office for National Statistics data reveals since 1970, England's population has snowballed to over forty-two-million in 2007, but contrary to immense investment in automation and I.T, GDP per capita has markedly declined since the early nineteen-seventies."

"A well-known fact," Ed substantiated. "But why?"

"It's because, as a percentage, there are less of us working and generating taxable revenue, and conversely, a lot more either claiming short-term or lifetime welfare benefits. Also, the vast population explosion has largely been caused by immigration, frostily adding to overhead and making little or no contribution to GDP. But the nub is just forty-nine percent of England's 2007 population were net GDP contributors, and of that number over ninety-eight percent were indigenous English. It is this core cadre that generates England's wealth. However, as a percentage of their income, the same coterie has to be pro-rata taxed over six times as much as they were in 1970, to maintain the fifty-one percent balance."

"What Bill says is true," Colin approved, a virtual spectator up to that distinction. "Government taxation revenues have boomed astronomically with England's economic growth over the past thirty-five years. But the money pot originally ring-fenced to finance the age of leisure, has been used to fund political agendas and vanity projects. Appending to the huge and ever escalating cost to the taxpayer of mass inward migration, the provocations of the nanny state, political correctness, multiculturalism, and

New Labour creating the chav subculture with lifetime welfare dependency, has enlarged the burden."

"*And*," Steve bemoaned, "we have to cough up to the EU and the Third World begging bowls every year."

"Correct," Colin validated. "EU membership cost English taxpayers nine-billion pounds in 2006/7, overseas aid six-point-eight billion pounds, but there are other contributory factors."

"Such as?" Steve pressed.

"Since 1970, we have been fiscally encumbered year-on-year by the ever-accruing cost of big government upkeep. Under Blair and Brown, civil servants form over sixty percent of the working population, but its private sector taxation funding them, and their huge, inflation-proof pensions. Sum up all this overhead, and it explains why the scientists' predicted age of leisure utopia never arrived. The accumulated taxation revenues have been squandered."

Disgruntled, Steve complained, "So, once again, the English have been royally screwed by politicians having a diverse roster, not centred on a utopia, but on governance and ultimately world-wide domination via the State."

Talking further about the missed age of leisure and its causes, the conversationalists' anger soared in their condemnation of successive British administrations, and the new world order, fostered by the Illuminati.

Balancing the unjust contradictions they had been underneath in Blighty, Glyn proclaimed, "There are some examples of the leisure age being attainable in principle."

"For example?" Tom enquired.

"Well, all the oil-rich, Middle East oligarchies. The petrodollars resultant from automation investment in oil exploration and production has raised the average income for the less than three-million Kuwaiti population, from $500 per year to $50,000 per year, and that's in less than twenty-five years. It's a similar story for other oil-rich, low population density realms such as Brunei, Saudi Arabia and the UAE."

"Perfectly true," Ed verified. "But what essentially defines those *nouveau riche* autonomies is a fully focused, homogeneous society, in which inward migration is not allowed, and foreign influences are only used to help generate oil revenues. Their indigenous populations take the full income, and their autocracies do not indulge in worldwide philanthropy, courtesy of the taxpayer." Hesitating as if anticipating a protest, none came. "I know what you're deliberating," he bellowed. "They are harsh and austere regimes, totally intolerant of anything beyond their ken. But there's none of the economic instability we see in the West. They are societies experiencing concerted economic upsurge throughout all social strata, independent of rigorous legislation and regulation by the governing bodies."

For those debating the controversy, it became clear but for the politicians' self-interested blueprints, England could have been on the same enviable economic and societal footing, through its automation investment. *Those scientists were right*, Glyn inwardly warranted. *We should have been in the age of leisure since the mid-nineteen-nineties. Instead, England is paying the price for Fabian policies, its people becoming life-long tax-slaves to fund the politicians' PC mentality.*

∽

By mid-afternoon, with Bill as *pro tem* music master, rock had sojourned into cool jazz, Miles Davis drenching the crew's ears in soft mellow tones, as Poseidon progressed across the Med at an improved twelve knots. Under full sail, she was a towering picture to behold, her sparkling superstructure and gigantic sails casting a dancing shadow on the water to port, as she gracefully negotiated the desired schema. Cutting through the sea, a swishing toll from her hull became the only indication of her presence, its hypnotic repercussion mesmerising the newcomers since Cadiz, her gentle, stern-to-bows rocking causing the occasional burst of sea spray reinvigorating those it hit. From its south-west, west post, the sun still emitted intense electric fluorescence, the on-watch basking in its comforting pizazz. After the automation discussion, the off watch dozed below deck, seductive jazz stimulating the ingress towards sleep, they roamed into contented malaise. Under a constant heading and only slight sea swell, the on-watch abided in standby mode, also close to dozing. If not for Ed's vigilant eye, they too could have lapsed into half sleep.

This was the nature of sea sailing. Commission and relaxation only separated by the watch timetable, the dodge being the ability to slip in and out of both states seamlessly. One moment, the on-watch could be battling against a north-easterly. When the watch-change bell rang, the capacity to *ad libitum* relax below deck became vital for recharging the body and mind, ready for the next watch duty. Conversely, when back on-watch, unlike pampered, modern day footballers, they had no warm-up time. Straight into the fray, a step-response was required to take charge instantly, the procedure sharpening mental and physical reaction times. When the newcomers got back to Blighty, they'd find it had affixed an extra dimension to their civilian lives.

Periodically, Ed roused the on-watch with a change of deck-roll or a sail trim, a check on this, a check on that, anything to keep the guard alert. Flying wise, it is said there are old pilots and bold pilots, but no old, bold pilots. The same with sea sailing, sailors never know what could loom into view from out of the blue, like the pirates or the Giuseppe Garibaldi, requiring agile evasive action. Unforgiving, the sea takes few prisoners, most catastrophic mistakes leading to a date with Neptune for the unfortunate crewmen, survival in the sea, singularly in colder waters, no more than thirty minutes before hypothermia sets in. Even in high summer, the Med fell into the dangerous category. If the boat goes down, the epigrammatic objective is to get out of the water and speedily into the dinghy, get dry and stay dry. With this in mind, even in clement conditions Poseidon's crew had been drilled to be watchful.

Five hours before docking in Algiers, with Poseidon off the Bouma'chouk headland, her crew had spotted wreckage in the water. Downing sails, they heaved to, gently floating adjacent to the capsized craft, a medium-sized fishing boat, upside down and splintered at the bows, with no sign of life.

"What on Earth has happened here?" Glyn exclaimed.

Pouring over the forlorn wreck, Jeff then squinted at the

headland, ten nautical miles south of their location. "Could have been anything," he verbalised. "There are submerged reefs just a few feet beneath the surface off the coast in this area. That could have been responsible for the crew's fate."

"Or," Ed began, "they could have been hit by a much larger vessel, possibly at night. It does happen."

Perturbed by the disquieting diorama, Tom recoiled. "Where are the bodies?"

"Oh, could have sunk," Jeff speculated, "or more probably, eaten. There are sharks and other meat-eaters in the Med. A drifting body represents a free meal. What they don't eat, every other little critter in the sea, will take a bite out of. Nothing is wasted."

"If not worm food, we end up as seafood," Steve philosophised, his remark not lost on the others, conspicuously David, his Falklands legacy still disconcerting him in the face of human tragedy.

"My god," he yawped, "we can't even say a prayer for them. There's nothing to pray over."

"Right," Jeff doggedly settled, not wanting the dispiriting prodigy to defocus the crew. "I'll call it in to the Algiers coastguard. Nothing more we can do here." Taking a gander at the newcomers, he logged their lifeless visages. Moments earlier, they'd been full of vim and vigour, joking about the pirate's stunner. Now they were overtaken by abject sadness. Peeking at the wreck again, he coaxed, "You'll have to get used to seeing sea accidents, like you see road accidents. There are a lot less of them, but when it does happen, there are few survivors."

Stung by the finality of the heartrending happenstance, it augmented the newcomer's vigilance. Becoming blasé, their seamanship confidence had grown before Algiers, daydreaming they could handle any eventuality, especially after the pirate attack. But taking in the fishing boat debris from Poseidon's deck, their minds in overdrive *vis-à-vis* what might have happened to the crew, the short ten nautical miles hop to dry land had all the aspects of an uncrossable chasm, the safety of *terra firma*, unreachable. Honing the newcomer's awareness, in terms of the fine margins between staying alive and perishing at sea, it made them acutely tune into seafaring disciplines. From then on, they needed little encouragement from the seniors to clinch on-watch duties were affected with diligence, and greater attention paid to safety standards.

~

Voyaging east-north-east through the Mediterranean, Poseidon perpetuated her trek to Sicily. Regenerated through Western fleshpot appetites and high-spirited activity, outwardly her crew had become cleansed from the previous night's escapade, though for Glyn, the Tunis landmark moment still lingered. Resting in his mind's mid recesses, he knew it could easily resurface, with fresh annoyances and more debate waiting to contradict perception. Moreover, was Bill's reading of *Heart of Darkness* purely coincidental, or did a more associative connection prompt it? From his tiller locus, Glyn peeped at him out of the corner of his eye, sat in the corner of the steering well deck, engrossed in Conrad's profound tale.

"I see you're reading *Heart of Darkness.*"

Nodding positively, Bill enounced, "Yes, I'm a big Conrad fan. I must have read this novella half a dozen times, but with each read I still find something new in it. It's not his best work. I'd put *Lord Jim* and maybe *The Secret Agent* above *Heart of Darkness*, but this little gem is a superb illustration of how little it takes for someone with delegated responsibility to abuse high office elevation, someday becoming a tyrant, and committing unfathomable, heinous acts."

"Do you find much crossover into *Apocalypse Now!?*" Glyn challenged whilst returning to eyeball frontwards, safeguarding Poseidon's sails were copiously bloomed and her compass heading on track. "Coppola freely admits his film draws heavily from Conrad's book."

"Hhmm, possibly. But there's more of *Lord Jim* in that film. Conrad wrote Charles Marlow into both *Lord Jim* and *Heart of Darkness*. Captain Willard from *Apocalypse Now!* is the equivalent Marlow character, charged with terminating Colonel Kurtz's command, with 'extreme prejudice', to quote from the film script, much in the same way Marlow relieves Kurtz of his ivory trader post command, albeit through illness. But the common thread running through both Conrad works and Coppola's film, is the temptation to play god with lesser beings."

Making sure they were not overheard, Glyn stipulated in a low voice, "I didn't want to bring this up again, Bill,

but—" He peered at him, his vision probing. "Do you see a parallel with last night's events and *Heart of Darkness* by way of dominion abuse?"

Bothered by the proposition, Bill's lineaments transformed into an agonising death mask, the motion plainly agitating him. Spying haphazardly as if searching, he became distracted gazing up at Poseidon's mainsail top, the sun glinting off the rotating radar antenna, directing a stroboscopic radiance into the stern well. For a moment he seemed nonplussed, on the verge of dissolving, then recovering hit Glyn with a wan examination.

"You're very perceptive. I picked up Conrad's novella again because of the Colonel Nassar interrogation and Lieutenant Ramiz's near-sadistic behaviour. Both made me recall *Heart of Darkness*."

"Me too."

"*Really?*"

"Yes," Glyn vehemently corroborated. "But I didn't want to say anything to the others. Collectively, we need to expunge that upsetting instalment from immediate memory, or at least archive it, so as not to let it jolt the remainder of the voyage. Doubtless the seniors won't like the wrangle reigniting."

"I agree," Bill endorsed, browsing about the deck again to ascertain no one lurked in earshot of their analysis, Ed in the radio room, Steve and Colin chatting in the bows, the remaining off-watch members curled-up in the saloon, relaxing. "Under an asymmetrical set of circumstances," he argued, "another side of Colonel Nassar might be inflamed. Given the right stimulus, say with a known terrorist, his delegated authority could absolve him of any accountability for the nasty methods chosen to extract the information he sought."

Hitting home, Glyn's own dark machinations on the issue were reawakened by the remark. What Bill inferred had weight, even the most benign of people capable of terrible acts under intensive predicaments. Jarred by the intuition, he turned to scrutinise Bill, only to find his shipmate already had him in his sightline.

"We're all perchance capable of the most primeval acts of depravity," Bill insisted. "Given the mandate from a perceived legal authority, elected or otherwise, history is strewn with good men reconstructed as maniacal torturers. Those convicted of war crimes at Nuremburg often cited they were acting under orders. Ostensibly, once given the go signal, normal people mutated into monsters."

"Yes, I'd go along with that. Granted the authorisation, there have been many lab experiments designed to test how far allegedly normal human beings will go to torture the truth out of a mark. One I read about in my teens, involved so-called, liberal-minded social workers, delegated to torture a supposed dupe with electricity." Combined with their spiky elocution, the salty air had dried up Glyn's mouth. Licking his lips to moisten them, he then resumed. "The detainee was strapped into a chair and electrodes attached to his most sensitive regions. In a control room, the inquisitor superintended the sufferer through CCTV. Behind the torturer, a psychoanalyst authorised him to conduct the Q&A. When the captive refused to answer questions, the inquisitor ramped up the electricity wick, intensifying torment and causing the gull to contort and scream, everything witnessed via CCTV and loudspeakers in the control room. One liberal-elitist torturer became so enthralled by the experiment, he started to laugh and guffaw as the sufferer's pain became more and more unbearable. Appealing to the psychoanalyst, should he keep going, he was given the green light. Turning the electrical current up to max, it produced a writhing and convulsing reaction in his patsy, making him collapse, his head hanging unmoving over his chest, his tongue slightly protruding. The psychoanalyst told the liberal he had killed the victim. Apparently, the liberal laughed, then defended he'd been legitimised to do it." Breaking, a wry manifestation evolved across Glyn's kisser before he surveyed forrard again. "What he didn't know was electricity had never been connected to the sufferer, an actor played out the part of the sap, including his own ugly death. The nucleus is, given delegated authority, even lily-livered, weak-kneed, heads up their own arse liberals, become as sadistic as what we picture the Nazis' to have been."

"That experiment was run at Harvard, wasn't it?"

"Yes," Glyn certified, glancing away from his steering post to clock Bill again. "When we were with Colonel Nassar, that depiction did cross my mind far more so than when Ramiz toyed with us on Majid's cruiser."

"Why?"

"Because Lieutenant Ramiz showed us most of his bad side. Apart from his anti-politician outbursts, the Colonel retained calmness, but I distinguished other shades to his makeup; traits out of necessity he embraced to do his job, should kismet dictate. He might not like his dark side, but I'd divine he'd be pragmatic when called upon to act as an inquisitor with uncooperative suspects."

"You mean like Saleh?"

"Maybe. It depends on how much of what Saleh told us was truth, and how much subsisted as lies, or hidden. It's the presumed hidden part Nassar would want to make a judgement on, regarding prospective upshots for Tunisian national security."

"I can see what you're driving at, but Saleh was all cosmetic gloss, shouting without backbone. Though he professed faith, I doubt the illusion could have persisted under the torturers' rack."

"Oh, for certain. It was a masquerade, a convenient bluff to solicit help. But if Saleh had been put at the disposal of Nassar's aid…what was his name?"

"Lieutenant Shamoun."

"Yes, he'd have confessed all in a heartbeat." Dwelling for a moment Glyn qualified, "But it's not the marrow I'm making, Bill. Saleh wouldn't be any worse than other felons, rapidly caving

in under the auspice of torture. We'd all come clean in the end."
Delaying, he frowned. "No, what disturbed me more was the
potential to metamorphose from *Mister Hyde* into *Doctor Jekyll*,
and the fine borderline between the two personas. It's why *Heart
of Darkness* crept into my anxieties at the police station."

"Mine to," Bill avowed. "It's through Conrad I can appreciate
the possibility of what we perceive to be spotlessly normal people
becoming homicidal maniacs."

"The thing of it is," Glyn began to outline, "they do not
necessarily announce themselves through the assumed stereotype
motif, menacing with a gleeful display, dressed in black uniforms
and jack boots, and baying over their pigeons. They come more
in the guise of cerebral, quietly spoken, professedly equitable
beings. It's why Steve is so concerned about Blair and Brown. He
imagines, and its palpable millions share the same supposition,
behind closed doors, they'd condone the same methods to bring
detractors in line with their new world order doctrine, used by
Hitler, Stalin and Pol Pot."

"I must admit, it has also crossed my mind, because basic
freedoms have been substantially reduced, even terminated since
New Labour came to office." Taking a breath, he then canvassed,
"But do you *really* think Blair and Brown, two of the biggest PC,
liberal lefties working world politics, could really authorise a
programme of torture?"

"I'm not schizoid about them, like Steve," Glyn elucidated.
"But yes, it's very possible. All the signs of convergence towards a
totalitarian regime are there. The thought police, laws benefiting
interlopers and penalising the English, surrender of sovereignty to
the EU, manipulation of the media, and a very snug rapport with
New Labour's publicity arm, the BBC. It doesn't take too much
more, to totally eradicate all opposition, does it?"

"No, and I suppose those steadfastly objecting, are disposed
of, or re-socialised by force. That's where the torture chambers
come in."

"Mmmm. So after last night, you'll understand why I kept
my misgivings to myself, though I daresay secretly, Steve has
already made all these connections."

"We all have."

Quivering his brow and devoured by reticence, Glyn counselled, "Best not to say anything more, Bill. We don't want the others hearing us, joining in, and the whole damned affair rekindling."

"Yes." Glowering, he pressed his lips together in an act of self-admonishment. "I'll put the Conrad away."

18

FINAL BRUSH WITH NEPTUNE

At about 16:30, Tom arrived on deck from the radio room. Monitoring the radar, he'd seen echo blips on the screen indicating vessels to the east, at seventy degrees to Poseidon's orientation, and on a near-parallel course. With Glyn off tiller assignment, Ed summoned him to climb the mainsail-mast, armed with binoculars to explore what lay off their starboard bow on the horizon.

In the spirit they had fused of not letting the side down, mast climbing duty became a ship's company expectation, everyone overcoming their perturbation to accept the task. Performing the undertaking several times, unlike naturals Steve and Bill, mounting the mainsail-mast for Glyn took grit and determination. Despite not being a vertigo sufferer, it was not like ascending a static ladder to inspect house guttering for him, the further up the mast, the more the boat pitch in both the yaw and roll axes became exaggerated. At the top of the mainsail, the swing could be as much as eight to ten feet about the vertical, though viewed from the deck it registered as tolerable.

"Ay, ay, Captain," Glyn assented.

Up he went, using securing points all the way up the mast to ensure even if he fell, the inexorable hard surface below never met him. Escalating to thirty-feet above the deck skating beneath him to the intersection of the mainsail top and the masthead, he then secured himself to the masthead top. With Ed peeking up at him, he indicated his readiness to perform the observational chore. More intense at masthead height, the prevailing wind made him screw up his eyes when he scouted to port at the shallow waves reflecting silver off the sun.

Settling into the crow's nest deployment, his powerful binoculars unmasked a flotilla of single-sail boats off starboard, about five nautical miles away at the navigational coordinates served up by radar.

"Looks like a bunch of very small sailing craft," he called to Ed.

Fixing his gaze on the targets, he tried to stay aligned as Poseidon pitched and rolled through the sea. As she closed on them, the image of the craft solidified with every passing moment.

Catching his ear, Ed shouted up, a further blip had been picked up on radar, two nautical miles further to the north east of the convoy. Adjusting the binocular's focus, Glyn identified a funnel gushing grey smoke and a bow wave, reminding him of the first occasion he climbed the mainsail-mast, when Poseidon approached Port de Mostaganem.

Coming out from the harbour, a tug pulling an old sailboat destined for the breakers yard at Oran came to his notice, the scene reminiscent of Turner's *The Fighting Temeraire*. As the tug and her load passed Poseidon, deep sorrow and regret overwhelmed him, her cold-hearted destruction plain to see. Once an august and noble wooden ship, her masts had been felled and laid on her deck, her sails ripped off to be used for rags, and her superstructure stripped, soon to be reduced to matchsticks.

Left naked and exposed, without prudence or apology she'd been humiliated after a lifetime's strenuous work. All that tarried of her glory was her vast carcass to be unceremoniously torn apart. Ships have souls. They are living entities loved by their crew like a family member. Tenderly maintained, every fibre of construction made to gleam and shine, they are nurtured, preened and painted to sustain celebrated glamour.

But in the end, it all comes to nought. Like for living things, they have a birth, a life and a burial. Goggling back at the tug until its smoke plume dissipated out of sight, Glyn had uttered a little prayer for the wooden ship's corpse, hoping she'd be treated with respect during her final indignation.

Persevering with the surveillance, his concentration returned to the seascape to his front. Peering through the eyepiece, he counted five small craft followed by a large motor vessel heading at them, some action about to take place.

Pinpointing those aboard the small craft taking desperate provisions to stay afloat, it became clear the task force was in trouble. Beckoning it to make haste, he picked out the odd arm waving at the larger vessel nearing from its north position. Though the sea swell hovered relatively smooth with little oblique wave mobility, the small craft bobbed up and down clearly shipping water, their occupants using bare hands and whatever else they had to return sea water overboard, but they were losing the battle.

To stabilise their boat, the preeminent craft's crew frantically tried to bring down its single sail. As they performed the action, it tipped to starboard throwing some of its occupants into the sea. Also starting to down sail, other boat crews ceased abruptly when they saw the fate of the leading craft. Ahead of the small boats, Glyn spied a man on the motor vessel with a loudhailer. Whatever he ordered had either spooked the fleet, or they were trying to obey his commands. With each of the sail craft taking measures to prevent capsizing, only to find themselves on a collision course with fellow travellers, the traffic ahead began to resemble a motorway accident happening in slow motion.

Investigating south of their track, then scanning the east and west horizons through the binoculars, Glyn established other vessels in the vicinity. Apart from a container vessel heading due west at least six nautical miles south of their bearing, and the gathering to the front of them, Poseidon remained alone.

Below, Glyn beheld the rest of the crew assembling in the stern to survey the imminent spectacle. Hearing them talking about the argosy, and replaying the previous evening's events, he knew what they were thinking. Absorbing his eye, Bill gave him a half-shrug, leaving Glyn picturing he re-visited their earlier *Heart of Darkness* dialogue, the playback also making him call to mind the esoteric novella, and correlating the trial of the small boats with Colonel Nassar's rasping words.

A while later, with Poseidon two nautical miles from the flotilla, the motor vessel heaved to and stood off before a crewman issued more instructions to the stricken craft through a loudhailer, its hollow ring barely discernible to Glyn.

Clocking a sign embossed in large, bold white letters against a black background on the motor vessel's flank reading Sicilian Coastguard, he shouted the identifying information down to Ed.

Immediately Jeff manned the radio making a ship-to-ship call to the coastguard vessel. Responding, the Sicilians communicated they were about to commence rescue operations for the people in the small boats.

Some occupants from the foremost sail craft clung on to her from the earlier tipping, those still onboard refusing to let them back for fear of toppling the craft again. Very low in the water, the four other pack members were near to overturning.

Tipped into the sea resultant from the earlier sail downing catastrophe, at least three people hung onto each of the craft, Glyn mentally filing their situation in the desperate category.

His shadowing stint complete, he descended the mainsail mast to join the on-watch. While Steve, Colin and Ed prolonged sailing duties, the off watch crowded into the radio room, listening to the congress between Poseidon and the Sicilian Coastguard. Broaching if they needed assistance, the coastguard declined Jeff's offer, saying they'd deal with the rescue in its entirety.

Losing the sea battle and nigh on sinking, without doubt, the small boat occupants were Sub-Saharan asylum seekers and economic migrants. Soon, the schooner was within short line-of-sight distance from the engagement. Her sails downed, she heaved to, her tiller positioned to mid-ships presenting her beam to the flotilla. From their starboard quarter, the on-watch witnessed the rescue operation unfolding.

Each of the small sailboats still contained seven or eight people, some holding on to their meagre possessions. Built for four occupants, and in-shore work, they had certainly come up against some rough weather.

Back on the radio, Jeff checked status, the coastguard radio operator responding, the illegals already aboard had told its captain, two small craft had sunk earlier in the voyage, with all hands lost. The coastguard would not be going in search of them. They were already dead.

One of the illegals reported they'd set sail from Tunis the previous night, originally in seven craft stolen from Halq al Wadi, each with at least eight occupants. One vessel had gone down during the night when rough sea swell swamped the craft, the surviving boat's inhabitants hearing the screams and wails of those in the water, but not stopping. Everyone knew the risks involved. If a boat turned turtle, there'd be no going back for those in the sea, besides, their boats were already overcrowded. Then a second suffered the same sequel at dawn, sheer overcrowding causing chaos and ultimately tragedy, leaving the five Glyn saw through the binoculars, still some sixty nautical miles from the Sicilian coast. As the morning progressed, a third had upended when a sudden gust dipped its sail, sending half its inexperienced crew into the sea. On that occasion, Neptune rested, its occupants managing to right it, and get those overboard back into the boat.

Later in the morning, a large container ship crossed the flotilla's course sending a giant wash-wave into their flank. None of the crews knew what to do, but instinctively the lead craft turned its bows into the wave. With the rest following suit, the manoeuvre saved the group from further misfortune. By noon, they were exhausted from their endeavours to keep the vessels upright. At sea for nearly twelve hours, for most, it became the worst twelve hours of their lives. None were sailors and had only worked out rudimentary sailing principles through trial and error during the voyage.

As the report came into Poseidon, Glyn visualised they must have compared the excesses of the sea to a bleak and distressing nightmare, the bow wave they took shocking, like when Don Giovanni sees the ghost of a dead commander and crumples before his presence.

Straying off course, the boats vectored in favour of the Capo Feto peninsula, entering the graveyard vicinity Jeff and Ed inspected where underwater currents joust with surface swell to generate very choppy waves. Already made unstable by overcrowding, it inserted a further alarming challenge to deal with for such small craft. Bobbing about in the sea for several hours, they tried to determine what was going on, and what action to take. Eventually, more through luck then judgment, the prevailing north-easterly wind sent the fleet away from Capo Feto towards Mazara del Vallo, where the Sicilian Coastguard happened upon them.

Silence reigned on Poseidon. Like watching an episode of a TV maritime drama from ringside seats, the crew stood on the starboard deck or in the stern well, impassively taking in the conclusion of the rescue being played out before them. Apart from the put-put noise of the coastguard vessel's diesel engines, little reverberation could be heard. Those being rescued were hauled aboard the coastguard ship without any real verve to avert further calamity. Rather than human rescuers, the coastguard crew acted more like fishermen, dispassionately pulling dead fish out of the sea, a duty actioned through obligation and legal necessity, without sympathy or enthusiasm. It became very obvious to Poseidon's crew that the Sicilian coastguard had performed the task on many occasions. Whereas once, a sense of helping humanity might have prevailed, the trait had long passed. Here was yet another party of unwanted asylum seekers and economic migrants, impacting not just Sicily, but Europe *en masse*, the flood never ceasing.

Concluding the operation, the coastguard crew waved to Poseidon, her ship's company reciprocating with a salute, Jeff offering a parting goodbye and good luck before signing off radio transmission.

Poseidon had drifted off course during the rescue. Quickly finding their GPS position, Ed then instructed the on-watch to hoist her sails and set the auto-tiller to take them straight into Marsala Harbour. Blankly staring back at the final part of the rescue from Poseidon's stern, they were all brooding on the same thing as Glyn. Was Saleh onboard the coastguard vessel, or was he shaking hands with Neptune?

That day became a watershed moment defining their subsequent lives. Were they crossing over to the dark side, with Priest's European dystopia vision just around the corner?

~

Don't miss out on your next favorite book!

Join the Melange Books mailing list at
www.melange-books.com/mail.html

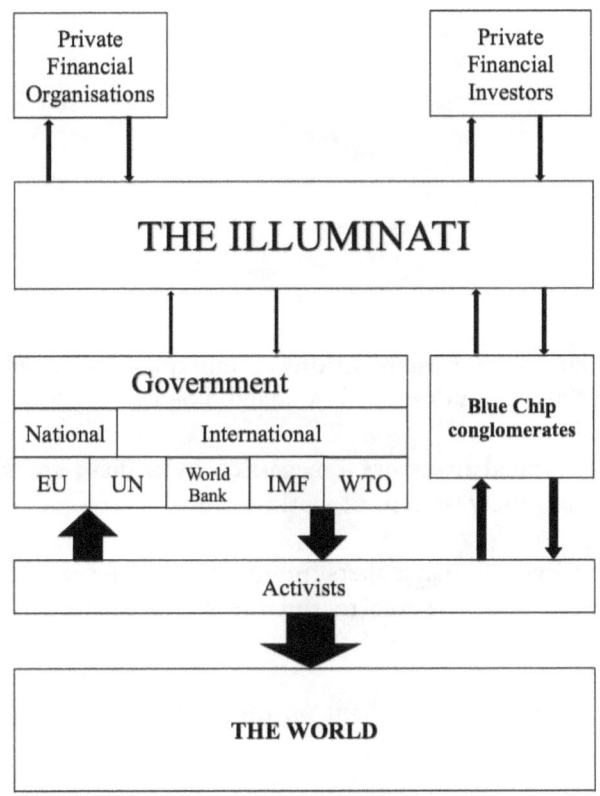

KEY

Private Financial Organisations - enterprise scale wholesale banks and hedge funds owned by shareholders.

Private Financial Investors - mega-rich individuals and families owning over ninety percent of world wealth.

The Illuminati - playmakers nominated by private financial organisations and investors to run the world economy on their behalf.

National government - reliant on the Illuminati for capitalising their vanity projects.

International government - a multiplicity of national government funded agencies with elected or nominated officials creating the cosmetic rules of engagement for international commerce.

EU - European Union, a non-elected, federalist cartel, aspiring to create the United States of Europe.

UN - United Nations, a quasi-neutral syndicate with consensus powers, only obeyed by top table stakeholders and lesser nations alike, if it suits their agendas.

World Bank - financed by Western national governments but mainly the Illuminati.

IMF - International Monetary Fund, in practice, devolves Western countries taxation funds to the Third World to facilitate trade.

WTO - World Trade Organisation, a jobs for the boys fraternity regulating international trade. Effectively, in competition with the IMF.

Blue Chip Conglomerates - enterprise scale intercontinental companies promulgating globalisation and internationalism for monetary gain.

Activists - worker ants in the pay of the Illuminati.

The World - everyone else.

THANK YOU FOR READING

Did you enjoy this book?

We invite you to leave a review at the website of your choice, such as Goodreads, Amazon, Barnes & Noble, etc.

∾

DID YOU KNOW THAT LEAVING A REVIEW...

- Helps other readers find books they may enjoy.
- Gives you a chance to let your voice be heard.
- Gives authors recognition for their hard work.
- Doesn't have to be long. A sentence or two about why you liked the book will do.

ABOUT THE AUTHOR

Clive Radford began writing at school, then university but mainly through subsequent life experience.

A series of his short stories and poems have been published by Ether Books. The Arts Council has sponsored publication of his novels 'One Night in Tunisia' and 'The Sounds of Silence'. His contemporary satire 'Doghouse Blues' was number one in Harper Collins Authonomy chart and has been awarded gold medal status. It has been published by Black Rose. His spy thriller 'Zavrazin' has been published by Triplicity Publishing. It's companion sequel 'Nexus Bullet' is published by Ex-L-Ence Publishing. His three-book series 'Disclosures of a Femme Fatale Addict' is published by Wild Dreams Publishing.

'One Night in Tunisia', 'Zavrazin' and 'Bullet' have all been converted into three-act screenplays.

The 'Zavrazin' screenplay is under contract with Story Merchant/Atchity Productions for film production.

Wild Dreams Publishing re-published 'Disclosures of a Femme Fatale Addict' as a deluxe edition, May 2020. Miraclaire Publishing has also re-published his 'Disclosures of a Femme Fatale Addict', October 2020.

Rogue Phoenix Press will be publishing his satire 'Doghouse Blues 2', March 2021. Melange Books will be publishing his 'The

Spiral Staircase and other Novellas', a mix of psychological, modern satire and rite of passage sagas, November 2021.

Currently, he is crafting a number of works including 'Doghouse Blues 3', 'Alpha Centauri', a contemporary thriller, 'Oklahoma City Looks Oh So Pretty', a rite of passage sojourn along Route 66, 'Three Cheshire Boys' a comedic thriller, and 'Colby Richmond: The University Years', the coming of age sequel to 'Disclosures of a Femme Fatale Addict'.

His work has a distinctive voice setting it apart and appealing to those fascinated by intrigue, and who question status quo accepted views.

 facebook.com/clive.radford.9